The Secon ... n

Lloyd Alexander ... in 1924 and attended ... ny during World Wa... to Wales, where he renewed his early fascination with Celtic mythology that forms the background to his stories of Prydain. After duties as a staff sergeant in Combat Intelligence in France and Germany, he was discharged in Paris and studied at the Sorbonne. He returned to Philadelphia with his Parisian wife, Janine, and worked as a cartoonist, layout artist, copywriter and magazine editor, whilst establishing a career as a writer.

He has written novels and non-fiction for both adults and young people. Awards for his work include the National Book Award for his *Marvelous Misadventures of Sebastian* and the Newbery Medal for the last book in the Prydain cycle, *The High King*. From 1970 to 1974 he served as author-in-residence at Temple University, Philadelphia and has lectured about his work at universities throughout the United States.

Available in Fontana by the same author

THE FIRST CHRONICLES OF PRYDAIN:
The Book of Three
The Black Cauldron
The Castle of Llyr

Lloyd Alexander

The Second Chronicles of Prydain

Taran Wanderer
The High King

FONTANA/Collins

Taran Wanderer and *The High King*
were first issued together as
The Second Chronicles of Prydain
in 1986 by Fontana Paperbacks,
8 Grafton Street, London W1X 3LA

Printed in Great Britain by
William Collins Sons & Co. Ltd, Glasgow

Taran Wanderer

First published in the USA 1967 by Holt Rinehart
First published in Great Britain by Fontana Lions 1979

Contents

1 Who Am I? 11
2 Cantrev Cadiffor 27
3 Goryon and Gast 35
4 A Matter of Cows 47
5 A Judgement 55
6 A Frog 64
7 Friends in Danger 73
8 The Wall of Thorns 82
9 The Hand of Morda 90
10 The Broken Spell 97
11 Dorath 104
12 The Wager 112
13 The Lost Lamb 119
14 The End of Summer 126
15 The Open Cage 133
16 Taran Wanderer 140
17 The Weir 149
18 The Free Commots 155
19 The Potter's Wheel 168
20 The Spoilers 176
21 The Mirror 183

For wayfarers still journeying,
for wanderers at rest.

Author's Note

This fourth chronicle of Prydain begins as a gallant, high-hearted quest, which soon becomes more intense and perhaps more essentially heroic than the preceding adventures. For here, Taran comes to grips with a merciless opponent: the truth about himself. No longer as Taran Assistant Pig-Keeper but as Taran Wanderer, he learns to reshape his life out of his own inner resources; for there must not only be an end to childhood but also a beginning of manhood. This is meant to be a serious tale – in the way that all humour is serious and all fantasy true – and if there is no conventionally happy ending in fairy-tale terms, there is still a most hopeful ending in human terms.

This does not imply any less humour or variety in the story. There is possibly more, as Taran's journey takes him from one end of Prydain to the other, from the Marshes of Morva to the Free Commots. However, instead of a clash of battle hosts, the underlying conflict between good and evil is stated in individual encounters: King Smoit, boisterous with being alive; Morda, deathlike, scornful of all humanity; Dorath the amoral; Annlaw Clay-Shaper the creator; Craddoc, in whose desolate valley Taran suffers the anguish of shame. The Princess Eilonwy, alas, is present only in memory, though it is hoped readers will miss her as much as Taran does – and the author himself, for that matter.

While certain inhabitants of Prydain were born of Welsh legend, in *Taran Wanderer* they have acquired characteristics more universal than specific. Morda's life secret, for example, is familiar in many mythologies. Orddu, Orwen, and Orgoch have appeared in other guises (as might well be expected of them): the Three Norns, the Moirae, the Triple Goddess, and very likely some other transformation they decline to admit. Prydain, of course, is part-memory and part-dream, the balance favouring the latter.

The Companions have gained many more friends than I had ever hoped, who are willing to follow these tales both as self-contained chronicles and as part of a larger pattern; and to them I promise in time all questions will be answered and all secrets revealed. To some friends of the Companions (especially Gypsy Reeves) I address a plea for clemency; to others, my sincere thanks for their hard but invaluable labour, insight, and encouragement when the straits seemed even more dire to an author than to an Assistant Pig-Keeper; and to all, my warmest affection.

L.A.

CHAPTER I

Who Am I?

It was full springtime, with promise of the richest summer the farm had ever seen. The orchard was white with fragrant blossoms; the newly planted fields lay light as green mist. Yet the sights and scents gave Taran little joy. To him, Caer Dallben was empty. Though he helped Coll with the weeding and cultivating, and tended the white pig, Hen Wen, with as much care as ever, he went about his tasks distractedly. One thought alone was in his mind.

'Now, my boy,' Coll said good-naturedly, as they finished the morning's milking, 'I've seen you restless as a wolf on a tether ever since you came back from the Isle of Mona. Pine for the Princess Eilonwy if you must, but don't upset the milk pail.' The stout old warrior clapped Taran on the shoulder. 'Come, cheer up. I'll teach you the high secrets of planting turnips. Or raising cabbages. Or whatever you might want to know.'

Taran shook his head. 'What I would know only Dallben can tell me.'

'Take my counsel, then,' said Coll. 'Trouble Dallben with none of your questions. His thoughts are on deeper matters. Have patience and bide your time.'

Taran rose to his feet. 'I can bide my time no longer. It is in my heart to speak with him now.'

'Have a care,' warned Coll as Taran strode to the door of the shed. 'His disposition rubs a little thin!'

Taran made his way through the cluster of low-roofed farm buildings. In the cottage, at the hearth-side, a black-robed woman crouched and tended the cooking fire. She did not raise her head or speak. It was Achren. Thwarted in her scheme to regain her ancient power, from the ruined Castle of Llyr the once-haughty Queen had accepted the refuge Dallben offered; though, by her own choice, she who had long ago ruled Prydain toiled now at the tasks Eilonwy had done before departing for Mona, and at day's end silently vanished to her pallet of straw in the granary.

Before Dallben's chamber Taran paused uneasily, then rapped quickly on the door. Entering at the enchanter's command, he found Dallben bent over *The Book of Three*, which lay open on the cluttered table. Much as he longed for a glimpse at even one page of this secret volume, Taran kept his distance from it. Once, in boyhood, he had dared touch the ancient, leather-bound tome, and his fingers smarted again at the memory.

'I never cease to wonder,' Dallben testily remarked, closing *The Book of Three* and glancing at Taran, 'that the young, with all their pride of strength, should find their own concerns such a weighty burden they must be shared with the old. Whereas, the old – ' he waved a frail, bony hand. 'But no matter, no matter. For the sake of my temper I hope your purpose in interrupting me is an excellent one.

'First, before you ask,' Dallben went on, 'I assure you the Princess Eilonwy is well and no more unhappy than any pretty young madcap obliged to turn a hand to sewing instead of sword-play. Second, you are as aware as I am that Kaw has not yet returned. By now, I daresay he has borne my potion to Glew's cavern, and the giant-by-accident who troubled you so much on Mona will shrink to the small stature he once had. But you also know your crow for a rascal and one to linger wherever he finds sport. Finally, an Assistant Pig-Keeper should have tasks enough to busy himself outdoors. What, then, brings you here?'

'One thing only,' Taran said. 'All that I have I owe to your kindness. You have given me a home and a name, and let me live as a son in your household. Yet who am I, in truth? Who are my parents? You have taught me much, but kept this always from me.'

'Since it has been always thus,' Dallben replied, 'why should it trouble you now?'

When Taran bowed his head and did not answer, the old enchanter smiled shrewdly at him. 'Speak up, my boy. If you want truth, you should begin by giving it. Behind your question I think I see the shadow of a certain golden-haired princess. Is that not so?'

Taran's face flushed. 'It is so,' he murmured. He raised his eyes to meet Dallben's. 'When Eilonwy returns, it – it is in my heart to ask her to wed. But this I cannot do,' he burst out, 'this I will not do until I learn who I am. An unknown foundling with a borrowed name cannot ask for the hand of a princess. What is my parentage? I cannot rest until I know. Am I lowly born or nobly?'

'To my mind,' Dallben said softly, 'the latter would please you better.'

'It would be my hope,' Taran admitted, a little abashed. 'But no matter. If there is honour – yes, let me share it. If there is shame, let me face it.'

'It takes as much strength of heart to share the one as to face the other,' Dallben replied gently. He turned his careworn face to Taran. 'But alas,' he said, 'what you ask I may not answer. Prince Gwydion knows no more than I,' he went on, sensing Taran's thought. 'Nor can the High King Math help you.'

'Then let me learn for myself,' Taran cried. 'Give me leave to seek my own answer.'

Dallben studied him carefully. The enchanter's eyes fell on *The Book of Three* and he gazed long at it, as though his glance penetrated deep into the worn leather volume.

'Once the apple is ripe,' he murmured to himself, 'no man can turn it back to a greening.' His voice grew heavy with sorrow as he said to Taran, 'Is this indeed your wish?'

Taran's heart quickened. 'I ask nothing more.'

Dallben nodded. 'So it must be. Journey, then, wherever

you choose. Learn what lies in your power to learn.'

'You have all my thanks,' Taran cried joyfully, bowing deeply. 'Let me start without delay. I am ready . . .'

Before he could finish the door burst open and a shaggy figure sped across the chamber and flung itself at Taran's feet. 'No, no, no!' howled Gurgi at the top of his voice, rocking back and forth and waving his hairy arms. 'Sharp-eared Gurgi hears all! Oh, yes, with listenings behind the door!' His face wrinkled in misery and he shook his matted head so violently he nearly sprawled flat on the floor. 'Poor Gurgi will be lone and lorn with whinings and pinings!' he moaned. 'Oh, he must go with master, yes, yes!'

Taran put a hand on Gurgi's shoulder. 'It would sadden me to leave you, old friend. But my road, I fear, may be a long one.'

'Faithful Gurgi will follow!' pleaded Gurgi. 'He is strong, bold, and clever to keep kindly master from harmful hurtings!'

Gurgi began snuffling loudly, whimpering and moaning more desperately than before; and Taran, who could not bring himself to deny the unhappy creature, looked questioningly at Dallben.

A strange glance of pity crossed the enchanter's face. 'Gurgi's staunchness and good sense I do not doubt,' he said to Taran. 'Though before your search is ended, the comfort of his kindly heart may stand you in better stead. Yes,' he added slowly, 'if Gurgi is willing, let him journey with you.'

Gurgi gave a joyous yelp, and Taran bowed gratefully to the enchanter.

'So be it,' Dallben said. 'Your road indeed will not be easy, but set out on it as you choose. Though you may not find what you seek, you will surely return a little wiser – and perhaps even grown to manhood in your own right.'

That night Taran lay restless. Dallben had agreed the two companions could depart in the morning, but for

Taran the hours until sunrise weighed like the links of a heavy chain. A plan had formed in his mind, but he had said nothing of it to Dallben, Coll or Gurgi; for he was half fearful of what he had decided. While his heart ached at the thought of leaving Caer Dallben, it ached more with impatience to begin his journey; and it was as though his yearning for Eilonwy, the love he had often hidden or even denied, now swelled like a flood, driving him before it.

Long before dawn Taran rose and saddled the grey, silver-maned stallion, Melynlas. While Gurgi, blinking and yawning, readied his own mount, a short, stocky pony almost as shaggy as himself, Taran went alone to Hen Wen's enclosure. As though she had already sensed Taran's decision, the white pig squealed dolefully as he knelt and put an arm around her.

'Farewell, Hen,' Taran said, scratching her bristly chin. 'Remember me kindly. Coll will care for you until I . . . Oh, Hen,' he murmured, 'shall I come happily to the end of my quest? Can you tell me? Can you give me some sign of good hope?'

In answer, however, the oracular pig only wheezed and grunted anxiously. Taran sighed and gave Hen Wen a last affectionate pat. Dallben had hobbled into the dooryard, and beside him Coll raised a torch, for the morning still was dark. Like Dallben's, the old warrior's face in the wavering light was filled with fond concern. Taran embraced them, and to him it seemed his love for both had never been greater than at this leave-taking as they said their farewells.

Gurgi sat hunched atop the pony. Slung from his shoulder was his leather wallet with its inexhaustible supply of food. Bearing only his sword at his belt and the silver-bound battle horn Eilonwy had given him, Taran swung astride the impatient Melynlas, constraining himself not to glance backward, knowing if he did, his parting would grieve him the more deeply.

The two wayfarers rode steadily while the sun climbed higher above the rolling, tree-fringed hills. Taran had spoken little, and Gurgi trotted quietly behind him, delving now and again into the leather wallet for a handful of food which he munched contentedly. When they halted to water their mounts at a stream, Gurgi clambered down and went to Taran's side.

'Kindly master,' he cried, 'faithful Gurgi follows as he leads, oh, yes! Where does he journey first with amblings and ramblings? To noble Lord Gwydion at Caer Dathyl? Gurgi longs to see high golden towers and great halls for feastings.'

'I, too,' answered Taran. 'But it would be labour lost. Dallben has told me Prince Gwydion and King Math know nothing of my parentage.'

'Then to kingdom of Fflewddur Fflam? Yes, yes! Bold bard will welcome us with meetings and greetings, with merry hummings and strummings!'

Taran smiled at Gurgi's eagerness, but shook his head. 'No, my friend, not to Caer Dathyl, nor to Fflewddur's realm.' He turned his eyes westward. 'I have thought carefully of this, and believe there is only one place where I might find what I seek,' he said slowly. 'The Marshes of Morva.'

No sooner had he spoken these words than he saw Gurgi's face turn ashen. The creature's jaw dropped; he clapped his hands to his shaggy head, and began gasping and choking frightfully.

'No, oh, no!' Gurgi howled. 'Dangers lurk in evil Marshes! Bold but cautious Gurgi fears for his poor tender head! He wants never to return there. Fearsome enchantresses would have turned him into a toad with hoppings and floppings! Oh, terrible Orddu! Terrible Orwen! And Orgoch, oh, Orgoch, worst of all!'

'Yet I mean to face them again,' Taran said. 'Orddu,

Orwen and Orgoch – she, or they, or whatever they may really be – are as powerful as Dallben. Perhaps more powerful. Nothing is hidden from them; all secrets are open. They would know the truth. Could it not be,' he went on, his voice quickening hopefully, 'could it not be that my parents were of noble lineage? And for some secret reason left me with Dallben to foster?'

'But kindly master *is* noble!' Gurgi cried. 'Noble, generous, and good to humble Gurgi! No need to ask enchanttresses!'

'I speak of noble blood,' Taran replied, smiling at Gurgi's protests. 'If Dallben cannot tell me, then Orddu may. Whether she will, I do not know,' he added. 'But I must try.

'I won't have you risk your poor tender head,' Taran continued. 'You shall find a hiding place at the edge of the Marshes and wait for me there.'

'No, no,' Gurgi moaned. He blinked wretchedly and his voice fell so low that Taran could scarcely hear his trembling whisper. 'Faithful Gurgi follows, as he promised.'

They set out again. For some days after fording Great Avren they bore quickly westward along the green slopes of the riverbank, leaving it reluctantly to wend north across a fallow plain. Gurgi's face puckered anxiously, and Taran sensed the creature's disquiet no less than his own. The closer they drew to the Marshes the more he questioned the wisdom of his choice. His plan which had seemed so fitting in the safety of Caer Dallben now struck him as rash, a foolhardy venture. There were moments when, Taran admitted to himself, had Gurgi spun the pony about and bolted homeward, he would have gladly done likewise.

Another day's travel and the marshland stretched before them, bleak, ugly, untouched by spring. The sight and scent of the bogs and the dull, stagnant pools filled Taran with loathing. The rotting turf sucked greedily at the hooves of Melynlas. The pony snorted fearfully. Warning Gurgi to stay close behind him and stray neither to the right nor left, Taran cautiously guided the stallion through beds of reeds shoulder-high, keeping to the firmer ground at the rim of the swamps.

The narrow neck at the upper reaches of the Marshes could be crossed with least danger, and the path indeed was burned into his memory. Here, when he and Eilonwy, Gurgi and Fflewddur had sought the Black Cauldron, the Huntsmen of Annuvin had attacked them, and Taran had lived the moment again and again in nightmares. Giving Melynlas rein, he beckoned to Gurgi and rode into the Marshes. The stallion faltered a sickening instant, then found footing on the chain of islands that lay beneath the brackish water. At the far side, without Taran's urging, Melynlas broke into a gallop, and the pony pelted after, as though fleeing for its life. Beyond the stunted trees at the end of a long gully, Taran halted. Orddu's cottage lay straight ahead.

Built against the side of a high mound, half-hidden by sod and branches, it seemed in even greater disrepair than Taran had remembered. The thatched roof, like a huge bird's nest, straggled down to block the narrow windows; a spider web of mould covered the walls, which looked ready to tumble at any moment. In the crooked doorway stood Orddu herself.

Heart pounding, Taran swung from the saddle. Holding his head high, in a silence broken only by the chattering of Gurgi's teeth, he strode slowly across the dooryard. Orddu was watching him with sharp, black eyes. If she was surprised, the enchantress gave no sign other than to bend forward a little and peer more closely at Taran. Her shapeless robe flapped about her knees; the jewelled clasps and pins glittered in her weedy tangle of dishevelled hair as she nodded her head rapidly and with evident satisfaction.

'Yes, and so it is!' Orddu called out pleasantly. 'The dear little fledgling and the – whatever-you-call-it. But you've grown much taller, my duck. How troublesome it must be should you ever want to climb down a rabbit hole. Come in, come in,' she hurried on, beckoning. 'So pale you are, poor thing. You've not been ill?'

Taran followed her not without uneasiness, while Gurgi, shuddering, clung to him. 'Beware, beware,' the creature whimpered. 'Warm welcomings give Gurgi frosty chillings.'

The three enchantresses, so far as Taran could see, had been busy at household tasks. Orgoch, her black hood shrouding her features, sat on a rickety stool, trying without great success to tease cockleburs from a lapful of wool shearings. Orwen, if indeed it was Orwen, was turning a rather lopsided spinning wheel; the milky white beads dangling from her neck seemed in danger of catching in the spokes. Orddu herself, he guessed, had been at the loom that stood amid piles of ancient, rusted weapons in a corner of the cottage. The work on the frame had gone forward somewhat, but it was far from done; knotted, twisted threads straggled in all directions, and what looked like some of Orgoch's cockleburs were snagged in the warp and weft. Taran could make out nothing of the pattern, though it seemed to him, as if by some trick of his eyes, that vague shapes, human and animal, moved and shifted through the weaving.

But he had no chance to study the curious tapestry. Orwen, leaving the wheel, hastened to him, clapping her hands delightedly.

'The wandering chicken and the gurgi!' she cried. 'And how is dear little Dallben? Does he still have *The Book of Three*? And his beard? How heavy it must be for him. The book, not the beard,' she added. 'Did he not come with you? More's the pity. But no matter. It's so charming to have visitors.'

'I don't care for visitors,' muttered Orgoch, irritably tossing the wool to the ground. 'They disagree with me.'

'Of course they do, greedy thing!' Orwen replied sharply. 'And a wonder it is that we have any at all.'

At this, Orgoch snorted and mumbled under her breath. Beneath her black hood Taran glimpsed a shadowy grimace.

Orddu raised a hand. 'Pay Orgoch no heed,' she said to Taran. 'She's out of sorts today, poor dear. It was Orwen's turn to be Orgoch, and Orgoch was so looking forward to being Orwen. Now she's disappointed, since Orwen at the last moment simply refused – not that I blame her,' Orddu whispered. 'I don't enjoy being Orgoch either. But we'll make it up to her somehow.

'And you,' Orddu went on, a smile wrinkling her lumpy face, 'you are the boldest of bold goslings. Few in Prydain have been willing to brave the Marshes of Morva; and of those few, not one has dared to return. Perhaps Orgoch disheartens them. You alone have done so, my chick.'

'Oh, Orddu, he is a brave hero,' Orwen put in, looking at Taran with girlish admiration.

'Don't talk nonsense, Orwen,' Orddu replied. 'There are heroes and heroes. I don't deny he's acted bravely on occasion. He's fought beside Lord Gwydion and been proud of himself as a chick wearing eagle's feathers. But that's only one kind of bravery. Has the darling robin ever scratched for his own worms? That's bravery of another sort. And between the two, dear Orwen, he might find the latter shows the greater courage.' The enchantress turned to Taran. 'But speak up, my fledgling. Why do you seek us again?'

'Don't tell us,' interrupted Orwen. 'Let us guess. Oh, but I do love games, though Orgoch always spoils them.' She giggled. 'You shall give us a thousand and three guesses and I shall be first to ask.'

'Very well, Orwen, if it pleases you,' Orddu said indulgently. 'But are a thousand and three enough? A young lamb can want for so much.'

'Your concern is with things as they are,' Taran said, forcing himself to look the enchantress in the eyes, 'and with things as they must be. I believe you know my quest from its beginning to its end, and that I seek to learn my parentage.'

'Parentage?' said Orddu. 'Nothing easier. Choose any parents you please. Since none of you has ever known each other, what difference can it possibly make – to them or to you? Believe what you like. You'll be surprised how comforting it is.'

'I ask no comfort,' Taran replied, 'but the truth, be it harsh or happy.'

'Ah, my sweet robin,' said Orddu, 'for the finding of that, nothing is harder. There are those who have spent lifetimes at it, and many in worse plight than yours.

'There was a frog, some time ago,' Orddu went on cheerfully. 'I remember him well, poor dear; never sure whether he was a land creature, who liked swimming under water, or a water creature, who liked sunning himself on logs. We turned him into a stork with a keen appetite for frogs, and from then on he had no doubts as to who he was – nor did the other frogs, for the matter of that. We would gladly do the same for you.'

'For both of you,' said Orgoch.

'No!' yelled Gurgi, ducking behind Taran. 'Oh, kindly master, Gurgi warned of fearsome changings and arrangings!'

'Don't forget the serpent,' Orwen told Orddu, 'all fretted and perplexed because he didn't know if he was green with brown spots or brown with green ones. We made him an invisible serpent,' she added, 'with brown and green spots, so he could be clearly seen and not trodden on. He was so grateful and much easier in his mind after that.'

'And I recall,' croaked Orgoch, huskily clearing her throat, 'there was a . . .'

'Do be still, Orgoch,' Orwen interrupted. 'Your tales

always have such – such untidy endings.'

'You see, my pullet,' Orddu said, 'we can help you in many ways, all quicker and simpler than any you might think of. What would you rather be? If you want my opinion, I suggest a hedgehog; it's a safer life than most. But don't let me sway your choice; it's entirely up to you.'

'On the contrary, let's surprise them,' cried Orwen in happy excitement. 'We'll decide among ourselves and spare them the tedious business of making up their minds. They'll be all the more pleased. How charming it will be to see the look on their little faces – or beaks or whatever it is they finally have.'

'No fowls,' grumbled Orgoch. 'No fowls, in any case. Can't abide them. Feathers make me cough.'

Gurgi's fright had so mounted he could only babble wordlessly. Taran felt his own blood run cold. Orddu had taken a step forward and Taran defensively reached for his sword.

'Now, now, my chicken,' Orddu cheerily remarked, 'don't lose your temper, or you may lose considerably more. You know your blade is useless here, and waving swords is no way to set anyone in a proper frame of mind. It was you who chose to put yourselves in our hands.'

'Hands?' growled Orgoch. From the depths of the hood her eyes flashed redly and her mouth began twitching.

Taran stood firm. 'Orddu,' he said, keeping his voice as steady as he could, 'will you tell me what I ask? If not, we will go our way.'

'We were only trying to make things easier for you,' said Orwen, pouting and fingering her beads. 'You needn't take offence.'

'Of course we shall tell you, my brave tadpole,' Orddu said. 'You shall know all you seek to know, directly we've settled another matter: the price to be paid. Since what you ask is of such importance – to yourself, at least – the cost may be rather high. But I'm sure you thought of that before you came.'

'When we sought the Black Cauldron,' Taran began, 'you took Adaon's enchanted brooch in fee, the one thing I treasured most. Since then I have found nothing I have prized more.'

'But, my chicken,' said Orddu, 'we struck that bargain long ago; it is over and done. Are you saying you brought nothing with you? Why, count yourself lucky to become a hedgehog, since you can afford little else.'

'Last time,' Orgoch hoarsely whispered in Orddu's ear, 'you would have taken one of the young lamb's summer days, and a tasty morsel it would have been.'

'You are always thinking of your own pleasures, Orgoch,' replied Orddu. 'You might at least try to think of what we all would like.'

'There was a golden-haired girl with him then,' Orwen put in, 'a pretty little creature. He surely has lovely memories of her. Could we not take them?' She went on eagerly. 'How delightful it would be to spread them out and look at them during long winter evenings. Alas, he would have none for himself, but I think it would be an excellent bargain.'

Taran caught his breath. 'Even you would not be so pitiless.'

'Would we not?' answered Orddu, smiling. 'Pity, dear gosling – as you know it, at least – simply doesn't enter into the question as far as we're concerned. However,' she went on, turning to Orwen, 'that won't answer either. We already have quite enough memories.'

'Hear me then,' cried Taran, drawing himself to his full height. He clenched his hands to keep them from trembling. 'It is true I own little to treasure, not even my name. Is there nothing you will have of me? This I offer you,' he went on quickly in a low voice. He felt his brow dampen. Though he had taken this decision at Caer Dallben and weighed it carefully, with the moment upon him, he nearly faltered and longed to turn from it.

'Whatever thing of value I may find in all my life to come,' Taran said, 'the greatest treasure that may come into my hands – I pledge it to you now. It shall be yours, and you shall claim it when you please.'

Orddu did not answer, only looked at him curiously. The other enchantresses were silent. Even Gurgi had ceased his whimpering. The shapes on the loom seemed to writhe before Taran's eyes as he waited for Orddu to speak.

The enchantress smiled. 'Does your quest mean so much that you will spend what you have not yet gained?'

'Or may never gain,' croaked Orgoch.

'No more can I offer,' Taran cried. 'You cannot refuse me.'

'The kind of bargain you propose,' said Orddu in a pleasant but matter-of-fact tone, 'is a chancy thing at best, and really satisfies no one. Nothing is all that certain, and very often we've found the poor sparrow who makes such a pledge never lives long enough to fulfil it. When he does, there is always the risk of his turning – well, shall we say – a little stubborn? It usually ends with unhappy feelings all around. Once, we might have accepted. But sad experience made us put a stop to it altogether. No, my fledgling, it won't do. We're sorry; that is, sorry as much as we can feel sorrow for anything.'

Taran's voice caught in his throat. For an instant the features of the enchantress shifted; he could not be sure whether it was Orddu, Orwen or Orgoch whom he faced. It was as though there had risen in front of him a wall of ice which force could not breach nor pleading melt. Despair choked him. He bowed his head and turned away.

'But, my dear gosling,' Orddu called cheerily, 'that's not to say there aren't others to answer your question.'

'Of course there are,' added Orwen, 'and the finding takes no more than the looking.'

'Who, then?' Taran asked urgently, seizing on this new hope.

'I recall a brown-and-orange ousel that comes once a year to sharpen his beak on Mount Kilgwyry,' said Orwen. 'He knows all that has ever happened. If you're patient you might wait and ask him.'

'Oh, Orwen,' Orddu interrupted with some impatience, 'sometimes I do believe you dwell too much in the past. Mount Kilgwyry has been worn down long ago with his pecking and the little darling has flown elsewhere.'

'You're so right, dear Orddu,' replied Orwen. 'It had slipped my mind for a moment. But what of the salmon of Lake Llew? I've never met a wiser fish.'

'Gone,' muttered Orgoch, sucking a tooth. 'Long gone.'

'In any case, ousels and fishes are flighty and slippery,' Orddu said. 'Something more reliable would serve better. You might, for example, try the Mirror of Llunet.'

'The Mirror of Llunet?' Taran repeated. 'I have never heard it spoken of. What is it? Where . . .'

'Best yet,' Orgoch broke in, 'he could stay with us. And the gurgi, too.'

'Do try to control yourself, dear Orgoch, when I'm explaining something,' Orddu remarked, then turned back to Taran. 'Yes, perhaps if you looked into it, the Mirror of Llunet would show you something of interest.'

'But where,' Taran began again.

'Too far,' grumbled Orgoch. 'Stay, by all means.'

'In the Llawgadarn Mountains,' replied Orddu, taking him by the arm, 'if it hasn't been moved. But come along, my gosling. Orgoch is growing restless. I know she'd enjoy having you here, and with two disappointments in the same day I shouldn't want to account for her behaviour.'

'But how may I find it?' Taran could do no more than stammer his question before he was outside the cottage, with Gurgi trembling at his side.

'Don't tarry in the Marshes,' Orddu called, while from within the cottage Taran heard loud and angry noises. 'Else you may regret your foolish boldness – or bold foolishness, whichever. Farewell, my robin.'

The crooked door closed tightly, even as Taran cried out for Orddu to wait.

'Flee!' Gurgi yelped. 'Flee, kindly master, while Gurgi's poor tender head is still on his shoulders!'

Despite the creature's frantic tugging at his arm, Taran stood staring at the door. His thoughts were confused, a strange heaviness had settled upon him.

'Why did she mock my bravery?' he said, frowning. 'Courage to scratch for worms? That task would be far easier than seeking the Mirror of Llunet.'

'Hasten!' Gurgi pleaded. 'Gurgi has his fill of questings. Now he is ready for returnings to safe and happy Caer Dallben, yes, yes! Oh, do not make useless peekings and seekings!'

Taran hesitated a moment longer. Of the Llawgadarn Mountains he knew only that they rose far to the east. With nothing to guide his search the journey might indeed prove useless. Gurgi looked imploringly at him. Taran patted the creature's shoulder, then turned and strode to Melynlas.

'The Mirror of Llunet is the only hope Orddu has given me,' Taran said. 'I must find it.'

While Gurgi hastily mounted his pony, Taran swung astride Melynlas. He glanced once again at the cottage, his heart suddenly uneasy. 'Given me?' he murmured. 'Does Orddu give anything for nothing?'

CHAPTER 2

Cantrev Cadiffor

The two companions left the Marshes of Morva, pressing south-eastward to the Valley Cantrevs along the Ystrad River, for Taran had decided to break his journey at Caer Cadarn, fortress of King Smoit, and ask the red-bearded king to refit them with gear sturdier than what they had brought from Caer Dallben. 'From there,' Taran told Gurgi, 'we can only search as the moment guides us. My poor tender head is full of questions,' he sighed, with a wry and regretful smile, 'but of plans, alas, none at all.'

With the Marshes many days behind, the two companions crossed the borders of Cadiffor, Smoit's realm and largest of the Valley Cantrevs. The countryside had long since changed from grey moors to green meadows and pleasantly wooded lands with farmholds nestled in the clearings. Though Gurgi eyed the dells longingly, sniffing the smoke of cookfires wafting from the cottage chimneys. Taran did not turn from the path he had chosen. By keeping a brisk pace, another three days of travel would bring them to Caer Cadarn. A little before sundown, seeing the clouds growing heavy and dark, Taran halted to find shelter in a pine grove.

He had scarcely dismounted, and Gurgi had only begun to unlash the saddlebags, when a band of horsemen cantered into the grove. Taran spun around and drew his blade. Gurgi, yelping in alarm, scurried to his master's side.

There were five riders, well-mounted and armed, their rough-bearded faces sun-blackened, their bearing that of men long used to the saddle. The colours they wore were not those of the House of Smoit, and Taran guessed the horsemen to be warriors in the service of one of Smoit's liegemen.

'Put up your blade,' commanded the leading rider, nevertheless drawing his own, reining up before the wayfarers and glancing scornfully at them. 'Who are you? Who do you serve?'

'They're outlaws,' cried another. 'Strike them down.'

'They look more like scarecrows than outlaws,' replied the leader. 'I take them for a pair of churls who have run away from their master.'

Taran lowered his sword but did not sheathe it. 'I am Taran Assistant Pig-Keeper . . .'

'Where then are your pigs?' cried the first rider with a coarse laugh. 'And why are you not at keeping them?' He gestured with a thumb towards Gurgi. 'Or will you tell me this – this sorry thing is one of your charges?'

'He is no piggy!' indignantly retorted Gurgi. 'No piggy at all! He is Gurgi, bold and clever to serve kindly master!'

The creature's outburst brought only more laughter from the horsemen. But now the first rider spied Melynlas. 'Your steed is above your station, pig-keeper,' he said. 'How do you come by it?'

'Melynlas is mine by right,' Taran replied sharply. 'A gift of Gwydion Prince of Don.'

'Lord Gwydion?' cried the warrior. 'Given? Stolen from him, rather,' he jeered. 'Have a care; your lies will cost you a beating.'

'I tell no lie and seek no quarrel,' Taran answered. 'We journey in peace to King Smoit's castle.'

'Smoit needs no pig-keeper,' one of the warriors broke in.

'Nor do we,' said the first rider. He swung around to his fellows. 'What say you? Shall we take his horse or his head? Or both?'

'Lord Goryon will welcome a fresh mount and reward us all the more for this one,' answered a rider. 'But the head of a pig-keeper serves no use, not even to himself.'

'Well said, and so be it!' cried the warrior. 'Besides, he can better mind his pigs afoot,' he added, reaching for the stallion's bridle.

Taran sprang between Melynlas and the horseman. Gurgi leaped forward and furiously grappled the rider's leg. The other warriors spurred their mounts, and Taran found himself in the midst of rearing horses, driven from the side of his own steed. He fought to bring up his sword. One of the riders wheeled and drove his mount's flank heavily against Taran, who lost his footing. At the same instant another of his assailants fetched him a blow that would surely have cost Taran his head had the warrior not struck with the flat of his sword. As it was, Taran fell stunned to the ground, his ears ringing, thoughts spinning, and the horsemen seeming to burst into comets before his eyes. He was dimly aware of Gurgi frantically yelling, of Melynlas whinnying, and it seemed to him that another figure had joined the fray. By the time he could stagger to his feet, the horsemen had vanished, dragging Melynlas with them.

Taran, crying out in dismay and anger, stumbled towards the path they had taken. A broad hand grasped his shoulder. He turned abruptly to see a man in a sleeveless jacket of coarse wool girt with a plaited rope. His bare arms were knotted and sinewy, and his back bent, though less by years than by labour. A shock of grey, uncropped hair hung about a face that was stern but not unkind.

'Hold, hold,' the man said. 'You'll not overtake them now. Your horse will come to no ill. The henchmen of Lord Goryon treat steeds better than strangers.' He patted the oaken staff he carried. 'Two of Goryon's border-band will have heads to mend. But so will you, from the look of you.' He picked up a sack and slung it over his shoulder. 'I am Aeddan Son of Aedd,' he said. 'Come, both of you. My farm is no distance.'

'Without Melynlas my quest will fail,' Taran cried. 'I must find – ' He stopped short. The warriors' mockery still rankled him, and he was reluctant to tell more than need be, even to this man who had befriended him.

But the farmer showed no interest in questioning him. 'What you seek,' replied Aeddan, 'is more your business than mine. I saw five set upon two and only put some fairness in the match. Will you heal your hurt? Then follow me.'

So saying, the farmer set off down the hillside, Taran and Gurgi behind him. Gurgi turned often to shake his fist in the direction of the departed horsemen, while Taran trudged along the darkening path, speaking not a word, deep in despair over Melynlas, and thinking bitterly that in his quest he had done no more than lose his horse and gain a broken head. His bones ached; his muscles throbbed. To worsen matters, the clouds had thickened; nightfall brought a pelting rain; and by the time he reached Aeddan's farmhold Taran was as drenched and bedraggled as ever he had been in all his life.

The dwelling into which Aeddan led the companions was only a hut of wattle and daub, but Taran was surprised at its snugness and neat furnishings. Never before in all his adventures had he shared hospitality with the farmer folk of Prydain, and he glanced around as wondering as a stranger in a new land. Now that he could look more closely at Aeddan, he sensed honesty and good nature in the man's weathered face. The farmer gave him a warm grin and Taran, despite the smart of his wounds, grinned back, feeling indeed that he had come upon a friend.

The farm wife, a tall, work-hardened woman with features as lined as her husband's, threw up her hands at the sight of Gurgi, whose dripping, matted hair had gathered a blanket of twigs and pine needles, and cried out at Taran's blood-smeared face. While Aeddan told of the fray, the woman, Alarca, opened a wooden chest and drew out a sturdy, warm jacket, well worn but lovingly mended, which Taran gratefully took in place of his own sodden garment.

Alarca set about mixing a potion of healing herbs, and Aeddan, meantime, poured on to a table the contents of his sack: hunches of bread, a cheese, and some dried fruit.

'You come to small comfort,' he said. 'My land yields little, so I toil part of my days in my neighbours' fields to earn what I cannot grow.'

'And yet,' Taran said, dismayed to learn Aeddan's plight, 'I have heard it told there was rich soil in the Valley Cantrevs.'

'Was, indeed,' replied Aeddan with a dour laugh. 'In the time of my forefathers, not in mine. As the Hill Cantrevs were famed for their long-fleeced sheep, so the Valley Cantrevs of Ystrad were known far and wide for the finest oats and barley, and Cantrev Cadiffor itself for wheat bright and heavy as gold. And golden days there must have been in all Prydain,' Aeddan went on, cutting the bread and cheese into portions and handing them to Taran and Gurgi. 'My father's father told a tale, already old when it was told to him, of ploughs that worked of themselves, of scythes that reaped a harvest without even the touch of a man's hand.'

'So, too, have I heard,' Taran said. 'But Arawn Death-Lord stole those treasures, and now they lie unused and hidden deep in the fastness of Annuvin.'

The farmer nodded. 'Arawn's hand chokes the life from Prydain. His shadow blights the land. Our toil grows heavier, and all the more because our skills are few. Enchanted tools did Arawn steal? Many secrets there were of making the earth yield richly, and of these, too, the Lord of Annuvin robbed us.

'Twice in two years have my crops failed,' Aeddan went on, as Taran listened with heartfelt concern. 'My granary is empty. And the more I must toil for others, the less I may work my own fields. Even so, my knowledge is too slight. What I most need is locked for ever in the treasure hoard of Annuvin.'

'It is not altogether your skill that lacks,' Alarca said, putting a hand on the farmer's knotted shoulder. 'Before the first planting the plough ox and cow sickened and died. And the second,' her voice lowered. 'For the second we were without the help of Amren.'

Taren glanced questioningly at the woman, whose eyes had clouded.

She said, 'Amren, our son. He was of your years, and it is his jacket you wear. He needs it no longer. Winter and summer are alike to him. He sleeps under a burial mound among other fallen warriors. Yes, he is gone,' the woman added. 'He rode with the battle host when they fought off raiders who sought to plunder us.'

'I share your sorrow,' Taran said; then, to console her, added, 'But he died with honour. Your son is a hero . . .'

'My son is slain,' the woman answered sharply. 'The raiders fought because they were starving; we, because we had scarcely more than they. And at the end all had less than when they began. Now, for us the labour is too great for one pair of hands, even for two. The secrets Arawn Death-Lord stole could well serve us. Alas, we cannot regain them.'

'No matter. Even without the secrets my harvest will not fail this year,' Aeddan said. 'All save one of my fields lies fallow; but in this one have I spent all my toil.' He looked proudly at Taran. 'When my wife and I could no longer pull the plough ourselves, I broke the earth with my own hands and sowed it grain by grain.' The farmer laughed. 'Yes, and weeded it blade by blade, as niggling as a granddam with her favourite patch of herbs. It will not fail. Indeed, it must not,' he added, frowning. 'This season our livelihood hangs on it.'

Little more was said then, and when the meagre meal ended, Taran gladly stretched his aching bones beside the hearth, while Gurgi curled up next to him. Weariness overcame even his despair for Melynlas, and with the patter of rain on the thatch and the hiss of the dying embers Taran soon fell asleep.

The companions woke before first light, but Taran found Aeddan already working in his field. The rain had stopped, leaving the earth fresh and moist. Taran knelt and took up a handful. Aeddan had spoken the truth. The soil had been tilled with utmost pains, and Taran watched the farmer with growing respect and admiration. The farm could indeed yield richly, and Taran stood a moment looking towards the fallow ground, barren for lack of hands to labour it. With a sigh he turned quickly away, his thoughts once more on Melynlas.

How he might regain the silver-maned stallion Taran could not foresee, but he had determined to make his way to the stronghold of Lord Goryon where, in Aeddan's judgement, the warriors had surely taken the animal. Though more than ever anxious over his beloved steed, Taran worked through the morning beside Aeddan. The farm couple had kept scarcely a morsel of the evening's fare for themselves, and Taran saw no other means to repay them. By midday, however, he dared delay no longer, and made ready to take his leave.

Alarca had come to the door of the hut. Like her husband, the woman had asked nothing beyond what little Taran had chosen to tell of his quest, but now she said, 'Will you still follow your own path? Have you turned from home and kinsmen? What mother's heart longs for her son as I long for mine?'

'Alas, none that I know,' Taran answered, folding Amren's jacket and gently putting it in her hands. 'And none that knows me.'

'You have been well taught in the ways of farming,'

Aeddan said. 'If you seek a place of welcome, you have already found one.'

'Whatever other welcomes I find, may they be as open-hearted as yours,' Taran replied, and it was not without regret that he and Gurgi said farewell.

CHAPTER 3

Goryon and Gast

Aeddan had pointed out the shortest path to Lord Goryon's stronghold, and the two wayfarers reached it by mid-afternoon. It was not a castle, Taran saw, but a large huddle of buildings circled by a barricade of wooden stakes lashed with osier and chinked up with hard-packed earth. The gate of heavy palings stood open, and there was much going and coming of horsemen, of warriors on foot, of herdsmen driving in their cows from pasture.

Though Gurgi was far from eager, Taran led on, keeping as bold a face as he could, and amid the busy crowd the two entered the stronghold unnoticed and unchallenged. Without difficulty Taran found the stables, which were larger, cleaner, and in better repair than the rest of the buildings; and strode quickly to a young boy raking straw, calling out in a firm voice, 'Tell me, friend, is there not a grey stallion here that Lord Goryon's warriors captured? A handsome steed, they say, and a rare one.'

'Grey stallion?' cried the stable boy. 'Grey dragon, rather! The beast half-kicked his stall down and gave me a bite I'll not forget. Lord Goryon will have broken bones before the day ends.'

'How then?' Taran hurriedly asked. 'What has he done with the steed?'

'What has the steed done with him!' answered the boy, grinning. 'Thrown him the most of a dozen times already! The Master of Horse himself cannot sit three moments on the creature's back, but Goryon tries to ride it even now. Goryon the Valorous he is called,' the boy chuckled; then added behind his hand, 'though to my mind he has little stomach for this task. But his henchmen egg him on, and so Goryon means to break the beast to his will even if he must first break its back.'

'Master, master,' Gurgi whispered frantically, 'hasten to King Smoit for helpings!'

Taran's face had paled at the boy's words. Caer Cadarn was too far; Smoit's help would come too late. 'Where is the steed?' he asked, hiding his concern. 'This would be a sight worth the seeing.'

The stable boy pointed his rake towards a long, low-roofed building. 'In the training field behind the Great Hall. But take heed,' he added, rubbing his shoulder, 'keep your distance, or the beast will give you worse than he gave me.'

Setting off instantly Taran no sooner passed the Great Hall than he heard shouting and the furious whinny of Melynlas. His pace quickened into a run. A grassless, hoof-beaten turf was ahead. He glimpsed warriors circling the grey stallion who reared, bucked, and spun about with heels flying. In another moment the burly, thickset figure atop the stallion's back was flung loose; then, arms and legs flailing, Lord Goryon plummeted to earth and lay there like a sack of lead.

Melynlas galloped desperately, seeking escape from the circle of warriors, one of whom hastened to snatch at the horse's reins. All caution forgotten, Taran cried out and raced to the stallion's side. He grasped the bridle before the surprised man could think of drawing his sword, and threw his arms about the neck of Melynlas, who whickered in greeting. The other onlookers ran towards Taran, as he strove to mount and pull Gurgi up after him. A hand seized his jacket. Taran fought free and set his back against the stallion's flank. Lord Goryon had meanwhile picked himself up and now burst through the press of warriors.

'Insolence! Impudence!' roared Goryon. His dark, grey-shot beard bristled like a furious hedgehog. His heavy face was mottled purple, whether from bruises, lack of breath, blind anger, or all three at once Taran could not judge. 'Does a churl lay hand on my horse? Away with him! Thrash him soundly for his insult!'

'I do no more than claim my own steed,' Taran cried. 'Melynlas foal of Melyngar . . .'

A tall, raw-boned man with one arm bound up in a sling, whom Taran guessed to be the Master of Horse, peered sharply at him. 'Foal of Melyngar, Prince Gwydion's war horse? That is noble lineage. How do you know this?'

'I know it as well as I know Melynlas was stolen from me,' Taran declared, 'near Aeddan's farmhold at the borders of your cantrev, and my comrade robbed of his pony.' He tried then to explain who he was and the purpose of his journey, but the cantrev lord, unheeding, broke in angrily.

'Impudence!' cried Goryon, his beard bristling all the more furiously. 'How dares a pig-keeper insult me with a liar's tale? My border-band gained these mounts nearly at the cost of their lives.'

'The cost of our lives,' Taran retorted, glancing hurriedly at the faces around him. 'Where are the riders? I beg you call them to witness.'

'More insolence!' snapped the cantrev lord. 'They ride the borders, as they are commanded. Do you mean to tell me I keep idle men and shirkers in my service?'

'And full service have they given you,' one of the warriors said to Goryon. 'Heroes, all of them, to stand against six giants . . .'

'Giants?' repeated Taran, scarcely believing his ears.

'Giants indeed!' cried Goryon. 'It will not be forgotten how the brave riders of Goryon the Valorous were beset by enemies, outnumbered two to one. By worse than giants! For one was a fierce monster with sharp claws and fangs. Another carried an oak tree in his fist and swept it about him as if it were no more than a twig. But the riders of Goryon overcame them all with glory and honour!'

'The stallion, too, was bewitched,' put in another of Goryon's henchmen, 'and fought as fiercely as the giants. The beast is a man-killer, vicious as a starving wolf.'

'But Goryon the Valorous will tame the creature,' added another, turning to the cantrev lord. 'You'll ride the brute, will you not, Goryon?'

'Eh?' said Goryon, a painful and unhappy grimace suddenly marking his face. 'So I will, so I will,' he growled; then flung out angrily, 'You insult my honour if you think I cannot.'

As Taran stood among these rough warriors, he began to despair of finding any means of convincing the prickly-tempered cantrev lord; the thought crossed his mind to draw blade and fight his way out as best he could. But another glance at the stern faces of the henchmen gave him only more cause for dismay.

'My lord,' Taran said firmly, 'I speak the truth. There were no giants, but my companion and myself, and a farmer who fought beside us.'

'No giants?' shouted Goryon. 'But more insults!' He stamped his foot as if the turf itself had given him some impertinence. 'You call my men liars? As well call me one!'

'My lord,' Taran began again, bowing deeply, for it was growing clear to him that Goryon's touchy honour could scarcely allow the cantrev lord to believe an account of simple horse-stealing; and there was, Taran realized, even for the border-band themselves, considerably more honour in overcoming giants than in robbing Assistant Pig-Keepers. 'I call no man liar and your men spoke the truth. The truth,' he added, 'as they saw it.'

'Insolence!' cried Goryon. 'The truth as it is! There were giants, monsters, uprooted oaks. My men were well rewarded for their valour, but you shall have a beating for your impudence!'

'What I believe, my lord, is this,' Taran went on, choosing his words carefully, since all he had thus far managed to say Goryon had turned into one kind of insult or another. 'The sun was low and our shadows made our number seem twice as great. Indeed, your men saw double what we truly were.

'As for giants,' Taran hurried on before the cantrev lord could cry out against another impertinence, 'again, the long shadows of sunset gave us such height that any man could mistake our size.'

'The oak-tree cudgel,' Lord Goryon began.

'The farmer bore a stout oaken staff,' Taran said. 'His arm was strong, his blows quick, as two of your men had good reason to know. He smote with such a mighty hand, small wonder they felt a tree had fallen on them.'

Lord Goryon said nothing for a moment, but sucked a tooth and rubbed his bristling beard. 'What of the monster? A raving, ferocious creature they saw with their own eyes?'

'The monster stands before you,' Taran answered, pointing to Gurgi. 'He has long been my companion. I know him to be gentle, but the fiercest foe when roused.'

'He is Gurgi! Yes, yes!' Gurgi shouted. 'Bold, clever, and fierce to fight for kindly master!' With this he bared his teeth, shook his hairy arms, and yelled so frightfully that Goryon and his henchmen drew backward a pace.

The face of the cantrev lord had begun to furrow in deep perplexity. He shifted his bulk from one foot to the other and glared at Taran. 'Shadows!' he growled. 'You mean to shadow the bravery of those who serve me. Another insult . . .'

'If your warriors believed they had seen what they claimed,' Taran said, 'and fought accordingly, their bravery is no less. Indeed,' he added, half under his breath, 'it is every bit as great as their truthfulness.'

'These are no more than words,' interrupted the Master of Horse. 'Show me deeds. There is no creature on four hooves that I cannot ride, save this one. You, churl, will you dare to mount?'

For answer, Taran swung quickly into the saddle. Melynlas whinnied, pawed the ground, then stood calmly. Lord Goryon choked with amazement, and the Master of Horse stared in disbelief. A surprised murmur rose from Goryon's henchmen, but Taran heard a rough laugh as one of them called, 'So ho, Goryon! A lout rides a steed a lord has not mastered, and takes your horse and honour both!'

Taran thought he had seen a faint flicker of relief in Goryon's bruised face, as though he were not altogether displeased to avoid riding Melynlas, but at the henchman's words the cantrev lord's features began to darken furiously.

'Not so!' Taran hastily cried out to the circle of men. 'Would you have your liege lord ride a pig-keeper's nag? Is that fitting to his honour?' He turned now to Goryon, for a bold thought had come to him. 'And yet, my lord, were you to take him as a gift from me . . .'

'What?' shouted Goryon at the top of his voice, his face turning livid. 'Insults! Impertinence! Insolence! How dare you! I take no gifts from pig-keepers! Nor will I lower myself to mount the beast again.' He flung up an arm. 'Begone! Out of my sight – your nag, your monster, and his pony along with you!'

Goryon snapped his jaws shut and said no more. Gurgi's pony was led from the stable, and under the eyes of the cantrev lord and his henchmen the two companions passed unhindered through the gate.

Taran rode slowly, head high, with all the assurance he could muster. But once out of sight of the stronghold, the companions clapped heels into their horses' flanks and galloped for dear life.

'Oh, wisdom that wins horses from prideful lord!' Gurgi

cried, when they had ridden far enough to be safe from any change of heart on the part of Goryon. 'Even Gurgi could not have been so clever. Oh, he wishes to be wise as kindly master, but his poor tender head has no skill in such thinkings!'

'My wisdom?' Taran laughed. 'Barely enough to make up for losing Melynlas in the first place.' He scanned the valley anxiously. Night was falling and he had hoped by this time to have come upon a farmhold where they might shelter, for the encounter with Goryon's border-band had given him no wish to learn what others might be roving the hills. But he saw neither cottage nor hut, and so pressed on through the purpling dusk.

Lights flared in a clearing ahead, and Taran reined Melynlas to a halt near a stronghold much like Lord Goryon's. But here torches blazed at every corner of the palisade, from sockets set high on either side of the gate, even at the rooftree of the Great Hall, as if in token of feasting and revelry within.

'Dare we stop here?' Taran said. 'If this cantrev lord shows us Goryon's courtesy, we'd sleep sounder in a gwythaint's nest.' Nevertheless, the hope of a comfortable bed and the torches' inviting glow made his weariness weigh all the heavier. He hesitated a moment, then urged Melynlas closer to the gate.

To the men in the watchtower Taran called out that here were wayfarers journeying to Caer Cadarn and known to King Smoit. He was relieved when the portal creaked open and the guards beckoned the pair to enter. The Chief Steward was summoned, and he led Taran and Gurgi to the Great Hall.

'Beg hospitality of my Lord Gast,' the Steward told them, 'and he will grant what he deems fitting.'

As he followed the Steward, Taran's spirits rose at the thought of a warm meal and a comfortable couch. Loud voices, laughter and the merry notes of a harp came from the Hall. Stepping through the doorway Taran saw crowded tables on either side of a low-ceilinged room. At the far end, flanked by his henchmen and their ladies, sat a richly garbed war lord, a drinking horn in one fist and most of a joint of meat in the other.

Taran and Gurgi bowed deeply. Before they could draw closer, the harper standing in the middle of the Hall turned, cried out in surprise, and ran to them. Taran, whose hand was being shaken half off his arm, found himself blinking with happy astonishment at the long pointed nose and spiky yellow hair of his old companion, Fflewddur Fflam.

'Well met, the two of you,' cried the bard, pulling them to the high table. 'I've missed you ever since we parted. Did you not stay at Caer Dallben? When we sailed from Mona,' Fflewddur hurriedly explained, 'I really meant to leave off wandering and settle down in my own realm. Then I said to myself, Fflewddur old fellow, spring's only once a year. And here it is. And here am I. But what of yourselves? First, food and drink, and your tidings later.'

Fflewddur had brought the companions to stand before Lord Gast, and Taran saw a heavy-featured warrior with a beard the colour of muddy flax. A handsome collar-piece dangled from his neck; rings glittered on fingers stout enough to crack walnuts; and bands of beaten silver circled his arms. The cantrev lord's raiment was costly and well-cut, but Taran saw it bore the spots and spatters not only of this feast but of many others long past.

The bard, with a sweep of his harp, named the companions to Lord Gast. 'These are two who sought the Black Cauldron from Arawn of Annuvin and fought at the side of Gwydion Prince of Don. Let your hospitality match their boldness.'

'And so it shall!' Gast loudly cried. 'No wayfarer can fault the hospitality of Gast the Generous!' He made place for the companions at his table and, sweeping aside the empty bowls and dishes before him, clapped his hands and bawled for the Steward. When the servitor arrived, Lord

Gast commanded him to bring such an array of food and drink that Taran could hardly imagine himself eating half of it. Gurgi, hungry as always, smacked his lips in gleeful anticipation.

As the Steward left, Lord Gast took up a tale, whose matter Taran found difficult to follow, concerning the costliness of his food and his open-handedness towards travellers. Taran listened courteously through it all, surprised and delighted at his good luck in finding Gast's stronghold. Feeling more at ease, thanks to the presence of Fflewddur, Taran at last ventured to speak of his meeting with Lord Goryon.

'Goryon!' snorted Gast. 'Arrogant boor! Crude lout! Braggart and boaster! To boast of what?' He snatched up a drinking horn. 'See this?' he cried. 'The name of Gast carved upon it and the letters worked in gold! See this cup! This bowl! These ornament my common table. My storehouse holds even finer, as you shall see. Goryon! Horseflesh is all he knows, and little enough of that!'

Fflewddur, meanwhile, had raised the harp to his shoulder and began to strike up a tune. 'It's a small thing I composed myself,' he explained. 'Though I must say it's been cheered and praised by thousands . . .'

No sooner were the words past his lips than the harp bent like an overdrawn bow and a string broke with a loud twang. 'Drat the thing!' muttered the bard. 'Will it give me no peace? I swear it's getting worse. The slightest bit of colour added to the facts and it costs me a string. Yes, as I meant to say, I know full half a dozen who deemed the song – ah – rather well done.' With deftness born of long, sad practice, Fflewddur knotted up the broken string.

Taran, glancing around the Hall this while, was surprised to realize the plates and drinking horns of the guests were more than half empty and, in fact, showed no sign of ever having been full. His perplexity grew when the Steward returned to set the food-laden tray before Lord Gast, who planted his elbows on either side of it.

'Eat your fill,' cried Gast to Taran and Gurgi, pushing a small hunch of gravy-spotted bread towards them and keeping the rest for himself. 'Gast the Generous is ever openhanded! A sad fault that may turn me into a pauper, but it's my nature to be free with all my goods; I can't fight against it!'

'Generous?' Taran murmured under his breath to Fflewddur, while Gurgi, swallowing the skimpy fare, looked hopelessly around for more. 'I think he'd make a miser seem a prodigal in comparison.'

So passed the meal, with Gast loudly urging the companions to stuff themselves, yet all the while grudgingly offering them no more than a few morsels of stringy meat from the heaped platter. Only at the end, when Gast had swallowed all he could and his head nodded sleepily and his beard straggled into his drinking horn, were the companions able to down the meagre leavings. At last, disheartened and with bellies still hollow, the three groped their way to a meanly furnished chamber, where they nevertheless dropped into sleep like stones.

In the morning Taran was impatient to start once more for Caer Cadarn, and Fflewddur agreed to ride with him. But Lord Gast would hear none of it until the companions marvelled at his storerooms. The cantrev lord flung open chests of goblets, ornaments, weapons, horse trappings and many things Taran judged of high value, but in such a muddled heap that he could scarcely tell one from another. Among all these goods Taran's eyes lingered on a gracefully fashioned wine bowl, the most beautiful Taran had ever seen. He had, however, little chance to admire it, for the cantrev lord quickly thrust a garishly ornamented horse bridle into Taran's hands and as quickly replaced it with a pair of stirrups which he praised equally.

'That wine bowl is worth all the rest put together,' Fflewddur whispered to Taran, as Lord Gast now led the three companions from the storehouse to a large cow pen just outside the barricade. 'I recognize the work from the hand of Annlaw Clay-Shaper, a master craftsman, the most skilled potter in Prydain. I swear his wheel is enchanted! Poor Gast!' Fflewddur added. 'To count himself rich and know so little of what he owns!'

'But how has he gained such treasure?' Taran said.

'On that score, I should hesitate to ask,' Fflewddur murmured with a grin. 'Very likely the same way Goryon gained your horse.'

'And this,' cried the cantrev lord, halting beside a black cow who stood peacefully grazing amid the rest of the herd, 'and this is Cornillo, the finest cow in all the land!'

Taran could not gainsay the words of the cantrev lord, for Cornillo shone as if she had been polished and her short, curving horns sparkled in the sun.

Lord Gast proudly stroked the animal's sleek flanks. 'Gentle as a lamb! Strong as an ox! Swift as a horse and wise as an owl!' Gast went on, while Cornillo, calmly munching her cud, turned patient eyes to Taran, as though hoping not to be mistaken for anything other than a cow.

'She leads my cattle,' declared Lord Gast, 'better than any herdsman can. She'll pull a plough or turn a grist mill, if need be. Her calves are always twins! As for milk, she gives the sweetest! Cream, every drop! So rich the dairy maids can scarcely churn it!'

Cornillo blew out her breath almost in a sigh, switched her tail, and went back to grazing. From the pasture Lord Gast pressed the companions to the hen roost, and from there to the hawk mews, and the morning was half spent and Taran had begun to despair of ever leaving the stronghold, when Gast finally ordered their mounts readied.

Fflewddur, Taran saw, still rode Llyan, the huge, golden-tawny cat who had saved the companions' lives on the Isle of Mona. 'Yes, I decided to keep her – rather, she's decided to keep me,' said the bard, as Llyan, recognizing Taran, padded forward and began happily rubbing her head against his shoulder. 'She loves the harp more than ever,'

Fflewddur went on. 'Can't hear enough of it.' No sooner did he say this than Llyan flicked her long whiskers and turned to give the bard a forceful nudge; so that Fflewddur then and there had to unsling his instrument and strike a few chords, while Llyan, purring loudly, blinked fondly at him with great yellow eyes.

'Farewell,' called the cantrev lord as the companions mounted. 'At the stronghold of Gast the Generous you'll ever find an openhanded welcome!'

'It's a generosity that could starve us to death,' Taran, laughing, remarked to the bard as they rode eastward again. 'Gast thinks himself openhanded, as Goryon thinks himself valorous; and as far as I can judge, neither one has the truth of it. Yet,' he added, 'they both seem pleased with themselves. Indeed, is a man truly what he sees himself to be?'

'Only if what he sees is true,' answered Fflewddur. 'If there's too great a difference between his own opinion and the facts – ah – then, my friend, I should say that such a man had no more substance to him than Goryon's giants!

'But don't judge them too harshly,' the bard went on. 'These cantrev nobles are much alike, prickly as porcupines one moment and friendly as puppies the next. They all hoard their possessions, yet they can be generous to a fault if the mood strikes them. As for valour, they're no cowards. Death rides in the saddle with them and they count it nothing, and in battle I've seen them gladly lay down their lives for a comrade. At the same time,' he added, 'it's also been my experience, in all my wanderings, that the farther from the deed, the greater it grows, and the most glorious battle is the one longest past. So it's hardly surprising how many heroes you run into.

'Had they harps like mine,' said Fflewddur, warily glancing at his instrument, 'what a din you'd hear from every stronghold in Prydain!'

CHAPTER 4

A Matter of Cows

Late that afternoon the companions sighted the crimson banner of the House of Smoit, its black bear emblem flying bravely above the towers of Caer Cadarn. Unlike the palisaded strongholds of the cantrev lords, Smoit's castle was a fortress with walls of hewn stone and iron-studded gates thick enough to withstand all attack; the chips in the stones and the dents in the portal told Taran the castle had indeed thrown back not a few assaults. For the three travellers, however, the gates were flung open willingly and an honour guard of spearmen hastened to escort the companions.

The red-bearded King sat at the dining table in his Great Hall, and from the array of dishes, platters and drinking horns both full and empty Taran judged Smoit could scarcely have left off eating since morning. Seeing the companions, the King leaped from his throne of oakwood, fashioned in the shape of a gigantic bear looking much like Smoit himself.

'My body and bones!' Smoit roared so loudly the dishes rattled on the table. 'It's better than a feast to see all of you!' His battle-scarred face beamed with delight and he flung his burly arms around the companions in a joint-cracking hug. 'Scrape out a tune from that old pot of yours,' he cried to Fflewddur. 'A merry tune for a merry meeting! And you, my lad,' he went on, seizing Taran's shoulders with his heavy, red-furred hands, 'when last we met you looked scrawny as a plucked chicken. And your shaggy friend – what, has he rolled in the bushes all the way from Caer Dallben?'

Smoit clapped his hands, shouted for more food and

drink, and would hear nothing of Taran's news until the companions had eaten and the King had downed another full meal.

'The Mirror of Llunet?' said Smoit, when Taran at last was able to tell of his quest. 'I've heard of no such thing. As well seek a needle in a haystack as a looking glass in the Llawgadarn Mountains.' The King's heavy brow furrowed and he shook his head. 'The Llawgadarns rise in the land of the Free Commots, and whether the folk there will be of a mind to help you . . .'

'The Free Commots?' Taran asked. 'I've heard them named, but know little else about them.'

'They're hamlets and small villages,' Fflewddur put in. 'They start to the east of the Hill Cantrevs and spread as far as Great Avren. I've never journeyed there myself; the Free Commots are a bit far even for my ramblings. But the land itself is the pleasantest in Prydain – fair hills and dales, rich soil to farm, and sweet grass for grazing. There's iron for good blades, gold and silver for fine ornaments. Annlaw Clay-Shaper is said to dwell among the Commot folk, as do many other craftsmen: master weavers, metalsmiths – from time out of mind their skills have been the Commots' pride.'

'A proud folk they are,' said Smoit. 'And a stiff-necked breed. They bow to no cantrev lords, but only to the High King Math himself.'

'No cantrev lords – ' asked Taran, puzzled. 'Who, then, rules them?'

'Why, they rule themselves,' answered Smoit. 'Strong and steadfast they are, too. And, by my beard, I'm sure there's more peace and neighbourliness in the Free Commots than anywhere else in Prydain. And so what need have they for kings or lords? When you come to the meat of it,' he added, 'a king's strength lies in the will of those he rules.'

Taran, who had been listening closely to these words

of Smoit, nodded his head. 'I had not thought of it thus,' he said, half to himself. 'Indeed, true allegiance is only given willingly.'

'Enough talk!' cried Smoit. 'It hurts my head and dries my gullet. Let's have more meat and drink. Forget the Mirror. Tarry with me in my cantrev, lad. We'll ride to the hunt, feast and make merry. You'll put more flesh on your bones here than scrambling about on a fool's errand. And that, my boy, is good counsel to you.'

Nevertheless, when he finally saw that Taran would not be dissuaded, Smoit goodnaturedly agreed to give the companions all they needed for the journey. Next morning, after a huge breakfast, which Smoit declared would serve to whet their appetites for dinner, the King threw open his storehouse to them and went with them to be sure they chose the best of gear.

Taran had only begun sorting through coils of rope, saddlebags and harness leather when one of the castle guards burst into the storeroom, calling, 'Sire! A horseman of Lord Gast is come. Raiders from Lord Goryon's stronghold have stolen Gast's prize cow and the rest of the herd with her!'

'My pulse!' roared Smoit. 'My breath and blood!' The King's tangled bush of eyebrows knotted and his face turned as red as his beard. 'How does he dare stir trouble in my cantrev!'

'The men of Gast have armed. They ride against Goryon,' the guard hastened on. 'Gast craves your help. Will you speak to his messenger?'

'Speak to him?' bellowed Smoit. 'I'll clap his master in irons for breaking the peace. And worse! For breaking it without my leave!'

'Put Gast in irons?' Taran asked with some perplexity. 'But Goryon stole his cow . . .'

'*His* cow?' cried Smoit. 'His cow, indeed! Gast stole her from Goryon himself last year. And before that, the other way around. Neither of them knows whose beast it rightly is. Those two brawlers have ever been at loggerheads. Now the warm weather heats their blood again. But I'll cool their tempers. In my dungeon! Gast and Goryon both!'

Smoit snatched up a mighty double-edged battle-axe. 'I'll fetch them back by the ears!' he roared. 'They know my dungeons; they've been there often enough. Who rides with me?'

'I will!' cried Fflewddur, his eyes lighting up. 'Great Belin, a Fflam never shuns a fight!'

'If you ask our help, Sire,' Taran began, 'we give it willingly. But . . .'

'Mount up, then, my lad!' shouted Smoit. 'You'll see justice done. And I'll have peace between Gast and Goryon if I have to break their heads to gain it!'

Swinging his battle-axe, Smoit bolted from the storeroom bellowing orders right and left. A dozen warriors sprang to horse. Smoit leaped astride a tall, barrel-chested steed, whistled through his teeth almost loudly enough to break them, and waved his men onward; amid the shouting and confusion Taran, bewildered, found himself atop Melynlas galloping across the courtyard and out the castle gate.

The red-bearded King set such a pace through the valleys that it put even Llyan on her mettle to keep up; while Gurgi, with most of the wind pounded out of him, clung to the neck of his frantically galloping pony. Smoit's war horse was in a lather, and so was Melynlas before the cantrev King signalled a halt.

'To meat!' Smoit cried, swinging out of the saddle and looking as unwearied as if he had just begun a morning's trot. The companions, still catching their breath, had by no means found their appetites, but Smoit clapped his hands to the heavy bronze belt around his middle. 'Hunger makes a man gloomy and saps all the spirit from a battle.'

'Sire, must we battle with Lord Gast?' Taran asked with some concern, for Smoit's war band numbered only the dozen who had ridden from Caer Cadarn. 'And if Lord Goryon's men have armed, we may be too few to stand against all of them.'

'Battle?' Smoit retorted. 'No, more's the pity. I'll have those troublemakers by the nose and into my dungeons before nightfall. They'll do as I command. I'm their king, by my beard! There's brawn enough here,' he added, shaking a mighty fist, 'to make them remember it.'

'And yet,' Taran ventured to say, 'you yourself told me a king's true strength lay in the will of those he ruled.'

'How's that?' cried Smoit, who had settled his bulk against a tree trunk and was about to attack the joint of meat he had pulled from his saddlebag. 'Don't puzzle me with my own words! My body and bones, a king is a king!'

'I meant only that you've locked Gast and Goryon in your dungeon many times before,' Taran answered. 'And still they quarrel. Is there no way to keep peace between them? Or make them understand . . .'

'I'll reason them reasons!' bellowed Smoit, clutching his battle-axe. He knitted his jutting brows. 'But, true enough it is,' he admitted, frowning and seeming to chew at the thought as if it were gristle in his meat, 'they go surly to the dungeon and surly leave it. You've struck on something, my lad. The dungeon's useless against that pair. And, my pulse, I know why! It needs more dampness, more draught. So be it! I'll have the place well watered down tonight.'

Taran was about to remark that his own thought was otherwise, but Fflewddur called out and pointed to a horseman galloping across the meadow.

'He wears the colours of Goryon,' shouted Smoit, jumping to his feet, still holding the joint in one hand and the battle-axe in the other. Two of the warriors quickly mounted and, drawing swords, spurred to engage the rider. But the horseman, brandishing his weapon hilt downward, cried out that he bore tidings from the cantrev lord.

'You rogue!' Smoit bellowed, dropping both meat and axe and collaring the rider to haul him bodily from the saddle. 'What other mischief's afoot? Speak! Give me your news, man, or I'll have it out of you along with your gizzard!'

'Sire!' gasped the messenger, 'Lord Gast attacks in strength. My Lord Goryon is hard-pressed; he has ordered more of his warriors to arm and calls on you to help him as well.'

'What of the cows?' cried Smoit. 'Has Gast won them back? Does Goryon still hold them?'

'Neither, Sire,' answered the messenger as well as he could with Smoit shaking him between every word. 'Lord Gast attacked Lord Goryon to regain his own herd and take Lord Goryon's, too. But as they fought, all the beasts frighted and ran off. The cows? Sire, both herds are gone, lost, every soul of them, and Cornillo herself!'

'Let that be the end of it!' declared Smoit, 'and a good lesson for all cow-robbers. Gast and Goryon shall cry peace and I'll spare them from my dungeon.'

'Sire, the fighting grows hotter,' the messenger said urgently. 'Neither one will leave off. Each blames the other for loss of his herd. Lord Goryon swears vengeance on Lord Gast; and Lord Gast swears vengeance on Lord Goryon.'

'They've both been itching for battle,' Smoit burst out. 'Now they find their excuse!' He summoned one of his warriors, ordering him to take Goryon's messenger to Caer Cadarn, there to be held as hostage. 'To horse, the rest of you,' Smoit commanded. 'My body and bones, we'll see sport after all.' He gripped his axe. 'Oh, there'll be heads broken today!' he cried with relish, and his battered face brightened as if he were on his way to a feast.

'The bards will sing of this,' exclaimed Fflewddur, carried away by Smoit's ardour. 'A Fflam in the thick of battle! The thicker the better!' The harp shuddered and a string snapped in two. 'I mean,' Fflewddur hastily added, 'I hope we're not too badly outnumbered.'

'Sire,' Taran called as Smoit strode to his war horse. 'If Gast and Goryon won't stop because their herds are lost, shouldn't we try to find the cows?'

'Yes, yes!' Gurgi put in. 'Find cows gone with strayings! And put an end to fightings and smitings!'

But Smoit had already mounted and was shouting for the war band to follow; and Taran could do no more than gallop after him. To which stronghold Smoit was leading them, Taran did not know. As far as Smoit was concerned, Taran decided, it made little difference whether Gast or Goryon fell first into the King's hands.

In a while, however, Taran recognized the path he and Gurgi had taken from Aeddan's farm, and he judged now that Smoit would make for Goryon's stronghold. But as they pounded across an open field, the King veered sharply left and Taran glimpsed a troop of mounted warriors some distance away.

At the sight of their banners, Smoit bellowed furiously and spurred his steed to overtake the horsemen. But the riders, themselves galloping at top speed, quickly vanished into the woodland. Smoit reined up, shouting after them and shaking his huge fist.

'Has Goryon put more warriors in the fray?' roared Smoit, his face crimson. 'Then Gast has done the same! Those louts wore his colours!'

'Sire,' Taran began, 'if we can find the cows – '

'Cows!' burst out Smoit. 'There's more than cows in this, my lad. Such a brawl can spread like a spark through tinder. Those thick-skulled ruffians will set the whole of Cadiffor ablaze and the next thing you know we'll all be at one another's throats! But, by my beard, they'll learn my fist smites harder than theirs!'

Smoit hesitated and his face darkened with deep concern. He scowled and tugged at his beard. 'The lords of the next cantrev,' he muttered. 'They'll not stand idle, but strike against us when they see we're fighting each other!'

'But the cows,' Taran urged. 'The three of us can seek them, while you – '

'The dungeon!' cried Smoit. 'I'll have Gast and Goryon in it before their squabble gets further out of hand.'

Smoit clapped heels to his horse and charged forward, making no attempt to hold to any pathway, dashing at breakneck speed through bramble and thicket. With the companions and the train of warriors pelting behind, Smoit clattered over the stones of a riverbank and plunged his horse into the swift current. The King had ill chosen his fording place, for in another moment Taran found himself in water up to his saddlehorn. Smoit, shouting impatiently, pressed on across the river. Taran saw the King rise up in his stirrups to beckon his followers and urge more haste. But an instant later the war horse lost footing and lurched sideways; steed and rider toppled with a mighty splash, and before Taran could spur Melynlas to him, Smoit had been torn loose from his mount and, like a barrel with arms and legs, was being borne quickly downstream.

Behind Taran some of the warriors had turned back, seeking to overtake the King by following along the riverbank. Taran, closer to the opposite bank, urged all strength from Melynlas, leaped from the saddle to dry ground, and raced along the shore after Smoit. The sound of rushing water filled his ears, and with dismay Taran realized the King was being pulled relentlessly to a waterfall. Heart bursting in his chest, Taran doubled his pace; though before he could set foot in the rapids, he saw the King's red beard sink below the churning water, and he cried out in despair as Smoit vanished over the brink.

CHAPTER 5

A Judgement

Taran scrambled down the rocks jutting beside the high cascade. In a pool hammered into white spray he could hardly make out Smoit's burly form spinning in the eddies. Heedless of the pounding water, Taran pitched through the falls and sprang into the pool. He groped for Smoit's belt and seized it at last. Battling the whirlpool and nearly drowning himself with his own efforts, Taran painfully strove to drag the half-conscious King into the shallows.

Smoit was bleeding heavily from the forehead and his ruddy face had gone chalky pale. Taran tugged at the King's waterlogged bulk, hauling him safely from the rolling waters. In another moment Gurgi and Fflewddur were beside him, helping to drag the King ashore. Smoit, like a beached whale, collapsed on the bank.

Gurgi, moaning anxiously, loosened the King's garments, while Taran and the bard hastily saw to Smoit's injuries.

'He can count himself lucky he's only cracked his skull and half his ribs,' Fflewddur said. 'Another man would have been snapped in two. But we're in a fine pickle,' he added under his breath to Taran, glancing at the warriors who had come to gather near the unconscious Smoit. 'He'll not lay Gast or Goryon by the heels now. He needs more healing than we can give. We'd best take him to Caer Cadarn.'

Taran shook his head. He remembered Smoit's words about the neighbouring cantrev lords who would seize the opportunity to attack. It was in his mind, too, that finding Cornillo could best bring Gast and Goryon to terms and thus end their battle. But his thoughts were as tangled as Orddu's weaving and he fervently wished himself in the place of Smoit, whose unconsciousness at that moment seemed a most enviable state.

'Aeddan's farmhold is closer,' Taran said. 'We'll bring him there and Gurgi shall stay with him. You and I must seek out Gast and Goryon and do what we can to stop their quarrel. As for Cornillo and the herd, I doubt we may hope to find them.'

The companions, tearing their cloaks into strips, set about binding up Smoit's wounds. The King's eyelids fluttered and he groaned loudly.

'Give me to eat!' gasped Smoit. 'I may be half drowned, but I'll not be half starved.' He put a hand on Taran's shoulder. 'Good lad, good lad. You've saved my life. Another moment and I'd have been beaten into a pudding. Claim any favour, it is yours.'

'I ask none,' Taran replied, knotting the bandages around Smoit's huge chest. 'Alas,' he murmured, 'what I most want, none can grant.'

'No matter,' panted Smoit. 'What you wish of me, you shall have.'

'Sire, you cannot travel far,' Taran began as Smoit tried painfully to climb to his feet. 'Give us leave to ride with your warriors and – '

'Kind master! Hear!' Gurgi called excitedly. 'Hear with listenings!'

Llyan, too, had caught some sound, for her ears cupped forward and her whiskers twitched.

'It's my gizzard calling for meat and drink!' cried Smoit. 'Loud it must be, for I'm empty as a drum!'

'No, no,' shouted Gurgi, seizing Taran's arm and drawing him past the trees along the riverside. 'Gurgi hears no thrummings and drummings but cooings and mooings!'

Leaning on the bard, Smoit stumbled after them. Gurgi had spoken the truth; the creature's sharp ears had not deceived him. Now Taran himself heard a faint lowing. Gurgi raced towards the sound. Beyond the trees the land dipped into a shady dell watered by a streamlet. Taran cried aloud. There stood the herd, grazing calmly around Cornillo.

'My pulse!' bellowed Smoit, so loudly that a dozen horned heads turned and stared as alarmed as if some strange new kind of bull had burst into their quiet pasture.

'Great Belin!' cried Fflewddur. 'Cornillo's led them all to safety. She's wiser than either of her masters!'

Cornillo raised her head as Taran hurried to her side. She blew out her breath gently and rolled her eyes in a look of long-suffering patience. Smoit, heedless of his grievous bruises, clapped his hands triumphantly and shouted at the top of his voice for his warriors.

'Sire, let us drive the herd to Aeddan's farm,' Taran urged. 'Your own hurts must be tended better than we've done.'

'Drive them where you please, lad,' answered Smoit. 'My body and bones, we have them now! That will fetch Gast and Goryon to me at a gallop!' He summoned two horsemen, commanding them to bear a message to the cantrev lords. 'Tell those two troublemakers where I'll await them,' cried Smoit. 'And tell each to call truce, for his cows are found!'

'And Gurgi found them!' shouted Gurgi, capering wildly. 'Yes, yes! Bold, clever, sharp-eared Gurgi finds all that is lost, oh, yes!' He flung his hairy arms around himself and seemed close to bursting with pride and delight at his own deed. 'Oh, bards will sing of clever Gurgi with rantings and chantings!'

'I'm sure they will, old friend,' Taran said. 'You've found the herd. But don't forget we still have Gast and Goryon to deal with – and there's only one Cornillo.'

The cows were at first reluctant to quit the dell, but after much coaxing Taran was able to lead Cornillo along the valley pathways towards Aeddan's farm. The others followed her, lowing and tossing their horns; it was a strange procession that wended its way across the meadows and rolling hillocks. Smoit's warriors rode on either side of the herd, and the red-bearded King himself brandished a spear as if it were a drover's staff; Llyan padded after the cattle, alert for strays; and Gurgi perched proud as a shaggy rooster on Cornillo's back.

When Aeddan's hut came in sight Taran galloped ahead calling to the farmer, but he had no sooner dismounted when the door burst open and he fell back, surprised. Aeddan stood with a rusted sword in his hand. Behind the farmer, Taran glimpsed Alarca weeping into her apron.

'Is this how you repay kindness?' Aeddan cried, recognizing Taran immediately. His eyes blazed as he pointed the ancient weapon at the approaching war band. 'Do you come with them to spoil our land? Begone! It is already done!'

'How then?' Taran stammered, shocked at these words from one he held to be a friend. 'I ride with King Smoit and his men. We seek peace between Gast and Goryon – '

'Does it matter whose warriors trampled my crops?' Aeddan flung back. 'What Gast has destroyed, Goryon has doubly destroyed, warring back and forth across my field till not a blade of wheat stands! Battle is their pride, but my farm is my life. Do they seek vengeance? I sought only a harvest.' In the weariness of despair Aeddan bowed his head and cast his sword to the ground.

Taran stared in dismay at the field where Aeddan had so painfully laboured. The hooves of steeds had churned the earth to mud, uprooting the young shoots which now lay torn to shreds. The harvest on which Aeddan had staked his livelihood would never come, and Taran felt the farmer's heartbreak as if it were his own.

Before he could speak, a troop of horsemen galloped from the woods edging the farm. Taran recognized Lord Goryon at their head. In another moment Lord Gast and his riders appeared. Catching sight of his rival, the cantrev lord spurred his mount and galloped frantically to the cottage, flung himself out of the saddle, and with a furious shout raced towards Goryon.

'Robber!' cried Gast. 'Do you mean to steal Cornillo from me again?'

'Thief!' cried Goryon. 'I took what was mine to begin with!'

'Liar!' roared Gast. 'Never was she yours!'

'Insults! Insolence!' roared Goryon, his face turning purple, his hand snatching for his sword.

'Be silent!' bellowed Smoit. He shook his battle-axe at the cantrev lords. 'Your King speaks! How dare you quarrel and insult each other, you pig-headed brawlers!' Smoit gestured to his warriors, who strode to seize Gast and Goryon. The riders of the two war bands cried out angrily and made to unsheathe their swords; for an instant Taran feared another battle would rage then and there. But Smoit's warriors stood their ground, and the sight of the enraged King himself caused the horsemen to draw back submissively.

'My dungeon will teach you to be good neighbours,' cried Smoit. 'You'll stay there till you learn. As for Cornillo – I've split my skull, cracked my bones, and ridden to the edge of starvation this day, and so I claim her for myself! A prize of war! And small recompense it is for the vexation you've given me! Another day and you'd have set the whole cantrev ablaze!'

At this, Gast and Goryon both roared in furious protest; and Taran could no longer hold his tongue. He strode to the King's side.

'Sire, even a lifetime in your dungeon will not raise one grain of wheat on a ruined field. Aeddan has lost all he hoped to gain, one harvest to keep himself and his wife alive. You offered me a favour,' Taran went on. 'I refused it then; will you let me claim it now?'

'Ask what you please, my lad,' replied Smoit. 'It is already given.'

Taran hesitated a moment as he stepped forward and

stood facing the cantrev lords. Then he turned to Smoit. 'I ask you this,' he said. 'Set Gast and Goryon free.'

While Smoit blinked in astonishment, Goryon, glimpsing Taran for the first time, exclaimed, 'It's the pig-keeper who cozened me out of my horse! I took him for a lout, but he asks a noble favour. Grant it, Smoit. He speaks wisdom!'

'Set them free,' Taran continued, 'to labour beside Aeddan and strive to mend what they have destroyed.'

'What?' cried Gast. 'I took him for a hero, but he's no more than a lout! How dare he ask Gast the Generous to delve the ground like a mole and for no reward!'

'Impudence! Impertinence! Insolence!' shouted Goryon. 'I'll not have a pig-keeper pass judgement on Goryon the Valorous!'

'Nor on Gast the Generous!' exclaimed Gast.

'Pass judgement on yourselves, then,' Taran answered, picking up two handfuls of earth and torn shoots and holding them before the furious cantrev lords. 'This is what remains of Aeddan's livelihood. As well take a sword and slay him. Look on this, Lord Goryon, for there is more truth here than in your tales of giants and monsters. And this he treasured, Lord Gast, more than you treasure any of your possessions – and it was more truly his own, for he toiled to make it so.'

Gast and Goryon had fallen silent; the two rough cantrev lords stared at the ground like sheepish boys.

Aeddan and his wife looked on without speaking.

'The lad has a better head on his shoulders than I do,' exclaimed Smoit, 'and his judgement is wiser. Kinder, too, for my choice would have been the dungeon, not the delving!'

The cantrev lords reluctantly nodded agreement.

Taran turned to Smoit. 'The rest of my favour is this: grant most where need is greatest. Do you claim Cornillo for your own? Sire, give her to Aeddan.'

'Give up Cornillo?' Smoit began, sputtering and choking. 'My prize of war . . .' He finally nodded his head. 'So be it, lad.'

'Aeddan shall keep her,' Taran went on, 'and Gast and Goryon shall have her next calves.'

'What of my herd?' cried Goryon.

'And mine!' cried Gast. 'They're so mixed together no man can tell his own from another's.'

'Lord Goryon shall divide the herds in equal portions,' Taran said.

'He shall not!' Lord Gast broke in. 'He'll give me all the scrawny ones and keep the fat for himself. It's I who'll divide them!'

'Not so!' shouted Goryon. 'You'll fob off none of your rawboned creatures on me!'

'Lord Goryon shall divide the herds,' Taran repeated. 'But Lord Gast shall be first to choose his half.'

'Well said!' Smoit burst out, roaring with laughter. 'My breath and blood, you have them there! Goryon divides and Gast chooses! Ho, oho! It takes two thieves to strike an honest bargain!'

Aeddan and Alarca had come to stand before Taran and King Smoit. 'Who you may truly be, I do not know,' the farmer said to Taran. 'But you befriended me far better than I befriended you.'

'Oh, wisdom of kindly master!' cried Gurgi, as the cantrev lords set about dividing their herds and Smoit's warriors made ready to return to Caer Cadarn. 'Gurgi finds cows, but only wise master knows what to do with them!'

'If indeed I did rightly,' Taran replied, 'Gast and Goryon will be waiting for Cornillo's calves. Gast said they were always twins. I only hope,' he added with a grin, 'that she doesn't disappoint us.'

It was long after nightfall when the companions at last reached Caer Cadarn. Fflewddur and Gurgi were too exhausted to do more than fling themselves on to their couches. Taran would gladly have followed them, but Smoit took his arm and drew him to the Great Hall.

'Count your day well spent, my lad,' cried Smoit. 'You've spared the cantrev from a war and me from being drubbed into jelly. As for Gast and Goryon, how long they'll stay at peace with each other I'll not guess. But you've taught me one thing: my dungeons are useless. My body and bones, I'll have them walled up directly. From this day I'll try my hand at speaking instead of smiting!

'And yet, lad,' Smoit went on, furrowing his brow, 'my wits are slow. I need no man to tell me that, and I am easier in my mind when I have a blade in my hand. Will you return favour for favour? Stay with me in Cantrev Cadiffor.'

'Sire,' Taran answered, 'I seek to learn who my kinsmen are. I cannot . . .'

'Kinsmen!' shouted Smoit, slapping his great girth. 'There's enough of me to make all the kinsmen you could want! Hear me well,' he added, his voice quieter now, 'a widower am I, and childless. Do you yearn for parents? No less do I yearn for a son. When the horn of Gwyn the Hunter sounds for me, there shall be none to take my place, and none would I choose but you. Stay, lad, and you shall one day be King of Cadiffor.'

'King of Cadiffor?' Taran cried. His heart leaped. What need to seek the Mirror when he could offer Eilonwy a royal throne, the proudest gift he could ever lay at her feet? Taran King of Cadiffor. The words rang more sweetly in his ears than Taran Assistant Pig-Keeper. Yet suddenly his joy turned cold. While Eilonwy might honour his rank, could she respect him for abandoning his quest even before it had begun? Could he respect himself? For a long while Taran did not answer, then with fond admiration he turned his eyes to Smoit.

'The honour you would give me,' Taran began, 'there is

nothing I would value more highly. Yes – I long to accept it.' His voice faltered. 'Yet I would rather hold kingship by right of noble birth, not as a gift. It may be,' he went on slowly, 'that in truth I am nobly born. If it should prove thus, then gladly would I rule Cadiffor.'

'How then?' cried Smoit. 'My body and bones, I'd rather see a wise pig-keeper on my throne than a blood prince who's a fool!'

'But there is this, as well,' Taran answered. 'It is in my heart to learn the truth about myself. I will not stop short of it. Were I to do so, who I truly am would for ever be unknown and through all my life I would feel a part of me lacking.'

At these words Smoit's battle-scarred face fell with sadness and regretfully he bowed his head. But after a moment he clapped Taran heartily on the back. 'My breath, blood and beard!' he cried. 'You've a will to chase the wild goose, will-o'-the-wisp, looking-glass, or whatever it may be; and I'll say no more to keep you from it. Seek it out, lad! Whether or not you find it, come back and Cadiffor will welcome you. But hasten, for if Gast and Goryon are ever at loggerheads again, I'll not vouch for how much of the cantrev will be left!'

Thus Taran, with Gurgi and Fflewddur Fflam, set off once more. In his secret heart Taran cherished the hope he might return to Smoit's realm with proud tidings of his parentage. Yet he did not foresee how long it would be until he set foot in Cantrev Cadiffor again.

CHAPTER 6

A Frog

From Caer Cadarn the companions made good progress and within a few days crossed the Ystrad River, where Fflewddur led them for a time along the farther bank before turning north-eastward through the Hill Cantrevs. Unlike the Valley Cantrevs, these lands were greyish and flinty. What might once have been fair pastureland Taran saw to be overlaid with brush, and the long reaches of forest were close-grown and darkly tangled.

Fflewddur admitted his roving seldom brought him to these parts. 'The cantrev nobles are as glum as their domains. Play your merriest tune and the best you can hope for is a sour smile. Yet, if the old lore is true, these realms were as rich as any in Prydain. The sheep of the Hill Cantrevs – Great Belin, it's said they had fleece so thick you could sink your arm in it up to the elbow! Nowadays, alas, they tend to be a little scruffy.'

'Aeddan told me Arawn Death-Lord stole many secrets from the farmers of the valley,' Taran replied. 'Surely he robbed the shepherds of the Hill Cantrevs as well.'

Fflewddur nodded. 'Few treasures he hasn't spoiled or stolen save those of the Fair Folk, and even Arawn might think twice before trifling with them. Be that as it may,' he went on, 'I'd not change the Northern Realms, where my own kingdom is, for any of these. There, my boy, we raise no sheep, but famous bards and warriors! Naturally, the House of Fflam has held its throne there for – well, for a remarkably long time. In the veins of a Fflam,' declared the bard, 'flows royal blood of the Sons of Don! Prince Gwydion himself is my kinsman. Distant – distant, it's true,' he added hastily, 'but a kinsman nonetheless.'

'Gurgi does not care for famous sheep or fleecy bards,' Gurgi wistfully murmured. 'He is happy at Caer Dallben, oh, yes, and wishes he is soon there.'

'As for that,' answered Fflewddur, 'I'm afraid you'll have hard travel before you see home again. It's anyone's guess how long it will take to find your mysterious Mirror. I'll go with you as far as I can,' he said to Taran, 'though sooner or later I shall have to get back to my kingdom. My subjects are always impatient for my return . . .'

The harp shuddered violently as a string snapped in two. Fflewddur's face reddened. 'Ahem,' he said, 'yes, what I meant was: I'll be anxious to see *them* again. The truth of it is, I often have the feeling they manage quite well even when I'm not there. Still, a Fflam is dutiful!'

The companions halted while Fflewddur slid from Llyan's back and squatted on the turf to repair his broken string. From his packet the bard took the large key which he used to tighten the harp's wooden pegs, and began patiently retuning the instrument.

A raucous cry made Taran glance quickly skyward. 'It's Kaw!' he exclaimed, pointing to the winged shape plummeting swiftly towards the companions. Gurgi shouted joyfully and clapped his hands as the crow alighted on Taran's wrist.

'So you've found us, old friend,' cried Taran, delighted to have the crow with him once again. 'Tell me,' he went on quickly, 'how does Eilonwy fare? Does she miss – all of us?'

'Princess!' Kaw croaked, beating his wings. 'Princess! Eilonwy! Taran!' He clacked his beak, hopped up and down on Taran's wrist, and set up such a jabbering and chattering that Taran could barely make out one word from another. The best he could understand was that Eilonwy's indignation at being forced to learn royal behaviour had by no means dwindled, and that indeed she missed him – tidings that both cheered Taran and sharpened his yearning for the golden-haired princess.

In the cavern on Mona, Kaw also managed to convey, Glew the giant had been restored to his original size by Dallben's potion.

Kaw himself was in the best of spirits. Still gabbling at the top of his voice, he flapped his glossy black wings, hopped from Taran's wrist to greet the other companions, and even perched on Llyan's head, where he busily ran his beak through the great cat's tawny fur.

'His eyes will help our search,' Taran said to Fflewddur, who had left his harp to come and stroke the bird's sleek feathers. 'Kaw can scout the land better than any of us.'

'So he can,' agreed Fflewddur, 'if he has a mind to and if you can make him heed you. Otherwise the scamp will have his beak in everyone's business but his own.'

'Yes, yes,' Gurgi added, shaking a finger at the crow. 'Heed commands of kindly master! Help him with flyings and spyings, not pryings and lyings!'

In answer, the crow impudently thrust out a sharp black tongue. With a flirt of his tail he fluttered to the harp and began rapidly twanging the strings with his beak. At the bard's cry of protest, Kaw hopped from the instrument's curved frame and snatched up the tuning key, which he began dragging across the turf.

'He's brazen as a magpie!' cried Fflewddur, setting off after the crow. 'He's thieving as a jackdaw!'

No sooner did Fflewddur come within half a pace of him than Kaw nimbly hopped away again, bearing the key in his beak. Squawking merrily, the crow stayed always out of Fflewddur's grasp, and Taran could not help laughing at the sight of the long-shanked bard vainly racing in circles, while Kaw danced ahead of him. When Gurgi and Taran joined the pursuit and Taran's fingers had come within a hair's breadth of the crow's tail feathers, Kaw shot upwards and flapped teasingly a short distance into the woods. There he lighted on the gnarled branch of a tall, ancient oak, and peered with bright beady eyes at the companions gathered below.

'Come down,' Taran ordered as sternly as he could, for the bird's comical antics made it impossible for him to be seriously angry. 'I've tried to teach him to behave,' Taran sighed, 'but it's no use. He'll bring it back when he feels like it and not before.'

'Hi, hi! Drop it!' called Fflewddur, waving his arms. 'Drop it, I say!'

At this Kaw bobbed his head, hunched up his wings, and dropped the key – not into the bard's outstretched hands but into a hollow of the tree trunk.

'Dropped it! Dropped it!' croaked Kaw, rocking back and forth on the branch, jabbering and chuckling gleefully at his own jest.

Fflewddur snorted. 'That bird's ill-mannered as a starling! He's had his merriment, now I shall have the toil.' Muttering hard comments about the impudence of waggish crows, the bard flung his arms about the trunk and tried to haul himself upward. Less than half-way, his grip loosened and he came tumbling down to land heavily amid the roots.

'A Fflam is agile!' Fflewddur panted, ruefully rubbing his back. 'Great Belin, there's not a tree I can't climb – ah, except this one.' He mopped his brow and glared at the high trunk.

'Gurgi climbs, yes, yes!' cried Gurgi, springing to the oak. With shaggy arms and legs working all at once, in a trice the creature clambered up the tree. While Fflewddur shouted encouragement, Gurgi thrust a skinny hand into the hollow.

'Here is tuneful key, oh yes!' he called. 'Clever Gurgi finds it!' He stopped short. Taran saw the creature's face wrinkle in surprise and perplexity. Tossing the key down to Fflewddur, Gurgi turned once more to the hollow. 'But what is this? What else does Gurgi find with gropings?

Kindly master,' he shouted, 'here is strange something all set away in hidings!'

Taran saw the excited creature tuck an object under his arm and slide down the oak tree.

'See with lookings!' cried Gurgi as Taran and the bard pressed around him.

Kaw's prank was forgotten in the moment and the crow, not abashed whatever, flew to Taran's shoulder, stretched out his neck, and crowded forward as if determined to be first to glimpse Gurgi's discovery.

'Is it treasure?' Gurgi exclaimed. 'Oh, treasure of great worth! And Gurgi finds it!' He stamped his feet wildly. 'Open it, kindly master! Open and see what riches it holds!'

What Gurgi pressed into Taran's hand was a small, squat iron coffer no wider than Taran's palm. Its curved lid was heavily hinged, bound with iron strips, and secured by a stout padlock.

'Is it jewels with winkings and blinkings? Or gold with shimmerings and glimmerings?' cried Gurgi, as Taran turned the coffer over and over; Fflewddur, too, peered at it curiously.

'Well, friends,' the bard remarked, 'at least we'll have some reward for the trouble that pilfering jackdaw has given us. Though from the size of it, I fear it shan't be very much.'

Taran, meantime, had been struggling with the lock which refused to give way. The lid resisted all his battering, and finally he had to set the coffer on the ground where Gurgi held it tightly while the bard and Taran pried at the hinges with the points of their swords. But the coffer was surprisingly strong, and it took all their strength and effort before the lid at last yielded and fell away with a loud, rasping snap. Within lay a packet of soft leather which Taran carefully untied.

'What is it? What is it?' yelped Gurgi, jumping up and

down on one leg. 'Let Gurgi see shining treasure!'

Taran laughed and shook his head. The packet held neither gold nor gems, but no more than a slender piece of bone as long as Taran's little finger. Gurgi groaned in disappointment.

Fflewddur snorted. 'I should say our shaggy friend has found a very small hairpin or a very large toothpick. I doubt we'll have much use for either one.'

Taran had not ceased examining the strange object. The sliver of bone was dry and brittle, bleached white and highly polished. Whether animal or human he could not tell. 'What value can this have?' he murmured, frowning.

'Great value,' replied Fflewddur, 'if one should ever need a toothpick. Beyond that,' he shrugged. 'Keep it, if you like, or toss it away; I can't see it would make any difference. Even the chest is beyond repair.'

'But if it's worthless,' Taran said, still studying the bone closely, 'why should it be so carefully locked up? And so carefully hidden?'

'It's been my long experience that people can be very odd about their belongings,' said Fflewddur. 'A favourite toothpick, a family heirloom – but, yes, I see what you're driving at. A Fflam is quick-thinking! Whoever put it away didn't want it found. As I was about to remark, there's considerably more here than meets the eye.'

'And yet,' Taran began, 'a hollow tree seems hardly the safest place to keep anything.'

'On the contrary,' answered the bard. 'What better way to hide something? Indoors, it could be found without too much difficulty. Bury it in the ground and there's the problem of moles, badgers, and all such. But a tree like this,' he continued, glancing upward, 'I doubt that anyone but Gurgi could climb it without a ladder, and it's hardly probable that anyone strolling through this forest would be carrying a ladder with them. If the birds or squirrels nest on top, they'd only cover it up all the more. No, whoever put it there gave the matter careful thought and took as much pains as if . . .'

Fflewddur's face paled. 'As if . . .' He swallowed hard, choking on his own words. 'Get rid of it,' he whispered urgently. 'Forget we ever found the thing. I can sniff enchantment a mile away. Toothpick, hairpin, or what have you, there's something queer about it.' He shuddered. 'As I've said time and time again: don't meddle. You know my mind on that score. Two things never mix: one is enchantments and the other is meddling with them.'

Taran did not answer immediately, but stared for a time at the polished fragment. At last he said, 'Whatever it may be, it's not ours to take. Yet, if there is enchantment, good or evil, dare we leave it?'

'Away with it!' cried Fflewddur. 'If it's good there's no harm done. If it's evil there's no telling what beastly thing might happen. Put it back, by all means.'

Taran reluctantly nodded. Wrapping the bone once more, he replaced it in the coffer, set the broken lid loosely on top, and asked Gurgi to return it to the hollow. Gurgi, who had been listening closely to Fflewddur's talk of enchantment, was loath to touch the coffer; and only after much urging and pleading by the companions did he agree to do so. He hastily climbed the oak and scuttled down even faster than he had clambered up.

'And good riddance to it,' muttered Fflewddur, striding as quickly as he could from the forest, Taran and Gurgi after him, the latter casting fearful backward glances until the oak was well out of sight.

The companions returned to their steeds and prepared to mount. Fflewddur picked up his harp, looked about him, and called, 'I say, where's Llyan? Don't tell me she's wandered off.'

Taran's alarm quickly changed to reassurance, for a moment later he saw the huge cat plunge from the underbrush and lope to Fflewddur, who clapped his hands and made loud whispering noises through his teeth.

'Sa! Sa! So there you are, old girl,' cried the bard, beaming happily as Llyan frisked about him. 'Now, what have *you* been after?'

'I think she's caught a – why, yes – she's caught a frog!' Taran exclaimed, catching sight of a pair of long legs with webbed feet dangling from Llyan's mouth.'

'Yes, yes,' put in Gurgi. 'A froggie! A froggie with thumpings and jumpings!'

'I should hardly think so,' said the bard. 'We've seen no swamps or pools, and very little water at all, for the matter of that.'

Proudly purring, Llyan dropped her burden at Fflewddur's feet. It was indeed a frog, and the biggest Taran had ever seen. The bard, after patting Llyan's head and fondly rubbing her ears, knelt and with a certain squeamishness picked up the motionless creature.

'Yes, well, I'm delighted, old girl,' he said, holding it at arm's length between his thumb and forefinger. 'It's lovely; I don't know how to thank you. She often does this,' he explained to Taran. 'I don't mean dead frogs necessarily, but odds and ends – an occasional mouse, that sort of thing. Little gifts she fancies I might enjoy. A sign of affection. I always make a fuss over them. It's the thought, after all, that counts.'

Taran, curious, took the frog from the bard's hand. Llyan, he saw, had carried the creature gently and had in no way harmed it. Instead, the frog had suffered from lack of water. Its skin, splotched in green and yellow, was sadly parched. Its legs feebly splayed; its webbed toes had begun to curl and wither like dry leaves; and its great bulging eyes were tightly shut. Regretfully, Taran was about to return the creature to the bushes when the faint tremor of a heartbeat touched his palm.

'Fflewddur, the poor thing's alive,' Taran said. 'There

may still be time to save him.'

The bard shook his head. 'I doubt it. He's too much the worse for wear. A shame, for he's a jolly-looking fellow.'

'Give poor froggie a drink,' Gurgi suggested. 'Give him water with sloshings and washings.'

In Taran's hand the frog stirred as in a last, painful effort. One eye flickered, the wide mouth gaped, and its throat trembled like a faint pulse. 'Arrad!' croaked the frog.

'I say, there is life in him yet!' exclaimed Fflewddur. 'But he must be desperately sick. I've never heard a frog make a noise like that.'

'Urgghi!' the frog croaked. 'Ood!'

The creature was struggling to make a further sound, but its croaking dwindled to a hoarse and scarcely audible rasping.

'Elpp! Elpp!'

'He is an odd one,' remarked Fflewddur, as Taran, more puzzled than ever, held the frog close to his ear. The creature had forced its eyes open and stared at Taran with what seemed a most pitiful, pleading expression.

'I've known them to go "chug-a-chug",' continued Fflewddur, 'and at times "thonk". But this fellow – if frogs could talk, I'd swear he was saying "help"!'

Taran gestured the bard to silence. From deep in the frog's throat came another sound, hardly more than a whisper but clear and unmistakable. Taran's jaw fell. His eyes wide with bewilderment, he turned to Fflewddur. Barely able to speak, he held the frog in his outstretched hand and gasped, 'It's Doli!'

CHAPTER 7

Friends in Danger

'Doli!' echoed the astonished bard, falling back a pace. His eyes bulged like the frog's and he clapped his hands to his head. 'It can't be! Not Doli of the Fair Folk! Not good old Doli!'

Gurgi had just then come up with a leather water flask and, hearing Fflewddur's words, began yelping in terror and dismay. Taran took the flask from Gurgi's trembling hand, unstoppered it, and with all haste began drenching the frog.

'Oh, terrible! Oh, horrible!' moaned Gurgi. 'Unlucky Doli! Unhappy dwarfish companion! But how did this froggie swallow him with gulpings?'

Under the stream of water the frog had begun to revive, and now kicked mightily with its long hind legs.

'Skin! Skin!' came Doli's voice. 'Pour it on my skin! Not down my throat, you clot! Are you trying to drown me?'

'Great Belin,' murmured Fflewddur. 'At first I thought it was just a frog who happened to have the same name as Doli. But I'd know that temper anywhere.'

'Doli!' Taran cried. 'Is it really you?'

'Of course it is, you long-legged beanpole!' snapped Doli's voice. 'Just because I look like a frog on the outside doesn't mean I'm not myself on the inside!'

Taran's head spun at the thought of Doli in this form. Gurgi was speechless, his eyes as round and wide open as his mouth. Fflewddur, as stunned as the other companions, had recovered somewhat from his first shock and now dropped to his hands and knees on the damp turf where Taran had set the frog.

'You've chosen a strange way to travel about,' said Fflewddur. 'Did you weary of turning yourself invisible? I can understand how that might be tiresome. But – a frog? Though you do make a handsome one. I remarked on it the moment I saw you.'

The frog rolled up his eyes in utter exasperation and his green-spotted body began to swell as if it might burst. 'Chosen? Do you think I chose this? I'm bewitched, you ninny! Can't you see that?'

Taran's heart skipped a beat. 'Who bewitched you?' he cried, aghast at the weird fate which had befallen his old companion. 'Was it Orddu? She's threatened us before. Did you, too, journey to the Marshes?'

'Idiot! Numbskull!' retorted Doli. 'I've better sense than to trifle with her.'

'Who then has done this to you?' Taran exclaimed. 'How can we help? Dallben surely has power against such enchantment. Have courage! We'll take you to him.'

'No time!' Doli answered. 'I don't know if Dallben can break the spell. I don't even know if King Eiddileg of the Fair Folk can do it. Right now it doesn't matter.

'If you want to help me,' Doli went on, 'dig a hole and put some water in it. I'm dry as a bone, and that's the worst thing that can happen to me – I mean, to a frog. I learned that quickly enough.' He blinked at Fflewddur. 'If that giant cat of yours hadn't found me, I'd be dead as a stump. Where did you ever get such a big one?'

'It's a long story,' began the bard.

'Don't tell me then,' snapped Doli. 'As for what brings you here, of all places, you can explain when there's more time.' He settled into the muddy basin Taran and Fflewddur had scraped out with their swords and filled with water from the flask. 'Ah – ah, that's better. I owe you my life. Ah – what a relief. Thank you, friends, thank you.'

'Doli, we can't let you stay in this plight,' Taran insisted.

'Tell us who cast this evil spell. We'll find him and make him lift it.'

'At sword point, if need be!' cried Fflewddur. He stopped and peered with renewed fascination at Doli. 'I say, old boy, what's it really like, being a frog? I've often wondered.'

'Damp is what it's like,' retorted Doli. 'Damp! Clammy! If I thought turning myself invisible was uncomfortable, this is a hundred times worse. It's like – oh, don't boggle me with stupid questions! It doesn't matter. I'll manage somehow. There's more important work afoot.

'Yes, you can help me,' Doli quickly went on. 'If anyone can help at all. Strange things have been happening . . .'

'So it would seem,' agreed the bard, 'to say the very least.'

'Fflewddur, let him speak,' Taran broke in. 'His life may be at stake.'

'Strange things,' Doli resumed. 'Peculiar, unsettling. First, not long ago, word reached King Eiddileg in our realm at the bottom of Black Lake that someone had plundered a Fair Folk treasure trove. Broke into it! Made off with the most valuable gems. It's rarely happened in all the history of Prydain.'

Fflewddur gave a whistle of surprise. 'Knowing Eiddileg, I can imagine he was rather sour about it.'

'Not for loss of the gems,' replied Doli. 'We've more than enough. It's that someone was able to find the trove in the first place; and, in the second, dared to lay hands on Fair Folk treasure. Most of you mortals have better sense.'

'Could it have been Arawn or any of his servants?' Taran asked.

'I shouldn't think so,' put in Fflewddur. 'As I remarked only today, even the Lord of Annuvin would be more than cautious with Fair Folk.'

'For once you're right,' Doli answered. 'No, not Arawn. We were sure of that. But we had only one report, incomplete, from a Fair Folk watcher in the Hill Cantrevs. No tidings from the guardian of the way post here – that, in itself, was very odd.

'Eiddileg sent a messenger to scout around and get to the root of things. He never came back. Not a word from him. Eiddileg sent another. Same thing. Silence. Dead silence.

'You can guess who was chosen to go next. That's right. Good old Doli. Anything disagreeable to be done? Any unpleasant task?'

Until now, Taran had never been aware that a frog's face could show such a look of indignation and of being much put upon.

Doli snorted, as well as he was able in his present shape. 'Naturally, send for good old Doli.'

'But you found who did it?' Taran asked.

'Of course I did,' Doli retorted. 'But I failed in the end. Look at me! Now, of all times, of all the useless things to be! Oh, if I had only had my axe!

'The Fair Folk are in danger,' he went on hurriedly. 'Terrible danger. Yes, I learned who found our trove and stole our treasure. The same who cast this spell on me: Morda!'

'Morda!' Taran repeated, frowning. 'Who is Morda? How could he have done so? Why would he dare to risk Eiddileg's wrath?'

'Why? Why?' Doli's eyes popped furiously and he began to swell up again. 'Don't you understand? Morda, this foul villain of a wizard! Oh, he's shrewder than a serpent! Don't you see? He's found a way of bewitching Fair Folk! No enchanter has ever been able to cast a spell on *us*. Unheard of! Unthinkable!

'And if he's gained the power to turn us into animals – fish, frogs, no matter – we're at his mercy. He could slay us out of hand, if he chose. That's surely what happened to the way post guardian, to the messengers who vanished without a trace. It can happen to any of us. To Eiddileg himself! Not one of the Fair Folk can be safe from Morda. He's the worst threat ever to fall upon our realm.'

Doli sank back exhausted by his own outburst, and the companions glanced fearfully at each other. 'What his scheme is, I couldn't discover,' Doli continued at last. 'Oh, I tracked him to his hiding place easily enough. He lives in a sort of enclosure not too far from here. I'd gone invisible, needless to say. But it was making my ears buzz so much, worse than a pair of hornets' nests! In the darkness I thought I could chance turning visible – just for a moment, to escape that awful buzzing. Next thing I knew, there I was, as you see me now.

'Morda could have crushed me then and there. Instead, he mocked my plight. It amused him to see a helpless frog. Then he threw me down among the rocks. He savoured my lingering agony more than the mercy of killing me out of hand. He was sure I'd perish in these dry hills, withering little by little to my death. And if by some chance I didn't – what difference could it make? How could a frog hope to prevail against a wizard? I crept away, trying to find water. I kept on until I could go no farther. Your cat found me then. If she hadn't, I can tell you it would have been the end of me.

'One thing Morda forgot,' Doli added, 'one tiny thing he overlooked: I could still speak. I myself didn't know it at the time. The shock of being turned into a frog quite took away my voice for a while.'

'Great Belin,' murmured Fflewddur, 'I've heard of *people* having frogs in their throats, but never . . . Forgive me, forgive me, old boy,' he added quickly, as Doli glared at him. 'I didn't mean to ruffle your feelings.'

'Doli, tell us what we must do,' Taran cried, horror-stricken at the dwarf's account. It was not Doli's plight alone that turned his blood cold; he saw clearly the fate in store for all the Fair Folk. 'Lead us to Morda. We'll try to take him prisoner, or slay him if we must.'

'So we shall!' exclaimed Fflewddur, drawing his sword. 'I'll not have my friends turned into frogs!'

'No, no!' shouted Gurgi. 'Froggies are froggies, but friends are friends!'

'Attack Morda?' Doli replied. 'Are you out of your heads? You'll end up in the same pickle as me. No, you can't risk it. Eiddileg must be warned, but before that I must finish my task. Find out more of Morda's powers and how he means to use them. There's no hope of Fair Folk standing against him unless we know better what we have to deal with. Take me back to Morda's stronghold. Somehow I'll get to the bottom of his scheme. Then carry me to a way post, so I can get word to Eiddileg and spread the alarm.'

A sudden spasm convulsed him; for an instant Doli seemed about to choke, then a racking sneeze nearly flung him out of the puddle. 'Curse this dampness!' he sputtered. 'Curse that black-hearted Morda! He's given me all the bad points of being a frog and none of the good!' Doli began coughing violently. 'Blast it! Dow I ab losigg by voice! Bake haste! Bake haste! Pick be up. I'll show you the way. There's doe tibe to waste!'

The companions hurriedly mounted. With Doli clinging to his saddle horn, Taran galloped where the dwarf commanded. But the forest thickened and slowed their pace, and often in the tangle of branches they were forced to dismount and go afoot. Doli had assured them the distance was not great, but his usually unfailing sense of direction had grown confused. At times the dwarf was uncertain which path to follow, and twice the companions reined up and retraced their steps.

'Dote blade be!' snapped Doli. 'I cabe over this ladd crawligg odd by belly. It's dot the sabe, seeigg it frob up here.'

To make matters worse, Doli began to shake and shudder. His eyes bleared; his nostrils streamed; and even as a frog he looked altogether miserable. With constant fits of sneezing and coughing, Doli's voice grew so hoarse he could barely force out a feeble, croaking whisper, which did nothing to improve the state of his disposition or the clarity of his directions to Taran.

Until now there had been no sign of Kaw. When the companions had first hastened to follow Doli's orders, the crow had chosen this of all moments to be exasperatingly disobedient. He flapped into the woods, stubbornly refusing to heed Taran's pleas to come back. At last Taran left him behind, sure the crow would rejoin them when he saw fit; but as the companions made their way deeper into the forest, Taran had grown more anxious for the impudent bird. Thus, when they halted to set Doli on the ground – where the dwarf insisted he could better regain his bearings – Taran was too relieved to scold the crow when Kaw finally appeared. The prankster, Taran saw, had been up to his old tricks, for he bore some glittering find in his beak.

Squawking proudly, Kaw dropped the object into the surprised Taran's hands. It was the fragment of polished bone.

'What have you done?' Taran cried in dismay, as Kaw, overweeningly pleased with himself, rocked back and forth and bobbed his head.

'The jackanapes!' burst out Fflewddur. 'He's gone back and rifled the coffer. I thought us well rid of that enchanted toothpick, now we've got it again. A sour jest, you magpie!' he exclaimed, flapping his cloak at the bird, who nimbly dodged away. 'A Fflam is fun-loving, but I see no joke in this at all. Throw it away,' he urged Taran, 'toss it into the bushes.'

'I dare not, if indeed it's a thing of enchantment,' Taran replied, though he felt as uneasy as the bard, and heartily wished Kaw had left the coffer undisturbed. A strange thought, vague and unformed, stirred in his mind, and he knelt, holding out the fragment to Doli. 'What can this be?' he asked, after briefly telling how the sliver had first come into their hands. 'Could Morda himself have hidden it?'

'Who dose?' croaked Doli. 'I've dever seed eddythigg like it. But it's edchadded, you cad be sure. Keep it, id eddy case.'

'Keep it?' cried the bard. 'We'll have nothing but ill luck from the cursed thing. Bury it!'

Swayed by Fflewddur's vehemence yet reluctant not to follow Doli's counsel, Taran stood uncertain what to do. At last, with strong misgivings, he tucked the fragment into his jacket.

Fflewddur groaned. 'Meddling! We'll only gain trouble, mark my words. A Fflam is fearless, but not when there's unknown enchantment lurking in someone's pocket.'

As they pressed on Taran shortly came to believe he had decided wrongly and that Fflewddur's unhappy prediction was well-founded. Doli had taken a turn for the worse; he could gasp no more than a word or two at a time. The frog's body trembled as in the grip of a painful ague; a sickness, Taran was sure, owing to Doli's gruelling crawl overland. To keep his skin from parching, the companions drenched him regularly; while the treatment, on the one hand, kept him alive, on the other it added to his misery. Under the stream of water he sneezed, choked and sputtered. Soon he sprawled listlessly, too feeble even to be bad-tempered.

The day had waned quickly and the companions halted in a glade, for Doli had given them to understand that from now on they must travel with utmost caution. Setting the frog carefully in the folds of a dampened cloak, Taran drew Fflewddur aside and spoke hurriedly with him.

'He has no strength for his task,' Taran murmured. 'We

dare not let him go on.'

Fflewddur nodded. 'I doubt he could, even if he wanted to.' The bard's face, like Taran's, was drawn tightly with concern.

Taran was silent. What he must do was plain to him; yet, despite himself, he shrank from facing it. His mind groped for another, better plan, but found none, returning always to the same answer. What kept him from taking the clear course was not reluctance to help a close companion, for this he would have done gladly. Nor was it fear for his life, but terror that he might share Doli's fate; not only that his own quest would fail but that he might himself be imprisoned, hapless in some pitiful creature shape, captive for ever.

He knelt at Doli's side. 'You must stay here. Fflewddur and Gurgi will watch over you. Tell me how I may find Morda.'

CHAPTER 8

The Wall of Thorns

Hearing this, Doli kicked weakly and croaked an incomprehensible protest, though nothing else could he do but agree to Taran's plan. With Kaw on his shoulder, Taran set off afoot through the woods. Behind him loped Gurgi, who had insisted on going with him.

After a time Taran shortened his stride and finally halted to glance around him at the forest now thick with brambles. High thorn bushes rose amid the trees in a tangled, impassable screen. Taran realized he had found what he sought. The tall bushes were no haphazard growth, but had been craftily twined into a dense barrier, a living wall nearly twice his height, bristling with spines sharper than the talons of a gwythaint. Taran drew his sword and strove to cut an opening in the thicket.

The brambles were hard as cold iron and Taran blunted both his strength and his blade against them. All he gained for his labour was a tiny hole to which he pressed his eye; he made out nothing more than a dark mound of boulders and black turf surrounded by rank weeds and burdock. What first seemed the lair of a wild beast he saw to be a rambling, ill-shaped dwelling of low, squat walls roofed with sod. There was no movement, no sign of life, and he wondered if the wizard had left his fastness and the companions had come too late. The thought only put a sharper edge to his uneasiness.

'Somehow Doli forced his way in,' Taran murmured, shaking his head. 'But his skill is greater than mine; he must have struck on an easier passage. If we try climbing over,' Taran added, 'we risk being seen.'

'Or caught on brambles with jabbings and stabbings!'

Gurgi replied. 'Oh, bold Gurgi does not like climbing walls without knowing what lies in lurkings beyond.'

Taran took the crow from his shoulder. 'Morda surely has his own passage: a breach in the thorns or perhaps a tunnel. Find it for us,' he said urgently to Kaw. 'Find it for us, old friend.'

'And hasten, too,' Gurgi put in. 'No jokings and trickings!'

Silent as an owl, the crow flew upward, circled the barrier, then dropped out of sight. Taran and Gurgi crouched waiting in the shadows. After some while, when the sun had dipped below the trees and dusk had gathered with still no tidings from Kaw, Taran began to fear for the bird. Prankster though he was, Kaw understood the seriousness of his mission, and Taran knew it was more than whim that delayed the crow's return.

At last Taran dared wait no longer. He strode to the barrier and carefully began to climb. The branches writhed like serpents and tore viciously at his hands and face. Wherever he sought a foothold the thorns turned against him as with a will of their own. Just below, he heard Gurgi panting, as the sharp points struck through the creature's matted hair. Taran paused to catch his breath while Gurgi clambered up beside him. The top of the wall was almost within reach.

With a sudden lashing and rattling among the thorns, a slipnoose tightened around Taran's upraised arm. He shouted in alarm and in that instant glimpsed the terrified face of Gurgi as loops of finely knotted cords whipped over the creature's body. A bent sapling sprang upright, pulling the ropes with it. Taran felt himself ripped from the brambles and, dangling on the end of the strong cord, flung upward and over the barrier. Now he understood the words Doli had striven to gasp out: traps and snares. He fell, and darkness swallowed him.

*

A bony hand gripped his throat. In his ears rasped a voice like a dagger drawn across a stone. 'Who are you?' it repeated. 'Who are you?'

Taran struggled to pull away, then realized his hands were bound behind him. Gurgi whimpered miserably. Taran's head spun. The guttering light of a candle stabbed his eyes. As his sight cleared, he saw a gaunt face the colour of dry clay, eyes glittering like cold crystals deep set in a jutting brow as though at the bottom of a well. The skull was hairless, the mouth a livid scar stitched with wrinkles.

'How have you come here?' demanded Morda. 'What do you seek of me?'

In the dimness Taran could make out little more than a low-ceilinged chamber and a fireless hearth filled with dead ashes. He himself had been propped in the angle of a low wall. Gurgi lay sprawled on the flagstones beside him. He glimpsed Kaw pinioned in a wicker basket set on a heavy oaken table, and he cried out to the bird.

'What then,' snapped the wizard, 'is this crow yours? He found one of my snares, as you did. None enters here without my knowledge. This much have you already learned. Now it is I who shall learn more of you.'

'Yes, the bird is mine,' Taran answered in a bold voice, deciding his only hope lay in telling as much of the truth as he dared. 'He flew beyond the thicket and did not return to us. We feared some mishap and went in search of him. We journey to the Llawgadarn Mountains. You have no cause to hinder us.'

'You have hindered yourselves,' replied Morda, 'foolish creatures without the wits of a fly. To the Llawgadarn Mountains, you say? Perhaps. Perhaps not. In the race of men is much greed and envy; but of truth, little. Your face speaks for you and calls you liar. What do you hope to hide? No matter. Your paltry store of days you call life is spun out. You shall not leave here. And yet – now you are in my hands, it may be that you shall serve me. I must ponder that. Your lives indeed may have some small use – to me, if not to yourselves.'

More than the wizard's words filled Taran with horror. As he watched, unable to take his own eyes away, Taran saw that Morda's gaze was unblinking. Even in the candle flame the shrivelled eyelids never closed; Morda's cold stare never wavered.

The wizard straightened and drew the grimy, threadbare robe closer about his wasted body. Taran gasped, for from Morda's withered neck hung a silver chain and crescent moon. Only one other he knew wore such an ornament: Princess Eilonwy, Daughter of Angharad. Unlike Eilonwy's, the horns of this crescent held a strangely carved gem, clear as water, whose facets sparkled as though lit by an inner fire.

'The emblem of the House of Llyr!' Taran cried.

Morda started and drew back. With fingers lean as spider's legs he clutched at the gem. 'Fool,' he hissed, 'did you think to gain this from me? Is that why you were sent? Yes, yes,' he muttered, 'so it must be.' His bloodless lips twitched faintly as he fixed Taran with his unlidded eyes. 'Too late. The Princess Angharad is long dead, and all its secrets are mine.'

Taran stared at him, bewildered to hear the name. 'Angharad Daughter of Regat?' he whispered. 'Eilonwy never knew her mother's fate. But it was you – at your hands,' he burst out, 'at your hands she met her death.'

Morda said nothing for a time, seeming as one gripped by a black dream. When he spoke, his voice was heavy with hatred. 'Think you the life or death of one of you feeble creatures should concern me? I have seen enough of the human kind and have judged them for what they are: lower than beasts, blind and witless, quarrelsome, caught up in their own small cares. They are eaten by pride and senseless striving; they lie, cheat and betray one another. Yes, I was born among the race of men. A human!' He spat the word scornfully. 'But long have I known it is not my destiny to be one with them, and long have I dwelt apart from their bickerings and jealousies, their little losses and their little gains.'

Deep in their shrunken sockets the wizard's eyes glittered. 'As I would not debase myself to share their lives, neither would I share their deaths. Alone, I studied the arts of enchantment. From the ancient lore I learned the Fair Folk held certain gems hidden in their secret troves; he who possessed one gained life far longer than any mortal's mayfly span of days. None had found these treasure troves, and few had even dared to search. Yet I knew that I would learn the means to find them.

'As for her who called herself Angharad of Llyr,' the wizard continued, 'of a winter's night she begged refuge in my dwelling, claiming her infant daughter had been stolen, that she had journeyed long in search of her.' The wizard's lips twisted. 'As if her fate or the fate of a girl child mattered to me. For food and shelter she offered me the trinket she wore at her throat. I had no need to bargain; it was already mine, for too weak was she, too fevered to keep it from me if I chose to take it. She did not live out the night.'

In loathing Taran turned his face away. 'You took her life, as surely as if you put a dagger in her heart.'

Morda's sharp, bitter laugh was like dry sticks breaking. 'I did not ask her to come here. Her life was worth no more to me than the book of empty pages I found among her possessions. Though in its way the book proved to be not without some small value. In time a whining weakling found his way to me. Glew was his name, and he sought to make an enchanter of himself. Little fool! He beseeched me to sell him a magic spell, an amulet, a secret word of power. Snivelling upstart! It pleased me to teach him a lesson. I sold him the empty book and warned him not to open it or look upon it until he had travelled far from here lest the spells vanish.'

'Glew!' Taran murmured. 'So it was you who cheated him.'

'Like all your kind,' answered Morda, 'his own greed and ambition cheated him, not I. His fate I know not, nor do I care to know. This much he surely learned: the arts of enchantment are not bought with gold.'

'Nor stolen through heartlessness and evil, as you robbed the Princess Angharad,' Taran flung back.

'Heartlessness? Evil?' said Morda. 'These words are toys for creatures such as you. To me they mean nothing; my powers have borne me beyond them. The book served to make a fool taste his folly. But the jewel, the jewel served me, as all things will do at the end. The woman Angharad had told me the gem would lighten burdens and ease harsh tasks. And so it did, though years I spent in probing its secrets until I gained mastery of its use. At my command it dwindled the heaviest faggots to no more than twigs. With the gem's help I raised a wall of thorns. As my skill grew, I found the waters of a hidden spring.'

The wizard's unblinking eyes glittered triumphantly. 'At last,' he whispered, 'at last the gem led me to what I had ever sought: a Fair Folk treasure trove.

'This trove held none of the life-giving stones,' Morda went on. 'But what matter! If not here, then would I find them elsewhere. Now all Fair Folk treasure, mines, hidden pathways – all lay open to me.

'One of the Fair Folk watchers came upon me then. I dared not let him raise an alarm. Though none had ever stood against any of them, I did so!' cried Morda. 'My jewel was more than a trinket to lighten a scullery maid's toil. I had grasped the heart of its power. At my command this Fair Folk spy turned to a sightless, creeping mole! Yes,' Morda hissed, 'I had gained power even beyond what I sought. Who now would disobey me when I held the means to make men into the weak, grovelling creatures they truly are! Did I seek only a gem? The whole kingdom of the Fair Folk was within my grasp. And all of Prydain! It was then I understood my true destiny. The race of men at last had found its master.'

'It's master?' Taran cried, aghast at Morda's words. 'You are viler than those you scorn. Dare you speak of greed and envy? The power of Angharad's gem was meant to serve, not enslave. Late or soon, your life will be forfeit to your evil.'

The glint in Morda's lidless eyes flickered like a serpent's tongue. 'Think you so?' he answered softly.

From beyond the chamber came a shout, a sudden crashing amid the wall of thorns. Morda nodded curtly. 'Another fly finds my web.'

'Fflewddur!' Taran gasped as Morda strode from the chamber. He flung himself closer to Gurgi and the two tore at each other's bonds; in vain, for within a few moments the wizard returned, half-dragging a figure he trussed securely and threw to the ground beside the companions. It was, as Taran feared, the luckless bard.

'Great Belin, what's happened to you? What's happened to me?' groaned Fflewddur, stunned. 'You didn't come back . . . I went to have a look – feared you'd got caught somehow in those brambles.' The bard painfully shook his head. 'What a jolt! My neck will never be the same.'

'You shouldn't have followed us,' Taran whispered. 'I had no way to warn you. What of Doli?'

'Safe enough,' replied Fflewddur. 'Safer, at least, than we are now.'

Morda had been intently watching the companions. 'So it was the Fair Folk who sent you to spy on me. You are leagued with the dwarfish creature foolish enough to think he could escape me. So be it. Did I think to spare you? You will share his fate.'

'Yes, Doli of the Fair Folk is our companion,' Taran cried. 'Unloose him from your spell. I warn you: harm none of us. Your plan will fail, Morda. I am Taran of

Caer Dallben, and we are under the protection of Dallben himself.'

'Dallben,' spat Morda. 'Grey-bearded dotard! His powers cannot shield you now. Even Dallben will bow before me and do my bidding. As for you,' he added. 'I will not slay you. That would be paltry punishment. You will live – as long as you are able to live in the shapes you will soon have; live and know, during every moment of your wretched days, the cost of defying me.'

Morda took the jewel and chain from about his neck and turned to Fflewddur. 'Let your boldness in seeking your fellows now be cowardice. Flee at the barking of hounds or the tread of hunters. Crouch in fear at the flutter of a leaf and the passing of every shadow.'

The gem flashed blindingly. Morda's hand shot forward. Taran heard Fflewddur cry out, but the bard's voice died in his throat. Gurgi screamed and Taran, horror-stricken, saw the bard no longer at his side. Kicking frantically in Morda's grasp was a dun-coloured hare.

With a harsh laugh Morda held the animal aloft and stared scornfully at it a moment before flinging it into a wicker basket near Kaw's cage. The wizard strode to the companions and stood above Gurgi whose eyes rolled in terror and who could only gibber wordlessly.

Taran struggled against his bonds. Morda raised the gem. 'This creature,' said the wizard, 'this half-brute serves no use. Feeble cringing beast, be weaker still, and prey to owls and serpents.'

With all his strength Taran fought to break the thongs holding him. 'You destroy us, Morda!' he shouted. 'But your own evil will destroy you!'

Even as Taran cried these words, the gem flashed once again. Where Gurgi had lain, a grey field mouse reared on its hind legs, then fled squeaking to a corner of the chamber.

Morda turned his unlidded eyes on Taran.

CHAPTER 9

The Hand of Morda

'And you,' said Morda, 'your doom will not be to lose yourself in forest or burrow. My plan fail? Here shall you stay prisoner and see my triumph. But what shape shall I give you? A dog whining for scraps from my table? A caged eagle eating out his heart for the freedom of the skies?'

Angharad's gem dangled from Morda's fingers. Despair choked Taran as he stared at the ornament like a bird fascinated by a serpent. He envied the wretched Gurgi and Fflewddur. A hawk's talons or a fox's jaws would shortly put a merciful finish to their days; his own would wear themselves out in the slow agony of captivity, like stone grinding against stone, until Morda was pleased to end them.

The wizard's taunts burned like drops of venom; but as Morda spoke, Taran felt a furry body press against his bound wrists. Startled, he almost cried out. His heart leaped and pounded. It was the mouse that had once been Gurgi.

Heedless of its plight, the creature had scurried noiselessly on tiny paws to the corner where Taran lay. Unseen by the wizard, the mouse flung himself on Taran's bonds and with his sharp teeth began hurriedly gnawing at the thongs.

Morda, as if undecided, toyed with the jewel. Gurgi, Taran felt, was chewing desperately at the stubborn bonds; time pressed, and despite the creature's brave efforts the thongs held fast. Taran strove to draw the leather taut to aid the frantic mouse, but there was no sign of loosening, and now the wizard raised the glittering gem.

'Hold!' Taran cried. 'If my fate is to be a beast, grant me this much: let me choose which it must be.'

Morda paused. 'Choose?' His bloodless lips tightened in a scornful smile. 'What can your wishes matter to me? And yet – perhaps it would be fitting if you chose your own prison. Speak!' he commanded. 'Quickly.'

'At Caer Dallben,' Taran began, speaking as slowly as he dared, 'I was Assistant Pig-Keeper. In my charge was a white pig . . .' At his wrists one strand parted. But Gurgi's strength had begun to ebb.

'What, then,' interrupted Morda, laughing harshly, 'do you crave to be a swine? To wallow in mire and grub for acorns? Yes, pig-keeper, your choice indeed is fitting.'

'It is my only wish,' said Taran, 'for it may at least remind me of a happier time.'

Morda nodded. 'Yes. And for that very reason, your wish will not be granted. Clever pig-keeper,' he jeered. 'You have told me what you most desire. Now I may be all the more sure you will not have it.'

'Will you not give me the shape I ask?' Taran replied. Another strand gave way as Gurgi, fighting weariness, redoubled his efforts. Suddenly the thongs yielded. Taran's hands burst free. 'Then,' Taran cried, 'then I will keep my own!'

In the instant Taran sprang to his feet. He snatched his blade from its sheath and lunged towards the wizard who, startled, had taken a backward pace. Before Morda could raise the gem, with a shout Taran drove his sword full into the wizard's breast. He plucked the weapon free. But his shout turned to a cry of horror and he stumbled back against the wall.

Morda stood unharmed. His gaze never faltered. The wizard's mocking laughter rang through the chamber.

'Foolish pig-keeper! Had I feared your sword I would have taken it from you!'

The wizard held Angharad's gem aloft. Taran's head

spun with fresh terror. In Morda's grasp the jewel gleamed coldly. In the sudden clarity of his fear Taran saw the sharp facets of the crystal and the bony claw that held it. He was aware now, for the first time, that the hand of Morda lacked a little finger; in its place was an ugly stump of scarred and withered flesh.

'Do you seek my life?' hissed Morda. 'Seek, then, pig-keeper. My life is not prisoned in my body. No, it is far from here, beyond the reach of death itself.

'One last power did I gain,' said the wizard. 'As my jewel could shape the lives of mortal men, so could it shield my own. I have drawn out my very life, hidden it safely where none shall ever find it. Would you slay me? Your hope is useless as the sword you hold. Now, pig-keeper, suffer for your defiance. Hound or eagle would be too proud a fate. Crawl in the darkness of earth, least of all creatures, a spineless, limbless blind worm!'

Light flared in the heart of the gem. Taran's sword dropped from his grasp and he flung his arm across his face. He staggered as though a thunderbolt had struck him. Yet he did not fall. His body was still unchanged, still his own.

'What blocks my spell?' cried Morda in a terrible voice. A shadow of fear crossed his face. 'As if I struggled against myself.' His lidless eyes stared unbelieving at Taran, and his hand with its lacking finger gripped the gem more tightly.

In Taran's mind a strange thought raced. The wizard's life safely hidden? Where none would find it? Taran could not take his eyes from Morda's hand. A little finger. The coffer in the hollow tree. Slowly, terrified lest his hope betray him, Taran thrust a hand into his jacket and drew out the fragment of polished bone.

At the sight of it Morda's face seemed to crumble in decay. His jaw dropped, his lips trembled, and his voice came in a rasping whisper. 'What do you hold, pig-keeper?

Give it into my hands. Give it, I command you.'

'It is a small thing my companions and I found,' replied Taran. 'How should this have worth to you, Morda? With all your power, do you covet such a trifle?'

A sickly sweat had begun to pearl on the wizard's brow. His features twitched and his voice took on a gentleness all the more horrible coming from his lips. 'Bold lad to stand against me,' he murmured. 'I did no more than test your courage to see if you were worthy to serve me, worthy of rich rewards. You shall have gold in proof of my friendship. And in proof of yours, you shall give me – the small thing, the trifle you hold in your hand . . .'

'This worthless shard?' Taran answered. 'Will you have it for a token? Then let us share it, half for me and half for you.'

'No, no, do not break it!' screamed Morda, his face turning ashen. He thrust out a skinny claw and took a step towards Taran, who quickly drew back and raised the fragment of bone above his head.

'A worthless thing it is,' Taran cried. 'Your life, Morda! Your life I hold in my hand!'

Morda's eyes rolled madly in their wasted sockets, a violent shudder gripped him and his body quaked as though buffeted by a gale. 'Yes, yes!' he cried in a voice racked with terror. 'My life! Poured into my finger! With a knife I cut it from my own hand. Give! Give it back to me!'

'You set yourself above the human kind,' Taran replied. 'You scorned their weakness, despised their frailty, and could not see yourself as one of them. Even I, without birthright or name of my own, know that if nothing else I am of the race of men.'

'Kill me not!' cried Morda, writhing in anguish. 'My life is yours; take it not from me!' The wizard flung himself to his knees and stretched out his trembling arms. His bloodless lips quivered as the words burst from his mouth. 'Hear me! Hear me! Many secrets are mine, many enchantments. I will teach them to you. All, all!'

Morda's hands clasped and unclasped. His fingers knotted around each other and he rocked back and forth at Taran's feet. His voice had taken on a wheedling, whining tone. 'I will serve you, serve you well, Master Pig-Keeper. All my knowledge, all my powers at your bidding.' Angharad's jewel dangled from its silver chain at Morda's wrist, and he clutched it and held it up before Taran. 'This! Even this!'

'The gem is not yours to give,' Taran answered.

'Not mine to give, Master Pig-Keeper?' The wizard's voice grew soft and sly. 'Not mine to give. But yours to take. Would you know its secret workings? I alone can tell you. Would you gain mastery of its use? Have you never dreamed of power such as this? Here, it awaits you. The race of men at your beck and call. Who would dare disobey your smallest wish? Who would not tremble in fear of your displeasure? Promise me my life, Master Pig-Keeper, and I shall promise you . . .'

'Do you bargain with enchantment you stole and corrupted?' Taran cried angrily. 'Let its secrets die with you!'

At this Morda howled horribly and pressed himself almost flat on the ground. Barking sobs racked his body. 'My life! Spare it! Spare it! Do not give me to death. Take the gem. Change me to the lowest crawling thing, to foulest vermin, only let me live!'

The sight of the cowering wizard turned Taran sick at heart, and for a long moment he could not speak. At last he said, 'I will not kill you, Morda.'

The wizard left off his frightful sobbing and lifted his head. 'You will not, Master Pig-Keeper?' He crept forward and made as though to fling his arms about Taran's feet.

'I will not kill you,' repeated Taran, drawing back in revulsion, 'though it is in my heart to do so. Your evil is too deep for me to judge your punishment. Restore my companions,' he commanded. 'Then you will go prisoner with me to Dallben. He alone can give whatever justice you may hope for. Stand, wizard. Cast Angharad's jewel from you.'

Morda, still crouching, slowly and reluctantly pulled the chain from his wrist. His pasty cheeks trembled as he fondled the winking gem, murmuring and muttering to himself. Suddenly he leaped upright and sprang forward. With all his might he swung the jewel at the end of its chain like a whip across Taran's face.

The sharp edges of the stone slashed Taran's forehead. With a cry he stumbled backward. Blood streamed into his eyes, blinding him. The shard of bone flew from his fingers and went spinning and skittering over the floor. Under the force of the wizard's blow, the jewel snapped from its silver chain and rolled into a corner.

In another moment the wizard was upon him growling and snarling like a mad beast. Morda's fingers clawed at Taran's throat. His yellow teeth were bared in a ghastly grin. Taran strove to tear himself from the wizard's grasp, but the frenzy of Morda's attack staggered him; he lost his footing and tumbled to earth. Uselessly he sought to break the deadly grip that stifled him. His head whirled. Through blood-filled eyes he glimpsed the wizard's face twisted in hate and fury.

'Your strength will not save you,' Morda hissed. 'It is no match for mine. You are weak as all your kind. Did I not warn you? My life is not in my body. Strong as death am I! So shall you die, pig-keeper!'

With sudden horror Taran knew the wizard spoke the truth; Morda's wasted arms were hard as gnarled branches, and though Taran struggled desperately the wizard's relentless grip tightened. Taran's lungs heaved to bursting and he felt himself drowning in a black sea. Morda's features blurred; only the wizard's baleful, unlidded gaze stayed fixed.

A crash of splintering wood shattered in Taran's ears.

Morda's grip suddenly slackened. Shouting in alarm and rage, the wizard leaped to his feet and spun about. His head still reeling, Taran clutched at the wall and tried to draw himself up. Llyan had burst into the chamber.

Growling fiercely, her eyes blazing gold fires, the huge cat sprang forward. Morda turned to meet her attack.

'Llyan! Beware of him!' Taran cried.

The force of Llyan's charge bore the wizard to his knees, but Morda in his unyielding strength grappled with the animal.

Llyan flung her tawny body right and left. Her powerful hind legs, their claws unsheathed, lashed vainly at the wizard, who twisted from her paws and now clung to her arching back. Yowling and spitting, the great cat tossed her head furiously, her sharp teeth flashed in her massive jaws; yet, with all her might, she could not free herself from the wizard's clutches. Taran knew even Llyan's strength would soon ebb, just as his own had failed. She had given him a moment more of life, but now Llyan herself was doomed.

The bone! Taran dropped to hands and knees seeking the shard. Nowhere did he see it. He flung aside wooden stools, upturned earthen vessels, scrabbled in the ashes of the hearth. The bone had vanished.

From behind him rose a high twittering and squeaking and he spun to see the mouse bobbing frantically on its hind legs. In its jaws the creature held the splinter of bone.

Instantly Taran caught up the polished fragment to snap it between his fingers. He gasped in dismay. The bone would not break.

CHAPTER 10

The Broken Spell

The polished splinter was unyielding as iron. Teeth clenched and muscles trembling with his effort, Taran felt he struggled against the wizard himself. Llyan had dropped weakly to her haunches; Morda sprang free of the unconscious cat and set upon Taran once more, snatching at the fragment. The wizard's fingers locked on the middle of the shard, but Taran clung with all his strength to the ends of it. He felt the splinter bend as Morda strove to wrest it from his grasp.

Suddenly the bone snapped in two. A sound sharper than a thunderclap split Taran's ears. With a horrible scream that stabbed through the chamber, Morda toppled backward, stiffened, clawed the air, then fell to the ground like a pile of broken twigs.

That same instant the mouse vanished. Gurgi stood at Taran's side. 'Kind master saves us!' he yelled, flinging his arms about Taran. 'Yes, yes! Gurgi is Gurgi again! No more a mouse with shriekings and squeakings!'

In Taran's hand the sundered bone had turned to grey dust, which he cast aside. Too exhausted and bewildered to speak, he could only pat Gurgi fondly and gratefully. Llyan, her deep chest heaving, climbed to her feet near Morda's broken, lifeless form. Her tawny fur still bristled furiously and her long tail looked twice its thickness. As Gurgi hastened to unloose Kaw, who jabbered at the top of his voice and beat his wings excitedly against the cage, Llyan's golden eyes darted about the chamber and from her throat rose an anxious, questioning trill.

'Great Belin!' came Fflewddur's voice. 'I'm trapped as badly as before!'

Llyan loping ahead of him, Taran ran to a corner of the chamber. The basket in which Morda imprisoned the hare now held the bard, squeezed into it along with his harp and stuck fast with his long shanks dangling over one side and his arms flapping helplessly over the other.

With some difficulty Taran and Gurgi set about freeing the bard, who hardly left off stammering incoherently all the while. Fflewddur's face was ashen from fright; he blinked, shook his ragged yellow head, and heaved huge sighs of relief.

'What humiliation!' he burst out. 'A Fflam! Turned into a rabbit! I felt I'd been stuffed in a woolsack! Great Belin, my nose still twitches! Never again! I told you no good comes from meddling. Though in this case, Taran old friend, it's lucky you had that bone. Ah, ah! Easy there, that wicker's jabbing me. A rabbit, indeed! If I could only have got my paws – I mean hands – on that foul Morda!'

At last out of the basket Fflewddur threw his arms around Llyan's powerful neck. 'And you, old girl! If you hadn't come looking for us . . .' He shuddered and clapped hands to his ears. 'Yes, well, let's not think of that.'

In the doorway stood a short, stocky, stoutly booted figure dressed in russet leather; on his head a round, close-fitting leather cap. Thumbs hooked into his belt, he turned bright crimson eyes on each of the companions. Instead of his customary scowl, a grin stretched across his broad face.

'Doli!' Taran cried, first catching sight of the dwarf. 'It's you again!'

'Again?' snapped Doli, trying to make his voice as gruff as he could. 'It always was.' He strode into the chamber. For a moment he looked down at Morda and nodded curtly. 'So that's the way of it,' he said to Taran. 'I thought as much. One moment I was a frog wrapped in a sopping wet cloak, sure all of you had been slain, and the next – as you see me.

'That cat of yours grew restless after a time,' Doli went on, turning to Fflewddur. 'She picked me up, cloak and all, and went off on your trail.'

'She won't let me out of her sight,' replied Fflewddur. 'For which,' he added, fondly rubbing Llyan's ears, 'we've all to thank her.'

'But how did she get through the thorns?' Taran asked. 'Morda's traps . . .'

'Through?' answered Doli. 'She didn't go through, she went over!' He shook his head. 'In one bound! With me in her mouth! I've never seen a creature jump so high. On the other hand, I've never seen a creature like this. But what of the rest of you? What of Morda?'

'If you don't mind,' Fflewddur interrupted before Taran could finish telling the dwarf of their ordeal, 'I suggest leaving here immediately. A Fflam is steadfast, but there's something about enchantments, even broken ones, that tends to – ah – disturb me.'

'Wait,' cried Taran. 'The jewel! Where is it?'

As Doli watched, puzzled, the companions hastily set about searching every corner of the chamber to no avail. Taran's concern mounted, for he was reluctant to leave the gem unfound. However, when almost ready to admit the jewel was hopelessly lost, he heard a raucous laugh above his head.

Kaw, perched on an oaken rafter, rocked back and forth chuckling and squawking, delighted with himself. The jewel glittered in his beak.

'Hi, hi!' shouted Fflewddur, alarmed. 'Give it up! Great Belin, you'll have us all with paws and tails again!'

After much coaxing by Taran and indignant retorts by the bard, Kaw flapped to Taran's shoulder and dropped the gem in his hand.

'Now it belongs to wise and kindly master!' Gurgi exclaimed. 'Gurgi fears stone of winkings and blinkings but not when kindly master holds it.'

Doli peered at the gem as Taran held it up. 'So that's how Morda meant to enslave us. I should have guessed. This comes from the Fair Folk realm,' he added. 'We always honoured the House of Llyr and gave the stone to Princess Regat as our wedding gift. She must have handed it down to her daughter; and when Angharad vanished, the jewel vanished with her.'

'And now it comes to my hands,' Taran said. He cupped the gem in his palm watching the play of light in the depths of the crystal. 'Morda has turned a thing of usefulness and beauty to evil ends. Whether it may ever serve its true purpose again, I do not know. To speak truth, it draws me. And frightens me, too. Its power is vast – too vast, perhaps, for any man to hold. Even if I could learn its secrets, I would not choose to do so.' He smiled at Gurgi. 'Do you call me wise? At least I'm wise enough to know I'll never have wisdom enough to use it.

'Still, it may serve one purpose,' Taran went on. 'With this to bargain, Orddu will surely tell me who I am. Yes!' he cried. 'This is a treasure she won't refuse.' He stopped abruptly and paused a long moment. In his grasp lay means to gain the knowledge he craved. But his heart sank. Though he had won the gem fairly, never could he claim to be its rightful owner. It was his to bargain with no more than it had been Morda's. If Orddu accepted it, and if he should learn he was of noble birth – was a royal robe enough to hide a dishonourable deed?

He looked at Doli. 'The gem is mine,' Taran said. 'But only mine to give, not mine to keep.' Slowly he pressed the jewel into Doli's hand. 'Take this. It belonged once to the Fair Folk. It belongs to them once more.'

The dwarf's usual scowl softened. 'You've done us a service,' he answered. 'Very likely the greatest service any of you mortals have done for the Fair Folk. Without your help Morda could have destroyed us all. Yes, the gem must return to our realm; it's too dangerous in other hands.

You chose well. King Eiddileg will ever remember you for this. You have his thanks – and mine.' Doli nodded with satisfaction and tucked the stone carefully into his jacket. 'It's made a long journey. At last it comes back to us.'

'Yes, yes!' shouted Gurgi. 'Take it for keepings. If kindly master will not have it, then Gurgi wants to see no more of wicked stone. Away with it, away! Do not let it turn faithful Gurgi to a mouse again!'

Taran, with a fond laugh, put a hand on Gurgi's shoulder. 'Morda couldn't have changed what you truly are, any more than he could have changed Doli. Mouse though you might have seemed, you still had the heart of a lion. But what of me?' he murmured thoughtfully. 'As a caged eagle, as a blind worm – could I indeed have stayed myself? Would I still have been Taran, when I scarcely know who Taran is?'

The sun had begun to climb, promising a day blue and fresh, when the companions left the wizard's fastness. The wall of thorns had fallen, shattered like the evil power that raised it, and the companions breached it without difficulty. They untethered Melynlas and Gurgi's pony, but it was not until they had gone a considerable distance that Fflewddur agreed to halt and rest. Even then, the bard appeared uncomfortable and, while Gurgi opened the wallet of food, Fflewddur sat distractedly on a hummock, meditatively fingering his ears, as though to make certain they were indeed his own.

'Rabbits!' the bard murmured. 'I'll never chase another.'

Taran sat apart with Doli, for there was much he had to tell and much he wanted to ask. Though Doli had regained his long frown and short patience, the occasional flicker of a grin betrayed his delight at seeing the companions again. Yet, learning of Taran's quest, Doli scowled more deeply than usual.

'The Free Commots?' said the dwarf. 'We're on the best of terms with the Commot folk; they respect us and we respect them. You'll not find many in Prydain to match their stout hearts and good will, and no man lords it over his fellows because he had the luck to be born in a king's castle instead of a farmer's hut. What matters in the Free Commots is the skill in a man's hands, not the blood in his veins. But I can tell you no more than that, for we have few dealings with them. Oh, we keep a way post open here and there, just in case they might need our help. But it seldom happens. The Commot folk would rather count on themselves, and they do quite well at it. So we're more than pleased, for our own sake, as well as theirs, for we have burden enough keeping an eye on the rest of Prydain.

'As for the Mirror you speak of,' Doli continued, 'never heard of it. There's a *Lake* of Llunet in the Llawgadarn Mountains. More than that I can't tell you. But what have you there?' the dwarf suddenly asked, noticing Taran's battle horn for the first time. 'Where did you get that?'

'Eilonwy gave it to me when I left Mona,' Taran replied. 'It was her pledge that we . . .' He smiled sadly. 'How long ago it seems.' He unslung the horn from his shoulder and handed it to Doli.

'That's Fair Folk craftsmanship,' said the dwarf. 'Can't mistake it.' To Taran's surprise Doli squinted into one end, then the other, and raised the horn into the sunlight as though trying to peer through the mouthpiece. As Taran watched, puzzled, Doli rapped the horn sharply with his knuckles and thumped it against his knee.

'Empty!' the dwarf grumbled. 'All used up. No! Hold on a moment.' He pressed the bell of the horn against his ear and listened intently. 'There's one left, no more than that.'

'One what?' cried Taran, more than ever perplexed at Doli's words.

'One call, what did you think?' snapped Doli.

Fflewddur and Gurgi had come closer, drawn by Doli's odd behaviour, and the dwarf turned to them. 'This was crafted long ago, when men and Fair Folk lived in closer friendship and each was glad to help the other. The horn holds a summons to us.'

'I don't understand,' began Taran.

'If you'd listen to me, you would,' retorted Doli, handing back the battle horn. 'And I mean listen. Hard.' He pursed his lips and whistled three long notes of a pitch and sequence strange to Taran. 'Hear that? Sound those notes on the horn – just so, mind you, and no other way. They'll bring you the nearest Fair Folk who will do whatever they can if you need help. Now, do you remember the tune?' Doli whistled the notes again.

Taran nodded and unthinkingly raised the horn to his lips.

'Not now, you clot!' shouted Doli. 'Keep it in your head. I told you there was only one summons. Save it. Don't waste it. Some day, your life may hang on that call.'

Taran stared in wonder at the horn. 'Eilonwy herself knew nothing of this. You've done me a priceless favour, Doli.'

'Favour?' snorted the dwarf. 'No favour at all. The horn serves whoever happens to have it – in this case, you. I've done nothing but show you how to gain a little more use from something already yours. Favour? Humph! It's only common courtesy. But guard it well, Squander it like a fool at the first whiff of danger and you'll regret it when you really are in trouble.'

'Ahem,' Fflewddur whispered to Taran. 'My own counsel to you is: trust your wits, your sword, or your legs. Enchantment is enchantment, and if you'd been through what I've been through, you'd want no part of it.' He frowned uneasily at the battle horn and turned away. 'I'll never be the same, that's sure!' he muttered, nervously patting his ears. 'Great Belin, they still feel twice as long as before!'

CHAPTER II

Dorath

After eating, the companions stretched themselves on the turf and slept solidly the rest of the day and all that night. In the morning Doli took his leave of them. Kaw, at Doli's request, had already begun flying to the Fair Folk realm with tidings that all was well; from there, the crow would rejoin Taran.

'I'd go with you if I could,' the dwarf said to Taran. 'The thought of an Assistant Pig-Keeper blundering his way through the Llawgadarn Mountains makes my hair stand on end. But I dare not. Eiddileg must have the jewel safely. And who's to bring it to him? Good old Doli! Humph!'

'It saddens me to part with you,' Taran said, 'but you've helped me more than I could hope. The Lake of Llunet bears the same name as the Mirror and perhaps will lead me to it.'

'Farewell, then,' said Doli. 'You've kept us all from being frogs or worse and restored a treasure to us. You'll not regret it. We Fair Folk have long memories.'

The dwarf clasped hands with the travellers, and pulled his leather cap tighter on his head. Doli waved one last time, and Taran watched the dwarf's stumpy figure trudging steadily across a broad meadow, growing smaller in the distance until he vanished into the skirting woods and Taran saw him no more.

Through the day the companions bore north-eastward again. Taran would have been glad for Doli's guidance and keenly missed the gruff dwarf, but his spirits had never been higher; he rode eagerly, light-heartedly; the battle horn swinging from his shoulder gave him fresh courage and confidence.

'Eilonwy's gift is more precious even than I thought,' he told Fflewddur. 'I'm grateful to Doli for telling me its power. And, more than that, for telling me of the Lake of Llunet. It's a strange thing, Fflewddur,' Taran went on, 'but somehow I feel closer to the end of my quest. I believe more than ever that I'll find what I'm looking for.'

'Eh? How's that?' Fflewddur answered, blinking as if he had just come awake. Though Gurgi had put all thoughts of Morda behind him, the bard seemed still shaken by his ordeal, and often lapsed into thoughtful silence when he would morosely finger his ears as though expecting them to lengthen at any moment. 'Dreadful experience!' he muttered now. 'A Fflam into a rabbit! What were you saying? The quest? Yes, of course.'

'Smell with whiffings!' interrupted Gurgi. 'Someone cooks tasty crunchings and munchings!'

'You're right,' Fflewddur agreed, sniffing the air. 'Oh, blast! There goes my nose twitching again!'

Taran reined Melynlas to a walk. Llyan, too, had caught the scent; her ears forward, she licked hungrily at her whiskers.

'Shall we see who it is?' asked Fflewddur. 'I wouldn't say no to a hot meal – so long as it isn't rabbit!'

Taran nodded and the companions rode cautiously through the glade. He had meant to catch a first glimpse of the strangers without himself being seen; but he had gone no more than a few paces when two roughly bearded men rose from the shadows of the bushes. Taran started. The two, evidently posted as guards, quickly drew their swords. One of the men whistled a bird call and stared sharply at the companions, but made no attempt to hinder them.

In the clearing Taran saw some dozen men sprawled around a cookfire, where collops of meat hung sizzling on a spit. Though armed heavily as warriors, the men wore neither the badge nor colours of any cantrev lord. Some were chewing at their food, some sharpening their blades or waxing their bowstrings. Closest to the fire, stretched at his ease, a heavy-faced man leaned on one elbow and toyed with a long dagger, which he tossed and twirled, catching it first by the hilt, then by the point. He wore a horsehide jacket whose sleeves had been ripped out; his muddy boots were thick-soled and studded with iron nails. His yellowish hair fell below his shoulders; his cold blue eyes seemed to measure the three companions with an unhurried glance.

'Welcome, lordships,' he drawled as Taran dismounted. 'What lucky wind blows you to the camp of Dorath?'

'I am no lord,' replied Taran. 'I am Taran Assistant Pig-Keeper . . .'

'No lord?' Dorath interrupted in mock surprise, a half-smile on his mouth. 'If you hadn't told me, I'd never have guessed.'

'These are my comrades,' Taran went on, vexed that he had let Dorath make sport of him. 'Gurgi. Fflewddur Fflam – he wanders as a bard of the harp, but in his own land he is a king.'

'And Dorath is king wherever he rides,' answered the yellow-haired man, laughing. 'Now, Lord Swineherd, will you share humble fare?' With his dagger he gestured towards the roasting collops. 'Eat your fill. Dorath's Company never goes short of commons. Then we'll want to know more about three such as you.'

'The harper rides a strange steed, Dorath,' called a man with a badly scarred face. 'I wager my mare could stand against the beast, no matter, for she's an evil-tempered brute and a killer born. Would it not be a merry match? What say you, Dorath? Will you have the cat show us some sport?'

'Hold your tongue, Gloff,' Dorath answered, carefully eyeing Llyan. 'You're a fool and always were.' He pulled the meat from the spit and thrust it towards the companions. Fflewddur, having assured himself the roast was not rabbit, ate with a good will; Gurgi, as usual, needed no urging to finish his meal; and Taran was glad to swallow his own share, washed down with a mouthful of harsh-tasting wine Dorath poured from a leather flask. The sun was dropping quickly. One of the band flung more branches on the fire. Dorath stuck his dagger into the ground before him and looked up sharply at Taran.

'And so, Lord,' said Dorath, 'have you no traveller's tales to pass the time for my friends and me? Where do you come from? Where do you go? And why? The Hill Cantrevs are dangerous unless a man knows what he's about.'

Taran did not answer immediately; Dorath's tone and the look of the men around the fire made Taran guard his words. 'We journey northward – through the Llawgadarn Mountains.'

Dorath grinned at him. 'And where then?' he asked. 'Or do you call my questions discourteous?'

'To the Lake of Llunet,' Taran answered with some reluctance.

'I've heard of treasure in those parts,' put in the man called Gloff. 'Is that what they seek?'

'Is it indeed?' Dorath said to Taran. 'Treasure?' He laughed loudly. 'Small wonder you're a miser with your words!'

Taran shook his head. 'If I find what I seek, it will be more to me than gold.'

'So?' Dorath bent close to him. 'But what would such a treasure be, Lord? Jewels? Fine-fashioned ornaments?'

'Neither,' Taran answered. He hesitated, then said, 'I seek my parents.'

Dorath was quiet a moment. The grin did not leave his face, but when he spoke again his voice was cold. 'When Dorath asks a question, he wants a truthful answer, Lord Swineherd.'

Taran flushed angrily. 'I have given you one. Say I have not and you call me liar.'

There was a sudden silence between the two. Dorath had half-risen, his heavy face darkened. Taran's hand moved to the pommel of his sword. But in that instant a merry burst of music rose from Fflewddur's harp and the bard called out, 'Gently, friends! Hear a gay tune to settle our supper!'

He leaned the beautifully curved harp against his shoulders and as his fingers danced over the strings the men around the fire clapped their hands and urged him on. Dorath settled back on the turf, but he glanced at the bard and spat into the fire.

'Have done, harper,' Dorath said after a time. 'Your tune jangles from that crooked pot. We'll take our rest. You'll stay with us and in the morning my Company will guide you to the Lake of Llunet.'

Taran glanced at Fflewddur and caught the bard's quick frown. He rose to his feet. 'We thank you for your courtesy,' he said to Dorath, 'but time presses and we mean to travel during the night.'

'Ah, yes – so we do,' Fflewddur put in, while Gurgi vigorously agreed. 'As for the Lake – yes, well – we wouldn't think of putting you to the trouble. It's a long journey, far beyond your cantrev.'

'Prydain is my cantrev,' Dorath answered. 'Have you not heard of Dorath's Company? We serve any who pay us to serve: a weak lord who craves a strong war band, or three wayfarers who need protection against the dangers of their journey. The many dangers, harper,' he grimly added. 'Llunet is no more than a step and a jump for my men; and I know how the land lies. Will you go safely? I ask only a little part of the treasure you seek, a small reward to your humble servants.'

'We thank you,' Taran said again. 'It is already past nightfall and we must find our path.'

'How then!' cried Dorath in a great show of indignation. 'Do you scorn my poor hospitality? You wound my feelings, lords. Is it beneath you to sleep beside the likes of us? Ah, ah, swineherd, do not insult my men. They might take it amiss.'

Indeed, as Dorath spoke, an ugly grumble rose from the band, and Taran saw some of the warriors finger their swords. He stood uncertain, though well aware of the bard's discomfort. Dorath watched him closely. Two of the men had drifted quietly to the horse lines, and Taran could imagine that in the shadows they were easing their weapons from their sheaths.

'So be it,' Taran said, looking Dorath squarely between the eyes. 'We welcome your hospitality for the night, and tomorrow we take leave of you.'

Dorath grinned. 'There will be time to speak of that again. Sleep well.'

'Sleep well?' muttered Fflewddur as they wrapped themselves in their cloaks and uneasily stretched out on the ground. 'Great Belin, I'll not sleep a wink. I never liked the Hill Cantrevs and this is one reason more for liking them less.' He glanced around him. Dorath had flung himself down near the fire; undoubtedly following his leader's order, the man named Gloff lay close by the companions. 'I know of such roaming war bands,' Fflewddur went on in a hushed voice. 'Ruffians and looters, all of them. The cantrev lord who hires their swords to fight his neighbour soon finds them at his own throat. Dorath protect us from dangers? The worst danger is Dorath himself!'

'He's sure we're after treasure,' Taran whispered. 'It's in his mind and he'll not believe otherwise. Lucky it is, in a way,' he added ruefully. 'As long as he thinks we can lead him to gold or jewels he won't kill us out of hand.'

'Perhaps so, perhaps not,' answered Fflewddur. 'He may not cut our throats, but he might just as well decide to – ah – shall we say persuade us to tell him where the treasure is, and I fear he'd do considerably more than tweak our toes.'

'I'm not sure,' Taran replied. 'If he meant to torture us, I think he'd have tried before this. He's put us in a tight corner and we dare not let him travel with us. Still, I don't believe Dorath is all that sure of himself. We're only three against a dozen, but don't forget Llyan. If it comes to a fight, Dorath has an excellent chance of killing us all. Yet I think he's shrewd enough to see it would cost him too dearly, perhaps most of his band and himself as well. I doubt he'll risk it unless he has to.'

'I hope you're right,' sighed the bard. 'I'd rather not stay to find out. I'd sooner spend the night in a nest of serpents. We must get free of these villains! But how?'

Taran frowned and bit his lip. 'Eilonwy's horn,' he began.

'Yes, yes!' whispered Gurgi. 'Oh, yes, magic horn of tootings and hootings! Help comes with rescuings! Sound it, wise master!'

'Eilonwy's horn,' Taran said slowly. 'Yes, that was first in my thoughts. Must I use it now? It's a precious gift, too precious to waste. If all else fails . . .' He shook his head. 'Before I sound it let us try with our own strength. Sleep now,' he urged. 'Rest as much as you can. Before first light Gurgi can go silently to the horse lines and cut the tethers of all Dorath's steeds while Fflewddur and I try to stun the guards. Frighten the mounts, scatter them in all directions. Then . . .'

'We ride for dear life!' put in Fflewddur. He nodded. 'Good. It's our best chance. Without blowing that horn of yours, I daresay it's our only chance. Dorath!' he added, cradling his harp fondly in his arms. 'My tunes jangle indeed! My harp a crooked pot! That ruffian has neither ears nor eyes! A Fflam is forbearing, but when he insults my harp Dorath goes too far. Though, alas,' Fflewddur admitted, 'I've heard the same opinion from a few others.'

While Gurgi and Fflewddur drowsed fitfully, Taran stayed wakeful and uneasy. The campfire burned to embers. He heard the heavy breathing of Dorath's men. Gloff sprawled motionless, snoring atrociously. For a little time Taran closed his eyes. Had he chosen wrongly by not sounding the battle horn? He knew, painfully, that three lives hung in the balance. Doli had warned him not to squander the gift. But was the gamble too great? Should the gift be spent now, when its need was clearest? These thoughts pressed upon him heavier than the moonless night.

As the black sky began to show the first pale traces of grey, Taran silently roused Gurgi and the bard. Cautiously they made their way to the tethered steeds. Taran's heart leaped with hope. The two guards were sleeping soundly, their swords across their knees. He turned, meaning to help Gurgi cut the lines. The dark bole of an oak tree loomed, and he clung to the safety of its shadow.

A booted leg thrust out to bar Taran's way. Dorath was leaning against the tree, a dagger in his hand.

CHAPTER 12

The Wager

'What, are you so impatient to be gone, Lord Swineherd?' said Dorath, an edge of mockery in his tone. The dagger twirled in his hands and he clicked his tongue against his teeth. 'Without a farewell? Without a word of thanks?' He shook his head. 'This is grave discourtesy to me and to my men. Their feelings are tender. I fear you've deeply wounded them.'

The men of Dorath's Company had begun to stir. In a moment of panic Taran glanced at Fflewddur and Gurgi. Gloff had climbed to his feet and held his sword lightly, almost carelessly. Taran knew the man could bring up the blade in a flash before his own weapon left its sheath. Taran's eyes darted to the horse lines. Another of Dorath's band had drifted close by the steeds, where he stood idly paring his nails with the point of a hunting knife. Taran gestured for the companions to make no move.

Dorath straightened. His eyes were cold. 'Truly, do you mean to part with us? Even warned of the dangers in the hills?' He shrugged. 'Never say Dorath forces hospitality on unwilling guests. Go, if that's in your head. Seek your treasure and a speedy journey to you.'

'We meant you no discourtesy,' Taran answered. 'Bear us no ill will, for we bear you none. Farewell to you and your Company.'

Much relieved, he beckoned Gurgi and the bard and turned away.

Dorath's hand gripped his shoulder. 'How then?' Dorath cried. 'Will you go your way without settling the small matter between us?'

Taran halted, surprised, as Dorath went on.

'Why, there is payment to be reckoned, Lord Swineherd. Will you cheat me of my fee? We are poor men, Lord; too poor to give where we do not receive.'

The warriors laughed harshly. Dorath's heavy face had twisted into a leering humility, which Taran found all the more fearsome by its falsity, and the man cried out in an accusing, begging tone, 'You have eaten our meat and drunk our wine. All night you slept safely under our protection. Is this worth nothing to you?'

Taran stared at him in astonishment and sudden alarm. Dorath's men had come to gather near their leader. Gurgi edged closer to Taran. 'Protection!' Fflewddur muttered under his breath. 'Who'll protect us from Dorath? Protection? Great Belin, I'd call it robbery!'

'And there is more, Lord Swineherd,' Dorath quickly continued. 'The matter of payment for guiding you to the Lake of Llunet. It is no light journey for my Company; the paths are long and harsh . . .'

Taran faced the man squarely. 'You have given us food, drink and shelter,' he said, his thoughts racing to seek escape from Dorath's trap. 'We will pay their worth. As for your protection on our journey, we neither ask it nor want it.'

'My men are willing, waiting, and ready to guide you,' replied Dorath. 'It is you who breaks the bargain.'

'I struck no bargain with you, Dorath,' Taran answered.

Dorath's eyes narrowed. 'Did you not? But you will keep it nonetheless.'

The two watched each other in silence for a moment. The warriors stirred restlessly. From Dorath's expression Taran could not judge whether the man indeed meant to risk battle. If he did, Taran realized coldly, the companions had little chance to escape unharmed. At last he said, 'What do you want from us?'

Dorath grinned. 'Now you speak wisely. Small scores are quickly settled. We are humble men, Lord. We ask little, far less than what our fee should be. But, for the sake of the friendship between us, Dorath will be generous. What shall you give me?' His eyes went to Taran's belt. 'You carry a fair blade,' he said. 'It will be mine.'

Taran's hand clenched on the pommel. 'That you shall not have,' he answered quickly. 'I offer you bridles and harness from our gear, and even these we can ill afford. Dallben my master gave me this blade, the first that was truly mine and the first of my manhood. The one I love girded it on me with her own hands. No, Dorath, I do not bargain with my sword.'

Dorath threw back his head and laughed. 'You make much ado for a piece of iron. Your sweetling girded it to your side! Your first blade! This adds no worth. It is a fair weapon, no more. I've cast away better than that. But the look of this one suits me well enough. Give it into my hand and we are quit.'

Dorath's face filled with cruel pleasure as he reached out. Sudden anger goaded Taran. Caution forgotten, he snatched the blade from its sheath and drew back a pace.

'Have a care, Dorath!' Taran cried. 'Will you take my sword? It will be a costly bargain. You may not live to claim it.'

'Nor you to keep it,' Dorath answered, undisturbed. 'We know each other's thoughts, swineherd. Am I fool enough to risk lives for a trinket? Are you fool enough to stop me?

'We can learn this easily,' Dorath added. 'To your grief or to mine. Will you try me? My Company against yours?' When Taran did not answer, Dorath continued. 'My trade is to spill another's blood, not waste my own. And here the matter is easily settled. Pit one of your number against one of mine. A friendly wager, swineherd. Do you dare? The stakes? Your sword!'

Gloff had been listening all this while; his villainous face lit up and he struck his hands together. 'Well spoken,

Dorath! We'll see sport after all!'

'The choice is yours, swineherd,' Dorath said to Taran. 'Who is your champion? Will that hairy brute you call comrade stand against Gloff? They're both ill-favoured enough to be well-matched. Or the harper . . .'

'The matter is between you and me, Dorath,' Taran replied, 'and none other.'

'All the better,' Dorath answered. 'Do you take the wager, then? We two unarmed, win or lose, and the score paid. You have Dorath's word.'

'Is your word as true as your claim?' Taran flung back. 'I trust no bargain with you.'

Dorath shrugged. 'My men will withdraw beyond the trees where they'll be no help to me, if that's what you fear. And so will yours. What say you now? Yes or no?'

'No, no!' shouted Gurgi. 'Kindly master, beware!'

Taran looked long at the sword. The blade was plain, the hilt and pommel unadorned, yet even Dorath had seen the craftsmanship in its making. The day Dallben had put it in his hands shone bright in Taran's memory as the untarnished metal itself; and Eilonwy – her tart words had not hidden her blush of pride. Still, treasure it though he did, he forced himself to see the blade coldly as indeed no more than a strip of metal. Doubt rose in his heart. Win or lose, he felt unsure whether Dorath would let the companions free without a pitched battle. He nodded curtly. 'So be it.'

Dorath signalled to his band and Taran watched cautiously until all had made their way a good distance into the woods. At Taran's orders Fflewddur and Gurgi untethered Llyan and the two steeds and reluctantly withdrew in the opposite direction. Taran flung down his cloak and dropped Eilonwy's horn beside it. Dorath waited, a crafty glint in his eyes, as Taran slowly ungirded the scabbard and thrust the sword into the ground.

Taran stepped back. In the instant Dorath sprang upon

him without warning. The force of the burly warrior's charge drove the breath from Taran's lungs and nearly felled him. Dorath grappled with him and Taran realized the man strove to seize him by the belt and hurl him to earth. Taran flung up his arms and slipped downward out of Dorath's clutches. Cursing, Dorath struck at him with a hard fist, and though Taran escaped the full weight of the blow it glanced painfully from the side of his head. Ears ringing, Taran sought to disengage himself and regain sure footing, but Dorath pressed his attack without respite.

He dared not, Taran understood, let his heavier opponent come to grips with him, for Dorath's powerful arms could snap him in two; as the warrior plunged once more against him, Taran snatched the man's forearm and with all his strength swung Dorath head over heels to send him crashing to the ground.

But Dorath was on his feet in a flash. Taran crouched to meet the warrior's new attack. For all his weight, Dorath moved quick as a cat; he dropped to one side, spun quickly, and suddenly Taran saw the man's thick fingers gouging at his eyes. As Taran struggled to escape the blinding thrust, Dorath seized him by the hair and wrenched his head backward. The warrior's fist was raised to strike. Taran, gasping at the painful shock, flailed at the man's grinning face. Dorath's hold loosened; Taran tore himself away. For an instant Dorath seemed bewildered by the rains of blows, and Taran pressed his slight advantage, darting from one side to the other, giving Dorath no chance to gain the upper hand again.

Dorath dropped suddenly to one knee and caught at Taran with an outflung arm. Striving to tear himself away, Taran felt a sharp, stinging blow to his side. He fell backwards, clutching at the hurt. Dorath rose up. He gripped a short-bladed knife drawn from his boot.

'Disarm!' Taran cried. 'We fight weaponless! You betray me, Dorath!'

The warrior looked down at him. 'Have you learned which of us is the fool, Lord Swineherd?'

Eilonwy's horn lay within Taran's grasp and his fingers reached for it. How long, he thought hurriedly, how long before the Fair Folk might answer his call? Could he hope to keep Dorath at bay, or, at the last, could he do no more than turn and flee? He yearned desperately to sound the notes, but with an angry shout he cast aside the battle horn, snatched up his cloak for a shield, and plunged straight against Dorath.

The warrior's knife tangled in the folds of the garment. Gaining strength from his anger, Taran ripped the blade from the hand of Dorath, who staggered under the fury of the onslaught and fell to the ground. Taran followed him, seized Dorath by the shoulders, and braced his knee against the warrior's chest.

'Cut-throat!' Taran shouted through clenched teeth. 'You'd have taken my life for the sake of a bit of iron.'

Dorath's fingers scrabbled in the earth. His arm shot up. A handful of dirt and stones pelted against Taran's face.

'Find me now!' cried Dorath with a mighty heave. Taran clapped hands to his smarting eyes; tears streamed down his face; and he groped for the warrior who sprang away in an instant.

Taran stumbled forward on hands and knees. Dorath's heavy boot drove into his ribs. Taran cried out, then fell doubled up and panting. He strove to rise, but even the strength of his anger could not bring him to his feet. He sank down, his face pressed against the ground.

Dorath strode to the sword and plucked it from the turf. He turned to Taran. 'I spare your life, swineherd,' he cried scornfully. 'It means naught to me and I have no wish for it. Should we meet again, it may not go as well for you.'

Taran raised his head. In Dorath's eyes he saw only cold hatred that seemed to reach out to blight or shatter all it touched. 'You have won nothing,' Taran whispered. 'What have you gained worth more to you than to me?'

'The getting pleased me, swineherd. The taking pleases me all the more.' Dorath tossed the sword in the air, caught it again, then threw back his head and burst into raw laughter. He turned on his heel and strode into the forest.

Even after his strength had come back and the pain in his side had dwindled to a dull ache, Taran sat a long while on the ground before gathering up his belongings – the torn cloak, the battle horn, the empty scabbard, and setting off to join Fflewddur and Gurgi. Dorath had gone. There was no sign of him, but the laughter still rang in Taran's ears.

CHAPTER 13

The Lost Lamb

Under fair skies and gentle weather, the companions travelled deeper into the Hill Cantrevs. Gurgi had bandaged Taran's wound and the smart of it eased more quickly than the sting of losing his sword. As for the bard, the encounter with Dorath had driven away his concern for the length of his ears; he hardly mentioned the word 'rabbit', and had begun to share Taran's belief in a good ending to a hard journey. Gurgi still grumbled bitterly about the ruffians and often turned to shake an angry fist in the air. Fortunately, the companions had seen no more of the band, though Gurgi's furious grimaces might well have been enough to keep any marauders at a safe distance.

'Shameful robbings!' muttered Gurgi. 'Oh, kindly master, why did you not sound helpful horn and be spared beatings and cheatings?'

'The blade meant a great deal to me,' Taran answered, 'but I'll find another that will serve me. As for Eilonwy's horn, once used, its power is gone beyond regaining.'

'Oh, true!' Gurgi cried, blinking in amazement, as if such a thought had never entered his shaggy head. 'Oh, wisdom of kindly master! Will humble Gurgi's wits never grow sharper?'

'We've all wits enough to see Taran chose rightly,' put in Fflewddur. 'In his place I'd have done the same – ah, no, what I meant,' he quickly added, glancing at the harp, 'I'd have blown that horn till I was blue in the face. Ho, there! Steady, old girl!' he cried as Llyan suddenly plunged ahead. 'I say, what are you after now?'

At the same time Taran heard a forlorn bleating coming from a patch of brambles. Llyan was already there, crouching playfully, her tail waving in the air and one of her paws outstretched to tug at the briars.

A white lamb was caught in the thicket and, seeing the enormous cat, bleated all the louder and struggled pitifully. While Fflewddur, strumming his harp, drew Llyan away, Taran quickly dismounted. With Gurgi's help he bent aside the brambles and picked up the terrified animal.

'The poor thing's strayed – from where?' Taran said. 'I saw no farm near by.'

'Well, I suppose it knows its home better than we do,' answered Fflewddur, while Gurgi eyed the lost animal and delightedly patted the creature's fleecy head. 'All we can do is let it go to find its own path.'

'The lamb is mine,' called a stern voice.

Surprised, Taran turned to see a tall, broad-shouldered man making his way with great difficulty down the rocky slope. Grey streaked his hair and beard, scars creased his wide brow, and his dark eyes watched the companions intently as he toiled over the jutting stones. Unarmed save for a long hunting knife in his leather belt, he wore the rude garb of a herdsman; his cloak was rolled and slung over his back; his jacket was tattered at the edges, begrimed and threadbare. What Taran had first taken to be a staff or shepherd's crook he now saw to be a roughly fashioned crutch. The man's right leg was badly lamed.

'The lamb is mine,' the herdsman said again.

'Why, then it is yours to claim,' Taran answered, handing the animal to him.

The lamb ceased its frightened bleating and nestled comfortably against the shoulder of the herdsman, whose frown of distrust turned to surprise, as if he had fully expected to be obliged to fight for possession of the stray. 'My thanks to you,' he said after a moment, then added, 'I am Craddoc Son of Custennin.'

'Well met,' Taran said, 'and now farewell. Your lamb is safe and we have far to go.'

Craddoc, taking a firm grip on his crutch, turned to

climb the slope, and had gone but little distance when Taran saw the man stumble and lose his footing. Under his burden Craddoc faltered and dropped to one knee. Taran strode quickly to him and held out his hands.

'If the way to your sheepfold is as stubborn as the ones we've travelled,' Taran said, 'let us help you on your path.'

'No need!' the herdsman gruffly cried. 'Do you think me so crippled I must borrow strength from others?' When he saw that Taran still offered his hands, Craddoc's expression softened. 'Forgive me,' said the herdsman. 'You spoke in good heart. It was I who took your words ill. I am unused to company or courtesy in these hills. You've done me one service,' he went on, as Taran helped him to his feet. 'Now do me another. Share my hospitality.' He grinned. 'Though it will be small payment for saving my lamb.'

As Fflewddur led the mounts and Gurgi happily bore the lamb in his arms, Taran walked close by the herdsman who, after his first reluctance, was willing now to lean on Taran's shoulder as the path steepened and twisted upward before dropping into a deep vale among the hills.

The farmstead Taran saw to be a tumbledown cottage, whose walls of stone, delved from the surrounding fields, had partly fallen away. Half a dozen ill-shorn sheep grazed over the sparse pasture. A rusted plough, a broken-handled mattock and a scant number of other implements lay in an open-fronted shed. In the midst of the high summits, hemmed in closely by thorny brush and scrub, the farm stood lorn and desolate, yet clung doggedly to its patch of bare ground like a surviving warrior flinging his last, lone defiance against a pressing ring of enemies.

Craddoc, with a gesture almost of shyness and embarrassment, beckoned the companions to enter. Within, the cottage showed scarcely more cheer than the harsh land around it. There were signs Craddoc had sought to repair his fireplace and broken hearthstone, to mend his roof and chink up the crannies in the wall, but Taran saw the herdsman's labour had gone unfinished. In a corner a spinning wheel betokened a woman's tasks; but if this were so, her hand had ceased to guide it long since.

'Well, friend herdsman,' Fflewddur remarked heartily, seating himself on a wooden bench by a narrow trestle table, 'you're a bold man to dwell in these forsaken parts. Snug it is,' he quickly added, 'very snug but – ah, well – rather out of the way.'

'It is mine,' Craddoc answered, and his eyes flashed with pride. Fflewddur's words seemed to stir him, and he bent forward, one hand gripping his crutch and the other clenched upon the table. 'I have stood against those who would have taken it from me; and if I must, so shall I do again.'

'Why, indeed I've no doubt of that,' replied Fflewddur. 'No offence, friend, but I might say I'm a little surprised anyone would fancy taking it from you in the first place.'

Craddoc did not answer for a time. Then he said, 'The land was fairer than you see it now. Here we lived among ourselves, untroubled and at peace, until certain lords strove to claim our holdings for themselves. But those of us who prized our freedom banded together against them. Hotly fought was the battle and much was destroyed. Yet we turned them back.' Craddoc's face was grim. 'At high cost to us. Our dead were many, and my closest friends among them. And I,' he glanced at his crutch, 'I gained this.'

'What of the others?' Taran asked.

'In time, one by one, they quit their homes,' Craddoc replied. 'The land was no longer worth the keeping or the taking. They made their way to other cantrevs. In despair they took service as warriors or swallowed their pride and hopes and laboured for any who would give them bed and board.'

'Yet you stayed,' Taran said. 'In a ruined land? Why so?'

Craddoc lifted his head. 'To be free,' he answered curtly. 'To be my own man. Freedom was what I sought. I had found it here, and I had won it.'

'You are luckier than I, friend herdsman,' Taran answered. 'I have not yet found what I seek.'

When Craddoc glanced enquiringly at him, Taran told of his quest. The herdsman listened intently, saying no word. But as Taran spoke, a strange expression came upon Craddoc's face, as though the herdsman strove against disbelief and sought to reach out beyond his own wonder.

When Taran finished, Craddoc seemed about to speak. But he hesitated, then set the crutch under his arm, and rose abruptly, murmuring that he must see to his sheep. As he hobbled out, Gurgi trotted after him to gaze with pleasure at the gentle animals.

The day had grown shadowed. Taran and Fflewddur sat quietly at the table. 'I pity the herdsman as much as I admire him,' Taran said. 'He fought to win one battle only to lose another. His own land is his worst foe now, and little can he do against it.'

'I'm afraid you're right,' agreed the bard. 'If the weeds and brambles press him any closer,' he wryly added, 'he must soon graze his sheep on the turf of his rooftop.'

'I would help him if I could,' Taran replied. 'Alas, he needs more than I can give.'

When the herdsman came back Taran made ready to take his leave. Craddoc, however, urged the companions to stay. Taran hesitated. Though anxious to be gone, he well knew that Fflewddur disliked travelling at night; as for the herdsman, his eyes more than his words bespoke his eagerness, and at last Taran agreed.

Craddoc's provisions being scant, the companions shared out the food from Gurgi's wallet. The herdsman ate silently. When he had done, he cast a few dry, thorny branches on the small fire, watched them flare and crackle, then turned his gaze on Taran.

'A lamb of my flock strayed and was found again,' Craddoc said. 'But another once was lost and never found.' The herdsman spoke slowly and with great effort, as though the words came from his lips at some painful cost. 'Long past, when all had left the valley, my wife urged that we, too, should do the same. She was to bear our child; in this place she saw naught but hardship and desolation, and it was for the sake of our unborn that she pleaded.'

Craddoc bowed his head. 'But this I would not do. As often as she besought me, as often I refused. In time the child was born. Our son. The infant lived; his mother died. My heart broke, for it was as if I myself had slain her.

'Her last wish,' Craddoc said, his voice heavy with grief, 'was that I take the child from here.' His weathered features tightened. 'Even that wish I did not heed. No,' he added, 'to my mind, I had paid in blood, and more than blood, for my freedom. I would not give it up.'

The herdsman was silent a while. Then he said, 'Alone I sought to raise the child. But it was beyond my skill. A sturdy boy he was, yet in less than a year I saw him sicken. Only then did I understand his mother had spoken wisely, and I, like a proud fool, had not listened. At last I was willing to quit this valley.

'Too late was my choice,' Craddoc said. 'I knew the babe could not live out the journey. Nor could he live out another winter here. He was the lamb of my heart, already given to death.

'But on a certain day,' Craddoc went on, 'a wayfarer came by chance to my door. A man of deep knowledge he was and of many secret healing arts. In his hands alone the child could live. This he told me, and I knew he spoke the truth. He pitied the infant and offered to raise him for me. Grateful was I for his kindness as I put the child in his arms.

'He went his way then, and my son with him. No more

did I see or hear of either, as the years passed, and often did I fear both had surely perished in the hills. Yet, I still hoped, for the stranger vowed by every oath my son one day would return to me.'

The herdsman looked closely at Taran. 'The name of the wayfarer was Dallben.'

In the fireplace a thorny branch split and crackled. Craddoc said no more, but his eyes never left Taran's face. Fflewddur and Gurgi stared wordlessly. Slowly Taran rose to his feet. He felt himself trembling, for an instant feared his legs would give way under him, and he put a hand to the edge of the trestle table. He could neither think nor speak. He saw only Craddoc silently watching him, and this man he had met as a stranger now seemed a stranger all the more. Taran's lips moved without sound, until at last the words came brokenly and he heard his voice as though it were another's.

'Do you say,' Taran whispered, 'do you say then, you are father to me?'

'The promise has been kept,' Craddoc answered quietly. 'My son has come back.'

CHAPTER 14

The End of Summer

It was near dawn. The fire in the hearth had long since burned out. Taran rose silently. He had slept only fitfully, his head crowded with so many thoughts he could not sort one from another: Fflewddur's cry of astonishment, Gurgi's joyful yelps, Craddoc's embrace of welcome to a son he had scarcely seen, and Taran's bewildered embrace to a father he had never known. There had been harp playing and singing. Fflewddur had never been in better voice or spirits, and the herdsman's cottage had surely never rung with so much merriment; yet Taran and Craddoc had been more quiet than gay, as if striving to sense each other's mind and heart. At last, all had slept.

Taran stepped to the door. The sheep were silent in their fold. The mountain air was chill. Dew glistened, a net of cold silver on the sparse pasture, and the stones twinkled like stars fallen to earth. Taran shivered and drew his cloak about him. He stood a while in the dooryard before he sensed he was not alone. Fflewddur moved to join him.

'Couldn't sleep, eh?' Fflewddur said cheerily. 'Neither could I. Too excited. Didn't close my eyes for three winks – ah, yes, well – perhaps a few more than that. Great Belin, but it's been a day and a half! It's not everyone who finds his long-lost father sitting out in the middle of nowhere. Taran, my friend, your search is ended; and ended well. We're spared a journey to the Lake of Llunet – I don't mind telling you I'm just as pleased. Now we must set our plans. I say we should ride north to the Fair Folk realm and get hold of good old Doli; then, on to my kingdom for some feasting and revelry. And I suppose you'll want to sail to Mona and tell Eilonwy the good news. So be it! Now your quest is over, you're free as a bird!'

'Free as the caged eagle that Morda would have made me!' Taran cried. 'This valley will destroy Craddoc if he stays alone even a little longer. His burden is too great. I honour him for trying to bear it. Indeed, I honour him for that, and nothing else. His deeds cost my mother her life, and nearly cost me mine. Can any son love such a father? Yet as long as Craddoc lives, I am bound to him by ties of blood – if truly his blood runs in my veins.'

'If?' replied Fflewddur. He frowned and looked closely at Taran. 'You say *if*, as though you doubted . . .'

'Craddoc speaks truth when he says he is my father,' Taran answered. 'It is I who do not believe him.'

'How's that again?' asked Fflewddur. 'You know he's your father and doubt it at the same time? Now you really baffle me.'

'Fflewddur, can you not see?' Taran spoke slowly and painfully. 'I don't believe him, because I don't *want* to believe him. In my heart, secretly, I had always dreamed, even as a child, that – that I might be of noble lineage.'

Fflewddur nodded. 'Yes, I take your meaning.' He sighed. 'Alas, there's no choosing one's kinsmen.'

'Now,' Taran said, 'my dream is no more than a dream, and I must give it up.'

'His tale rings true,' answered the bard. 'But if there's doubt in your heart, what shall you do? Ah, that rascal Kaw! If he were only here we could send him with word to Dallben. But I doubt he'll find us in this dreary wasteland.'

'Wasteland?' said the voice of Craddoc.

The herdsman stood in the doorway. Taran quickly turned, ashamed of his own words and wondering how many of them Craddoc had overheard. But if the man had been there longer than a moment, he gave no sign of it. Instead, his weather-beaten face smiled as he hobbled to the companions. Gurgi followed behind him.

'Wasteland you see it now,' Craddock said, 'but soon as fair as ever it was.' He set a hand proudly on Taran's shoulder. 'My son and I. We will make it so.'

'I had thought,' Taran began slowly, 'I had hoped you would return with us to Caer Dallben. Coll and Dallben will welcome you. The farm is rich, and can be richer still if you help us with your labour. Here, the land may be worn out past restoring.'

'How then?' Craddoc answered, his features growing stern. 'Leave my land? To be another's servant? Now? When there is hope for us at last?' His eyes filled with pain as he looked at Taran. 'My son,' he said quietly, 'you do not say all that is in your heart. Nor have I said all that is in mine. My happiness blinded me to the truth. Your life has been too long apart from me. Caer Dallben is your home, more than this may ever be, this wasteland, this fallow ground – and the master of it a cripple.'

The herdsman had not raised his voice, but the words echoed in Taran's ears. Craddoc's face had gone hard as stone and a terrible pride flamed in his eyes. 'I cannot ask you to share this, nor beg duty from a son who is a stranger to me. We have met. We shall part, if that is your wish. Go your own path. I do not keep you from it.'

Before Taran could answer, Craddoc turned and made his way to the sheepfold.

'What must I do?' Taran cried in dismay to the bard.

Fflewddur shook his head. 'He'll not leave here, that's for certain. It's easy enough to see where your stubborn streak comes from. No, he won't budge. But if you'd set your mind at rest, then you yourself might go to Caer Dallben. Find out the truth from Dallben. He alone can tell you.'

'Winter would be upon us before I could return,' Taran answered. He gazed at the harsh land and desolate cottage. 'My – my father is at the end of his strength. The tasks are long. They must begin now, and be done before the first snowfall.'

He said no more for a time. Fflewddur waited silently; Gurgi was quiet, his brow wrinkled with concern. Taran looked at the two and his heart ached. 'Hear me well, my friends,' he said slowly. 'Fflewddur, if you are willing, ride to Caer Dallben. Tell that my search is ended and how this has come about. As for me, my place must be here.'

'Great Belin, you mean to stay in this wilderness?' Fflewddur cried. 'Even though you doubt . . . ?'

Taran nodded. 'My doubts may be of my own making. One way or another, I pray you send word speedily to me. But Eilonwy must be told nothing of this, only that my quest is over, my father found.' His voice faltered. 'Craddoc needs my help; his livelihood and his life depend on it, and I will not withhold it from him. But to have Eilonwy know I am a herdsman's son . . . No!' he burst out. 'That would be more than I could bear. Bid her my farewell. She and I must never meet again. It were better the Princess forget the shepherd boy, better that all of you forget me.'

He turned to Gurgi. 'And you, best of good friends, ride with Fflewddur. If my place is here, yours must be in a happier one.'

'Kindly master!' Gurgi shouted, flinging his arms desperately about Taran. 'Gurgi stays! So he promised!'

'Call me master no more!' Taran bitterly flung back. 'No master am I, but a low-born churl. Do you long for wisdom? You will not find it here with me. Take your freedom. This valley is no beginning but an ending.'

'No, no! Gurgi does not listen!' shouted Gurgi, clapping his hands over his ears. He threw himself flat on the ground and lay stiff as a poker. 'He does not go from side of kindly master. No, no! Not with pullings and pushings! Not with naggings and draggings!'

'So be it,' Taran said at last, seeing nothing else would

sway the determined creature.

When Craddoc returned, Taran told him only that he and his companion would stay, and that Fflewddur could no longer delay his own journey.

When Llyan was ready to travel, Taran put his arms about the cat's mighty shoulders and pressed his cheek into her deep fur as she mewed unhappily. Silently, he and Fflewddur clasped hands, and he watched while the bard, with many a backward glance, rode slowly from the valley.

Leaving Melynlas and the pony tethered in the shed, Taran and Gurgi bore the saddlebags holding their few possessions into the tumbledown cottage. Taran stood a moment, looking at the crumbling walls of the narrow chamber, the dead fire and broken hearthstone. From the pasture Craddoc was calling to him.

'And so,' Taran murmured, 'and so have we come home.'

In the weeks that followed, Taran believed he could have fared no worse had Morda done as he had threatened. Tall grey summits rose about him like the unyielding bars of a cage. Prisoner, he sought freedom from his memories in the harsh toil of the long days. There was much to be done, indeed there was all to be done; the land to clear, the cottage to repair, the sheep to tend. At first he had dreaded the dawns that brought him, weary as if he had not slept, from the straw pallet by the hearth to the seemingly endless labour awaiting him; but soon he rediscovered, as Coll had told him long ago, that he could force himself to plunge into it as into an icy stream, and find refreshment even in his exhaustion.

With Gurgi and Craddoc, he strained and sweated to uproot boulders from the field and haul them to the cottage, where they would later serve to mend the walls. The spring where the sheep watered had dwindled to a slow trickle. Taran saw a way to unblock it, shore up the damp ground, and dig a channel which he lined with flat stones. As the sparkling stream rushed into its new course,

Taran, forgetting all else, knelt and drank of it from his cupped hands. The cool draught filled him with wonder, as though never had he tasted water until now.

One day the three set about burning away the overgrowth and thorns. Taran's portion of the field took flame too slowly and he pressed his way to thrust his torch deeper amid the brambles. As he did, a sudden gust of wind turned the fire against him. Quickly he drew back, but the thorns caught at his jacket; he stumbled and fell, crying out as the flames rose in a scarlet wave.

Gurgi, at some distance, heard the shout. Craddoc, seeing Taran's plight, swung about on his crutch, and even before Gurgi could reach him, flung himself to Taran's side. The herdsman dropped to the ground, and, shielding Taran with his body, seized him by the belt and dragged him clear. Where Taran had been trapped, the flaming thorns roared and crackled.

The herdsman, gasping from the effort, climbed painfully to his feet.

Though Taran was unscathed, the fire had seared Craddoc's brow and hands. But the herdsman grinned, clapped Taran on the shoulder, saying with rough affection, 'I've not found a son only to lose him,' and with no more ado went back to his work.

'My thanks to you,' Taran called. But in his voice there was as much bitterness as gratitude, for the man who had saved his life was the same man who had broken it.

Thus it was in the days that followed. When a sheep sickened, Craddoc cared for it with an unexpected tenderness that went to Taran's heart. Yet Craddoc it was who had torn asunder Taran's dream of noble birth and destroyed every hope he had cherished for Eilonwy. When danger threatened the flock, Craddoc turned fierce as a wolf, heedless of his own safety with a courage Taran could only admire. Yet this man held him prisoner, in fetters of blood right. Craddoc would touch no food until Taran and Gurgi had their fill, and often went hungry as a result, all the while insisting his appetite was dull. Yet the gift stuck in Taran's throat, and he scorned the generosity he would have honoured in any other man.

'Are there two herdsman in this valley?' Taran cried to himself. 'One I can only love, and one I can only hate?'

So passed the summer. To forget the anguish of his divided heart, Taran laboured for the sake of the labour itself. Many tasks were still to be done, and the flock always to be tended. Until now Craddoc had been hard-pressed to keep the new lambs from straying and, as the sheep roved farther afield seeking better pasture, to gather all into the fold at evening. Gurgi pleaded to be given charge of them, and the flock seemed as pleased as he was.

He gambolled happily with the lambs, clucked and fussed over the ewes, and even the ancient, bad-tempered ram turned gentle in his presence. As the days grew cooler Craddoc gave him a jacket of unshorn fleece, and as Gurgi moved among his charges Taran could hardly distinguish the shaggy creature bundled in his woolly garb from the rest of the flock. Often Taran came upon him sitting on a boulder, the sheep in an admiring circle around their guardian. They followed him everywhere and would even have trotted after him into the cottage. Marching at the head of the flock, Gurgi looked as proud as a war leader. 'See with lookings!' Gurgi shouted. 'See them heed Gurgi with bleatings! Is kindly master Assistant Pig-Keeper? Then bold, clever Gurgi now is Assistant Sheep-Keeper!'

But Taran's eyes still turned beyond the barrier of the hills. At the end of each day he scanned the passes for a sign of Fflewddur and the clouds for a glimpse of Kaw. The crow, he feared, had flown to the Lake of Llunet; not finding the companions there, Kaw might still be waiting or, impatient, be seeking them elsewhere. As for the bard, Taran sensed more than ever that Fflewddur would not return; and as the days shortened and autumn drew closer, he gave up his vigil and looked no longer at the sky.

CHAPTER 15

The Open Cage

Throughout summer and autumn the three had worked unstintingly to finish the cottage, their only refuge against the oncoming winter. Now, as the first snow whirled from the heavy sky to powder the crags with dry, white flakes, it was done. The walls of new stone rose firm and solid; the roof had been thatched anew and tightly chinked against wind and weather. Within, a fire cheerily blazed in the new hearth. The wooden benches had been mended; the door no longer sagged on broken hinges. Though Craddoc had given himself unsparingly to the toil, the cottage for the most part was Taran's labour. The rusted tools, sharpened and refurbished, served him to make what other tools he needed. The planning as well as the doing had been his, and as he stood in the dooryard, the fine snow clinging like chaff to his uncropped hair, it was not without pride that he watched the smoke rising from the rebuilt chimney.

Craddoc had come to stand beside him, and the herdsman put a hand fondly on Taran's shoulder. For a time neither spoke, but at last Craddoc said, 'For all the years I strove to keep what was mine, it is mine no longer.' His bearded face furrowed in a smile. 'Ours,' he said.

Taran nodded, but made no further answer.

Since the winter tasks were short, the brief days seemed longer. Evenings by the fire, to while away the time, Craddoc told of his youth, of his settling in the valley. As the herdsman spoke of his hopes and hardships, Taran's admiration quickened, and for the first time he saw Craddoc as a man who had been not unlike himself.

Thus, at Craddoc's urging, Taran was willing to tell of

his days at Caer Dallben and all that had befallen him. Craddoc's face brightened with fatherly pride as he heard of these adventures. Yet, often Taran would stop in the midst of his recounting when memories of Eilonwy and all his life long past would surge suddenly and break upon him like a wave. Then would he break off abruptly, turn his face away, and stare at the fire. Those times Craddoc pressed him to speak no further.

A bond of affection, born of their common toil, had grown among all three. Craddoc never failed to treat Gurgi with much kindness and gentleness, and the creature, more than ever pleased with his duties as shepherd, was well content. But once, at the beginning of winter, Craddoc spoke apart with Taran, saying, 'Since the day you came to dwell here I have called you my son, yet never have you called me Father.'

Taran bit his lip. At one time, he had yearned to shout aloud his bitterness, to fling it angrily in the herdsman's face. It still tormented him, but now he could not bring himself to wound the feelings of one he scorned as a father yet honoured as a man.

Seeing Taran's distress, Craddoc nodded briefly. 'Perhaps,' he said, 'perhaps one day you shall.'

Snow turned the grey summits glistening white, yet the tall peaks Taran once had seen as bars now shielded the valley from the brunt of the storms, and against the wolf-wind howling through the icebound passes the cottage stood fast. Late of an afternoon, when Craddoc and Gurgi had gone to see to the flock, the gale sharpened and Taran set about stretching a heavier sheepskin across the narrow window.

He had only begun when the door was flung open as though ripped from its hinges. Shouting frantically, Gurgi burst into the cottage.

'Help, oh help! Kindly master, come with hastenings!'

Gurgi's face was pale as ashes, his hands shook violently as he clutched at Taran's arm. 'Master, master, follow Gurgi! Quickly, oh, quickly!'

Taran dropped the sheepskin, hurriedly donned a fleece jacket and, as Gurgi moaned and wrung his hands, snatched up a cloak and raced through the open door.

Outside, the wind caught at him and nearly flung him backward. Gurgi pressed on, wildly waving his arms. Taran bent forward against the gale and ran beside his desperate companion, stumbling across the snow-swept field. At the edge of the pasture they had cleared during the summer the land fell sharply away into stony slopes, and he followed close behind Gurgi as the creature scrambled past a rocky draw, then along a twisting path where he soon halted.

Taran gasped in dismay as Gurgi, whimpering fearfully, pointed downward. A narrow ledge jutted from the sheer side of the gorge. A figure, arms outflung, lay motionless, one leg twisted under his body, partly covered with fallen stones. It was Craddoc.

'Gone with stumblings!' Gurgi moaned. 'Oh, miserable Gurgi could not save him from slippings!' He clapped his hands to his head. 'Too late! Too late for helpings!'

Taran's head spun with shock; grief struck him like a sword. But then, beyond his will, terrifying in its sudden onrush, a wild sense of freedom flooded him as though rising from the most hidden depths of his heart. In one dizzying glance he seemed to see his cage of stone crumble.

The still form on the ledge stirred painfully and lifted an arm.

'He lives!' Taran cried.

'Oh, master! How do we save him?' Gurgi wailed. 'Terrible crags are steep! Even bold Gurgi fears to climb down!'

'Is there no way?' Taran exclaimed. 'He's badly hurt; dying, perhaps. We cannot leave him.' He pressed his fists to his reeling forehead. 'Even if we could make our way to him, how should we bear him up? And if we fail – not one life lost but three.'

His hands were shaking. It was not despair that filled him, but terror, black terror at the thoughts whispering in his mind. Was there the slimmest hope of saving the stricken herdsman? If not, even Prince Gwydion would not reproach Taran's decision. Nor would any man. Instead, they would grieve with him at his loss. Free of his burden, free of the valley, the door of his cage opened wide, and all his life awaited him; Eilonwy, Caer Dallben. He seemed to hear his own voice speak these words, and he listened in shame and horror.

Then, as if his heart would burst with it, he cried out in terrible rage, 'What man am I?'

Blind with fury at himself, he sprang down the slope and clawed for a handhold amid the ice-covered stones, while Gurgi, panting fearfully, clambered after him. Taran's numbed fingers clutched vainly at an outcropping as a rock gave way beneath his feet. Downward he pitched, and cried out as a jagged stone drove against his chest. Black suns burst in his head and he choked with pain. Above, Gurgi was sliding down in a shower of ice and pebbles. Taran's heart pounded. He was on the ledge. Craddoc lay within arm's reach.

Taran crawled to his side. Blood streamed down Craddoc's brow as the herdsman struggled to raise his head. 'Son, son,' he gasped, 'you have lost your life for me.'

'Not so,' Taran answered. 'Don't try to move. We'll find a way to bring you to safety.' He raised himself to his knees. Craddoc was even more grievously hurt than Taran had feared. Carefully he lifted away the heavy stones and shale that pressed against the herdsman, and gently drew him closer to the protecting face of the cliff.

Gurgi had dropped to the ledge and scurried to join Taran. 'Master, master,' he cried, 'Gurgi sees a pathway upward. But it is steep, oh, steep, with dangers of hurtful stumblings and tumblings!'

Taran glanced at where the creature pointed. Amid the rocks and snow-filled crevices he could make out a narrow passageway, free of ice. Yet, as Gurgi had warned, it rose nearly straight up. One man at a time could scale it; but what of two, burdened with a third? He gritted his teeth. The sharp stone had wounded him sorely as a blade, and each breath he drew filled his lungs with fire. He gestured for Gurgi to lay hold of Craddoc's legs, while he edged unsteadily along the sheer drop and slid his hands under the herdsman's shoulders. As gently as the companions strove to lift him, Craddoc cried out in agony, and they were forced to halt, fearful their efforts would do him further harm.

A wind had risen, screaming through the valley, lashing at the companions and nearly tearing them from the ledge. Once more they struggled to bear Craddoc to the upward passage, and once more fell back as the gale battered them. The early twilight had begun deepening and shadows filled the gorge. The face of the cliff wavered before Taran's eyes. His legs trembled as he forced himself again to lift the herdsman.

'Leave me,' Craddoc murmured hoarsely. 'Leave me. You waste your own strength.'

'Leave you?' Taran burst out. 'What son forsakes his own flesh and blood?'

Hearing this, Craddoc smiled for an instant, then his face drew taut in anguish. 'Save yourselves,' he whispered.

'You are my father,' Taran replied. 'I stay.'

'No!' the herdsman cried out with all his strength. 'Do as I ask, and go from here. Heed me now, or it will be too late. The duty of kinship? You owe me none. No bond of blood holds you.'

'How then?' Taran gasped, staring wildly at the herdsman. His head spun and he clutched at the ledge. 'How then? Do you tell me I am not your son?'

Craddoc looked at him a moment, his eyes unwavering. 'Never have I been false to any man. Save once. To you.'

'A lie?' Taran stammered in dismay. 'Did you lie to me then – or do you lie to me now?'

'Half-truth is worse than lie,' Craddoc answered brokenly. 'Hear me. Hear this part of the truth. Yes, long past, as he journeyed through Prydain, Dallben sheltered with me. But of what he sought he never spoke.'

'The child,' Taran cried. 'There was none?'

'There was,' Craddoc answered. 'A son. Our first born, even as I told you. He did not live beyond the day of his birth. His mother died with him,' he murmured. 'And you – I needed your strength to keep what remained to me. I saw no other way. Even as I spoke the lie, I was ashamed, then more ashamed to speak the truth. When your companion left, I could only hope that you would follow with him, and gave you freedom so to do. You chose to stay.

'But this, as well, is true,' Craddoc said hurriedly. 'At first I leaned upon you as on my crutch, because you served my need, but no father came to love a son more dearly.'

Taran's head sank to his breast. He could not speak, and his tears blinded him.

Craddoc, who had half-raised himself, fell back to the stones of the ledge. 'Go from here,' he murmured.

Taran's hand dropped to his side. His fingers touched the rim of the battle horn. With a sudden cry he straightened. Eilonwy's horn! Unthinking, he had slung it about his shoulder when he had run from the cottage. Hastily he drew it from beneath his cloak. The summons to the Fair Folk, the call he had treasured! It alone could save Craddoc. He stumbled to his feet. The ledge seemed to sway beneath him. The notes Doli had taught him blurred in his mind and he strove desperately to recall them. Suddenly they rang once more in his memory.

He raised the horn to his lips. The notes sprang loud and clear and even before the signal faded, the wind caught them and seemed to fling the call through all the valley, where it returned in echo after echo. Then whirling shadows engulfed him and Taran dropped to the ledge.

How long they clung there he did not know; whether moments or hours, he was only dimly aware of strong hands bearing him up, of a rope lashed about his waist. He glimpsed vaguely, as between the flickering of a dark flame, the broad faces of dwarfish mountaineers, whose number he could not judge.

When next he opened his eyes he was in the cottage, the fire blazing, Gurgi beside him. Taran started up. Pain seared his chest, which he saw had been carefully bandaged.

'The signal!' he murmured feebly. 'It was answered . . .'

'Yes, yes!' Gurgi cried. 'Fair Folk save us with mighty haulings and heavings! They bind up kindly master's hurtful wounds and leave healing herbs for all that is needful!'

'The summons,' Taran began. 'Good old Doli. He warned me not to waste it. For Craddoc's sake, I'm glad I kept it as long as I did. Craddoc – where is he? How does he fare?' He stopped suddenly.

Gurgi was looking at him silently. The creature's face wrinkled miserably and tears stood in his eyes as he bowed his shaggy head.

Taran fell back. His own cry of anguish rang in his ears. Beyond that was only darkness.

CHAPTER 16

Taran Wanderer

Fever came, sweeping over him, a blazing forest through which he staggered endlessly; tossing on the straw pallet, he knew neither day nor night. Often there were dream faces half-glimpsed, half-recognized, of Eilonwy, of his companions, of all whom he had loved; yet they slipped away from him, shifting and changing like wind-driven clouds, or were swallowed by nightmares that made him cry out in terror. Later, he seemed to see Fflewddur, but the bard had turned gaunt, hollow-eyed, his yellow hair matted on his forehead, his mouth pinched and his long nose thin as a blade. His garments hung ragged and stained. Kaw perched on his shoulder and croaked, 'Taran, Taran!'

'Yes, well, indeed it's about time you're waking up,' said Fflewddur, grinning at him. Beside the bard, Gurgi squatted on a wooden stool and peered at him anxiously.

Taran rubbed his eyes, unsure whether he was asleep or awake. This time the faces did not vanish. He blinked. The sheepskin had been taken from the window and sunlight streamed over him.

'Gurgi? Kaw?' Taran murmured. 'Fflewddur? What's happened to you? You look like half of yourself.'

'You're hardly one to talk about appearances, old friend.' The bard chuckled. 'If you could see yourself, I'm sure you'd agree you look worse than I do.'

Still baffled, Taran turned to Gurgi who had leaped up joyously and clapped his hands.

'Kindly master is well again!' Gurgi shouted. 'He is well, without groanings and moanings, without shiverings and quiverings! And it is faithful, clever Gurgi who tends him!'

'That's true,' agreed Fflewddur. 'For the past two weeks he's fussed over you like a mother hen, and he couldn't have given you more care if you'd been one of his pet lambs!

'I rode straight as an arrow from Caer Dallben,' the bard continued. 'Ah – well – the truth of it is, I got lost for a time; then it began snowing. Llyan ploughed through drifts up to her ears, and even she finally had to stop. For a while we sheltered in a cave – Great Belin, I thought I'd never see the light of day again.' Fflewddur gestured at his tattered clothing. 'It was the sort of journey that tends to make one rather unkempt. Not to mention three-fourths starved. Kaw was the one who happened to find us, and he guided us along the clearer trails.

'As for Dallben,' Fflewddur went on, 'he was upset, considerably more than he wanted to show. Though all he said was, "Taran is not the herdsman's son, but whether or not he stays is a matter entirely of his own choosing."

'And so I came back as fast as I could,' the bard concluded. 'Alas, I didn't reach you sooner.' He shook his head. 'Gurgi told me what happened.'

'Craddoc longed for a son,' Taran answered slowly, 'as I longed for parentage. I wonder if I would not have been happier had I believed him. Though at the end, I think I did. Gurgi and I could have climbed to safety. For the sake of Craddoc, I sounded Eilonwy's horn. Had I done it sooner, perhaps he might have lived. He was a man of courage and good heart, a proud man. Now he is dead. I saved the signal to use in a worthy cause, and when I found one it was wasted.'

'Wasted?' answered Fflewddur. 'I think not. Since you did your best and didn't begrudge using it, I shouldn't call it wasted at all.'

'There is more that you do not know,' Taran said. He looked squarely at the bard. 'My best? At first I thought to leave Craddoc on the ledge.'

'Well, now,' replied the bard, 'each man has his moment of fear. If we all behaved as we often wished to there'd be sorry doings in Prydain. Count the deed, not the thought.'

'In this I count my thought as much,' Taran said in a cold voice. 'It was not fear that held me back. Will you know the truth? I was ashamed to be base-born, so ashamed it sickened me. I would have left Craddoc to his death. Yes, left him to die!' he burst out. 'Because I believed it would have set me free of him. I was ashamed to be the son of a herdsman. But no longer. Now my shame is for myself.' He turned his face away and said no more.

The companions wintered in the cottage, and little by little Taran's strength came back. At the first thaw, when the valley sparkled with melting snow and the streams burst from their ice-bound courses, Taran stood silently in the dooryard and looked at the pale green summits, pondering what had long been in his heart.

'We'll soon be ready,' said Fflewddur, who had come from seeing to Llyan and the steeds. 'The passes should be clear. The Lake of Llunet can't be too far, and with Kaw to help us, we should reach it in no time.'

'I've thought carefully on this,' Taran replied. 'All winter I've tried to decide what I should do, and never have I found an answer. But one thing is clear, and my mind is made up. I will not seek the Mirror.'

'What's that you say?' cried Fflewddur. 'Do I hear you aright? Give up your search? Now, of all times? After all you've gone through? Taran, my boy, you've regained your health, but not your wits!'

Taran shook his head. 'I give it up. My quest has brought only grief to all of you. And for me, it's led me not to honour but to shame. Taran? Taran makes me sick at heart. I longed to be of noble birth, longed for it so much I believed it was true. A proud birthright was all that counted for me. Those who had none – even when I admired them, as I admired Aeddan, as I learned to admire Craddoc – I deemed them lesser because of it. Without knowing them, I judged them less than what they were. Now I see them as true men. Noble? They are far nobler than I.

'I am not proud of myself,' Taran went on. 'I may never be again. If I do find pride, I'll not find it in what I was or what I am, but what I may become. Not in my birth, but in myself.'

'All things considered, then,' replied the bard, 'the best thing would be to pack our gear and start for Caer Dallben.'

Taran shook his head. 'I cannot face Dallben or Coll. One day, perhaps. Not now. I must make my own way, earn my own keep. Somehow, the robin must scratch for his own worms.' He stopped suddenly and looked, wondering, at the bard. 'Orddu – those were her words. I heard them only with my ears. Until now, I did not understand with my heart.'

'Scratching for worms is unappetizing, to say the best of it,' Fflewddur answered. 'But it's true, everyone should have a skill. Take myself, for example. King though I am, as a bard you'll find none better – ' A harp string snapped, and for a moment it appeared that several others might give way.

'Yes, well, aside from all that,' Fflewddur said hastily, 'if you don't mean to go home, then I suggest the Free Commots. The craftsmen there might welcome a willing apprentice.'

Taran thought for some moments, then nodded. 'So shall I do. Now will I scorn no man's welcome.'

The bard's face fell. 'I – I fear I can't go with you, old friend. There's my own realm waiting. True enough, I'm happier wandering as a bard than sitting as a king. But already I've been too long away.'

'Then our ways must part again,' Taran replied. 'Will there ever be an end to saying farewell?'

'But Gurgi does not say farewell to kindly master,' cried Gurgi, as Fflewddur went to gather up his gear. 'No, no, humble Gurgi toils at his side!'

Taran bowed his head and turned away. 'If the day comes when I deserve your faithfulness that will be prize enough for me.'

'No, no!' protested Gurgi. 'Not prizings! Gurgi only gives what is in his heart to give! He stays and asks nothing more. Once you comforted friendless Gurgi. Now let him comfort sorrowful master!'

Taran felt the creature's hand on his shoulder. 'Dallben spoke truth, old friend,' he murmured. 'Staunchness and good sense? All that and more. But your comfort stands me in better stead than all the cleverness in Prydain.'

Next morning Taran and Fflewddur took leave of one another for the second time. Despite the bard's protest that a Fflam could always find his way, Taran insisted on Kaw's going along as a guide. Once this task was done, Taran urged the crow to return to Caer Dallben or, if it pleased him better, to fly freely as he chose. 'I'll not bind you to my journey,' Taran said to Kaw, 'for even I don't know where it may end.'

'Then how do we fare?' cried Gurgi. 'Faithful Gurgi follows, oh, yes! But where does kindly master begin?'

The valley seemed suddenly empty as Taran stood, unanswering, looking at the silent cottage and the small mound of stones marking Craddoc's resting place. 'Times there were,' Taran said, almost to himself, 'when I believed I was building my own prison with my own hands. Now I wonder if I shall ever labour as well and gain as much.'

He turned to the waiting Gurgi. 'Where?' He knelt, plucked a handful of dry grass from the turf, and cast it into the air. The freshening wind bore the blades eastward, towards the Free Commots.

'There,' Taran said. 'As the wind blows, so do we follow it.'

Since neither Taran nor Gurgi wished to leave the sheep behind, the wayfarers departed from the valley with the small flock bleating after them. Taran intended offering the animals to the first farmstead with good grazing land, yet several days passed and he saw no inhabited place. The two companions had started in a south-easterly direction, but Taran soon gave Melynlas free rein and, though aware the stallion was bearing more east than south, he paid little heed until they drew near the banks of a wide, rapid-flowing river.

Here, the pasture stretched broad and fair. Ahead he glimpsed an empty sheepfold; he noticed no flock, but the gate of the enclosure stood open as though awaiting the animals' return at any moment. The low-roofed cottage and sheds were neat and well-kept. A pair of shaggy goats browsed near the dooryard. Taran blinked in surprise, for set about the cottage were all manner of woven baskets, some large, some small, some rising on stilts, and others seemingly dropped at random. Several trees by the river held wooden platforms, and along the riverbank itself Taran caught sight of what appeared to be a weir of carefully woven branches. Wooden stakes secured a number of nets and fishing lines drifting in the current.

Puzzling over this farmhold, surely the strangest he had seen, Taran drew closer, dismounted, and as he did so a tall figure ambled from the shed and made his way towards the companions. Taran glimpsed the farm wife peering from the cottage window. At the same time, as if out of nowhere, half a dozen children of different ages burst into sight and began running and skipping towards the flock, laughing gaily and shouting to one another: 'They're here! They're here!' Seeing Gurgi, they turned their attention from the sheep to cluster around him, clapping their hands in delight and calling out such merry-hearted greetings that the astonished creature could only laugh and clap his own hands in return.

The man who stood before Taran was thin as a stick with lank hair tumbling over his brow and blue eyes bright as a bird's. Indeed, his narrow shoulders and spindly legs made him look like a crane or stork. His jacket was too short in the arms, too long in the body, and his garments seemed pieced together with patches of all sizes, shapes and colours.

'I am Llonio Son of Llonwen,' he said, with a friendly grin and a wave of his hand. 'A good greeting to you, whoever you may be.'

Taran bowed courteously. 'My name – my name is Taran.'

'No more than that?' said Llonio. 'As a name, my friend, it's cropped a little short.' He laughed good-naturedly. 'Shall I call you Taran Son of Nobody? Taran of Nowhere? Since you're alive and breathing, obviously you're the son of two parents. And you've surely ridden here from somewhere else.'

'Call me, then, a wanderer,' Taran replied.

'Taran Wanderer? So be it, if that suits you.' Llonio's glance was curious, but he asked no further.

When Taran then spoke of seeking pasture for the sheep, Llonio nodded briskly.

'Why, here shall they stay, and my thanks to you,' he exclaimed. 'There's no grazing fresher and sweeter, and no sheepfold safer. We've seen to that and laboured since the first thaw to make it so.'

'But I fear they may crowd your own flock,' Taran said, though he admired Llonio's pastureland and the stoutly built enclosure, and would have been well content to leave the sheep with him.

'My flock?' Llonio answered, laughing. 'I had none until this moment! Though we've been hoping and waiting and the children have been talking of little else. A lucky wind it was that brought you to us. Goewin, my wife, needs wool to clothe our young ones. Now we'll have fleece and to spare.'

'Wait, wait,' put in Taran, altogether baffled, 'do you mean you cleared a pasture and built a sheepfold without having any sheep at all? I don't understand. That was work in vain – '

'Was it now?' asked Llonio, winking shrewdly. 'If I hadn't, would you be offering me a fine flock in the first place; and in the second, would I have the place to keep them? Is that not so?'

'But you couldn't have known,' Taran began.

'Ah, ah,' Llonio chuckled, 'why, look you, I knew that with any kind of luck a flock of sheep was bound to come along one day. Everything else does! Now honour us by stopping here a while. Our fare can't match our thanks, but we'll feast you as best we can.'

Before Taran could answer, Llonio bent down to one of the little girls who was staring round-eyed at Gurgi. 'Now then, Gwenlliant, run see if the brown hen's chosen to lay us an egg today.' He turned to Taran. 'The brown hen's a moody creature,' he said. 'But when she has a mind to, she puts down a handsome egg.' He then set the rest of the children running off on different tasks, while Taran and Gurgi watched astonished at the hustle and bustle in this most peculiar household. Llonio led the two into the cottage where Goewin gave them a warm welcome and bade them sit by the hearth. In no time Gwenlliant was back holding an egg in outstretched hands.

'An egg!' cried Llonio, taking it from her, raising it aloft, and peering as if he had never seen one before. 'An egg it is! The finest the brown hen's given us! Look at the size! The shape! Smooth as glass and not a crack on it. We'll feast well on this, my friends.'

At first Taran saw nothing extraordinary in the egg which Llonio praised so highly; but, caught up by the man's good spirits, Taran to his own surprise found himself looking at the egg as though he, too, had never seen one. In Llonio's hands the shell seemed to sparkle so brightly, to curve so gracefully and beautifully that even Gurgi marvelled at it, and Taran watched almost with regret as Goewin cracked such a precious egg into a large earthen bowl. Nevertheless, if Llonio intended sharing it among his numerous family, Taran told himself, the fare would indeed be meagre.

Yet, as Goewin stirred the contents of the bowl, the children crowded one after the other into the cottage, all bearing something that made Llonio call out cheerily at each discovery.

'Savoury herbs!' he cried. 'That's splendid! Chop them up well. And here – what's this, a handful of flour? Better and better! We'll need that pot of milk the goat's given us, too. A bit of cheese? Just the thing!' Then he clapped his hands delightedly as the last and smallest child held up a fragment of honeycomb. 'What luck! The bees have left us honey from their winter store.'

Goewin, meanwhile, was busy popping all these finds into the bowl and, before Taran's eyes, the contents soon filled it nearly to the brim. Even then, his surprise did not end. Goewin deftly poured the mixture on to a sheet of metal which, Taran was quite certain, was nothing else but a warrior's shield hammered flat, and held it over the glowing embers. Within moments, the scent of cooking filled the cottage, Gurgi's mouth watered, and in no time the farm wife drew a dappled golden cake nearly as big as a cartwheel from the fireplace.

Llonio quickly sliced it into pieces and to Taran's amazement there was not only enough for all but some left over. He ate his fill of the most delicious egg he ever tasted – if egg it could now be called – and not even Gurgi could eat more.

'Now then,' said Llonio, when they had finished, 'I'll see to my nets. Come along, if you like.'

CHAPTER 17

The Weir

While Gurgi lingered in the cottage, Taran followed Llonio to the riverbank. On the way, whistling merrily through his teeth, Llonio stopped to peer into the baskets, and Taran noticed one of them held a large beehive, undoubtedly the source of the honey which had sweetened Goewin's cake. The rest, however, stood empty. Llonio merely shrugged his shoulders.

'No matter,' he said. 'Something will surely fill them later. Last time a flock of wild geese flew down to rest. You should have seen the feathers left after they'd gone. Enough to stuff cushions for every one of us!'

By now they reached the river, which Llonio named as Small Avren since, farther south, it flowed into Great Avren itself. 'Small it is,' he said, 'but sooner or later whatever you might wish comes floating along.' As if to prove his words he began hauling vigorously at the net staked along the bank. It came up empty, as did the fishing lines. Undismayed, Llonio shrugged again. 'Tomorrow, very likely.'

'How then,' Taran exclaimed, feeling perplexed as he had ever been, 'do you count on baskets and nets to bring you what you need?' He looked at the man in astonishment.

'That I do,' replied Llonio, laughing good-naturedly. 'My holding is small; I work it as best I can. For the rest – why, look you, if I know one thing, it's this: life's a matter of luck. Trust it, and a man's bound to find what he seeks, one day or the next.'

'Perhaps so,' Taran admitted, 'but what if it takes longer than that? Or never comes at all?'

'Be that as it may,' answered Llonio, grinning. 'If I fret over tomorrow, I'll have little joy today.'

So saying, he clambered nimbly on to the weir, which Taran now saw was made not to bar the flow of water but to strain and sift the current. Balancing atop this odd construction, seeming more cranelike than ever as he bobbed up and down, bending to poke and pry among the osiers, Llonio soon gave a glad cry and waved excitedly.

Taran hurriedly picked his way across the dam to join him. His face fell, however, when he reached Llonio's side. What had caused the man's joyful shout was no more than a discarded horse bridle.

'Alas,' said Taran, disappointed, 'there's little use in that. The bit's missing and the rein's worn through.'

'So be it, so be it,' replied Llonio. 'That's what Small Avren's brought us today, and it will serve, one way or another.' He slung the dripping bridle over his shoulder, scrambled from the dam, and with Taran following him set off with long strides through the grove of trees fringing the river.

In a while Llonio, whose sharp eyes darted everywhere at once, cried out again and stooped at the bottom of a gnarled elm. Amid the roots and for some distance around, mushrooms sprouted abundantly.

'Pluck them up, Wanderer,' Llonio exclaimed. 'There's our supper for tonight. The finest mushrooms I've seen! Tender and tasty! We're in luck today!' Quickly gathering his finds, Llonio popped them into a sack dangling from his belt and set off again.

Following Llonio's rambling, halting now and then to cull certain herbs or roots, the day sped so swiftly it was nearly over before Taran realized it had begun. Llonio's sack being full, the two turned their step back to the cottage, taking a path different from the way they had come. As they ambled along, Taran caught his foot on a jutting edge of stone and he tumbled head over heels.

'Your luck is better than mine,' Taran laughed ruefully.

'You've found your mushrooms, and I, no more than a pair of bruised shins!'

'Not so, not so!' protested Llonio, hastily scraping away the loam partly covering the stone. Look you, now! Have you ever seen one so shaped? Round as a wheel and smooth as an egg. A windfall it is that needs only the picking up!'

If a windfall, Taran thought, it was the hardest and heaviest he had stumbled on, for Llonio now insisted on unearthing the flat rock. They did so with much digging and heaving and, carrying it between them, struggled back to the farmhold, where Llonio rolled it into the shed already bursting with an odd array of churn handles, strips of cloth, horse trappings, thongs, hanks of cord, and all the harvest of his weir, nets and baskets.

Over the cookfire, the mushrooms, eked out with the left-over griddle cake and a handful of early vegetables the children had found, simmered so deliciously that Taran and Gurgi needed no urging to stay for the repast. As night fell Taran welcomed the family's invitation to rest by the hearth. Gurgi, stuffed and contented, began snoring instantly. And Taran, for the first time in many days, slept soundly and dreamlessly.

The next morning was bright and crisp. Taran woke to find the sun high, and though he had meant to saddle Melynlas and be on his way he did not do so. If Llonio's weir had yielded little the day before, the night current had more than made up for it. A great sack of wheat had somehow become tangled with a cluster of dead branches which served as a raft and thus had floated downstream undampened by the river. Goewin, without delay, brought out a large stone quern to grind the grain into meal. All took a hand in the task, the children from eldest to youngest, even Llonio himself; Taran did his share willingly, though he found the quern heavy and cumbersome, as did Gurgi.

'Oh, tiresome millings,' Gurgi said. 'Gurgi's poor fingers

are filled with achings, and his arms with strainings and painings!'

Nevertheless, he finished his turn; although by the time enough meal had been ground, another day had nearly sped by, and once more Llonio urged the wayfarers to share his hospitality. Taran did not refuse. Indeed, as he stretched by the fire, he admitted to himself he had secretly hoped Llonio would suggest it.

During the next few days, Taran's heart was easier than it had been since he chose to abandon his quest. The children, shy with him at first as he with them, had become his fast friends, and frolicked with him as much as they did with Gurgi. With Llonio, each day he visited the nets, the baskets and the weir, sometimes returning empty-handed and sometimes laden with whatever strange assortment the wind or current brought. In the beginning he had seen no value in these odds and ends, but Llonio found a use for nearly all. A cartwheel was turned into a spinning wheel, parts of the horse bridle made belts for the children, a saddlebag became a pair of boots; and Taran shortly realized there was little the family needed that did not, late or soon, appear from nowhere; and there was nothing – an egg, a mushroom, a handful of feathers delicate as ferns – that was not held to be a treasure.

'In a way,' Taran told Gurgi, 'Llonio's richer than Lord Gast is or ever will be. Not only that, he's the luckiest man in Prydain! I envy no man's riches,' Taran added. Then he sighed and shook his head. 'But I wish I had Llonio's luck.'

When he repeated this to Llonio, the man only grinned and winked at him. 'Luck, Wanderer? One day, if you're lucky, I'll tell you the secret of it.' Beyond that, Llonio would say no more.

At this time a thought had begun taking shape in Taran's mind. Nearly all of Llonio's finds had been put to one use or another – save the flat stone which still lay in the shed. 'But I wonder,' he told Llonio, 'I wonder if it couldn't serve to grind meal better than the quern . . .'

'How then?' cried Llonio, greatly pleased. 'If you think it can, do as you see fit.'

Still pondering his idea, Taran roamed the woods until he came upon another stone of much the same size as the first. 'That's a stroke of luck,' he laughed, as Llonio helped him drag it back.

Llonio grinned. 'So it is, so it is.'

During the several days following, Taran, with Gurgi's eager help, toiled unceasingly. In a corner of the shed he set one stone firmly in the ground and the other above it. In this, he laboriously hollowed out a hole and, using the left-over harness leathers, in it he affixed a long pole that reached up through an opening in the roof. At the top of the pole he attached frames of wood, over which he stretched large squares of cloth.

'But this is no quern,' Gurgi cried when at last it was done. 'It is a ship for boatings and floatings! But there is no ship, only mast with sails!'

'We shall see,' Taran answered, calling Llonio to judge his handiwork.

For a moment the family stood puzzled at Taran's peculiar structure. Then, as the wind stirred, the roughly fashioned sails caught the current of the breeze. The mast-like pole shuddered and creaked, and for a breathless instant Taran feared all his work would come tumbling about his ears. But it held fast, the sails bellied out and began turning, slowly at first, then faster and faster, while below, in the shed, the upper stone whirled merrily. Goewin hastened to throw grain into Taran's makeshift mill. In no time, out poured meal finer than any the quern had ground. The children clapped their hands and shouted gleefully; Gurgi yelped in astonishment; and Llonio laughed until the tears ran down his cheeks.

'Wanderer,' he cried, 'you've made much from little, and

done it better than ever I could!'

Over the next few days the mill not only ground the family's grain, Taran also struck on a means of using it as a sharpening stone for Llonio's tools. Looking at his handiwork, Taran felt a stirring of pride for the first time since leaving Craddoc's valley. But with it came a vague restiveness.

'By rights,' he told Gurgi, 'I should be more than happy to dwell here all my life. I've found peace and friendship – and a kind of hope, as well. It's eased my heart like balm on a wound.' He hesitated. 'Yet, somehow Llonio's way is not mine. A spur drives me to seek more than what Small Avren brings. What I seek, I do not know. But, alas, I know it is not here.'

He spoke then with Llonio and regretfully told him he must take up his journeying again. This time, sensing Taran's decision firmly made, Llonio did not urge him to stay, and they bade each other farewell.

'And yet,' Taran said, as he swung astride Melynlas, 'alas, you never told me the secret of your luck.'

'Secret?' replied Llonio. 'Have you not already guessed? Why, my luck's no greater than yours or any man's. You need only sharpen your eyes to see your luck when it comes, and sharpen your wits to use what falls into your hands.'

Taran gave Melynlas rein, and with Gurgi at his side rode slowly from the banks of Small Avren. As he turned to wave a last farewell, he heard Llonio calling after him, 'Trust your luck, Taran Wanderer. But don't forget to put out your nets!'

CHAPTER 18

The Free Commots

From Small Avren they wended eastward at an easy pace, halting as it pleased them, sleeping on the turf or sheltering at one of the many farmsteads among the rich green vales. This was the land of the Free Commots, of cottages clustering in loose circles, rimmed by cultivated fields and pastures. Taran found the Commot folk courteous and hospitable. Though he named himself only as Taran Wanderer, the dwellers in these hamlets and villages respected his privacy and asked nothing of his birthplace, rank or destination.

Taran and Gurgi had ridden into the outskirts of Commot Cenarth when Taran reined up Melynlas at a long, low-roofed shed from which rang the sound of hammer on anvil. Within, he found the smith, a barrel-chested, leather-aproned man with a stubbly black beard and a great shock of black hair bristly as a brush. His eyelashes were scorched, grime and soot smudged his face; sparks rained on his bare shoulders but he seemed to count them no more than fireflies. In a voice like stones rattling on a bronze shield he roared out a song in time with his hammer strokes so loudly that Taran judged the man's lungs as leathery as his bellows. While Gurgi cautiously drew back from the shower of sparks, Taran called a greeting, scarcely able to make himself heard above the din.

'Master smith,' he said, bowing deeply as the man at last caught sight of him and put down the hammer, 'I am called Taran Wanderer and journey seeking a craft to help me earn my bread. I know a little of your art and ask you to teach me more. I have no gold or silver to pay you, but name any task and I will do it gladly.'

'Away with you!' shouted the smith. 'Tasks I have aplenty, but no time for teaching others to do them.'

'Is time what lacks?' Taran said, glancing shrewdly at the smith. 'I've heard it said that a man must be a true master of his craft if he would teach it.'

'Hold!' roared the smith as Taran was about to turn away, and he snatched up the hammer as if he meant to throw it at Taran's head. 'You doubt my skill? I've flattened men on my anvil for less! Skill! In all the Free Commots none has greater than Hevydd Son of Hirwas!'

With that he seized the tongs, drew a bar of red-hot iron from the roaring furnace, flung it on the anvil, and set to hammering with such quick strokes that Taran could hardly follow the movement of Hevydd's muscular arm; and suddenly there formed at the end of the bar a hawthorn blossom perfect in every turn of leaf and petal.

Taran looked at it in astonishment and admiration. 'Never have I seen work so deftly done.'

'Nor will you see it elsewhere,' Hevydd answered, at pains to hide a proud grin. 'But what tale do you tell me? You know the shaping of metal? The secrets are not given to many. Even I have not gained them all.' Angrily he shook his bristly head. 'The deepest? They lie hidden in Annuvin, stolen by Arawn Death-Lord. Lost they are. Lost for ever to Prydain.

'But here, take these,' ordered the smith, pressing the tongs and hammer into Taran's hands. 'Beat the bar smooth as it was, and quickly, before it cools. Show me what strength you have in those chicken wings of yours.'

Taran strode to the anvil and, as Coll had taught him long ago, did his best to straighten the rapidly cooling iron. The smith, folding his huge arms, eyed him critically for a time, then burst into loud laughter.

'Enough, enough!' cried Hevydd. 'You speak truth. Of the art, indeed, you know little. And yet,' he added, rubbing his chin with a battered thumb nearly as thick as a fist, 'and yet, you have the sense of it.' He looked closely at Taran. 'But have you courage to stand up to fire? To fight hot iron with only hammer and tongs?'

'Teach me the craft,' Taran replied. 'You'll have no need to teach me courage.'

'Boldly said!' cried Hevydd, clapping Taran on the shoulder. 'I'll temper you well in my forge! Prove yourself to me and I'll vow to make a smith of you. Now, to begin . . .' His eye fell on Taran's empty scabbard. 'Once, it would seem, you bore a blade.'

'Once I did,' Taran answered. 'But it is long gone, and now I journey weaponless.'

'Then you shall make a sword,' commanded Hevydd. 'And when you've done, you'll tell me which is harder labour: smiting or smithing!'

To this Taran learned the answer soon enough. The next several days were the most toilsome he had ever spent. He thought, at first, the smith would set him to work shaping one of the many bars already in the forge. But Hevydd had no such intention.

'What, start when half the work is done?' Hevydd snorted. 'No, no, my lad. You'll forge a sword from beginning to end.'

Thus, the first task Hevydd gave Taran was gathering fuel for the furnace, and from dawn to dusk Taran stoked the fire until he saw the forge as a roaring, flame-tongued monster that could never eat its fill. Even then the work had only begun, for Hevydd soon put him to shovelling in a very mountain of stones, then smelting out the metal they bore. By the time the bar itself was cast, Taran's face and arms were scorched and blackened, and his hands were covered with more blisters than skin. His back ached; his ears rang with all the clank and clatter and with Hevydd's voice shouting orders and instructions. Gurgi, who had offered to pump the bellows, never faltered even when a cloud of sparks burst and flew into his shaggy hair, singeing it away in patches until he looked as if a flock of birds had plucked him to make their nests.

'Life's a forge!' cried the smith, as Taran, his brow streaming, beat at the strip of metal. 'Yes, and hammer and anvil, too! You'll be roasted, smelted and pounded, and you'll scarce know what's happening to you. But stand boldly to it! Metal's worthless till it's shaped and tempered!'

Despite the weariness that made him drop gratefully at day's end to the straw pallet in the shed, Taran's heart quickened and his spirits rose as the blade little by little took shape on the anvil. The heavy hammer seemed to weigh more each time he lifted it; but at last, with a joyous cry, he flung it down and raised the finished sword, well-wrought and balanced, gleaming brightly in the light of the forge.

'A handsome weapon, master smith!' he cried. 'As fair as the one I bore!'

'What then?' Hevydd exclaimed. 'Have you done your work so well? Would you trust your life to a blade untried?' He flung out a burly arm towards a wooden block in a corner of the forge. 'Strike hard,' he commanded. 'The flat, the edge, and the point.'

Proudly Taran raised the sword high and swung it down to the block. The weapon shuddered with the force of the blow, a sharp crack and clang smote his ears as the blade shattered and the shards went flying in all directions.

Taran shouted in dismay and could have wept as he stared, disbelieving, at the broken hilt still clutched in his hand. He turned and gave Hevydd a despairing glance.

'So ho!' cried the smith, not at all distressed by Taran's wretched and rueful expression. 'Did you think to gain a worthy blade at first go?' He laughed loudly and shook his head.

'Then what must I do?' Taran cried, appalled at Hevydd's words.

'Do?' the smith retorted. 'What else but start anew?'

And so they did, but this time for Taran there remained little of his joyous hopes. He laboured grimly and doggedly, all the more dejected when Hevydd ordered him to cast aside two new blades even before they were tempered, judging them already flawed. The reek of hot metal clung in his nostrils and flavoured even the food he hastily swallowed; the billows of steam from the great quenching tub choked him as if he were breathing clouds of scalding fog; the ceaseless din almost addled his wits; until indeed he felt it was himself, not the blade, being hammered.

The next blade he shaped seemed to him ugly, dinted and scarred, without the fair proportions of the first, and this too he would have cast aside had not the smith ordered him to finish it.

'This may well serve,' Hevydd told him confidently, despite the doubtful look Taran gave him.

Again Taran strode to the block and raised the sword. brought it down with all his strength. The blade rang like a bell. This time it was the block that split in two.

'Now,' said Hevydd quietly. 'That's a blade worth bearing.'

Then he clapped his hands and seized Taran's arm. 'You've strength in those chicken wings after all! You've proved yourself as well as you proved the blade. Stay, lad, and I'll teach you all I know.'

Taran said nothing for a time, but looked, not without pride, at the new-forged blade. 'You have already taught me much,' he said at last to Hevydd, 'though I lost what I had hoped to gain. For I had hoped I was indeed a swordsmith. I have learned that I am not.'

'How then!' cried Hevydd. 'You've the makings of an honest swordsmith, as good as any in Prydain.'

'It cheers me to think that may be true,' Taran answered. 'But I know in my heart your craft is not mine. A spur drove me from Small Avren, and it drives me now. And so must I journey, even if I wished to stay.'

The smith nodded. 'You are well-named, Wanderer. So be it. I ask no man to go against his heart. Keep the blade in token of friendship. Yours it is, more so than any other, for you forged it with you own hands.'

'It's not a noble weapon, and thus it suits me all the more,' Taran laughed, glancing at the ungainly sword. 'Lucky it was that I didn't have to make a dozen before it.'

'Luck?' snorted Hevydd, as Taran and Gurgi took leave of him. 'Not so! More labour than luck. Life's a force, say I! Face the pounding; don't fear the proving; and you'll stand well against any hammer and anvil!'

With Hevydd the Smith waving a sooty hand in farewell, the companions travelled on, bearing northwards along the rich valley of Great Avren. A few days of easy riding through pleasant countryside brought them to the edge of Commot Gwenith. Here, a shower suddenly began pelting down on them, and the wayfarers galloped for the first shelter they could find.

It was a cluster of sheds, stables, chicken roosts and storehouses seeming to ramble in all directions, but as Taran dismounted and hastened to the cottage amid the maze of buildings, he realized all were linked by covered walkways or flagstoned paths, and whichever he followed would sooner or later have brought him to the doorway that opened almost before he knocked on it.

'Come in, and a good greeting to you!' called a voice crackling like twigs in a fire.

As Gurgi scuttled inside to escape the teeming rain, Taran saw a bent old woman cloaked in grey beckoning him to the hearth. Her long hair was white as the wool on the distaff hanging from her belt of plaited cords. Below her short-girt robe, her bony shins looked thin and hard as spindles. A web of wrinkles covered her face; her cheeks were withered; but for all her years she gave no sign of frailty, as though time had only toughened and seasoned her; and her grey eyes were sharp and bright as a pair of new needles.

'I am Dwyvach Weaver-Woman,' she replied, as Taran bowed courteously and told her his name. 'Taran Wanderer?' she repeated with a tart smile. 'From the look of you, I'd say you've indeed been wandering. More than you've been washing. And that's clear as the warp and weft on my loom.'

'Yes, yes!' cried Gurgi. 'See loom of weavings! See windings and bindings! So many it makes Gurgi's poor tender head swim with twirlings and whirlings!'

Taran for the first time noticed a high loom standing like a giant harp of a thousand strings in a corner of the cottage. Around it were stacked bobbins of thread of all colours; from the rafters dangled skeins of yarn, hanks of wool and flax; on the walls hung lengths of finished fabrics, some of bright hue and simple design, others of subtler craftsmanship and patterns more difficult to follow. Taran gazed astonished at the endless variety, then turned to the weaver-woman of Gwenith.

'This calls for skill beyond anything I know,' he said admiringly. 'How is such work done?'

'How done?' The weaver-woman chuckled. 'It would take me more breath to tell than you have ears to listen. But if you look, you shall see.'

So saying, she hobbled to the loom, climbed to the bench in front of it, and with surprising vigour began plying the shuttle back and forth, all the while working her feet on the treadles below, hardly pausing to glance at her handiwork. At last she stopped, cocked her head at Taran, fixed him with her sharp grey eyes, and said, 'Thus is it done, Wanderer, as all things are, each in its own way, thread by thread.'

Taran's amazement had grown all the more. 'This would I gladly learn,' he said eagerly. 'The craft of the swordsmith was not mine. Perhaps the craft of the weaver may be. I pray you, will you teach it to me?'

'That I will, since you ask,' replied Dwyvach. 'But mind you: it is one thing to admire a well-woven bit of cloth and another to sit yourself before the loom.'

'My thanks to you,' Taran exclaimed. 'I'll not fear to labour at your loom. With Hevydd the Smith, I didn't shrink from hot iron or the flames of his forge, and a weaver's shuttle is a lighter burden than a smith's hammer.'

'Think you so?' Dwyvach asked, with a dry chuckle that sounded like knitting needles clicking together. 'Then what shall you weave to begin with?' she went on, eyeing him sharply. 'Taran Wanderer you call yourself? Taran Threadbare would be more like it! Would you weave yourself a new cloak? Thus you'll gain something to put on your back, and I'll see what skill you have in your fingers.'

Taran willingly agreed; but next day, instead of teaching him weaving, Dwyvach led the companions to one of her many chambers, which Taran saw full nearly to bursting with piles of wool.

'Tease out the thorns, pick out the cockleburs,' the weaver-woman ordered. 'Comb it, card it – carefully, Wanderer, or when your cloak is done you'll feel it's made of thistles instead of wool!'

The size of the task ahead of him made Taran despair of ever finishing, but he and Gurgi started the painstaking work, with Dwyvach herself lending a hand. The aged weaver-woman, Taran soon learned, had not only a tart tongue but a keen eye. Nothing escaped her; she spied the smallest knot, speck or flaw, and brought Taran's attention to it with a sharp rap from her distaff to his knuckles. But what smarted Taran more than the distaff was to learn that Dwyvach, despite her years, could work faster, longer and harder than he himself. At the end of each day Taran's eyes were bleary, his fingers raw, and his head nodded wearily; yet the old weaver-woman was bright and spry as if the day had scarce begun.

Nevertheless, the work at last was finished. But now Dwyvach set him in front of a huge spinning wheel. 'The finest wool is useless until it's spun to thread,' the weaver-woman told him. 'So you'd best begin learning that, as well.'

'But spinnings are woman's toilings!' Gurgi protested. 'No, no, spinnings are not fitting for bold and clever weaver-men!'

'Indeed!' snorted Dwyvach. 'Then sit you down and learn otherwise. I've heard men complain of doing woman's work, and women complain of doing man's work,' she added, fastening her bony thumb and forefinger on Gurgi's ear and marching him to a stool beside Taran, 'but I've never heard the *work* complain of who did it, so long as it got done!'

And so, under Dwyvach's watchful eye, Taran and Gurgi spun thread and filled bobbins during the next few days. Chastened by Dwyvach's words, Gurgi did his best to help, though all too often the hapless creature managed only to tangle himself in the long strands. Next, Dwyvach took the companions to a shed where pots of dye bubbled over a fire. Here, Taran fared no better than Gurgi, for when the yarn was at last dyed, he was bespattered from head to toe with colours, and Gurgi himself looked like a rainbow suddenly sprouting hair.

Not until all these other tasks were done to Dwyvach's satisfaction did she take Taran to a weaving room; and there his heart sank, for the loom stood bare and stark as a leafless tree.

'How then?' clucked the weaver-woman as Taran gave her a rueful glance. 'The loom must be threaded. Did I not tell you: all things are done step by step and strand by strand?'

'Hevydd the Smith told me life was a forge,' Taran sighed, as he laboriously tried to reckon the countless threads needed, 'and I think I'll be well-tempered before my cloak is finished.'

'Life a forge?' said the weaver-woman. 'A loom, rather, where lives and days intertwine; and wise he is who can learn to see the pattern. But if you mean to have a new cloak, you'd do better to work more and chatter less. Or did you hope for a host of spiders to come and labour for you?'

Even after deciding on the pattern, and threading the loom, Taran still saw only a hopeless, confusing tangle of threads. The cloth was painfully slow in forming and at the end of a long day he had little more than a hand's breadth of fabric to show for all his toil.

'Did I ever think a weaver's shuttle a light burden?' Taran sighed. 'It feels heavier than hammer, tongs and anvil all together!'

'It's not the shuttle that burdens you,' answered Dwyvach, 'but lack of skill, a heavy burden, Wanderer, that only one thing can lift.'

'What secret is that?' Taran cried. 'Teach it to me now or my cloak will never be done.'

But Dwyvach only smiled. 'It is patience, Wanderer. As for teaching it, that I cannot do. It is both the first thing and the last thing you must learn for yourself.'

Taran gloomily went back to work, sure he would be as ancient as Dwyvach before finishing the garment. Nevertheless, as his hands became used to the task the shuttle darted back and forth like a fish among reeds, and the cloth grew steadily on the loom; though Dwyvach was satisfied with his progress, Taran, to his own surprise, was not.

'The pattern,' he murmured, frowning. 'It – I don't know, somehow it doesn't please me.'

'Now then, Wanderer,' replied Dwyvach, 'no man put a

sword to your throat; the choice of pattern was your own.'

'That it was,' Taran admitted. 'But now I see it closely, I would rather have chosen another.'

'Ah, ah,' said Dwyvach, with her dry chuckle, 'in that case you have but one of two things to do. Either finish a cloak you'll be ill-content to wear, or unravel it and start anew. For the loom weaves only the pattern set upon it.'

Taran stared for a long while at his handiwork. At last he took a deep breath, sighed, and shook his head. 'So be it. I'll start anew.'

Over the next few days he ruefully unthreaded and rethreaded the loom. But after it was ready and he began weaving once again, he was delighted to find the cloth grow faster than ever it had done before, and his spirits rose with his new-found skill. When the cloak at last was done, he held it up proudly.

'This is far better than what I had,' he cried. 'But I doubt I'll ever be able to wear a cloak again without thinking of every thread!'

Gurgi shouted triumphantly and Dwyvach bobbed her head in approval.

'Well-woven,' she said. Her expression had lost much of its tartness and she looked fondly at Taran, seeming to smile within herself. 'You have skill in your fingers, Wanderer,' she said, with unaccustomed gentleness. 'Enough to make you one of the finest weavers in Prydain. And if my distaff and your knuckles met more often than you liked, it was because I deemed you worth reproving. Dwell in my house, if you choose, work at my loom, and what I know I will teach you.'

Taran did not answer immediately, and as he hesitated, the weaver-woman smiled and spoke again.

'I know what is in your heart, Wanderer,' she said. 'A young man's way is restless; yes, and a young girl's too – I'm not so gone in years that I've forgotten. Your face tells me it is not your wish to stay in Commot Gwenith.'

Taran nodded. 'As much as I hoped to be a swordsmith, so I hoped to be a weaver. But you speak truth. This is not the way I would follow.'

'Then must we say farewell,' answered the weaver-woman. 'But mind you,' she added, in her usual sharp tone, 'if life is a loom, the pattern you weave is not so easily unravelled.'

Taran and Gurgi set off again, still journeying northward, and soon Commot Gwenith was far behind them. Though Taran wore his new cloak on his shoulders and his new blade at his side, his pleasure in them shortly gave way to disquiet. The words of Dwyvach lingered in his mind, and his thoughts turned to another loom in the distant Marshes of Morva.

'And what of Orddu?' he said. 'Does she weave with more than threads? The robin has truly been scratching for his worms. But have I indeed chosen my own pattern, or am I no more than a thread on her loom? If that be so, then I fear it's a thread serving little purpose. At any rate,' he added, with a rueful laugh, 'it's a long and tangled one.'

But these gloomy thoughts flew from his mind when, some days later, Melynlas bore him to the top of a rise and he looked down on the fairest Commot he had ever seen. A tall stand of firs and hemlocks circled broad, well-tended fields, green and abundant. White, thatch-roofed cottages sparkled in shafts of sunlight. The air itself seemed different to him, cool and touched with the sharp scent of evergreens. His heart quickened as he watched, and a strange excitement filled him.

Gurgi had ridden up beside him. 'Kindly master, can we not stop here?'

'Yes,' Taran murmured, his eyes never leaving the fields and cottages. 'Yes. Here shall we rest.'

He urged Melynlas down the slope, with Gurgi cantering eagerly behind him. Crossing a shallow stream, Taran reined up at the sight of a hale old man digging busily near the water's edge. Beside him stood a pair of wooden buckets on a yoke, and into these he carefully poured spadefuls of pale brown earth. His iron-grey hair and beard were cropped short; despite his age, his arms seemed as brawny as those of Hevydd the Smith.

'A good greeting to you, master delver,' Taran called. 'What place is this?'

The man turned, wiped his deeply lined brow with a forearm, and looked at Taran with keen blue eyes. 'The water your horse is standing in – and churning to mud, by the way – is Fernbrake Stream. The Commot? This is Commot Merin.'

CHAPTER 19

The Potter's Wheel

'I've told you where you are,' the man went on good-naturedly, as Taran dismounted at the bank of the stream. 'Now might you be willing to tell me who you are, and what brings you to a place whose name you must ask? Have you lost your way and found Merin when you sought another Commot?'

'I am called Wanderer,' Taran replied. 'As for losing my way,' he added with a laugh, 'I can't say that I have, for I'm not sure myself where my path lies.'

'Then Merin is as fair a place as any to break your journey,' the man said. 'Come along, if you'd see what hospitality I can offer the two of you.'

As the man dropped a last spadeful of clay into the wooden buckets, Taran stepped forward and offered to carry them; and, since the man did not refuse, set his shoulders under the yoke. But the buckets were heavier than Taran reckoned. His brow soon burst out in sweat; he could barely stagger along under the load he felt doubling at every pace; and the hut to which the man pointed seemed to grow farther instead of closer.

'If you seek daub to mend your chimney,' Taran gasped, 'you've come a long way to find it!'

'You've not caught the trick of that yoke,' said the man, grinning broadly at Taran's effort. He shouldered the buckets, which Taran gladly gave back, and strode along so briskly, despite the weight of his burden, that he nearly outdistanced the companions. Arriving at a long shed, he poured the clay into a great wooden vat, then beckoned the wayfarers to enter his hut.

Inside Taran saw racks and shelves holding earthenware

of all kinds, vessels of plain baked clay, graceful jars, and among these, at random, pieces whose craftsmanship and beauty made him catch his breath. Only once, in the treasure house of Lord Gast, had he set eyes on handiwork such as this. He turned, astonished, to the old man who had begun laying dishes and bowls on an oaken table.

'When I asked if you sought daub to mend your chimney I spoke foolishly,' Taran said, humbly bowing. 'If this is your work, I have seen some of it before, and I know you: Annlaw Clay-Shaper.'

The potter nodded. 'My work it is. If you've seen it, it may be that indeed you do know me. For I am old at my craft, Wanderer, and no longer sure where the clay ends and Annlaw begins – or, in truth, if they're not one and the same.'

Taran looked closer at the vessels crowding the hut, at the newly finished wine bowl shaped even more skilfully than the one in Lord Gast's trove, at the long clay-spattered tables covered with jars of paints, pigments and glazes. Now he saw in wonder that what he had first taken for common sculleryware was as beautiful, in its own way, as the wine bowl. All had come from a master's hand. He turned to Annlaw.

'It was told me,' Taran said, 'that one piece of your making is worth more than all of a cantrev lord's treasure house, and I well believe it. And here,' he shook his head in amazement, 'this is a treasure house in itself.'

'Yes, yes!' Gurgi cried. 'Oh, skilful potter gains riches and fortunes from clever shapings!'

'Riches and fortune?' replied Annlaw, smiling. 'Food for my table, rather. Most of these pots and bowls I send to the small Commots where the folk have no potter of their own. As I give what they need, they give what I need; and treasure is what I need the least. My joy is in the craft, not the gain. Would all the fortunes in Prydain help my fingers shape a better bowl?'

'There are those,' Taran said, half in earnest as he glanced at the potter's wheel, 'who claim work such as yours comes by enchantment.'

At this Annlaw threw back his head and laughed heartily. 'I wish it did, for it would spare much toil. No, no, Wanderer, my wheel, alas, is like any other. True it is,' he added, 'that Govannion the Lame, master craftsman of Prydain, long ago fashioned all manner of enchanted implements. He gave them to whom he deemed would use them wisely and well, but one by one they fell into the clutches of Arawn Death-Lord. Now all are gone.

'But Govannion, too, discovered and set down the high secrets of all crafts,' Annlaw went on. 'These, as well, Arawn stole, to hoard in Annuvin where none may ever profit from them.' The potter's face turned grave. 'A lifetime have I striven to discover them again, to guess what might have been their nature. Much have I learned – learned by doing, as a child learns to walk. But my steps falter. The deepest lore yet lies beyond my grasp. I fear it ever shall.

'Let me gain this lore,' Annlaw said, 'and I'll yearn for no magical tools. Let me find the knowledge. And these,' he added, holding up his clay-crusted hands, 'these will be enough to serve me.'

'But you know what you seek,' Taran answered. 'I, alas, seek without knowing even where to look.' He then told Annlaw of Hevydd the Smith and Dwyvach the Weaver-Woman, of the sword and cloak he had made. 'I was proud of my work,' Taran went on. 'Yet, at the end neither anvil nor loom satisfied me.'

'What of the potter's wheel?' asked Annlaw. When Taran admitted he knew nothing of this craft and prayed Annlaw to let him see the shaping of clay, the old potter willingly agreed.

Annlaw drew up his coarse robe and seated himself at the wheel, which he quickly set spinning, and on it flung a lump of clay. The potter bent almost humbly to his work, and reached out his hands as tenderly as if he were lifting an unfledged bird. Before Taran's eyes Annlaw began shaping a tall, slender vessel. As Taran stared in awe, the clay seemed to shimmer on the swiftly turning wheel and to change from moment to moment. Now Taran understood Annlaw's words, for indeed between the potter's deft fingers and the clay he saw no separation, as though Annlaw's hands flowed into the clay and gave it life. Annlaw was silent and intent; his lined face had brightened; the years had fallen away from it. Taran felt his heart fill with a joy that seemed to reach from the potter to himself, and in that moment understood that he was in the presence of a true master craftsman, greater than any he had ever known.

'Fflewddur was wrong,' Taran murmured. 'If there is enchantment, it lies not in the potter's wheel but in the potter.'

'Enchantment there is none,' answered Annlaw, never turning from his work. 'A gift, perhaps, but a gift that bears with it much toil.'

'If I could make a thing of such beauty, it is toil I would welcome,' Taran said.

'Sit you down, then,' said Annlaw, making room for Taran at the wheel. 'Shape the clay for yourself.' When Taran protested he would spoil Annlaw's half-formed vessel, the potter only laughed. 'Spoil it you will, surely. I'll toss it back into the kneading trough, mix it with the other clay, and sooner or later it will serve again. It will not be lost. Indeed, nothing ever is, but comes back in one shape or another.'

'But for yourself,' Taran said. 'The skill you have already put in it will be wasted.'

The potter shook his head. 'Not so. Craftsmanship isn't like water in an earthen pot, to be taken out by the dipperful until it's empty. No, the more drawn out the more remains. The heart renews itself, Wanderer, and skill grows all the better for it. Here, then. Your hands – thus. Your thumbs – thus.'

From the first moment Taran felt the clay whirling beneath his fingers, his heart leaped with the same joy he had seen on the potter's face. The pride of forging his own sword and weaving his own cloak dwindled before this new discovery that made him cry out in sudden delight. But his hands faltered and the clay went awry. Annlaw stopped the wheel. Taran's first vessel was so lopsided and misshapen that, despite his disappointment, he threw back his head and laughed.

Annlaw clapped him on the shoulder. 'Well tried, Wanderer. The first bowl I turned was as ill-favoured – and worse. You have the touch for it. But before you learn the craft, you must first learn the clay. Dig, sift and knead it, know its nature better than that of your closest companion. Then grind pigments for your glazes, understand how the fire of the kiln works upon them.'

'Annlaw Clay-Shaper,' Taran said in a low voice that hid nothing of his yearning, 'will you teach me your craft? This more than all else I long to do.'

Annlaw hesitated several moments and looked deeply at Taran. 'I can teach you only what you can learn,' said the potter. 'How much that may be, time will tell. Stay, if that is your wish. Tomorrow we shall begin.'

The two wayfarers made themselves comfortable that night in a snug corner of the pottery shed. Gurgi curled on the straw pallet, but Taran sat with knees drawn up and arms clasped about them. 'It's strange,' he murmured. 'The more of the Commot folk I've known, the fonder have I grown of them. Yet Commot Merin drew me at first sight, closer than all the others.' The night was soft and still. Taran smiled wistfully in the darkness. 'The moment I saw it, I thought it the one place I'd be content to dwell. And that – that even Eilonwy might have been happy here.

'And at Annlaw's wheel,' he went on, 'when my hands touched the clay, I knew I would count myself happy to be a potter. More than smithing, more than weaving – it's as though I could speak through my fingers, as though I could give shape to what was in my heart. I understand what Annlaw meant. There is no difference between him and his work. Indeed, Annlaw puts himself into the clay and makes it live with his own life. If I, too, might learn to do this . . .'

Gurgi did not answer. The weary creature was fast asleep. Taran smiled and drew the cloak over Gurgi's shoulders. 'Sleep well,' he said. 'We may have come to the end of our journey.'

Annlaw was as good as his word. In the days that followed, the potter showed Taran skills no less important than the working of the clay itself: the finding of proper earths, judging their texture and quality, sifting, mixing, tempering. Gurgi joined Taran in all the tasks, and soon his shaggy hair grew so crusted with dust, mud and gritty glaze that he looked like an unbaked clay pot set on a pair of skinny legs.

The summer sped quickly and happily, and the more Taran saw the potter at his craft the more he marvelled. At the kneading trough, Annlaw pounded the clay with greater vigour than Hevydd the Smith at his anvil; and at the wheel did the most intricate work with a deftness surpassing even that of Dwyvach the Weaver-Woman. As early as he rose in the mornings, Taran always found the potter already up and about his tasks. Annlaw was tireless, often spending nights without sleep and days without food, absorbed in labour at his wheel. Seldom was the potter content to repeat a pattern, but strove to better even what he himself had originated.

'Stale water is a poor drink,' said Annlaw. 'Stale skill is worse. And the man who walks in his own footsteps only ends where he began.'

Not until autumn did Annlaw let Taran try his hand at the wheel again. This time, the bowl Taran shaped was not as ill-formed as the other.

Annlaw, studying it carefully, nodded his head and told him, 'You have learned a little, Wanderer.' Nevertheless, to Taran's dismay, Annlaw cast the bowl into the kneading trough. 'Never fear,' said the potter. 'When you shape one worth the keeping, it will be fired in the kiln.'

Though Taran feared such a time might never come, it was not long before Annlaw judged a vessel, a shallow bowl simple in design yet well-proportioned, to be ready for firing. He set it, along with other pots and bowls he had crafted for the folk of Commot Isav, into a kiln taller and deeper than Hevydd's furnace. While Annlaw calmly turned to finishing other vessels for the Commot folk, Taran's anxiety grew until he felt that he himself was baking in the flames. But at last, when the firing was done and the pieces had cooled, the potter drew out the bowl, turned it around in his hands as Taran waited breathlessly, and tapped it with a clay-rimmed finger.

He grinned at Taran. 'It rings true. Beginner's work, Wanderer, but not to be ashamed of.'

Taran's heart lifted as if he had fashioned a wine bowl handsomer than ever Lord Gast had seen.

But his joy changed soon to despair. Through autumn Taran shaped other vessels; yet, to his growing dismay, none satisfied him, none matched his hopes, despite the painful toil he poured into the work.

'What lacks?' he cried to Annlaw. 'I could forge a sword well enough and weave a cloak well enough. But now, what I truly long to grasp is beyond my reach. Must the one skill I sought above all be denied me?' he burst out in an anguished voice. 'Is the gift forbidden me?' He bowed his head, and his heart froze even as he spoke the words, for he knew, within himself, he had touched the truth.

Annlaw did not gainsay him, but only looked at him for a long while with deep sadness.

'Why?' Taran whispered. 'Why is this so?'

'It is a heavy question,' Annlaw replied at last. He put a hand on Taran's shoulder. 'Indeed, no man can answer it. There are those who have laboured all their lives to gain the gift, striving until the end only to find themselves mistaken; and those who had it born in them yet never knew; those who lost heart too soon; and those who should never have begun at all.

'Count yourself lucky,' the potter went on, 'that you have understood this now and not spent your years in vain hope. This much have you learned, and no learning is wasted.'

'What then shall I do?' Taran asked. Grief and bitterness such as he had known in Craddoc's valley flooded over him.

'There are more ways to happiness than in the shaping of a pot,' replied Annlaw. 'You have been happy in Merin. You still can be. There is work for you to do. Your help is welcome and valuable to me, as a friend as much as an apprentice. Why, look you now,' he went on in a cheerful tone, 'tomorrow I would send my ware to Commot Isav. But a day's journey is long for one of my years. As a friend, will you bear the burden for me?'

Taran nodded. 'I will carry your ware to Isav.' He turned away, knowing that his happiness was ended, like a flawed vessel shattered in the firing.

CHAPTER 20

The Spoilers

Next morning, as Taran had promised, he loaded Melynlas and Gurgi's pony with the potter's ware and, Gurgi beside him, set out for Commot Isav. Annlaw, he knew, could as well have sent word to the Commot folk, asking them to come and bear away their own vessels.

'This is not an errand I do for him, but a kindness he does for me,' Taran told Gurgi. 'I think he means to give me time to myself, to find my own thoughts. As for that,' he added sorrowfully, 'so far I've found none. I long to stay in Merin, yet there's little to keep me here. I prize Annlaw as my friend and as a master of his craft. But his craft will never be mine.'

Still pondering and troubled at heart Taran reached Isav some while before dusk. It was the smallest Commot of all he had seen, with fewer than half a dozen cottages and a little grazing plot for a handful of sheep and cattle. A knot of men were gathered by the sheepfold. As Taran rode closer he saw their faces tightly drawn and grim.

Perplexed at this he called out his name and told them he brought pottery from Annlaw Clay-Shaper.

'Greetings to you,' said one man, naming himself as Drudwas Son of Pebyr. 'And farewell in the same breath,' he added. 'Our thanks to Annlaw and yourself. But stay to share our hospitality and you may stay to shed your blood.

'Outlaws rove the hills,' Drudwas went on quickly, answering Taran's questioning frown, 'a band, perhaps a dozen strong. We have heard they plundered two Commots already, and not content were they with a sheep or cow for their own food, but slaughtered all the herd for the joy of it. Today, not long past, I saw horsemen over the rise, and leading them a yellow-haired ruffian on a sorrel mare.'

'Dorath!' Taran cried.

'How then?' asked one of the Commot men. 'Do you know this band?'

'If it's Dorath's Company, I know them well enough,' Taran answered. 'They are paid swords; and if none will hire them, I judge them glad to kill even without fee. Hard warriors they are, as I have seen them, and cruel as the Huntsmen of Annuvin.'

Drudwas nodded gravely. 'So it is said. It may be they will pass us by,' he went on, 'but this I doubt. Commot Isav is small prey, but where defenders are few the reasons to attack are all the more.'

Taran glanced at the men. From their faces and bearing he knew their courage would not lack; but once more he heard Dorath's laughter and recalled the man's cunning and ruthlessness. 'And if they attack,' he asked, 'what shall you do?'

'What would you have us do?' Drudwas angrily burst out. 'Offer tribute and beg them to spare us? Give our animals to their swords and our homes to their torches? Commot Isav has ever been at peace; our pride is husbandry not warfare. But we mean to stand against them. Have we better choice?'

'I can ride back to Merin,' Taran replied, 'and bring you help.'

'Too far and too long,' Drudwas answered. 'Nor would I do so, even then, for it would leave Merin ill-defended. No, we stand as we are. Against twelve, seven. My son Llassar,' he began, indicating a tall, eager-faced boy scarcely older than Taran had been when Coll first dubbed him Assistant Pig-Keeper.

'Your count is amiss,' Taran interrupted. 'You are not seven, but nine. Gurgi and I stand with you.'

Drudwas shook his head. 'You owe us no service or duty, Wanderer. We welcome your swords, but will not ask for them.'

'They are yours nonetheless,' Taran replied, and Gurgi nodded agreement. 'Will you heed me? Nine may stand against a dozen and win the day. But with Dorath, number counts less than skill. Were he alone I would still fear him as much as twelve. He will fight shrewdly and strive to gain the most at least cost. We must answer him in kind.' The Commot men listened carefully as Taran then spoke of a ruse to make the raiders believe themselves outnumbered, and to attack where Dorath would expect no more than feeble defence.

'If two men were to lie waiting in the sheepfold and two in the cattle pen, ready to spring up,' Taran said, 'they might take the band unawares and hold them a few moments while the rest of us attack from ambush in the rear. At the same time, if the women of your households set up a din with rakes and hoes, it would seem other swordsmen had hastened to join us.'

Drudwas thought a long moment, then nodded. 'Your plan may be sound, Wanderer. But I fear for those in the pens, as they must bear the brunt for all of us. If aught should go awry, small chance of escape would they have.'

'I shall be one to keep watch in the sheepfold,' Taran began.

'And I the other,' Llassar broke in quickly.

Drudwas frowned. 'I would not spare you because you are my son. You are a good lad and gentle with the flock. I think of your years . . .'

'The flock is in my charge,' Llassar cried. 'By right my place is with the Wanderer.'

The men spoke hurriedly among themselves, at last agreeing that Llassar would keep watch with Taran, while Drudwas stood guard over the cattle along with Gurgi who, fearful though he was, refused to be any farther from Taran's side. By the time all plans were set and the Commot men posted among the trees just beyond the sheepfold, a full moon had risen above thin clouds. The cold light sharpened the edges of the shadows and the outlines of brush and branches. In the fold Taran and Llassar crouched amid the restless flock.

For a time neither spoke. In the bright moonlight the face of Llassar seemed to Taran more boyish than before; he saw the youth was afraid and making all effort to hide it. Though uneasy himself, he grinned reassuringly at Llassar. Drudwas had been right. The boy was young, untried. And yet – Taran smiled, knowing that he himself, at Llassar's age, would have claimed the same right.

'Your plan is good, Wanderer,' Llassar said at last in a hushed voice, speaking, Taran knew, more to ease his own disquiet than anything else. 'Better than we should have done. It cannot fail.'

'All plans can fail,' Taran said, almost harshly. He fell silent then. Fears had begun stirring in him like leaves in a chill wind. Sweat drenched his body under the fleece jacket. He had come to Isav unknown, unproven, yet the men of the Commot had willingly heeded him and willingly put their fate in his hands. They had accepted his plan when another might have served better; should it fail, though all their lives could be forfeit, the blame would be his alone. He gripped the hilt of his sword and strained his eyes to peer into the darkness. There was no movement, and even the shadows seemed frozen.

'You are called Wanderer,' Llassar went on quietly, with some shyness. 'To my mind, one who wanders must as well be one who seeks. Is this true?'

Taran shook his head. 'I sought once to be a smith and once to be a weaver. And once a potter. But that is over. Now, perhaps I must wander without seeking.'

'If you seek nothing,' Llassar said with a friendly laugh, 'then you have little chance of finding it. Our life is not easy here,' he went on. 'It is not willingness that lacks, but knowledge. The Sons of Don have long held Prydain against the Lord of Annuvin, and for their protection we are grateful; yet the secrets Arawn Death-Lord stole from us – to regain them, my father says, would give us stouter shield and sword than even the battle hosts of Prince Gwydion himself. But for all that, Isav is my home and I am well content in it.' Llassar grinned. 'I do not envy you, Wanderer.'

Taran did not answer for a time. Then he murmured, 'No, it is I who envy you.'

They said no more, listening alertly to every sound as the night wore away and the moon, fading behind thickening clouds, lost shape and its light spread like pale mist. In a while Llassar blew out his breath in relief. 'They will not come,' he said. 'They will pass us by.'

Even as he spoke, the darkness shattered in fragments that turned into the figures of armed warriors. Taran sprang to his feet as the gate burst open.

Taran sounded his battle horn, then flung himself upon the warrior who cried out in surprise and stumbled backward. Llassar had leaped up at the same instant as Taran, and the shepherd plunged against the press of the attackers at the gate, thrusting with his spear. Taran struck out blindly, struggling not only against the raiders but against the sudden terror that his plan had failed, that the outlaws had come too silently, too swiftly. In another moment, above the frantic bleating of the frightened animals, a great shout burst from the Commot men as they rose from the cover of the trees, and from the huts came the clash of iron upon iron.

At the sheepfold the outlaws hesitated. Llassar's opponent had fallen. Taran glimpsed the boy spring past him and strike again with his spear. The attack wavered at the gate, as the raiders turned their weapons against the men of Isav. But one warrior, growling like a wild beast, long knife upraised, raced into the pen as if to wreak all the destruction he could, and Taran grappled with the man who spun about and slashed at him. It was Gloff.

The warrior recognized him; Gloff's first astonishment changed to an ugly grin almost of pleasure and eagerness, as he shifted the knife in his hand. Gloff lunged and Taran flung up his weapon to ward against the blow. But the warrior leaped forward, his free hand clawing at Taran's eyes, and his blade flickered as its point drove swiftly in a killing stroke. A figure plunged between them. It was Llassar. Taran shouted a warning as the boy strove to catch the blow on his spear shaft. Snarling, Gloff turned his attack and struck viciously at Llassar. The shepherd fell. With a cry of rage Taran raised his sword. Suddenly, Drudwas was beside him. Gloff shrieked as the blade of the husbandman chopped downward.

Under the onslaught of the Commot folk Dorath's warriors fell back. Amid the turmoil of racing men Taran found himself borne away from the fold. During a backward glance he could glimpse neither Drudwas nor Llassar; in fury, he pressed onward. Torches flared, and he saw that the women and girls of Isav had joined their men, flailing with hoes, rakes and pitchforks at the raiders. Taran cast about for Gurgi and shouted his name, but his voice was drowned in the tumult.

A fierce bellowing had risen from the cattle pen as a dark shape burst through the bars. Taran gasped in astonishment to see a furious black bull heaving and plunging among the raiders. On its back clung Gurgi, yelling at the top of his voice, kicking his heels against the powerful animal's flanks, turning its charge against the terrified remainder of Dorath's band.

'They flee!' shouted one of the Commot men.

Taran pressed ahead. The raiders, who had left their mounts at the fringe of trees, now hastened to gain them, caught between the Commot folk and the slashing horns of the enraged bull. Taran glimpsed Dorath astride the sorrel mare and ran to overtake him. But Dorath spurred the steed and galloped into the wood.

Taran turned and raced to the stables, whispering for Melynlas. One of the Commot men caught at his arm and cried, 'The day is ours, Wanderer!' Only then did Taran realize the sounds of the fray had ceased. Dorath himself had vanished. Taran hurried to the sheepfold where the wife of Drudwas knelt, her arms about her son.

'Llassar!' Taran cried in dismay, dropping beside the shepherd. The boy's eyes opened and he strove to grin at Taran.

'His wound is not deep,' said Drudwas. 'He will live to tend his flock.'

'And so I will,' Llassar said to Taran, 'and thanks to you, I'll have a flock to tend.'

Taran put a hand on the boy's shoulder. 'And to you,' he answered, 'to you I owe much more than sheep.'

'Full half the band will plunder no longer,' said Drudwas, 'neither Commot Isav nor any Commot. The rest are scattered, and it will be long before their wounds heal. You have well served us, Wanderer, you and your companion. You came among us strangers. We count you strangers no longer, but friends.'

CHAPTER 21

The Mirror

Although the folk of Isav urged him to linger, Taran took leave of them and rode slowly back to Merin. The defeat of Dorath's Company held no savour, for his thoughts still turned restlessly; his questions still found no answers; and he was more downhearted than ever. To Annlaw he said little of his deeds in Isav, and it was Gurgi, bursting with pride, who told what had befallen them.

'Yes, yes!' cried Gurgi. 'Wicked robbers fled with yellings! Oh, they feared kindly master. And feared bold Gurgi, too! And great bull with stampings and trampings, sharp horns with jabbings and stabbings!'

'You should be well content, Wanderer,' Annlaw said to Taran, who had remained silent all the while. 'You've saved honest folk their lives and homes.'

'Drudwas told me I was no stranger, but a friend. For that I am glad,' Taran answered. 'I only wish,' he added, 'that I weren't a stranger to myself. What use am I?' he burst out. 'To myself, to anyone? None that I can see.'

'The folk of Isav would gainsay you,' the potter answered. 'And there might be others who would welcome a stout blade and a bold heart.'

'A hired sword?' Taran replied bitterly. 'And follow the same way as Dorath?' He shook his head. 'When I was a child I dreamed of adventure, glory, of honour in feats of arms. I think now that these things are shadows.'

'If you see them as shadows then you see them for what they are,' Annlaw agreed. 'Many have pursued honour, and in the pursuit lost more of it than ever they could gain. But I did not mean a hired sword . . .' He stopped abruptly and was thoughtful a moment. 'To see them for what they are,' he murmured, returning to his first words. 'Perhaps – perhaps . . .' The potter looked closely at Taran. 'The Commot lore tells how one may see himself for what he is. Whether it be true or no more than an old wives' tale I will not judge,' the potter went on slowly. 'But the lore says that he who would know himself need only gaze in the Mirror of Llunet.'

Though Annlaw had spoken quietly, Taran heard the potter's words like a thunderclap.

'The Mirror of Llunet?' Taran cried. Since leaving Craddoc's valley he had put away all thought of the Mirror, hidden and forgotten it, and the days had covered it as dead leaves on a burial mound. 'The Mirror,' he repeated in a stifled voice, 'the goal of my quest from the beginning. I had given up searching. Now do I find it when I seek it least of all?'

'Your quest?' Annlaw said, perplexed. He had risen and was watching Taran with concern. 'Of this you have told me nothing, Wanderer.'

'I would have no pride in the telling,' Taran replied.

But now, as Annlaw listened quietly, a look of kindness on his face, little by little Taran was able to speak of Caer Dallben, of Orddu, of where the quest had led him, of Craddoc's death and his own despair. 'Once,' Taran concluded, 'I would have asked nothing better than to find the Mirror. Now, even if it were in my hand, I would dread to look in it.'

'I understand your fears,' the potter answered quietly. 'The Mirror may put your heart at ease – or trouble you all the more. Such is the risk. The choice must be yours.

'But know this, Wanderer,' Annlaw went on, as Taran bit his lips in silence, 'it is not such a mirror as you think. It lies close by here in the Llawgadarn Mountains, no more than two days' distance, in a cave at the head of the Lake of Llunet. The Mirror of Llunet is a pool of water.'

'A pool of water?' Taran cried. 'What enchantment

gives it power? For enchanted it must be.'

'It is,' answered the potter, 'to those who deem it so.'

'What of yourself?' Taran asked in a low voice. 'Have you sought to look in it?'

'That I have not,' replied Annlaw. 'For I well know who I am. Annlaw Clay-Shaper. For better or worse, that knowledge must serve me my lifetime.'

'And I,' Taran murmured, 'what knowledge will serve mine?' He said nothing for a time. At last he raised his head. 'It is true. I fear to look in the Mirror, and fear to know what it might tell me. But I have already known shame,' he flung out bitterly. 'Must I know cowardice as well?

'In the morning,' Taran continued, 'in the morning I journey to the Mirror of Llunet.'

His decision gave him little comfort. At first light, as he and Gurgi saddled their mounts, his doubts chilled him more than the cold mist of late autumn. Nevertheless, having made his choice, he set a swift pace, riding northward from Merin to the Llawgadarn Mountains, taking his bearings on the high peak of Mount Meledin, for it was at the foot of Meledin, as Annlaw told him, that he would find the cave. The companions rode silently and steadily, halting only when the day had so far waned they could no longer guide the steeds along the paths. They camped on the soft carpet of pine needles, but a deep uneasiness had settled on the two wayfarers and they slept little.

At dawn of the next day they gathered up their gear and rode at a good pace along the crest of a ridge. Soon Taran called out and pointed downward. The Lake of Llunet stretched in a long oval, gleaming in the early sun. Its waters were calm, blue, and the Lake itself seemed a perfect mirror that held the tree-lined shore in its depths. At some distance Mount Meledin rose, tall but seeming almost weightless in the mist still clinging to its long slopes.

Taran's heart beat faster as the companions made their way downward to the shore. Closer to Meledin the land fell in sharp drops, and short stretches of meadow broke into shallow ravines. Near a stream tumbling from the upper reaches of the mountain the companions tethered their steeds. Taran had already sighted the cave and hastened towards it, with Gurgi scrambling after him.

'There!' Taran cried. 'There! The Mirror!'

At the foot of Meledin wind and weather had carved an arching cave little more than a few paces deep. Rivulets trickled from the moss-grown rocks of its overhanging brow. Taran raced towards it. His heart pounded; his pulse burnt in his wrists. Yet as he drew closer his pace slowed, and fear weighed heavy as a chain about his legs. At the mouth of the cave he halted a long moment. Gurgi glanced anxiously at him.

'It is here,' Taran murmured. He stepped forward.

Within, a shallow basin hollowed in the floor of smooth stones, lay the Mirror of Llunet like a shield of polished silver, gleaming of itself despite the shadows. Taran slowly knelt at the rim. The basin held no more than a finger's depth of water, fed drop by drop from a thread of moisture twining down the rocky wall. The passing of countless years had not filled it to the brim. Yet shallow though it was, the water seemed a depthless crystal whose facets turned one upon the other, each catching brilliant beams of white.

Scarcely daring to breathe lest he trouble the shining surface, Taran bent closer. The cave was utterly silent, and it seemed that even the falling of a wisp of dry moss would shatter the reflection. His hands trembled as he saw his own face, travel-worn and sun-scorched. With all his heart he longed to turn away, but forced himself to look more deeply. Were his eyes playing tricks on him? Closer he knelt. What he saw made him cry out in disbelief.

At the same instant Gurgi shrieked in terror. Taran

leaped to his feet and spun around as Gurgi ran and cowered at his side. Before him stood Dorath.

The man's face was stubble-bearded, his dirty yellow hair hung into his eyes. The horsehide jacket was slashed along one side and mud crusted his boots. In one hand he held food which he scooped up with his fingers and crammed into his mouth. He grinned at Taran.

'Well met, Lord Swineherd,' Dorath said between mouthfuls.

'Ill met, Dorath,' Taran cried, drawing his sword. 'Will you call your Company to set upon us? Call them, then, all who fled us at Commot Isav!' He raised the weapon and strode forward.

Dorath laughed harshly. 'Will you strike before my own blade is out?'

'Draw it, then,' Taran flung back at him.

'So I shall, when my meal is done,' Dorath said. He gave a scornful grunt. 'Your blade is ill-favoured, swineherd, uglier than Gloff's face.' He grinned slyly. 'Mine is the fairer weapon, yet gained at no cost. My Company?' he added. 'Would you have me call them? They are deaf. For half of them, the dirt of their graves stops their ears. I saw you at Isav, and guessed it was you who rallied the Commot clods. Alas, I had no time to linger and pay my greetings to you.'

Dorath wiped his mouth on the back of his hand. 'Of those who rode from Isav, two cowards fled and I've seen none of them. Two were heavily wounded. Those, I myself sped on their journey to the carrion crows, and they burden me no longer. But no matter. I'll soon find others to join me.

'Meantime, so much the better,' he went on. 'I'll share your treasure with none but myself.'

'Treasure?' Taran cried. 'There is no treasure! Draw your blade, Dorath, or I'll kill you unarmed as you'd have done to me.'

'An end to your lying, swineherd,' Dorath growled. 'Do you still take me for a fool? I've known of your travels, and the bent path you followed here did not deceive me. Your saddlebags hold nothing of worth; I've seen that for myself. So the prize is yet to be claimed.'

He strode to the Mirror. 'Is this your trove? What have you found, swineherd? A mud puddle? What does it hide?'

Taran cried out, though before he could fling himself upon Dorath the warrior stamped his heavy boot into the pool and, with a curse, sent the water spurting from the basin.

'It holds nothing!' Dorath burst out, his face twisting in rage.

Taran gasped and stumbled forward. Dorath drew his sword.

'My meal is ended, swineherd,' Dorath cried.

He struck heavily and the force of his onslaught sent Taran reeling from the cave. Gurgi yelled in fury and clutched at the warrior, who seized him with a powerful grasp and dashed him against the rocky wall. Snarling, Dorath sprang after Taran.

Scrambling to his feet, Taran brought up his blade to meet the warrior's attack. Dorath spat and lunged again, driving Taran towards the slope. As the warrior bore closer upon him, Taran lost his footing, stumbled backward, and dropped to one knee.

With a mocking laugh Dorath raised his weapon, and Taran saw the blade that once had been his own glint sharply as Dorath swung it down with all his strength. Taran saw his death upon him and flung up his sword in a last attempt to ward against the blow.

The blades met with a grating, ringing clash. Taran's weapon shuddered in his hand, the shock threw him to earth. Yet his blade held. The sword of Dorath shattered on it.

Cursing, Dorath flung the useless hilt at Taran's face, turned and ran to the cover of pines along the shore. Hearing her master's whistle, Dorath's sorrel mare broke from the trees. Taran sprang to pursue the fleeing warrior.

'Help, help!' Gurgi's voice cried from the cave. 'Kindly master! Oh, help wounded Gurgi!'

Hearing this, Taran halted even as Dorath leaped astride his mount and galloped away. Taran raced to the cave. Within, Gurgi moaned and tried to sit up. Taran knelt quickly and saw the creature's forehead was heavily gashed, but that Gurgi's pain came more from terror than from his hurts. He carried him from the cave and propped him against a boulder.

Taran did not return to the Mirror of Llunet. Already he had seen it empty, its spattered water spread over the stones, holding only the muddy print of Dorath's boot. He sank down beside Gurgi and put his head in his hands. For long he did not move or speak.

'Come,' he said at last, helping Gurgi to his feet. 'Come. We have far to journey.'

A light glowed in Annlaw's hut. The night was nearly spent, yet Taran saw the potter still bent over his wheel.

Annlaw rose to his feet as Taran slowly crossed the threshold. Neither spoke for some while. The potter anxiously studied Taran's face, and said at last, 'Have you looked into the Mirror, Wanderer?'

Taran nodded. 'For a few moments. But none shall look in it again. It is destroyed.' He told of Dorath and the happenings at the Lake of Llunet. When Taran had done, the potter sadly shook his head.

'You saw nothing then?' said Annlaw.

'I learned what I sought to learn,' Taran replied.

'I will not question you, Wanderer,' said Annlaw. 'But if it is in your heart to tell me, I will listen.'

'I saw myself,' Taran answered. 'In the time I watched, I saw strength – and frailty. Pride and vanity, courage and fear. Of wisdom, a little. Of folly, much. Of intentions, many good ones; but many more left undone. In this, alas, I saw myself a man like any other.

'But this, too, I saw,' he went on. 'Alike as men may seem, each is different as flakes of snow, no two the same. You told me you had no need to seek the Mirror, knowing you were Annlaw Clay-Shaper. Now I know who I am: myself and none other. I am Taran.'

Annlaw did not reply immediately. Then he said, 'If you have learned this you have learned the deepest secret the Mirror could tell you. Perhaps it was truly enchanted after all.'

'There was no enchantment,' Taran answered. He smiled. 'It was a pool of water, the most beautiful I have seen. But a pool of water, no more than that.

'At first,' he went on, 'I thought Orddu had sent a fool on a fool's errand. She did not. She meant me to see what the Mirror showed me. Any stream, any river would have given me the same reflection, but I would not have understood it then as I understand it now.

'As for my parentage,' he added, 'it makes little difference. True kinship has naught to do with blood ties, however strong they be. I think we are all kin, brothers and sisters one to the other, all children of all parents. And the birthright I once sought, I seek it no longer. The folk of the Free Commots taught me well, that manhood is not given but earned. Even King Smoit in Cantrev Cadiffor told me this, but I did not heed him.

'Llonio said life was a net for luck; to Hevydd the Smith life was a forge; and to Dwyvach the Weaver-Woman a loom. They spoke truly, for it is all of these. But you,' Taran said, his eyes meeting the potter's, 'you have shown me life is one thing more. It is clay to be shaped, as raw clay on a potter's wheel.'

Annlaw nodded. 'And you, Wanderer, how will you shape your clay?'

'I cannot stay in Merin,' Taran replied, 'much as I love it. Caer Dallben waits for me, as it has always waited. My life is there, and gladly I return to it, for I have been too long away.'

They sat silently then: Taran, Gurgi and Annlaw Clay-Shaper. As dawn lightened, Taran clasped the potter's hand and bade him farewell.

'Good journey to you, Wanderer,' called Annlaw, as Taran swung astride Melynlas. 'Do not forget us, for we shall not forget you.'

'I have the sword I fashioned,' Taran proudly cried, 'the cloak I wove, and the bowl I shaped. And the friendship of those in the fairest land of Prydain. No man can find greater treasure.'

Melynlas pawed the ground, impatient, and Taran gave the stallion rein.

Thus Taran rode from Merin with Gurgi at his side.

And as he did, it seemed he could hear voices calling to him. 'Remember us! Remember us!' He turned once, but Merin was far behind and out of sight. From the hills a wind had risen, driving the scattered leaves before it, bearing homeward to Caer Dallben. Taran followed it.

The High King

First published in the USA 1968 by Holt Rinehart
First published in Great Britain by Fontana Lions 1979

Contents

1	Homecomings	199
2	The Letter Sticks	210
3	The Prophecy	222
4	King Smoit's Castle	232
5	The Watcher	241
6	A Clutch of Eggs	252
7	The King of Mona	260
8	The Messengers	269
9	The Banner	275
10	The Coming of Pryderi	288
11	The Fortress	299
12	The Red Fallows	309
13	Darkness	322
14	Daylight	337
15	The River of Ice	347
16	The Enchanter	356
17	The Snowstorm	363
18	Mount Dragon	374
19	The Death Lord	380
20	The Gift	393
21	Farewells	402

For the boys who might have been Taran and
the girls who will always be Eilonwy.

Author's Note

Despite their shortcomings, no books have given me greater joy in the writing than the Chronicles of Prydain. I come sadly to the end of this journey, aware of the impossibility of commenting objectively on a work which has absorbed me so long and so personally.

I must, however, warn readers of this fifth chronicle to expect the unexpected. Its structure is somewhat different, its range wider. If there is more external conflict, I have tried to add more inner content; if the form follows that of the traditional hero-tale, the individuals, I hope, are genuinely human. And although it deals with a battle on an epic scale, where Taran, Princess Eilonwy, Fflewddur Fflam, even the oracular pig Hen Wen, are pressed to the limit of their strength, it is a battle whose aftermath is deeper in consequence than the struggle itself. The final choice, which even faithful Gurgi cannot avoid, is almost too hard to bear. Fortunately, it is never offered to us in the real world – not, at least, in such unmistakable terms. In another sense, we face this kind of choice again and again, because for us it is never final. Whether the Assistant Pig-Keeper chose well, whether the ending is happy, heartbreaking, or both, readers must decide for themselves.

Like the previous tales, this adventure can be read independently of the others. Nevertheless, certain long-standing questions are resolved here. Why was that sneering scoundrel Magg, allowed to escape from the Castle of Llyr? Whatever became of the small-hearted giant, Glew? Can Achren really be trusted in Caer Dallben? And, of course, the secret of Taran's parentage. Readers who have been asking me these questions will see why I could not, until now, answer them fully without spoiling the surprises.

As for Prydain itself, part Wales as it is, but more as it never was: at first, I thought it a small land existing only in my imagination. Since then, for me it has become much larger. While it grew from Welsh legend, it has broadened into my attempt to make a land of fantasy relevant to a world of reality.

The first friends of the Companions are as steadfast today as they were at the beginning; many I thought were new have turned out to have been old friends all along. I owe all of them considerably more than they may suspect; and, as always, I offer these pages to them fondly, hoping they will find the result not too far below the promise. If time has tried their patience with me, it has only deepened my affection for them.

L.A.

CHAPTER I

Homecomings

Under a chill, grey sky, two riders jogged across the turf. Taran, the taller horseman, set his face against the wind and leaned forward in the saddle, his eyes on the distant hills. At his belt hung a sword, and from his shoulder a silver-bound battle horn. His companion Gurgi, shaggier than the pony he rode, pulled his weathered cloak around him, rubbed his frost-nipped ears, and began groaning so wretchedly that Taran at last reined up the stallion.

'No, no!' Gurgi cried. 'Faithful Gurgi will keep on! He follows kindly master, oh yes, as he has always done. Never mind his shakings and achings! Never mind the droopings of his poor tender head!'

Taran smiled, seeing that Gurgi, despite his bold words, was eyeing a sheltering grove of ash trees. 'There is time to spare,' he answered. 'I long to be home, but not at the cost of that poor tender head of yours. We camp here and go no farther until morning.'

They tethered their mounts and built a small fire in a ring of stones. Gurgi curled up and was snoring almost before he had finished swallowing his food. Though as weary as his companion, Taran set about mending the harness leathers. Suddenly he stopped and jumped to his feet. Overhead, a winged shape plunged swiftly towards him.

'Look!' Taran cried, as Gurgi, still heavy with sleep, sat up and blinked. 'It's Kaw! Dallben must have sent him to find us.'

The crow beat his wings, clacked his beak, and began squawking loudly even before he landed on Taran's outstretched wrist.

'Eilonwy!' Kaw croaked at the top of his voice. 'Eilonwy! Princess! Home!'

Taran's weariness fell from him like a cloak. Gurgi, wide awake and shouting joyfully, scurried to unloose the steeds. Taran leaped astride Melynlas, spun the grey stallion about, and galloped from the grove, with Kaw perched on his shoulder and Gurgi and the pony pounding at his heels.

Day and night they rode, hardly halting for a mouthful of food or a moment of sleep, urging all speed and strength from their mounts and from themselves, ever southward, down from the mountain valley and across Great Avren until, on a bright morning, the fields of Caer Dallben lay before them once again.

From the instant Taran set foot across the threshold, such a commotion filled the cottage that he scarcely knew which way to turn. Kaw had immediately begun jabbering and flapping his wings; Coll, whose great bald crown and broad face shone with delight, was clapping Taran on the back; while Gurgi shouted in glee and leaped up and down in a cloud of shedding hair. Even the ancient enchanter Dallben, who seldom let anything disturb his meditations, hobbled out of his chamber to observe the welcomings. In the midst of it all, Taran could hardly glimpse Eilonwy, though he heard the voice of the Princess very clearly above the din.

'Taran of Caer Dallben,' she cried, as he strove to draw near her, 'I've been waiting to see you for days! After all the time I've been away learning to be a young lady – as if I weren't one before I left – when I'm home at last, you're not even here!'

In another moment he was at her side. The slender Princess still wore at her throat the crescent moon of silver, and on her finger the ring crafted by the Fair Folk. But now a band of gold circled her brow, and the richness of her apparel made Taran suddenly aware of his travel-stained cloak and muddy boots.

'And if you think living in a castle is pleasant,' Eilonwy went on, without a pause for breath, 'I can tell you it isn't. It's weary and dreary! They've made me sleep in beds with goosefeather pillows enough to stifle you; I'm sure the geese needed them more than I did – the feathers, that is, not the pillows. And servitors to bring you exactly what you don't want to eat. And washing your hair whether it needs it or not. And sewing and weaving and curtsying and all such I don't even want to think about. I've not drawn a sword for I don't know how long . . .'

Eilonwy stopped abruptly and looked curiously at Taran. 'That's odd,' she said. 'There's something different about you. It's not your hair, though it does look as if you'd cropped it yourself with your eyes shut. It's – well, I can't quite say. I mean, unless you told someone, they'd never guess you were an Assistant Pig-Keeper.'

Taran laughed fondly at Eilonwy's puzzled frown. 'Alas, it's been long since last I tended Hen Wen. Indeed, when we journeyed among the folk of the Free Commots, Gurgi and I toiled at nearly everything but pig-keeping. This cloak I wove at the loom of Dwyvach the Weaver-Woman; this sword – Hevydd the Smith taught me the forging of it. And this,' he said with a trace of sadness, drawing an earthen bowl from his jacket, 'such as it is, I made at the wheel of Annlaw Clay-Shaper.' He put the bowl in her hands. 'If it pleases you, it is yours.'

'It's lovely,' answered Eilonwy. 'Yes, I shall treasure it. But that's what I mean, too. I'm not saying you aren't a good Assistant Pig-Keeper, because I'm sure you're the best in Prydain, but there's something more – '

'You speak truth, Princess,' put in Coll. 'He left us a pig-keeper and comes back looking as if he could do all he set his hand to, whatever.'

Taran shook his head. 'I learned I was neither swordsmith nor weaver. Nor, alas, a shaper of clay. Gurgi and I were already homeward bound when Kaw found us, and here shall we stay.'

'I'm glad of that,' replied Eilonwy. 'All anyone knew about you was that you were wandering every which where. Dallben told me you were seeking your parents. Then you met someone you thought was your father but wasn't. Or was it the other way round? I didn't altogether understand it.'

'There is little to understand,' Taran said. 'What I sought, I found. Though it was not what I had hoped.'

'No, it was not,' murmured Dallben, who had been watching Taran closely. 'You found more than you sought, and gained perhaps more than you know.'

'I still don't see why you wanted to leave Caer Dallben,' Eilonwy began.

Taran had no chance to reply, for now his hand was seized and shaken vigorously.

'Hallo, hallo!' cried a young man with pale blue eyes and straw-coloured hair. His handsomely embroidered cloak looked as though it had been water-soaked, then wrung out to dry. His bootlacings, broken in several places, had been retied in large, straggling knots.

'Prince Rhun!' Taran had almost failed to recognize him. Rhun had grown taller and leaner, though his grin was as broad as it had ever been.

'King Rhun, actually,' the young man answered, 'since my father died last summer. That's one of the reasons why Princess Eilonwy is here now. My mother wanted to keep her with us on Mona to finish her education. And you know my mother! She'd never have left off with it, even though Dallben had sent word Eilonwy was to come home. And so,' he proudly added, 'I finally put my foot down. I ordered a ship fitted out, and off we sailed from Mona Haven. Amazing what a king can do when he sets his mind to it!

'We've brought someone else along, too,' Rhun continued, gesturing towards the fireside where Taran for the first time noticed a pudgy little man sitting with a cook-pot between his knees. The stranger licked his fingers and wrinkled a flabby nose at Taran. He made no attempt to rise, but only nodded curtly while the scraggly fringe of hair around his bulbous head stirred like weeds under water.

Taran stared, not believing what he saw. The little man drew himself up and sniffed with a mixture of haughtiness and wounded feelings.

'One should have no trouble remembering a giant,' he said testily.

'Remember you?' replied Taran. 'How could I not! The cavern on Mona! Last time I saw you, though, you were – bigger, to say the least. But it is you, nevertheless. It is, indeed! Glew!'

'When I was a giant,' Glew said, 'few would have forgotten me so quickly. Unfortunate that things worked out as they did. Now, in the cavern – '

'You've started him off again,' Eilonwy whispered to Taran. 'He'll go on like that until you're fairly wilted, about the glorious days when he used to be a giant. He'll only stop talking to eat, and only stop eating to talk. I can understand his eating, since he lived on nothing but mushrooms for so long. But he must have been wretched as a giant, and you'd think he'd want to forget it.'

'I knew Dallben sent Kaw with a potion to shrink Glew back to size,' Taran answered. 'Of what happened to him since then, I've had no word.'

'*That's* what happened to him,' said Eilonwy. 'As soon as he got free of the cavern, he made his way to Rhun's castle. No one had the heart to turn him away, though he bored us all to tears with those endless, pointless tales of his. We took him with us when we sailed, thinking he'd be grateful to Dallben and want to thank him properly. Not a bit of it! We almost had to twist his ears to get him aboard. Now that he's here, I wish we'd left him where he was.'

'But three of our companions are missing,' Taran said, glancing around the cottage. 'Good old Doli, and Fflewddur Fflam. And I had hoped Prince Gwydion might have come to welcome Eilonwy.'

'Doli sends his best wishes,' said Coll, 'but we shall have to do without his company. Our dwarf friend is harder to root out of the Fair Folk realm than a stump out of a field. He'll not budge. As for Fflewddur Fflam, nothing can keep him and his harp from any merry-making, whatever. He should have been here long since.'

'Prince Gwydion as well,' Dallben added. 'He and I have matters to discuss. Though you young people may doubt it, some of them are even weightier than the homecomings of a Princess and an Assistant Pig-Keeper.'

'Well, I shall put this on again when Fflewddur and Prince Gwydion arrive,' said Eilonwy, taking the golden circlet from her brow, 'just so they can see how it looks. But I won't wear it a moment longer. It's rubbed a blister and it makes my head ache – like someone squeezing your neck, only higher up.'

'Ah, Princess,' Dallben said, with a furrowed smile, 'a crown is more discomfort than adornment. If you have learned that, you have already learned much.'

'Learning!' Eilonwy declared. 'I've been up to my ears in learning. It doesn't show, so it's hard to believe it's there. Wait, that's not quite true, either. Here, I've learned this.' From her cloak she drew a large square of folded cloth and almost shyly handed it to Taran. 'I embroidered it for you. It's not finished yet, but I wanted you to have it, even so. Though I admit it's not as handsome as the things you've made.'

Taran spread out the fabric. As broad as his outstretched arms, the somewhat straggle-threaded embroidery showed a white, blue-eyed pig against a field of green.

'It's meant to be Hen Wen,' Eilonwy explained as Rhun and Gurgi pressed forward to study the handiwork more closely.

'At first, I tried to embroider you into it, too,' Eilonwy said to Taran. 'Because you're so fond of Hen and because – because I was thinking of you. But you came out looking like sticks with a bird's nest on top, not yourself at all. So I had to start over with Hen alone. You'll just have to make believe you're standing beside her, a little to the left. Otherwise, I'd never have got this much done, and I did work the summer on it.'

'If I was in your thoughts then,' Taran said, 'your work gladdens me all the more. No matter that Hen's eyes are really brown.'

Eilonwy looked at him in sudden dismay. 'You don't like it.'

'I do, in all truth,' Taran assured her. 'Brown or blue makes no difference. It will be useful – '

'Useful!' cried Eilonwy. 'Useful's not the point! It's a keepsake, not a horse blanket! Taran of Caer Dallben, you don't understand anything at all.'

'At least,' Taran replied, with a good-natured grin, 'I know the colour of Hen Wen's eyes.'

Eilonwy tossed her red-gold hair and put her chin in the air. 'Humph!' she said. 'And very likely forgotten the colour of mine.'

'Not so, Princess,' Taran answered quietly. 'Nor have I forgotten when you gave me this,' he added, taking up the battle horn. 'Its powers were greater than either of us knew. They are gone now, but I treasure it still because it came from your hands.

'You asked why I sought to know my parentage,' Taran went on. 'Because I hoped it would prove noble, and give me the right to ask what I dared not ask before. My hope was mistaken. Yet even without it – '

Taran hesitated, searching for the most fitting words. Before he could speak again, the cottage door burst open, and Taran cried out in alarm.

At the threshold stood Fflewddur Fflam. The bard's face was ashen, his ragged yellow hair clung to his forehead. On his shoulder he bore the limp body of a man.

Taran, with Rhun behind him, sprang to help. Gurgi and Eilonwy followed as they lowered the still figure to the ground. Glew, his pudgy cheeks quivering, stared speechless. At the first instant, Taran had nearly staggered at the shock. Now his hands worked quickly, almost of themselves, to unclasp the cloak and loosen the torn jacket. Before him, on the hard-packed earth, lay Gwydion Prince of Don.

Blood crusted the warrior's wolf-grey hair and stained his weathered face. His lips were drawn back, his teeth set in battle rage. Gwydion's cloak muffled one arm as though at the last he had sought to defend himself with this alone.

'Lord Gwydion is slain!' Eilonwy cried.

'He lives – though barely,' Taran said. 'Fetch medicines,' he ordered Gurgi. 'The healing herbs from my saddlebags – ' He stopped short and turned to Dallben. 'Forgive me. It is not for me to command under my master's roof. But the herbs are of great power. Adaon Son of Taliesin gave them to me long ago. They are yours if you wish them.'

'I know their nature and have none that will serve better,' Dallben answered. 'Nor should you fear to command under any roof, since you have learned to command yourself. I trust your skill as I see you trust it. Do as you see fit.'

Coll was already hurrying from the scullery with water in a basin. Dallben, who had knelt at Gwydion's side, rose and turned to the bard.

'What evil deed is this?' The old enchanter spoke hardly above a whisper, yet his voice rang through the cottage and his eyes blazed in anger. 'Whose hand dared strike him?'

'The Huntsmen of Annuvin,' replied Fflewddur. 'Two lives they almost claimed. How did you fare?' he urgently asked Taran. 'How did you outride them so quickly? Be thankful it went no worse for you.'

Taran, puzzled, glanced up at the distraught bard. 'Your words have no meaning, Fflewddur.'

'Meaning?' answered the bard. 'They mean what they say. Gwydion would have traded his life for yours when the Huntsmen set upon you not an hour ago.'

'Set upon me?' Taran's perplexity grew. 'How can that be? Gurgi and I saw no Huntsmen. And we have been at Caer Dallben this hour past.'

'Great Belin, a Fflam sees what he sees!' cried Fflewddur.

'A fever is working in you,' Taran said. 'You, too, may be wounded more grievously than you know. Rest easy. We shall give you all the help we can.' He turned again to Gwydion, opened the packet of herbs which Gurgi had brought, and set them to steep in the basin.

Dallben's face was clouded. 'Let the bard speak,' he said. 'There is much in his words that troubles me.'

'Lord Gwydion and I rode together from the northern lands,' Fflewddur began. 'We'd crossed Avren and were on our way here. A little distance ahead of us, in a clearing . . .' The bard paused and looked directly at Taran. 'I saw you with my own eyes! You were hard pressed. You shouted to us for help and waved us onward.

'Gwydion outdistanced me,' Fflewddur went on. 'You'd already galloped beyond the clearing. Gwydion rode after you like the wind. Llyan carried me swiftly, but by the time I caught up there was no sign of you at all, yet Huntsmen a-plenty. They had dragged Gwydion from his saddle. They would have paid with their own lives had they stood against me,' cried Fflewddur. 'But they fled when I rode up. Gwydion was close to death and I dared not leave him.'

Fflewddur bowed his head. 'His hurt was beyond my skill to treat. I could do no more than bring him here as you see him.'

'You saved his life, my friend,' Taran said.

'And lost what Gwydion would have given his life to keep!' cried the bard. 'The Huntsmen failed to slay him, but a greater evil has befallen him. They've stripped him of his sword – blade and scabbard!'

Taran caught his breath. Concerned only for his companion's wounds, he had not seen that Dyrnwyn, the black sword, hung no longer at Gwydion's side. Terror filled him. Dyrnwyn, the enchanted blade, the flaming weapon of ancient power, was in the Huntsmen's hands. They would bear it to their master: to Arawn Death-Lord, in the dark realm of Annuvin.

Fflewddur sank to the ground and put his head in his hands. 'And my own wits are lost, since you tell me it was not yourself who called out to us.'

'What you saw I cannot judge,' Taran said. 'Gwydion's life is our first care. We will talk of these things when your memory is clearer.'

'The harper's memory is clear enough.' A black-robed woman moved from the dark corner where she had been silently listening, and stepped slowly into the midst of the company. Her long, unbound hair glittered like pale silver; the deadly beauty of her face had not altogether vanished, though now it seemed shadowy, worn away, lingering as a dream only half-recalled.

'Ill fortune mars our meeting, Assistant Pig-Keeper,' Achren said. 'But welcome, nonetheless. What, then, do you still fear me?' she added, seeing Taran's uneasy glance. She smiled. Her teeth were sharp. 'Neither has Eilonwy Daughter of Angharad forgotten my powers, though it was she who destroyed them at the Castle of Llyr. Yet, since I have dwelt here, have I not served Dallben as well as any of you?'

Achren strode to the outstretched form of Gwydion. Taran saw a look almost of pity in her cold eyes. 'Lord Gwydion will live,' she said. 'But he may find life a crueller fate than death.' She bent and with her fingertips lightly touched the warrior's brow, then drew her hand away and faced the bard.

'Your eyes did not play you false, harper,' Achren said. 'You saw what was meant for you to see. A pig-keeper? Why not, if thus he chose to appear? Only one wields such a power: Arawn himself, Lord of Annuvin, Land of the Dead.'

CHAPTER 2

The Letter Sticks

Taran could not stifle a gasp of fear. The black-robed woman glanced at him coldly.

'Arawn dares not pass the borders of Annuvin in his true form,' Achren said. 'To do so would mean his death. But he commands all shapes, and they are both shield and mask. To the harper and Lord Gwydion, he showed himself as a pig-keeper. He could as well have appeared as a fox in the forest, an eagle, even a blind worm if he deemed that would best serve his ends. Yes, Pig-Keeper, with no less ease could he have chosen the form and features of any creature living. For Lord Gwydion, what better lure than the sight of a companion in danger – one who had fought often at his side, known to him, and trusted. Gwydion is too shrewd a warrior to be taken in a weaker snare.'

'Then all of us are lost,' Taran said, dismayed. 'The Lord of Annuvin can move among us as he pleases, and we are without defence against him.'

'You have reason to fear, Pig-Keeper,' replied Achren. 'Now you glimpse one of Arawn's subtlest powers. But it is a power used only when none other will serve him. Never will he leave his stronghold, save in the press of mortal danger; or, as today, when what he sought to gain far outweighed the risk.' Achren's voice lowered. 'Arawn has many secrets, but this one is most deeply guarded. Once he assumes a shape, his strength and skill are no greater than that of the guise he wears. Then can he be slain, like any mortal being.'

'Oh, Fflewddur, if I'd only been with you!' Eilonwy cried in despair. 'Arawn wouldn't have deceived me, no matter how much he looked like Taran. Don't tell me I couldn't have told the difference between a real Assistant Pig-Keeper and a false one!'

'Foolish pride, Daughter of Angharad,' Achren answered scornfully. 'No eyes can see behind the mask of Arawn Death-Lord. No eyes,' she added, 'but mine. Do you doubt me?' Achren went on quickly, seeing Eilonwy's surprise.

The woman's ravaged features held shreds of an old pride, and her voice sharpened with haughtiness and anger.

'Long before the Sons of Don came to dwell in Prydain, long before the lords of the cantrevs swore allegiance to Math, High King, and Gwydion, his war leader, it was I who commanded obedience to my rule, I who wore the Iron Crown of Annuvin.

'Arawn was my consort, who served me and did my bidding,' Achren said. 'And he betrayed me.' Her voice was low and harsh, and rage glittered in her eyes. 'He robbed me of my throne and cast me aside. Yet his powers are no secret to me, for it was I who taught them to him. Let him cloud your sight with whatever guise he chooses. From me, never can the face of Arawn be hidden.'

Gwydion stirred and groaned faintly. Taran turned again to the basin of healing herbs, while Eilonwy raised the warrior's head.

'Bear Prince Gwydion to my chamber,' Dallben ordered. The enchanter's careworn face was drawn, and the lines had deepened in his withered cheeks. 'Your skill has helped keep him from death,' he said to Taran. 'Now I must see if mine may help him to life.'

Coll lifted Gwydion in his burly arms.

Achren made to follow after him. 'I have little need of sleep and can best keep a vigil,' Achren said. 'I shall watch the night over Lord Gwydion.'

'I shall watch over him,' Eilonwy said, stepping to the side of Coll.

'Fear me not, Daughter of Angharad,' Achren said. 'I

bear no ill will against Lord Gwydion.' She bowed deeply, half-humble and half-mocking. 'The stable is my castle and the scullery my realm. I seek no other.'

'Come,' Dallben said, 'both of you shall help me. Wait – the others. Be patient and hopeful.'

Darkness had blinded the windows of the cottage. To Taran, it seemed the fire had lost its warmth and cast only cold shadows among the silent companions.

'At first I thought somehow we could overtake the Huntsmen and keep them from reaching Annuvin,' Taran said at last. 'But if Achren speaks truth, Arawn himself commanded them, and Gwydion's sword is already in his hands. I do not know his purpose, but I am deeply afraid.'

'I can't forgive myself,' Fflewddur said. 'The loss is my fault. I should have seen the trap instantly.'

Taran shook his head. 'Arawn worked a bitter ruse on you. Gwydion himself was deceived.'

'But not I!' cried the bard. 'A Fflam is keen-eyed! From the first moment, I saw differences. The way he sat his steed, the way . . .' The harp, slung at the bard's shoulder, tensed suddenly and a string snapped with such a twang that Gurgi, crouched near the hearth, started bolt upright. Fflewddur choked and swallowed. 'There it goes again,' he muttered. 'Will it never leave off? The slightest . . . ah, colouring of the facts, and the beastly strings break! Believe me, I meant no exaggeration. As I thought back it did seem that I could notice . . . No, the truth of it is: the guise was perfect. I could be snared again – and as easily.'

'Amazing!' murmured the King of Mona, who had been watching wide-eyed. 'I say, I wish I could do that sort of shape-changing myself. Unbelievable! I've always thought: how interesting to be a badger, or an ant. I should love to know how to build as well as they do. Since I've been king, I've tried to improve things here and there. I mean to put up a new seawall at Mona Haven. I've begun once already. My idea was to start from both ends at the same time and thus be done twice as quickly. I can't understand what went wrong, for I took charge of all the work myself, but somehow we didn't meet in the middle and I'll have to find a better way of going at it. Then I've planned a road to Glew's old cavern. It's an amazing place and I think the folk of Dinas Rhydnant will enjoy visiting it. Surprising how easy it is,' Rhun said, beaming proudly. 'The planning, at any rate. The doing, for some reason, always seems a little harder.'

Glew, hearing his name spoken, pricked up his ears. He had not left his place in the chimney corner; nor had his alarm at the happenings in the cottage made him loosen his hold on the cook-pot. 'When I was a giant,' he began.

'I see the little weasel is with you,' said Fflewddur to King Rhun, recognizing Glew immediately despite the former giant's present stature. 'When he was a giant,' the bard muttered, giving Glew a look of ill-concealed vexation, 'he was a paltry one. He'd have done anything to be free of that cavern – even to popping us into that foul stew he'd cooked up. A Fflam is forgiving! But I think he went a little too far.'

'When I was a giant,' Glew continued, either ignoring or not hearing the bard's remarks, 'no one would have humiliated me by taking me by the ears and hustling me aboard a smelly boat. I had no wish to come here. After what's happened today, I have less wish to stay.' Glew pursed his lips. 'Dallben shall see that I'm taken back to Mona without delay.'

'I'm sure he will,' Taran replied. 'But Dallben has graver concerns now, and so do we all.'

Mumbling something about shabby treatment and lack of consideration, Glew scraped a finger along the bottom of the pot and sucked his teeth with indignant satisfaction. The companions said no more, but settled down to wait out the night.

The fire burned to ashes. A night wind rose outside the cottage. Taran rested his head on his arms. At his homecoming he had longed to stand before Eilonwy, forgetting rank and birth, as any man before any woman, and ask her to wed. But now the disaster that had overtaken Gwydion made Taran's own wishes unimportant. Though he still did not know Eilonwy's heart, nor what her answer to him might be, he could not bring himself to learn it until all hearts were at peace again. He closed his eyes. The wind screamed as if it would rip to tatters the quiet meadows and orchards of Caer Dallben.

A hand on his shoulder aroused him. It was Eilonwy.

'Gwydion has wakened,' she said. 'He would speak with us.'

In Dallben's chamber the Prince of Don half-raised himself from the couch. His features were pale under their weathering, and tightly drawn, though more in anger than pain. His mouth was set, bitter, his green eyes burned with dark flashes, and his glance was that of a proud wolf scornful of his hurt, and scornful all the more of those who had given him his wounds. Achren was a silent shadow in the corner. The old enchanter stood anxiously beside the book-strewn table near the wooden bench where Taran, throughout boyhood, had sat for lessons. *The Book of Three*, the huge, leather-bound tome of secret lore forbidden to all but Dallben himself, lay closed atop a pile of other ancient volumes.

Taran, with Eilonwy, Fflewddur, and King Rhun behind him, strode to Gwydion and clasped the warrior's hand. The Prince of Don smiled grimly.

'No merry meeting, and no long one, Assistant Pig-Keeper,' Gwydion said. 'Dallben has told me of the Death-Lord's ruse. Dyrnwyn must be regained at all cost, and without delay. He spoke, too, of your wanderings,' Gwydion added. 'I would hear more of them from yourself, but that must wait another time. I ride to Annuvin before the day is out.'

Taran looked at the Prince of Don in surprise and concern. 'Your wounds are still fresh. You cannot make such a journey.'

'Neither can I stay,' Gwydion answered. 'Since Dyrnwyn first came into my hands, I have learned more of its nature. Only a little more,' he added, 'but enough to know its loss is fatal.

'Dyrnwyn's lineage lies beyond memory of living man,' Gwydion continued, 'and much of its history has been forgotten or destroyed. For long, the blade was thought no more than legend, and matter for a harper's song. Taliesin Chief Bard is wisest in the lore of Prydain, but even he could tell me only that Govannion the Lame, a master craftsman, forged and tempered Dyrnwyn at the behest of King Rhydderch Hael, as a weapon of greatest power and protection for the land. To safeguard it, a spell was cast upon the blade and a warning graven on the scabbard.'

'I remember the Old Writing,' Eilonwy said. 'Indeed, I shall never forget it, for I had an impossible time keeping Taran from meddling with things he didn't understand. *"Draw Dyrnwyn only thou of royal blood . . ."* '

'Closer to its true meaning is *"noble worth"*,' said Gwydion. 'The enchantment forbade the sword to all but those who would use it wisely and well. The flame of Dyrnwyn would destroy any other who sought to draw it. But the writing on the scabbard has been marred. The full message, which might have told more of the sword's purpose, is unknown.

'King Rhydderch bore the blade throughout his life,' Gwydion continued, 'and his sons after him. Their reigns were peaceful and prosperous. But here Dyrnwyn's history ends. King Rhitta, grandson of Rhydderch, was the last to hold the blade. He was lord of Spiral Castle before it became the stronghold of Queen Achren. He met his death, in a way unknown, with Dyrnwyn clutched in his hands. From that time on the sword was seen no more, forgotten as it lay buried with him in Spiral Castle's deepest chamber.' Gwydion turned to Eilonwy. 'Where you, Princess, found it. You gave it to me willingly; but it was not willingly that it left my hands. The blade is worth more than my life, or the lives of any of us. In Arawn's grasp, it can bring doom upon Prydain.'

'Do you believe Arawn can unsheathe the sword?' Taran asked hurriedly. 'Can he turn the weapon against us? Can he make it serve some evil end?'

'This I do not know,' replied Gwydion. The warrior's face was troubled. 'It may be that Arawn Death-Lord has found means to break the enchantment. Or, unable to use it himself, his purpose may be to keep the blade from any other use. He would have taken my life as well as the sword. Thanks to Fflewddur Fflam, I still have the one. Now I must find the other, though the path lead me to the depths of Annuvin itself.'

Achren, silent until now, raised her head and spoke to Gwydion. 'Let me seek Dyrnwyn in your stead. I know the ways of Annuvin; no stranger am I to its secret hoards, and where and how they are guarded. If the sword is hidden, I will find it. If Arawn himself bears it, Dyrnwyn will be taken from him. More than that. I swear by every oath to destroy him. Thus have I sworn already to myself, and swear it again to you. You forced life upon me, Gwydion, when I begged for death. Now give me what I live for. Give me my vengeance.'

Gwydion did not answer immediately. His green-flecked eyes searched the woman's face. He said, 'Vengeance is not a gift I may bestow, Achren.'

Achren stiffened. Her hands twisted into claws and Taran feared she would fling herself upon Gwydion. She did not move. 'You will not trust me,' Achren said hoarsely. Her bloodless lips turned in a smile of contempt. 'So be it, Prince of Don. Once you scorned to share a kingdom with me. Scorn me again to your own loss.'

'I do not scorn you,' Gwydion said. 'I only urge you to accept Dallben's protection. Stay here in safety. Among all of us, your hope of finding the sword is the least. Arawn's hatred of you can be no less than yours of him. He or his servants would slay you at sight, even before you set foot in Annuvin. No, Achren, what you offer is not possible.' He thought a moment. 'There may be another way to learn how Dyrnwyn shall be found.'

Gwydion turned to Dallben, but the enchanter sorrowfully shook his head.

'Alas,' Dallben said, '*The Book of Three* cannot tell us what we most need to know. I have searched carefully, every page, to understand its hidden meanings. They are dark, even to me. Fetch the letter sticks,' the enchanter said to Coll. 'Hen Wen alone can help us.'

From her enclosure the white pig watched the silent procession. On his bony shoulders Dallben bore the letter sticks, the ash-wood rods carved with ancient symbols. Glew, interested only in the provisions of the scullery, remained behind, as did Gurgi, who well remembered the former giant and chose to keep an eye on him. Achren had spoken no further, but hooded her face and sat motionless in the cottage.

Usually, at the sight of Taran, the oracular pig would squeal joyously and trot to the railing to have her chin scratched. Now she cowered in a far corner of the pen, her little eyes wide and her cheeks trembling. As Dallben entered the enclosure and planted the letter sticks upright in the earth, Hen Wen snuffled and crouched closer against the bars.

Dallben, murmuring inaudibly, moved to stand beside the ash-wood rods. Outside the enclosure, the companions waited. Hen Wen whimpered and did not stir.

'What does she fear?' Eilonwy whispered. Taran made no answer; his eyes were fixed on the aged enchanter in his wind-whipped robe, on the letter sticks, and the unmoving form of Hen Wen. Against the dull sky they seemed to him frozen together in their own moment, far beyond the silent watchers. This was the first time Taran had seen the enchanter seek a prophecy from the oracular pig. Of Dallben's powers he could only guess; but he knew Hen Wen, and knew she was too terrified to move. He waited what felt an age. Even Rhun sensed something amiss; the King of Mona's cheerful face was darkly clouded.

Dallben glanced uneasily at Gwydion. 'Never before has Hen Wen refused to answer when the letter sticks were shown her.'

Again he murmured words Taran could not distinguish. The oracular pig shuddered violently, shut her eyes, and sank her head between her stubby trotters.

'Perhaps a few notes on my harp?' Fflewddur suggested. 'I've had excellent success . . .'

The enchanter motioned the bard to be silent. Once more he spoke, softly yet commandingly. Hen Wen shrank into herself and moaned as though in pain.

'Her fear blinds her powers,' Dallben said gravely. 'Even my spells do not reach her. I have failed.'

Despair filled the faces of the watching companions.

Gwydion bowed his head, and his eyes were deeply troubled. 'We, too, shall fail,' he said, 'if we do not learn whatever she can tell us.'

Quickly and without a word Taran climbed the railing, walked steadily towards the frightened pig, and dropped to his knees beside her. He scratched her chin and gently stroked her neck. 'Don't be afraid, Hen. Nothing will harm you here.'

Dallben, surprised, started forward, then halted. Hearing Taran's voice, the pig had cautiously opened one eye.

Her snout twitched, she raised her head slightly and gave a faint 'Hwoinch!'

'Hen, listen to me,' Taran pleaded. 'I have no power to command you. But we need your help, all of us who love you.'

Taran spoke on; as he did, the oracular pig ceased her trembling. Though she did not attempt to rise, Hen Wen grunted fondly, wheezed, and made affectionate muttering sounds in her throat. She blinked her eyes and her wide face seemed nearly to grin.

'Tell us, Hen,' Taran urged. 'Please. Tell us what you can.'

Hen Wen moved uneasily. Slowly she climbed to her feet. The white pig snorted and glanced at the letter sticks. Step by step, on her short legs, she moved closer to them.

The enchanter nodded to Taran. 'Well done,' he murmured. 'This day, the power of an Assistant Pig-Keeper is greater than my own.'

As Taran stared, not daring to speak, Hen Wen paused at the first rod. Still hesitant, she pointed with her snout at one of the carved symbols, then at another. Dallben, watching intently, quickly wrote on a scrap of parchment the signs the oracular pig had indicated. Hen Wen continued a few moments, then suddenly left off and backed anxiously from the stick.

Dallben's face was grave. 'Can this be so?' he murmured, his voice filled with alarm. 'No . . . no. We must learn more than that.' He glanced at Taran.

'Please, Hen,' Taran whispered, coming to the side of the pig, who had begun to shudder again. 'Help us.'

Despite his words, Taran feared Hen Wen would turn away. She shook her head, squinted her eyes and grunted piteously. Nevertheless, at his pleading, she cautiously trotted to the second rod. There, in desperate haste, as if to make an end of it quickly, she pointed to other symbols.

The enchanter's hand trembled as he wrote. 'Now the third one,' he said urgently.

Hen Wen, stiff-legged, reared back and sank to her haunches. All of Taran's soothing words would not budge her for several moments. At last, however, she rose and more fearfully than ever trotted to the final ash-wood rod.

Even as Hen Wen approached and before she could point to the first letter, the ash-wood rods shook and swayed like living things. They twisted as though to uproot themselves, and with a sound that ripped the air like a thunder clap, they split, shattered, and fell to earth in splinters.

Hen Wen, squealing in terror, flung herself backwards and fled to a corner of the enclosure. As Taran hurried to her, Dallben bent, picked up the fragments of wood and studied them hopelessly.

'They are destroyed beyond repair, and useless now,' Dallben said in a heavy voice. 'The cause is dark to me, and Hen Wen's prophecy remains unfinished. Even so, I doubt its end could bode less ill than its beginning. She must have sensed this herself.'

The enchanter turned and walked slowly from the enclosure. Eilonwy had joined Taran, who strove to calm the terrified pig. Hen Wen still gasped and shook, and pressed her head between her forelegs.

'No wonder she didn't want to prophesy,' Eilonwy cried. 'And yet,' she added to Taran, 'Hen would have told nothing at all if it hadn't been for you.'

Dallben, with the parchment in his hand, had gone to the side of Gwydion. Coll, Fflewddur, and King Rhun gathered anxiously around them. Sure that Hen Wen was unharmed and wanted only to be left in peace, Taran and Eilonwy hurried to the companions.

'Help! Oh, help!'

Yelling, waving his arms frantically, Gurgi raced across the turf. He dashed into their midst and pointed towards the stables.

'Gurgi could do nothing!' he cried. 'He tried, oh yes, but there were only smackings and whackings for his poor tender head! Gone!' Gurgi shouted. 'With fast and speedful gallopings! Wicked Queen is gone!'

CHAPTER 3

The Prophecy

The companions hastened to the stable. As Gurgi had told them, one of King Rhun's horses was missing. Of Achren, there was no trace.

'Let me saddle Melynlas,' Taran urged Gwydion. 'I shall try to overtake her.'

'She's going straight to Annuvin,' burst out Fflewddur. 'I never trusted that woman. Great Belin, who knows what treachery she plans! She's off to feather her own nest, you can be sure of it.'

'Achren goes more likely to her death,' answered Gwydion, his face grim as he looked towards the hills and the leafless trees. 'There is no safety for her beyond Caer Dallben. I would protect her, but dare not delay my quest to seek her now.' He turned to Dallben. 'I must know Hen Wen's prophecy. It is my only guide.'

The enchanter nodded and led the companions to the cottage. The aged man still held the parchment and the splintered letter sticks. Now he cast them on the table and gazed at them for a long moment before he spoke.

'Hen Wen has told us what she can. All, I fear, that we shall ever learn from her. I have again studied the symbols she pointed out, hoping against hope I had misread them.' His expression was withdrawn, his eyes lowered, and he spoke with difficulty, as if each word wrenched his heart. 'I asked how Dyrnwyn might be recovered. Hear the answer given us:

Ask, sooner, mute stone and voiceless rock to speak.

'Such is Hen Wen's message as I have read it from the first letter stick,' Dallben said. 'Whether it is a refusal to speak, a prophecy in itself, or a warning to ask no further,

I cannot be sure. But the symbols of the second letter stick spell out the fate of Dyrnwyn itself.'

Dallben continued, and the enchanter's words filled Taran with cold anguish that struck deep as a sword thrust:

> Quenched will be Dyrnwyn's flame;
> Vanished, its power.
> Night turn to noon
> And rivers burn with frozen fire
> Ere Dyrnwyn be regained.

The ancient man bowed his head then and was silent for a time. 'The third stick,' he said at last, 'was destroyed before Hen Wen could complete her message. She might have told us more; but, judging from the first two, we would have cause for no more hope than we have now.'

'The prophecies mock us,' Taran said. 'Hen told us truly. We could as well have asked stones for help.'

'And got as much sense from them!' cried Eilonwy. 'Hen could have come straight out and said we'll never get Dyrnwyn back. Night can't be noon, and that's the end of it.'

'In all my travels,' added Fflewddur, 'I've never noticed even a small creek burning, not to mention a river. The prophecy is doubly impossible.'

'And yet,' said King Rhun, with innocent eagerness, 'it would be an amazing thing to see. I wish it could happen!'

'I fear you shall not see it come to pass, King of Mona,' Dallben said heavily.

Gwydion, who had been sitting thoughtfully at the table and turning the splintered rods back and forth in his hands, rose and spoke to the companions. 'Hen Wen's prophecy is disheartening,' he said, 'and far from what I had hoped. But when prophecies give no help, men must find it for themselves.' His hands clenched and snapped the fragment of ash wood. 'As long as life and breath are mine, I will seek Dyrnwyn. The prophecy does not change my plans, but makes them only more urgent.'

'Then let us go with you,' Taran said, rising to face Gwydion. 'Take our strength until your own returns.'

'Exactly so!' Fflewddur jumped to his feet. 'I'll pay no heed whether rivers burn or not. Ask stones to speak? I'll ask Arawn himself. He'll keep no secrets from a Fflam!'

Gwydion shook his head. 'In this task, the more men the greater risk. It is done best alone. If any life be staked against Arawn Death-Lord, it must be mine.'

Taran bowed, for Gwydion's tone forbade dispute. 'If such is your will,' he said. 'But what if Kaw were to fly ahead to Annuvin? Send him first. He will go swiftly and bring back whatever knowledge he can gain.'

Gwydion looked shrewdly at Taran and nodded approval. 'You have found some wisdom in your wanderings, Assistant Pig-Keeper. Your plan is sound. Kaw may serve me better than all your swords. But I shall not await him here. To do so would cost me too much time. Let him spy out Annuvin as far as he is able, then find me at King Smoit's castle in Cantrev Cadiffor. Smoit's realm lies on my path to Annuvin, and thus my journey will be half accomplished when Kaw rejoins me.'

'At least we can ride with you as far as King Smoit's castle,' Taran said, 'and guard you until you are well on your way. Between here and Cantrev Cadiffor, Arawn's Huntsmen may be abroad, still seeking your death.'

'The foul villains!' cried the bard. 'Treacherous murderers! They'll have a taste of my sword this time. Let them attack us. I hope they do!' A harp string snapped with a loud crack that set the instrument a-jingling. 'Ah, yes – well – that's only a manner of speaking.' Fflewddur said sheepishly. 'I hope we don't come upon them at all. They could be troublesome and delay our journey.'

'No one has considered the inconvenience to *me*,' said

Glew. The former giant had come out of the scullery and looked peevishly around him.

'Weasel!' muttered Fflewddur. 'Dyrnwyn is gone, we don't know if our lives are at stake, and he frets about inconvenience. He's a little man indeed, and always was.'

'Since no one has mentioned it,' said Eilonwy, 'it seems I'm not being asked to come along. Very well, I shan't insist.'

'You, too, have gained wisdom, Princess,' said Dallben. 'Your days on Mona were not ill-spent.'

'Of course,' Eilonwy went on, 'after you leave, the thought may strike me that it's a pleasant day for a short ride to go picking wildflowers which might be hard to find, especially since it's almost winter. Not that I'd be following you, you understand. But I might, by accident, lose my way, and mistakenly happen to catch up with you. By then, it would be too late for me to come home, through no fault of my own.'

Gwydion's haggard face broke into a smile. 'So be it, Princess. What I cannot prevent, I accept. Ride with me, all those who choose, but no farther than Smoit's stronghold at Caer Cadarn.'

'Ah, Princess,' Coll sighed, shaking his head. 'I will not gainsay Lord Gwydion, whatever. But it is hardly the conduct of a young lady to force her own way thus.'

'Certainly not,' Eilonwy agreed. 'That's the first thing Queen Teleria taught me: A lady doesn't insist on having her own way. Then, next thing you know, it all works out somehow, without one's even trying. I thought I'd never learn, though it's really quite easy once you get the knack.'

Without further delay, Taran lifted Kaw from his fireside perch and carried him to the dooryard. This time the crow did not clack his beak or gabble impudently. Instead of his customary scoldings, hoarse quackings, and mischievous foolery, Kaw hunched on Taran's wrist and cocked a beady, attentive eye, listening closely while Taran carefully explained the task.

Taran raised his arm and Kaw flapped his glossy wings in farewell.

'Annuvin!' Kaw croaked. 'Dyrnwyn!'

The crow flew aloft. Within moments Kaw was high over Caer Dallben. The wind bore him like a leaf, and he hung poised above the watching companions. Then, with a roguish flirt of his wings, Kaw sped northwestward. Taran strained his eyes to follow his flight until the crow vanished into the looming clouds. In sadness and disquiet, Taran at last turned away. Kaw, he was sure, would be alert to the perils of the journey: the arrows of the Huntsmen; the cruel talons and slashing beaks of the gwythaints, Arawn's fierce winged messengers. More than once had gwythaints attacked the companions, and even the fledglings could be dangerous.

Taran recalled, from his boyhood, the young gwythaint whose life he had saved, and he well remembered the bird's sharp claws. Despite Kaw's gallant heart and sharp wits, Taran feared for the safety of the crow; and feared, still more, for Gwydion's quest. And to him came the foreboding that an even heavier fate might ride on Kaw's outspread wings.

It had been agreed that when the travellers neared Great Avren, King Rhun would escort the disgruntled Glew to the ship anchored in the river, there to await his return, for Rhun was determined to ride with Gwydion to Caer Cadarn. Glew liked neither cooling his heels on the swaying vessel nor sleeping on the hard pebbles of the shore; but the protests of the former giant could not move the King of Mona to change his plan.

While Gwydion held a last, hurried council with Dallben, the companions began leading the horses from the stable. The wise Melyngar, Gwydion's white, golden-maned steed, waited calmly for her master. Melynlas,

Taran's stallion, snorted and impatiently pawed the ground.

Eilonwy was already mounted on her favourite, the bay mare, Lluagor. In a fold of her cloak the Princess carried her most treasured possession: the golden sphere that glowed brightly when she cupped it in her hands.

'I'm leaving that uncomfortable crown behind,' Eilonwy declared. 'There's no use for it at all, except to hold down my hair, and that's hardly worth the blisters. But I'd sooner walk on my hands than go without my bauble. Besides, if we need a light, we shall have one. That's much more practical than a hoop on top of your head.' In a saddlebag, she had packed the embroidery made for Taran, intending to finish it along the way. 'Perhaps,' Eilonwy added, 'I might fix the colour of Hen Wen's eyes while I'm at it.'

Fflewddur's mount was the huge, tawny cat, Llyan, herself tall as a horse. Seeing the bard, she purred loudly, and Fflewddur could barely keep the powerful animal from knocking him down with her nuzzling.

'Gently, old girl,' cried the bard, as Llyan thrust her great head between his neck and shoulder. 'I know you want a tune on my harp. I shall play one later, I promise you.'

Glew had recognized Llyan immediately. 'That's not fair,' he sniffed. 'By all rights she belongs to me.'

'Yes,' replied Fflewddur, 'if you count feeding her those vile potions you once brewed to make her grow bigger. If you care to ride her, you're welcome to try. Though I warn you – Llyan has a memory longer than her tail.'

Llyan, indeed, had begun lashing her tail at the sight of Glew. She towered over the pudgy little man, her yellow eyes blazed, her whiskers twitched, her tufted ears went flat against her head; and from her throat came a sound quite unlike her greeting to the bard.

Fflewddur quickly strummed a melody on his harp.

Llyan turned her eyes from Glew and her mouth curved in an enormous smile and she blinked fondly at the bard.

However, Glew's pale face had gone paler and he edged away from the cat. 'When I was a giant,' Glew muttered, 'things were considerably better managed.'

King Rhun saddled his dapple grey steed. Since Coll, who had also decided to accompany Gwydion, would ride the sorrel mare Llamrei, foal of Melynlas and Lluagor, Glew had no choice but to climb up behind Gurgi on his shaggy pony – a companionship unwelcome to all three. Taran, meanwhile, helped Coll rummage in the stables, forge, and tool sheds for weapons.

'Few enough of them there are,' said Coll. 'These spears have served me well as beanpoles,' the stout warrior added. 'I had hoped never to use them for another purpose. Alas, the only blade I can give Gwydion is rusted from propping up one of the apple trees. As for helmets, there are none save my leather cap; and the sparrows have a nest in it. I shall not disturb them. But my own old pate is tough as leather,' Coll said, winking. 'It can last me to Caer Cadarn and back.

'And you, my lad,' Coll went on cheerfully, though he had not failed to notice Taran's troubled frown, 'I remember a day when an Assistant Pig-Keeper would have been all flash and fire to ride with Lord Gwydion. Now you look as glum as a frostbitten turnip.'

Taran smiled. 'I myself would ride to Annuvin, if Gwydion allowed me. What you say is true, old friend. For the boy I was, this would have been a bold adventure, full of glory. This much have I learned: A man's life weighs more than glory, and a price paid in blood is a heavy reckoning.

'My heart is not easy,' Taran added. 'Long ago, you made your way to Annuvin, to rescue Hen Wen after she had been stolen from you. Tell me: What chance has Gwydion alone in Arawn's realm?'

'No man has better,' said Coll, shouldering the spears. And he was gone from the shed before Taran realized the old warrior had not really answered him at all.

Caer Dallben lay far behind them and the day was darkening when the companions made camp deep in the shadows of the forest.

Eilonwy happily flung herself to the ground. 'It's been long since I've slept on comfortable roots and rocks!' she cried. 'What a pleasant change from goosefeathers!'

Gwydion allowed a fire to be built; and while Coll saw to the mounts, Gurgi opened his wallet of food to share out provisions. For the most part the companions were silent, chilled, and stiff after the long day's journey. King Rhun, however, had lost none of his good spirits. As the travellers huddled closer to the pale flames, Rhun picked up a twig and scratched busily in the earth, covering the ground before him with a spider web of lines.

'About that seawall,' said Rhun. 'I think I see how it went wrong. Yes, exactly so. Now, here's the way to do it.'

From across the fire Taran saw Rhun's eyes brightly eager and on his face the familiar boyish grin. But Rhun, Taran sensed, was no longer the feckless princeling he had known on the Isle of Mona. As Rhun was absorbed in the tasks he had planned, so Taran had been caught up in his own labours at forge, loom, and potter's wheel. And if Rhun had found manhood in ruling a kingdom, Taran had found the same in toiling among the staunch folk of the Free Commots. He watched Rhun with new affection. The King of Mona spoke on and Taran's interest was drawn to the scratchings on the ground. He studied them as Rhun continued. Taran smiled. One thing had not changed, he realized; as usual, the King of Mona's intentions went somewhat beyond the King of Mona's skill.

'I fear your wall may tumble if you build it thus,' Taran said with a kindly laugh. 'See this part here.' He pointed.

'The heavier stones must be sunk deeper. And here . . .'

'Amazing!' exclaimed Rhun, snapping his fingers. 'Quite right! You shall come to Mona and help me finish it!' He began scratching new lines so vigorously he nearly pitched himself into the fire.

'Oh, great and kindly master!' cried Gurgi, who had been listening closely without altogether understanding what the two comrades had been discussing. 'Oh, clever scannings and plannings! Gurgi wishes he, too, had wisdom of wise speakings!'

Gwydion warned them to silence. 'Our fire is risk enough, without adding noise to it. I can only hope Arawn's Huntsmen are not abroad. We are too few to withstand even a handful of them. They are not common warriors,' Gwydion added, seeing Rhun's questioning expression, 'but an evil brotherhood. Slay one of their band, and the strength of the others grows that much greater.'

Taran nodded. 'They are as much to be feared as the Cauldron-Born,' he cautioned Rhun, 'the deathless, voiceless creatures that guard Annuvin. Perhaps more to be feared. The Cauldron-Born cannot be slain, yet their power dwindles if they journey too far, or stay too long beyond Arawn's realm.'

Rhun blinked and Gurgi fell silent, glancing behind him uncomfortably. Memory of the ruthless Cauldron-Born turned Taran's thoughts once more to Hen Wen's prophecy. 'The flame of Dyrnwyn quenched,' Taran murmured. 'Yet how shall Arawn achieve this? For all his power, I will not believe he can even draw the blade.'

'Prophecy is more than the words that shape it,' Gwydion said. 'Seek the meaning that underlies it. For us, the flame of Dyrnwyn will be as good as quenched if Arawn keeps it from my hands. Its power will indeed vanish, for all it may avail us, should the blade be locked forever in his treasure hoard.'

'Treasure?' said Glew, stopping his munching only long

enough to speak the word.

'The Death-Lord's domain is as much a treasure-house as a stronghold of evil,' Gwydion said. 'Long has it been filled with all the fair and useful things Arawn has stolen from Prydain. These treasures do not serve him; his purpose is to deprive, to keep their use from men, to sap our strength by denying us what might yield a richer harvest than any of us here has known.' Gwydion paused. 'Is this not death in but another guise?'

'I have been told,' Taran said, 'the treasure troves of Annuvin hold all that men could wish for. Ploughs, there are said to be, that work of themselves, scythes that reap with no hand to guide them, magical tools and more,' Taran went on. 'For Arawn stole the craft secrets of metalsmiths and potters, the lore of herdsmen and farmers. This knowledge, too, lies locked forever in his hoard.'

Glew sucked his teeth. The morsel of food stayed untouched in his chubby fingers. For a long while he said nothing. At last he cleared his throat. 'I mean to forgive your slights and humiliations. It would not have happened when I was a giant, I assure you. But no matter. I pardon you all. In token of my good will, I too shall journey with you.'

Gwydion looked at him sharply. 'Perhaps you shall,' he said quietly after a time.

'No question of it now!' Fflewddur snorted. 'The little weasel hopes to sniff out something for himself. I can see his nose trembling! I never thought the day would come when I should want him at our side. But I think that's safer than having him at our backs.'

Glew smiled blandly. 'I forgive you, too,' he said.

CHAPTER 4

King Smoit's Castle

At dawn, King Rhun made ready to part from the companions and ride farther westward to Avren Harbour, where he would advise his shipmaster of the change in plans. Fflewddur was to accompany him, for the bard knew the shallow fording places across the river and the swiftest paths on the opposite bank.

Eilonwy had decided to go with them. 'I've forgotten half my embroidery thread in Rhun's ship, and must have it if I'm to finish Hen Wen properly. Neither of you can find it, for I'm not sure myself where it might be. I believe I've left a warmer travelling cloak, too; and a few other things – I don't remember what they are right now, but I'm bound to think of them once I get there.'

Coll grinned and rubbed his bald crown. 'The Princess,' he remarked, 'becomes more the lady in every way.'

'Since I'm not staying on the ship,' said Glew, whose decision of the night before remained unshaken, 'I see no reason to be taken out of my way. I shall follow with Lord Gwydion.'

'That, my puny giant, is where you're wrong,' the bard replied. 'Mount up behind the King of Mona, if he can stand your company, and be quick about it. Don't think I'll let you out of my sight for a moment. Where I go, you go. And the other way around, too, for the matter of that.'

'Surely, Fflewddur,' Taran said, drawing the bard aside, 'Glew can't trouble us. I myself shall watch over him.'

The bard shook his tousled, yellow head. 'No, my friend. I'll be easier in my mind if I see him with my own eyes. And at all times. No, the little weasel is in my charge.

Ride on ahead, and we'll catch up with you on the other side of Avren well before midday.

'I'll be glad to see Smoit again,' Fflewddur added. 'That red-bearded old bear is dear to my heart. We shall feast well at Caer Cadarn, for Smoit eats as bravely as he fights.'

Gwydion had already mounted Melyngar and signalled them to hasten. Fflewddur clapped Taran on the shoulder and ran to climb astride Llyan, who was frisking gaily in the bright, cold sun and pouncing at the tip of her own tail.

King Rhun, Fflewddur, Eilonwy, and Glew soon were out of sight. Bearing westward, Taran rode between Gwydion and Coll, while Gurgi, on his pony, trotted at the rear.

They halted on the far bank of Great Avren. Midday passed without a sign of the other companions. Though Taran was anxious about them, he preferred to believe they had not come to harm. 'Rhun has likely stopped to look at a badger tunnel or anthill,' he said. 'I hope it is no more than that.'

'Never fear,' said Coll. 'Fflewddur will jog him along. They'll be here at any moment.'

Taran sounded his horn, hoping the signal would guide the bard in case Fflewddur had mistaken the path. Still they did not come. Gwydion, having waited as long as he dared, chose to press on to Caer Cadarn. They continued at a brisk pace for the rest of the day.

Taran turned often in his saddle, expecting always to glimpse Rhun and the other companions galloping up behind them, or suddenly to hear the King of Mona's cheerful 'Hallo, hallo!' However, as the day waned, Taran realized that Rhun, a slow horseman at best, was by now outdistanced. Fflewddur, he was sure, would not travel after nightfall.

'They have camped somewhere behind us,' Coll assured Taran. 'Were aught amiss, one of them would have reached us. Fflewddur Fflam knows the way to Smoit's castle. We shall all meet there. And if they seem too long delayed, Smoit will raise a searching party.' The stout warrior put a hand on Taran's shoulder. 'Ease your spirit until there is clear cause for alarm. Or,' he added, with a wink, 'is it the company of Princess Eilonwy you long for?'

'She should not have come with us,' Taran replied, half angrily.

'No doubt,' Coll grinned. 'Yet you were not the one to speak against her.'

Taran grinned back at him. 'As for doing that,' he said, 'I have given it up long since.'

At mid-morning of the following day, Caer Cadarn rose before them, and from a stone tower Smoit's crimson banner with its emblem of a black bear snapped in the wind. The stronghold had been built in a clearing, and the heavy walls jutted like the bearded King's own brows, scarred and pitted by many a battle. Coll, urging Llamrei ahead, shouted to the guards in the name of Gwydion Prince of Don. The massive gates opened and the companions galloped into the courtyard, where men-at-arms tethered the horses and a party of warriors led the way to Smoit's Great Hall.

Gwydion strode quickly down the corridor. Flanked by the guards, Taran, Coll, and Gurgi followed. 'Smoit will be at his meat,' Taran said. 'His breakfast lasts till high noon.' He laughed. 'He says it whets his appetite for the rest of his meals. Gwydion will get no word out of him until we ourselves are stuffed.'

'Yes, yes!' Gurgi cried. 'Gurgi longs for tasty crunchings and munchings!'

'You shall have them, old friend,' Taran answered. 'Be sure of it.'

They entered the Great Hall. At one end stood Smoit's

huge throne, cut from half an oak tree and carved in the shape of a bear with paws upraised on either side.

The man seated there was not King Smoit.

'Magg!' Taran gasped.

Guards fell upon them instantly. Taran's sword was ripped from his belt. With a great cry, Gwydion flung himself against the warriors, but they pressed about him and bore the Prince of Don to his knees. Coll, too, was borne down and a spear pressed against his back. Gurgi yelled in rage and terror. A guard seized him by the scruff of his shaggy neck, buffeting him until the poor creature could barely stagger to his feet.

Magg grinned like a skull. With a slight movement of his skinny fingers, he gestured the warriors to stand away. His grey, pinched face twitched with pleasure. 'Our meeting, Lord Gwydion, is one I did not foresee. My warriors hold Caer Cadarn, but this is an added prize, and a richer one than I had hoped.'

Gwydion's green eyes blazed. 'Have you dared even to enter King Smoit's cantrev? Begone from here before he returns. He shall deal with you less gently than I.'

'You will join King Smoit,' Magg replied. 'Though King I scorn to call this rude cantrev lord.' Magg's thin lips curled. Carelessly he put a hand to his embroidered cloak. Taran saw that Magg's garments were even richer than those the lank-haired man had worn as Chief Steward to the Court of Mona.

'More powerful than Smoit or the King of Mona, more powerful than Queen Achren is my liege lord,' Magg said with a yellow smile. 'And mightier now than the Prince of Don.' He touched the iron chain hanging from his neck and fondled the heavy badge of office. In horror Taran saw it bore the same symbol that was branded on the foreheads of the Huntsmen.

'I serve no lesser liege,' Magg said haughtily, 'than the King of Annuvin, Arawn Death-Lord himself.'

Gwydion's glance did not falter. 'You have found your true master, Magg.'

'When last we parted, Lord Gwydion,' said Magg, 'I believed you dead. It was my joy, later, to learn that you were not.' The Chief Steward licked his lips. 'Seldom is one given to savour his revenge twice, and I was patient until that day we should meet again.

'Patient, yes,' Magg hissed. 'Long I wandered after I sailed from the Isle of Mona. There were those I served humbly, biding my time. One sought even to cast me in a dungeon – I, Magg, who once held a kingdom in his grasp.' The voice of the Chief Steward rose shrilly. His face had gone livid and his eyes started from their sockets. But in a moment he gained control of his trembling hands and sank back on Smoit's throne. Now the words came from his lips as if he were tasting each one.

'At length, I made my way to Annuvin,' Magg said, 'to the very threshold of Dark Gate. Lord Arawn did not know me then, as he knows me now.' Magg nodded in satisfaction. 'There was much he learned from me.

'Lord Arawn knew the history of Dyrnwyn,' Magg continued. 'He knew it had been lost and found again, and that Gwydion Son of Don bore it. But it was I, Magg, who told him how best to gain it.'

'Even your treachery is paltry,' Taran said. 'Late or soon, with or without you, Arawn would have struck on that evil scheme himself.'

'Perhaps,' Magg said slyly. 'Perhaps what he learned from me was less than what I learned from him. For I soon discovered that his power was dangerously balanced. His champion, the Horned King, had long been defeated. Even the Black Crochan, the cauldron that gave him the deathless Cauldron-Born, was shattered.

'Lord Arawn has many secret liegemen among the cantrev kings,' Magg went on. 'He has promised them great riches and domains, and they are sworn to serve him. But his defeats turned them restive. It was I who showed him the means to win stronger allegiance. It was my plan, mine alone that put Dyrnwyn in his hands!

'Word now spreads throughout the cantrevs that Arawn Death-Lord holds the mightiest weapon in Prydain. He knows its secrets, far better than you do, Lord Gwydion, and knows he cannot be defeated. His liegemen rejoice, for they will soon taste victory. Other warlords will rally to his banner and his host of warriors will grow.

'I, Magg, have wrought this!' the Chief Steward cried. 'I, Magg, second only to the Death-Lord! I, Magg, speak in his name. I am his trusted emissary, and I ride from realm to realm, gathering armies to destroy the Sons of Don and those who give them allegiance. All Prydain will be his dominion. And those who stand against him – if Lord Arawn choose to be merciful, he will slay them. His Huntsmen will drink their blood. The others will grovel in bondage forever!'

Magg's eyes gleamed, his pale brow glistened and his cheeks quivered violently. 'For this,' he hissed, 'for this, Lord Arawn has sworn to me by every oath: one day I, Magg, will wear the Iron Crown of Annuvin!'

'You are as much a fool as a traitor,' Gwydion said, in a hard voice. 'And doubly so. First, to believe Arawn. Then to believe King Smoit would heed your serpent's words. Have you slain him? Only dead would he listen to you.'

'Smoit lives,' answered Magg. 'I care nothing for his allegiance. I seek the fealty of the liegemen in his cantrev. Smoit shall order them, in his name, to serve my cause.'

'King Smoit would sooner have his tongue ripped out,' Taran cried.

'And so perhaps he shall,' replied Magg. 'Mute, he will serve me as well. He will ride with me and I will speak on his behalf better than he would speak on his own. Yet,' he mused, 'I would prefer the commands to come from his lips rather than mine. There are ways to loosen his tongue instead of cutting it from his head. Some have already been tried.'

Magg narrowed his eyes. 'The best means stand before me now. You, Lord Gwydion. And you, Pig-Keeper. Speak with him. Let Smoit see that he must yield to me.' Magg smiled crookedly. 'Your lives hang on it.'

The Chief Steward moved his head slightly. The guards stepped forward.

Roughly the companions were prodded from the Great Hall. Shock and despair so filled Taran that he was hardly aware of the passage they were led down. The warriors halted. One flung open a heavy door. Others thrust the companions into a narrow chamber. The door grated shut and darkness swallowed them.

As they groped blindly Taran stumbled on a prostrate form that stirred and bellowed loudly.

'My body and blood!' roared the voice of King Smoit, and Taran was grappled by a pair of bone-cracking arms. 'Are you come again, Magg? You'll not take me alive!'

Taran was nearly smothered and crushed before Gwydion called out his name and the names of the companions. Smoit's grip loosened and Taran felt a huge hand on his face.

'My pulse, and so it is!' cried Smoit, as the companions gathered around him. 'The Pig-Keeper! Lord Gwydion! Coll! I'd know that bald pate of yours anywhere!' His hand fell on Gurgi's dishevelled head. 'And the little – whatever-it-is! Well met, my friends!' Smoit groaned heavily. 'And ill met, too. How has that simpering sop trapped you? The lard-lipped, squirming lackey has snared us all!'

Gwydion quickly told Smoit what had befallen them.

The red-bearded King growled furiously. 'Magg caught me as easily as he did you. Yesterday I was at breakfast, and had barely set myself to my meat, when my steward brought tidings that a messenger from Lord Goryon sought words with me. Now then, I knew Goryon was at odds with Lord Gast. A matter of cow-stealing, as usual. Ah, will the cantrev lords of Prydain ever stop their endless bickering! However, since I'd heard Gast's side of it, I deemed I should listen to Goryon's.'

Smoit snorted and struck his massive thigh. 'Before I could swallow another mouthful, Magg's warriors were about me. My heart and liver! Some of them will remember Smoit! Another troop had lain in ambush and stormed through the gate.' Smoit put his head in his hands. 'Of my own men those not slain are prisoned in the guardrooms and armouries.'

'And you,' Taran asked anxiously, 'are you in pain? Magg spoke of torture.'

'Pain!' Smoit bellowed so loudly, the chamber echoed. 'Torture? I suffer till I sweat. But not at the hands of that long-nosed worm! My skin's thick enough. Let Magg break his teeth on my bones! He troubles me no more than a fleabite or bramble scratch. Why, I've taken worse in a friendly scuffle.

'Do you speak of pain?' Smoit stormed on. 'By every hair of my beard, I swear it pains me more than hot iron to be mewed up in my own castle! My own stronghold, and a captive in it! Gulled in my own Great Hall! My own food and drink snatched from my lips, and my breakfast ruined. Torment? Worse than that! It's enough to sour a man out of his appetite!'

Gwydion and Coll, meantime, had made their way to the walls and, as far as the dim light allowed, were hastily examining them for any sign of weakness. Taran, now that his eyes had grown a little more used to the gloom, feared that his companions were wasting their labours. The cell was windowless; what little air reached them came only from the tiny, heavily barred grating of the door. The floor was not of hard-packed earth, but of flagstones joined with barely a crack.

Smoit himself, realizing the purpose of Gwydion's efforts, shook his head and pounded his iron-shod boots on the floor. 'Solid as a mountain,' he cried. 'I know, for I built it myself. Spare yourself pains, my friends. It will crack no sooner than I!'

'How far below ground is this dungeon?' Taran asked, though his hope for escape was fading with each moment. 'Is there no way we can dig upward?'

'Dungeon?' cried Smoit. 'I've no more dungeons in Caer Cadarn. When last we met, you called my dungeons useless. Right you were, and so I walled them up. Now there's no wrongdoing in my cantrev that I can't settle quicker and easier with a few words. Who hears my voice will mend his ways – or mend his head. Dungeons indeed! It's a spare larder.

'Would that I had stocked it as solidly as I built it,' groaned Smoit. 'Let Magg bring his irons and lashes. I'll heed them not a bit in the midst of this other fiendish torment. The larder lies beside my scullery! I've not lined my belly for two days. Two years, it feels! The vile traitor has not left off his feasting! And for me? No more than the sniff of it! Oh, he shall pay for this,' Smoit cried. 'I'll beg him one thing only: a moment with my paws about his skinny neck. I'll squeeze out all the puddings and pastries he's ever gobbled!'

Gwydion had come to crouch beside the furious Smoit. 'Your larder may be our tomb,' he said grimly. 'Not only for ourselves,' he added. 'Fflewddur Fflam leads our companions here. Magg's jaws will close on them as tightly as they are closed on us.'

CHAPTER 5

The Watcher

Although Fflewddur Fflam quickly led Eilonwy, King Rhun, and Glew to Avren Harbour, their return from the ship was less rapid. First, the King of Mona managed, against all likelihood, to tumble over his horse's neck when the dapple grey halted to drink at the riverbank. The ducking thoroughly soaked the unlucky King but did not dampen his spirits. However, Rhun's sword belt had come undone and the blade had sunk in the shallows. Rhun being unable to fish it out again because he had also got himself tangled in the steed's harness, Fflewddur was obliged to plunge into the river for the weapon. Glew now protested bitterly against riding behind the sopping bard.

'Walk, then, little weasel!' cried Fflewddur, shivering and beating his arms against his sides. 'By my choice, in the opposite direction!'

Glew only sniffed haughtily and refused to budge.

Eilonwy stamped her foot with impatience. 'Will you make haste, all of you! We came to look after Lord Gwydion, and we can hardly look after ourselves.'

The former giant consented to ride behind the Princess on Lluagor, and they set out once more. Llyan, however, had suddenly taken it into her head to be playful. She lunged forward on her huge padded paws and spun joyfully about while the desperate bard clung to her tawny neck. It was all Fflewddur could do to keep Llyan from rolling on to her back with himself astride her.

'She – seldom does this,' shouted the breathless bard, while Llyan, with great leaps, circled the companions. 'She's really been – quite well – behaved! No use – scolding her. Makes no – difference!'

At last Fflewddur was forced, with difficulty, to unsling his harp and pluck out a melody until Llyan grew calm again.

Soon after midday the bard heard the faint, distant notes of Taran's horn. 'They're worried over us,' Fflewddur said. 'I hope we shall soon rejoin them.'

The companions pressed on as quickly as they could, but the distance between the two bands increased rather than dwindled, and at nightfall they wearily halted and slept.

A fresh morning start brought them, according to Fflweddur's reckoning, less than half a day behind the others. King Rhun, more than ever eager to reach Caer Cadarn, urged all speed from the dapple grey; but the mare's pace was much slower than Llyan's and Lluagor's; Eilonwy and Fflewddur continually had to rein in their mounts.

Midway through the afternoon, King Rhun gave a glad cry. Caer Cadarn lay only a little distance off. They saw Smoit's crimson banner clearly beyond the trees. The companions were about to hasten onward, but Eilonwy frowned and looked once more at the fluttering standard.

'How odd,' the Princess remarked. 'I see King Smoit's jolly old bear. But Gwydion surely must be there by now, and I don't set the banner of the House of Don. Queen Teleria taught me it is courtesy for a cantrev noble to fly the Golden Sunburst of Don when one of the Royal House visits him.'

'True enough in ordinary circumstances,' agreed Fflewddur. 'But I doubt, at this point, that Gwydion wants anyone to know where he is. He's told Smoit to put aside the formalities. A most sensible precaution.'

'Yes, of course,' Eilonwy replied. 'I shouldn't have thought of that. How clever of you, Fflewddur.'

The bard beamed happily. 'Experience, Princess. Long experience. But never fear. Such wisdom will come to you, in time.'

'Even so,' Eilonwy said, as they rode farther. 'It's curious the gates are closed. Knowing King Smoit, you might suppose they'd be flung wide open and a guard of honour waiting for us, with King Smoit himself at their head.'

Fflewddur waved the girl's remark aside. 'Not a bit of it. Lord Gwydion follows a path of danger, not a round of festivals. I understand how such things are done. I've been on a thousand secret missions – ah, well, perhaps one or two,' he added hastily. 'I fully expected Caer Cadarn would be buckled, bolted, and shut tight as an oyster.'

'Yes,' Eilonwy said, 'I'm sure you know more about such things than I.' She hesitated, straining her eyes to take in the castle, which the companions were now rapidly approaching. 'But King Smoit isn't at war with his neighbours, as far as I've heard. Two watchmen on the walls would be more than enough. Does he need a whole party of bowmen?'

'Naturally,' replied Fflewddur, 'to protect Lord Gwydion.'

'But if no one is to know Gwydion's there – ' Eilonwy persisted.

'Great Belin!' cried the bard, reining up Llyan. 'Now you make my head spin. Are you trying to say Gwydion's not at Caer Cadarn? If he's not, we shall soon find out. And if he is, we shall find that out as well.' Fflewddur scratched his spiky yellow head. 'But if he's not, then, why not? What could have happened? And if he is, then there's nothing to worry about. Yet, if he isn't . . . Oh, drat and blast, you've turned me queasy. I don't understand . . .'

'I don't understand, either,' Eilonwy answered. 'All I know – and I don't even *know* it – is that, well, I can't explain. I – I see the castle all crooked-wise – no, not *see*. Taste? No . . . Well, no matter,' she burst out, 'I've come all over chills and creeps and I don't like it. You've had experience, I don't doubt. But my ancestors were enchantresses, every one. And so should I have been, if I hadn't chosen to be a young lady.'

'Enchantments!' the bard muttered uncomfortably. 'Stay away from them. Don't meddle. It's also been my experience they never turn out well.'

'I say,' put in Rhun, 'if the Princess feels there's something amiss, I'll be glad to ride ahead and find out. I shall frankly rap on the gates and demand to know.'

'Nonsense,' replied Fflewddur. 'I'm quite sure all is well.' A harp string broke and twanged loudly. The bard cleared his throat. 'No, I'm not sure at all. Oh, bother it! The girl has put an idea in my head and I can't shake it out. One way, everything looks all right; the other way, it looks all wrong.

'Just to ease your mind – ah, *my* mind, that is,' Fflewddur told the Princess, 'I shall be the one to find out. As a wandering bard I can go and come as I please. If anything's wrong, none will suspect me. If not, there's no harm done. Stay here. I'll be back directly. We shall laugh over this at King Smoit's table,' he added, but without great assurance.

The bard dismounted, considering it wiser not to draw attention by riding Llyan. 'And you try no mischief,' he warned Glew. 'I hate to let you out of my sight, but Llyan will keep an eye on you. Hers are sharper than mine. So are her teeth.'

On foot, the bard made his way to the castle. After a time, Eilonwy saw the gates swing open and Fflewddur disappear within. Then all was silent.

By nightfall the girl had grown seriously alarmed, for there had been no further sign from the bard. The companions had concealed themselves in a thicket, awaiting Fflewddur's return, but now Eilonwy rose and anxiously faced the castle. 'It *is* all wrong!' she cried, taking an impatient stride forward.

King Rhun drew her back. 'Perhaps not,' he said. 'Why, he'd have come back immediately to warn us if there was. No doubt Smoit's giving him supper, or . . .' Rhun loosened his sword in its sheath. 'I'll go and see.'

'No, you shall not!' Eilonwy cried. 'I should have gone in the first place. Oh, I should have known better than to let myself be put off by anyone.'

Rhun, however, insisted. Eilonwy refused. The heated, although whispered, dispute that followed was interrupted by the sudden arival of the bard himself. Breathless and gasping, he stumbled into the thicket.

'It's Magg! He has them all!' Fflewddur's voice was pale as his face in the moonlight. 'Caught! Trapped!'

Eilonwy and Rhun listened aghast at what Fflewddur had learned. 'The warriors themselves don't know who the prisoners are, only that there are four with Smoit locked up for treachery. Treachery indeed! They've been made to swallow some kind of tale! The game goes deeper than that. What it is, I couldn't discover. I think the guards had orders to lay hold of everybody entering the castle. Luckily, those orders didn't seem to apply to wandering bards. It's so usual for a bard to drift in and sing for his supper that the warriors never gave it a second thought, though they did keep an eye on me and wouldn't let me near Smoit's Great Hall or the larder where they've put the prisoners. But I caught a glimpse of Magg. Oh, the sneering, smirking spider! If only I could have run him through then and there!

'The warriors kept me harping until I thought my fingers would drop off,' he hurriedly concluded. 'Otherwise I should have been back long ago. I didn't stop, or they'd have smelled a rat. And there's a rat to be smelled!' he cried furiously.

'How shall we rescue them?' Eilonwy demanded. 'I don't care *why* they're locked up. Ask later. First get them out.'

'We can't,' Fflewddur answered in despair. 'Impossible. Not with only four of us. And that's four counting Glew, who can't be counted at all.'

Glew snorted. Usually the little man took no interest in anything not bearing directly on himself; now, his face was agitated. 'When I was a giant I could have torn the walls down.'

'Bother when you were a giant,' snapped Fflewddur. 'You're not one now. Our only hope is to go farther into the cantrev, tell one of the cantrev lords what's happened, and have him rally an attack force.'

'It will take too long,' cried Eilonwy. 'Oh, do be quiet and let me think!'

The girl strode again to the clearing, and turned her eyes defiantly towards the castle which flung its own dark defiance against her. Her mind raced, but with no clear plan. With half a sob and half a cry of anger she was about to turn away. A movement against a nearby tree caught her glance. She halted a moment. Not daring to turn her head, from a corner of her eye she grew aware of a strange, humped shadow, motionless now. As if to continue on her path she walked seemingly in the direction of Fflewddur and Rhun, but edged little by little towards the tree.

Suddenly, quick as Llyan, she leaped upon the humped figure. Part of it went rolling in one direction, and the rest of it set up a muffled shrieking. Eilonwy pummelled, kicked, and scratched. Fflewddur and King Rhun were at her side in an instant. The bard seized one end of the flailing shape, King Rhun the other.

Eilonwy drew back and quickly took the bauble from her cloak. As she cupped it in her hand the sphere began to glow. She held it closer to the struggling form. Her jaw dropped. The golden beams shone on a pale, wrinkled face with a long, drooping nose and mournful mouth. Wild wisps of cobweb-like hair floated above a pair of eyes that blinked wretchedly and tearfully.

'Gwystyl!' Eilonwy cried. 'Gwystyl of the Fair Folk!'

The bard loosened his grasp. Gwystyl sat up, rubbed his skinny arms, then climbed to his feet and pulled his cloak defensively about him.

'How nice to see you again,' he mumbled. 'A pleasure, believe me. I've thought of you often. Goodbye. Now I really must be on my way.'

'Help us!' Eilonwy pleaded. 'Gwystyl, we beg you. Our companions are prisoned in Smoit's castle.'

Gwystyl clapped his hands to his head. His face puckered miserably. 'Please, please,' he moaned, 'don't shout. I'm not well, I'm not up to being shouted at this evening. And would you mind not shining that light in my eyes? No, no, it's really too much. It's more than enough to be pulled down and sat on, without people picking at you and bellowing and half-blinding you. As I was saying – yes, it's been delightful running into you. Of course I'll be glad to help. But perhaps another time. When we're not feeling so upset.'

'Gwystyl, don't you understand?' Eilonwy cried. 'Have you been listening to me at all? Another time? You must help us *now*. Gwydion's sword is stolen. Dyrnwyn is gone! Arawn has it! Don't you see what that means? This is the most terrible thing that could ever happen. How can Gwydion get the sword back if he's locked up, with his own life in danger? And Taran – and Coll and Gurgi . . .'

'Some days are like that,' Gwystyl sighed. 'And what's to be done about it? Nothing, alas, but hope things will brighten, which they very likely won't. But, there you are, it's all one can do. Yes, I know Dyrnwyn is stolen. A sad misfortune, a disheartening state of affairs.'

'You already know?' exclaimed the bard. 'Great Belin, speak up! Where is it?'

'No idea whatever,' Gwystyl gasped in such desperation that Eilonwy believed the melancholy creature indeed spoke the truth. 'But that's the least of my concerns. What's happening around Annuvin – ' He shuddered and patted his pale forehead with a trembling hand. 'The Huntsmen are gathering. The Cauldron-Born have come out, whole troops of them. I've never seen so many Cauldron-Born altogether in my life. It's enough to make a decent person take to his bed.

'And that's not the half of it,' Gwystyl choked. 'Some of the cantrev lords are rallying their battle hosts, and their war leaders hold council in Annuvin. The place is thick with warriors, inside, outside, wherever you look. I was even afraid they'd discover my tunnels and spy holes. These days, I'm the Fair Folk's only watcher close to Annuvin – more's the pity, for the work piles up so.

'Believe me,' Gwystyl hurried on, 'your friends are better off where they are. Much safer. No matter what's being done to them, it can't be worse than stumbling into that hornet's nest. If, by chance, you do see them again, give them all my fondest greetings. I'm sorry, terribly sorry I can't stay longer. I'm on my way to the realm of the Fair Folk; King Eiddileg should learn of these matters without delay.'

'If King Eiddileg learns you wouldn't help us,' Eilonwy indignantly burst out, 'you'll wish you'd never left your waypost.'

'It's a long, hard journey,' Gwystyl sighed and shook his cobwebby head, completely ignoring Eilonwy's remark. 'I shall have to go above ground every step. Eiddileg will want to know all that's stirring along the way. I'm not up to journeying, not in my condition, not in this weather, least of all. Summer would have been much more agreeable. But – there's nothing to be done about that. Goodbye, farewell. Always a pleasure.'

Gwystyl stooped to pick up a bundle almost as large as himself. Eilonwy clutched him by the arm.

'Oh, no you don't!' she cried. 'You'll warn King Eiddileg after we free our companions. Don't try to deceive me, Gwystyl of the Fair Folk. You're cleverer than you care to let on. But if you won't give us your help, I know how to get it. I'll squeeze it out of you!'

The girl made a movement to seize the creature about his neck. Gwystyl gave a heartrending sob and feebly endeavoured to defend himself.

'No squeezing! No, please. I couldn't face up to it. Not now. Goodbye. Really, this is hardly the moment . . .'

Fflewddur, meanwhile, was staring curiously at the bundle. The large, lumpy pack had rolled near a bush when Eilonwy had first set upon Gwystyl and it lay partly undone on the ground.

'Great Belin,' murmured the bard, 'what a tangle of oddments. Worse than a snail with his household on his back.'

'It's nothing, nothing at all,' Gwystyl said hurriedly. 'A few little comforts to ease the journey.'

'We might do better squeezing this pack instead of Gwystyl's neck,' remarked Fflewddur, who had dropped to his knees and had begun to rummage through the bundle. 'There may be something here more useful than Gwystyl himself.'

'Take whatever you please,' Gwystyl urged, as Eilonwy turned the bauble's glow upon the heap. 'Have it all, if you like. It makes no difference. I shall manage without it. Painfully, but I shall manage.'

King Rhun knelt beside the bard, who thus far had pulled out a few mended sheepskin-lined jackets and several ragged cloaks. 'Amazing!' Rhun cried. 'Here's a bird's nest!'

'Yes,' Gwystyl sighed. 'Take it. It's something I've been saving; you never know when the need for one might arise. But it's yours now.'

'No thank you,' muttered the bard. 'I shouldn't want to deprive you.'

Their hasty search next revealed water flasks both empty and full, a walking staff in jointed sections allowing it to be folded up, a cushion with an extra bag of feathers, two lengths of rope, some fishing lines and large hooks, two tents, a number of iron wedges and a crooked iron bar, a wide piece of soft leather which, as Gwystyl reluctantly explained, could be set about a willow frame to serve as a small boat; several large bunches of dried vegetables and herbs, and numerous bags of lichens in all colours.

'For my condition,' Gwystyl mumbled, indicating the latter. 'The dampness and clamminess around Annuvin is dreadful. These don't help at all, but they're better than nothing. However, you're welcome . . .'

The bard shook his head in despair. 'Useless rubbish. We might borrow the ropes and fish hooks. But, for whatever good they may do us . . .'

'Gwystyl,' Eilonwy cried angrily, 'all your tents and boats and walking staves won't answer! Oh, I could squeeze you anyway, for I'm out of patience with you. Begone! Yes, goodbye indeed!'

Gwystyl, heaving huge sighs of relief, rapidly began packing his bundle. As he hoisted it to his shoulder, from his cloak fell a small sack which he tried desperately to recover.

'I say, what's this?' asked Rhun, who had already gathered up the bag and was about to hand it to the agitated creature.

'Eggs,' mumbled Gwystyl.

'Lucky they weren't smashed when you took your tumble,' said Rhun cheerfully. 'Perhaps we'd better have a look,' he added, untying the string around the mouth of the bag.

'Eggs!' said Fflewddur, brightening somewhat. 'I shouldn't mind eating one or two of them. I've had no food since midday – those warriors kept me harping, but they took no pains to feed me. Come, old fellow, I'm starved enough to crack one now and swallow it raw!'

'No, no!' squealed Gwystyl, snatching for the bag. 'Don't do it! They're not eggs. Not eggs, at all!'

'I say, they surely look like it,' remarked Rhun, peering into the sack. 'If they aren't, then what are they?'

Gwystyl choked, then went into a fit of violent coughing and sighing before he answered. 'Smoke,' he gasped.

CHAPTER 6

A Clutch of Eggs

'Amazing!' cried King Rhun. 'Smoke made of egg! Or is it egg made of smoke?'

'The smoke is inside,' Gwystyl muttered, drawing his shabby cloak about him. 'Goodbye. Crack the shell and the smoke comes out – in considerable quantity. Keep them. A gift. If you should ever see Lord Gwydion, warn him to shun Annuvin at all cost. For myself, I'm glad to leave the place behind me and hope never to return. Goodbye.'

'Gwystyl,' Eilonwy said sharply, gripping the melancholy creature's arm, 'something tells me there's more to that cloak of yours than meets the eye. What else have you hidden away? The truth, now. Or I promise you such squeezing . . .'

'Nothing!' Gwystyl choked. Despite the chill wind, he had begun perspiring heavily. His cobwebby hair hung limp and his brow dripped as if he had been caught in a downpour. 'Nothing, that is, but a few little personal things of my own. Odds and ends. If they interest you, by all means . . .'

Gwystyl raised his arms and spread his cloak on either side, a gesture which made him resemble a long-nosed and dismal bat. He sighed and groaned miserably while the companions stared in surprise.

'Odd indeed!' said Fflewddur. 'And, Great Belin, there's no end of them!'

Neatly attached within the folds of the cloak hung a dozen cloth sacks, mesh bags, and carefully wrapped packets. Most of them seemed to contain clutches of eggs of the sort Fflewddur had narrowly avoided eating.

Gwystyl pulled off one of the mesh bags and handed it to Eilonwy.

'I say,' exclaimed Rhun. 'First eggs, now mushrooms!'

As far as the Princess could see, the mesh bag held nothing more than a few large, brown-speckled toadstools; but Gwystyl waved his arm desperately, and moaned.

'Beware, beware! Break them and they'll singe your hair off! They make a handsome puff of flame, if you should ever need such a thing. Take them all. I'm well pleased to be rid of them.'

'It *is* what we need!' Eilonwy cried. 'Gwystyl, forgive me for threatening to squeeze you.' She turned to the bard who was examining the sacks with an air of uneasiness. 'Yes! These will help us. Now, if we can find a way into the castle . . .'

'My dear Princess,' replied Fflewddur, 'a Fflam is dauntless, but I hardly think it practical, overcoming a stronghold with little more than eggs and mushrooms in our hands, even eggs and mushrooms of this particular sort. And yet . . .' He hesitated, then snapped his fingers. 'Great Belin, we might pull it off at that! Wait! I'm beginning to see the possibilities.'

Gwystyl, meantime, had unfastened the remaining packets from his voluminous cloak. 'Here,' he sighed, 'since you have most of them, you might as well have the rest. All of it. Go on, it makes no difference to me now.'

The packets which Gwystyl held out in a trembling hand were filled with a quantity of what appeared to be dark, powdery earth. 'Put this on your feet, and no one can see your tracks – that is, if someone's looking for your tracks. That's really what it's for. But if you throw it into someone's eyes, they can't see anything at all – for a short while at least.'

'Better and better!' cried Fflewddur. 'We'll have our friends out of the spider's clutches in no time. A daring deed! Clouds of smoke! Billows of fire! Blinding powder!

And a Fflam to the rescue! That will give the bards something to sing about. Ah – tell me, old fellow,' he added uneasily to Gwystyl, 'you're quite sure those mushrooms work?'

The companions hurriedly returned to the cover of the thicket to set their plans. Gwystyl, after much coaxing and cajoling, as well as hints of further squeezing and suggestions of King Eiddileg's displeasure, at last agreed – with many a racking sigh and moan – to help in the rescue. The bard was eager to begin immediately.

'In my long experience,' Fflewddur said, 'I've found it best to go at this kind of business head-on. First, I shall return to the castle. Since the warriors know me, they'll open the gates without a second thought. Under my cloak I'll have Gwystyl's eggs and mushrooms. Directly the gates are open – clouds of smoke, a blast of fire! The rest of you will be lurking behind me in the shadows. At my signal, we all rush in, swords drawn, shouting at the top of our voices!'

'Amazing!' put in Rhun. 'It can't fail.' The King of Mona frowned. 'On the other hand, it would almost seem – not that I know anything about these matters – we'd be rushing into our own smoke and fire. I mean to say, the warriors couldn't see us; but neither could we see them.'

Fflewddur shook his head in disagreement. 'Believe me, my friend, this is the best and quickest way. I've rescued more captives than I have fingers on my hands.' The harp tensed and shuddered, and a number of strings would have given way had not Fflewddur added in the same breath: '*Planned* to rescue, that is. I've never, in strict point of fact, actually done so.'

'Rhun is right,' Eilonwy declared. 'It would be worse than stumbling over your own feet. Besides, we'd be risking everything at one go. No, we must have a better plan than that.'

King Rhun beamed, surprised and delighted that his words had found agreement. He blinked his pale blue eyes, grinned shyly, and ventured to raise his voice once more. 'I suddenly think of the seawall I've been rebuilding,' he began, in some hesitation. 'I mean, starting it from both ends. Unfortunately, it didn't turn out quite as I had hoped. But the *idea* was a good one. Now, if we might try the same kind of thing. Not building a wall, of course. I mean going at Caer Cadarn from different ways.'

Fflewddur shrugged, not a little crestfallen that his own suggestion had been dismissed.

But Eilonwy nodded. 'Yes. It's the only sensible thing.'

Glew snorted. 'The only sensible thing is to get an army behind you. When I was a giant, I'd have been willing to help you. But I mean to have no part in this scheme.'

The little man was about to say more, but a glance from the bard silenced him. 'Never fear,' said Fflewddur. 'You and I will be together at every moment. You'll be in good hands.'

'Now, then,' broke in Rhun, impatient to speak again. 'There are five of us. Some should climb over the rear wall, the others enter at the gate.' The young King rose to his feet and his eyes flashed eagerly. 'Fflewddur Fflam shall have the gates opened. Then, while the others attack from the far wall, I shall ride straight through the gates.'

Rhun's hand had gone to his sword. His head was thrown back and he stood before the companions as proudly as if all the Kings of Mona were at his side. He spoke on, firmly and clearly, with such joyful enthusiasm that Eilonwy had no heart to stop him.

But at last she interrupted. 'Rhun, I'm sorry,' Eilonwy said. 'But – and I think Fflewddur will agree with me – you will serve better if you stay out of the actual fighting unless it's absolutely necessary. That way, you'll be on hand when you're needed, but it won't be quite so dangerous for you.'

Rhun's face clouded with disappointment and dismay. 'But, I say . . .'

'You're not a Prince any more,' Eilonwy added, before Rhun could continue his protest. 'You're King of Mona. Your life isn't altogether your own, don't you see? You have a whole realm of people to think of, and we shan't let you take any more risks than you have to. You'll be in far too much danger as it is. If Queen Teleria could have guessed the way things would turn out,' Eilonwy added, 'you wouldn't have sailed to Caer Dallben in the first place.'

'I don't see what my mother has to do with it,' cried Rhun. 'I'm sure my father would have wanted . . .'

'Your father understood what it means to be a king,' Eilonwy said gently. 'You must learn as well as he did.'

'Taran of Caer Dallben saved my life on Mona,' Rhun said urgently. 'I am in his debt, and it is a debt that I alone can pay.'

'You owe another kind of debt to the fisher folk of Mona,' Eilonwy replied. 'And theirs is the greater claim.'

Rhun turned away and sat dejectedly on a hummock, his sword trailing at his side. Fflewddur gave him an encouraging clap on the shoulder.

'Don't despair,' said the bard. 'If our friend Gwystyl's eggs and mushrooms fail, you'll have more than your share of trouble. So will we all.'

It was nearly dawn and bitter cold when the little band left the concealment of the thicket and moved stealthily towards the lightless castle. Each carried a share of Gwystyl's mushrooms and eggs, and a packet of his black, loamy powder. Making a wide circle, they now approached Caer Cadarn from its darkest, most shadowed side.

'Remember the plan,' Fflewddur warned under his breath. 'It must go exactly as we set it. When we are all in position, Gwystyl is to pop open one of those famous mushrooms of his; the fire should draw the guards to the rear of the courtyard. That will be your signal,' he said to Eilonwy and Rhun. 'Then – and not before, mind you – be ready to force the gates open as soon as possible, for I imagine we shall be rather in a hurry to get out. At the same time, I'll free Smoit's men locked up in the guard-room. They'll help you if you need them, while I make my way to the larder and loose our friends. We must hope that villainous spider hasn't already taken them away somewhere. If he has, well, we shall have to make new plans on the spot.

'And you, old fellow,' Fflewddur added to Gwystyl, as the dark walls loomed ahead, 'I think it's time for you to do as you promised.'

Gwystyl sighed heavily and his mouth drooped more wretchedly than ever. 'I'm not up to climbing, not today. If only you could have waited. Next week, perhaps. Or when the weather turns better. Well, no matter. There's little a person can do about it.'

Still shaking his head dubiously, the gloomy creature set down the coils of rope he carried over his shoulder. The large fish hooks, taken from his bundle, he now attached at various angles to the end of a slender line. Fascinated, King Rhun watched as Gwystyl with a deft movement flung the line into the air. From the parapet high above came a faint rasping sound, then a dry click as the hooks caught on a projecting stone. Gwystyl tugged at the cord and slung the remaining coils of rope about his neck.

'I say,' Rhun whispered, 'will that fishing line hold you?'

Gwystyl sighed and looked mournfully at him. 'I doubt it.'

Nevertheless, mumbling and moaning, he quickly hoisted himself into the air, hanging an instant before his feet found the stones of the wall. Pulling himself up on the line and scrabbling with his feet against the sheer side of the castle, Gwystyl was soon out of sight.

'Amazing!' cried Rhun.

The bard frantically cautioned him to silence.

A moment later the fishing line was hauled up and the end of one of the heavier ropes came swinging down. The bard lifted Glew, who was protesting as loudly as he dared, and boosted him on to the dangling cord.

'Up you go,' Fflewddur muttered. 'I'll be right behind you.'

Rhun followed, as the bard and the former giant disappeared into the shadows. Eilonwy seized the rope and felt herself rapidly drawn aloft. She swung herself over the parapet and dropped to a projecting ledge. Gwystyl had already scuttled towards the rear of the castle. Fflewddur and Glew slid into the darkness below. King Rhun grinned at Eilonwy and crouched against the cold stones.

The moon was down; the sky had turned black. Amid the shadows of the silent buildings, the stables, and the long dark mass which Eilonwy guessed to be Smoit's Great Hall, the low flames of a watch fire gleamed. Farther along the parapet, in the direction of the gates, the figures of the guards stood motionless, drowsing.

'I say, it's dark enough!' Rhun whispered cheerfully. 'We shan't need Gwystyl's powder, at this rate. I can hardly see as it is.'

Eilonwy turned her eyes in the direction Gwystyl had taken, waiting from one endless moment to the next for the signal. Rhun was tensed, ready to fling himself down the rope.

A shout rang from the courtyard. At the same instant, a cloud of crimson flame burst in the shadows of the Great Hall.

Eilonwy jumped to her feet. 'Something's amiss!' she cried. 'Fflewddur attacks too soon!'

It was only then that she saw a burst of fire at the far

end of the castle. More shouts of alarm rose above the clatter of racing footsteps. But the warriors, Eilonwy saw with sinking heart, ran not to Gwystyl's false attack but to the Great Hall. The courtyard seethed with shadows. Torches sprang to light.

'Quickly!' Eilonwy shouted. 'The gates!'

Rhun swung from the ledge. Eilonwy was about to follow him when she glimpsed a bowman at one of the guard posts on the wall. He raced towards her, then halted to take aim.

Hastily, Eilonwy drew a mushroom from her cloak and flung it at the warrior. It fell short and split against the stones; fire spurted, blinding her. The flames leaped in a roaring, searing cloud. The bowman shouted in terror and staggered back. His arrow whistled past her head.

The girl seized the rope and dropped into the courtyard below.

CHAPTER 7

The King of Mona

In the larder which had become a prison, Gurgi was first to hear the shouts of alarm. Though muffled by the heavy walls, the cries brought him to his feet before the other companions were aware of the tumult beyond their cell. All night, fearing the arrival of Magg from one moment to the next, they had vainly sought escape. Exhausted from their efforts, they dozed fitfully by turns; hoping only to sell their lives dearly when the guards at last came for them.

'Fightings and smitings!' Gurgi cried. 'Is it for weary tired captives? Yes, yes, it must be! Yes, we are here!' He ran to the door and began shouting through the iron grating.

Now Taran heard what seemed to be a clash of swords. Coll and King Smoit were quickly beside him. Gwydion had already reached the door in two strides and drew away the excited Gurgi.

'Beware,' Gwydion sharply warned. 'Fflewddur Fflam may have found a way to free us, but if the castle is aroused, Magg may take our lives before our comrades can save us.'

Footsteps rang outside, the lock of the heavy door began to rattle, and the companions fell back, crouched and ready to set upon their captors. The door was flung open. Into the cell burst Eilonwy.

'Follow me!' she cried. In one upraised hand she held the brightly glowing bauble; and with the other, pulled a sack from her belt. 'Take these. The mushrooms are fire, the eggs are smoke. Throw them at anyone who attacks you. And this powder – it will blind them.

'I couldn't find weapons,' she hurried on. 'I've set Smoit's warriors free, but Fflewddur's trapped in the courtyard. Everything's gone wrong. Our plan has failed!'

Smoit, bellowing in rage, dashed to the door. 'Away with your toadstools and rooster eggs!' he roared. 'My hands are all I need to wring a traitor's neck!'

Gwydion sprang through the doorway. With Coll and Gurgi behind him, Taran sped after Eilonwy. From the corridors of the Great Hall, Taran raced into what was neither daylight nor darkness. Huge billows of dense, white smoke rose in the courtyard, blotting out the dawn sky. Like swaying, twisting waves, they shifted as the wind caught them, then flooded back in an impenetrable tide. Here and there roaring columns of fire writhed through the smoke.

Losing sight of Eilonwy, Taran plunged into the swirling clouds. A warrior brought up his sword and slashed at him. Taran stumbled to escape the blow. With outflung hand he cast his small store of powder in the man's face. The warrior fell back as if stunned; his wide-open eyes stared blankly at nothing. Taran snatched the blade from the baffled guard and raced on.

'A Smoit! A Smoit!' The red-bearded King's war cry rang from the stables. Before smoke filled his eyes again, Taran caught a fleeting glimpse of the furious Smoit, armed with a huge scythe and laying about him like a bear turned harvester.

The luckless Gurgi, however, had stumbled with his eggs still clutched in his hands. Smoke poured over him. For an instant all Taran could see of him was a pair of waving, hairy arms before these, too, vanished in the billows. Yelling at the top of his voice, Gurgi spun about and dashed frantically wherever his feet led him. Warriors shouted and fled from this fearsome whirlwind.

King Smoit, Taran realized, was trying to rally his own men around him, and Taran attempted to fight his way towards the stables. Coll, briefly, was at his side. The stout warrior had just gained a blade from a fallen opponent. Flinging aside the hoe which, until then, had served him as a weapon, Coll threw his bulk against the press of swordsmen besetting Fflewddur Fflam. Taran leaped into the fray, striking left and right with telling blows.

Magg's warriors fell back. The bard joined Taran as they raced across the court.

'Where is Rhun?' Taran cried.

'I don't know!' Fflewddur gasped. 'He and Eilonwy were to open the gates for us. But, Great Belin, what's happened since then I can't guess. Everything has changed. One of Magg's men trod on Glew, and we were discovered before we could go another step. From then on the fat was in the fire. Where Glew is now I have no idea – though the little weasel gave a fair account of himself, I must say. So did Gwystyl!'

'Gwystyl?' Taran stammered. 'How . . .'

'Never mind,' replied Fflewddur. 'We'll tell you later. If there is a later.'

They had nearly reached the stables. Taran caught sight of Gwydion. The Prince of Don's wolf-grey head towered above the milling warriors. But Taran's relief at Gwydion's safety turned to despair. He saw, through the shifting clouds, the tide of battle was turning against the companions. Only a handful of Smoit's men had been able to rally for an attack; the others were cut off, locked in combat throughout the courtyard.

'To the gates!' Gwydion commanded. 'Fly, all who can!'

With sinking heart Taran realized the little band was grievously outnumbered. Dimly, Taran saw the gates had been opened. But more of Magg's warriors had joined their fellows and the way to safety was blocked.

Suddenly a mounted figure galloped into the courytard. It was Rhun, astride his dapple grey. The King of Mona's boyish face shone with a furious light. As the steed reared and plunged, Rhun swung his sword about his head and shouted at the top of his voice:

'Bowmen! Follow me! All of you, into the court!' He spun the mare about and beckoned with his sword. His words rang above the clash of arms. 'Spearmen! This way! Make haste!'

'He's brought help!' Taran cried.

'Help?' echoed the amazed Lard. 'There's no one within miles!'

Rhun had not ceased to gallop back and forth amid the struggling warriors, shouting orders, as if a whole army streamed behind him.

Magg's men turned to face the unseen foe.

'A ruse!' exclaimed Fflewddur. 'He's a madman! It will never work!'

'But it does!' At a glance Taran saw their assailants had broken away, seeking, in confusion, to engage what they imagined to be fresh attackers. Taran brought his horn to his lips and sounded the charge. Magg's men faltered, believing the foe was now at their backs.

At that instant Llyan burst through the gates. The men who saw her shouted in terror as the huge cat leaped forward. Llyan paid no heed to the warriors, but raced across the court while the swordsmen dropped their weapons and fled at her approach.

'She's looking for me!' Fflewddur cried. 'Here I am, old girl!'

King Smoit's embattled fighting men seized this moment to press forward with a mighty surge. Many of Magg's warriors had already flown; fear-driven, they slashed and stabbed among themselves in blind panic. Rhun galloped on and vanished into the smoke.

'He's duped them well!' Fflewddur shouted jubilantly. 'For all the good those eggs and mushrooms did us – it was Rhun who turned the trick!'

The bard hastened to Llyan. Gwydion, Taran saw, was now on horseback. Golden-maned Melyngar streaked across the courtyard, as Gwydion urged the mare to overtake the retreating foe. Smoit and Coll had also leaped astride their steeds. Behind them galloped Gwystyl. Smoit's warriors, too, joined the pursuit. Taran ran to find Melynlas, but before he reached the stables, he heard Eilonwy call his name. He turned. The girl, her face smudged, her robe torn, beckoned urgently.

'Come!' she called. 'Rhun is badly hurt!'

Taran raced to follow her. Near the far wall the dapple grey stood riderless. The King of Mona was sitting on the ground, his legs stretched in front of him, his back resting against a cart still smouldering from Gwystyl's fiery mushrooms. Gurgi and Glew, both unharmed, were at his side.

'Hallo, hallo!' Rhun murmured and waved a hand. His face was deathly white.

'The day is ours,' Taran said. 'Without you, it would have gone differently. Don't move,' he cautioned, loosening the young King's bloodstained jacket. Taran frowned anxiously. An arrow had sunk deep in Rhun's side and the shaft had broken.

'Amazing!' Rhun whispered. 'I've never been in battle before, and I wasn't sure of – of anything at all. But, I say, the oddest things kept running through my head. I was thinking of the seawall at Mona Haven. Isn't it surprising? Yes, your plan will work very well.' Rhun murmured. His eyes wandered and suddenly he looked very young, very lost and a little frightened. 'And I think – I think I shall be glad to be home.' He made an effort to raise himself. Taran bent quickly to him.

Fflewddur had come up with Llyan loping at his heels. 'So there you are, old boy,' he called to Rhun. 'I told you we'd have more than our share of trouble. But you pulled us out of it! Oh, the bards will sing of you ...'

Taran lifted a grief-stricken face. 'The King of Mona is dead.'

Silent and heavy hearted, the companions raised a burial mound a little distance from Caer Cadarn. The warriors of Smoit joined them; and at dusk, horsemen bearing torches rode slowly circling the mound, to honour the King of Mona.

As the last flame died, Taran came to stand before the burial place. 'Farewell, Rhun Son of Rhuddlum. Your sea-wall is unfinished,' he said gently. 'But I promise you your work shall not be left undone. Your fisher folk shall have their safe harbour if I must build it for you with my own hands.'

Soon after nightfall Gwydion, Coll and King Smoit returned. Magg had eluded them, and the fruitless pursuit had left them worn and haggard. They, too, mourned the death of Rhun, and did honour to all the fallen warriors. Gwydion then led the companions to the Great Hall.

'Arawn Death-Lord gives us little time for grief, and we shall mourn others, I fear, before our tasks are done,' he said. 'I must tell you now of a choice carefully to be weighed.

'Gwystyl of the Fair Folk has left us, and continues his journey to King Eiddileg's realm. Before we parted, he told me further of the gathering of Arawn's hosts. Magg's words were not evil boasting. Gwystyl judges, as do I, that Arawn means to defeat us in one last battle. His armies gather even now.

'There is grave risk, and perhaps fatal risk, in leaving Dyrnwyn in Arawn's grasp,' Gwydion went on. 'Yet we must face the more pressing danger. No longer will I seek the black sword. Whatever strength it may yield him, in my own strength I will stand against him to the death. I ride not to Annuvin but to Caer Dathyl to rally the Sons of Don.'

No one spoke for some moments. At length Coll replied. 'To my mind, you have chosen wisely, Prince of Don.'

Smoit and Fflewddur Fflam nodded their agreement.

'Would that I were as sure of my wisdom,' Gwydion replied heavily. 'So be it then.'

Taran rose and faced Gwydion. 'Is there no way one of us can breach the Death-Lord's stronghold? Must the search for Dyrnwyn indeed be given up?'

'I read your thoughts, Assistant Pig-Keeper,' Gwydion replied. 'You will serve me best if you obey my commands. Gwystyl warns that a journey to Annuvin can mean only wasted life – and more than that: a loss of precious time. Gwystyl's nature is to conceal his nature, but among the Fair Folk none is shrewder or more trustworthy. I heed his warning, and so must all of you.

'Gwystyl has promised to do all in his power to gain help from the Fair Folk,' Gwydion went on. 'King Eiddileg has no great fondness for the race of men. Yet even he must see that Arawn's victory would blight all Prydain. The Fair Folk would suffer no less than we.

'But we dare not count too heavily on Eiddileg. Our own armies must be gathered, and our battle host raised. In this, our greatest help will come from King Pryderi of the West Domains. No lord in Prydain commands a mightier army. His allegiance to the House of Don is firm, and between us are strong bonds of friendship. I will send word to Pryderi, and pray him to join his host with ours at Caer Dathyl.

'There must we all meet,' Gwydion continued. 'Before then, I ask King Smoit to muster every loyal warrior in his cantrev and the dominions closest to his.' He turned to the bard. 'Fflewddur Fflam Son of Godo, you are a king in your own Northern Realms. Return there without delay. To you I entrust the rallying of the northern cantrevs.

'And you, Assistant Pig-Keeper,' Gwydion said, seeing the question in Taran's eyes, 'your own task is urgent. You are well known to the folk of the Free Commots. I charge you to raise whatever force you can among them. Lead all who will follow you to Caer Dathyl. Gurgi and Coll Son of Collfrewr will ride with you. So, too, will the Princess Eilonwy. Her safety is in your hands.'

'I'm glad,' Eilonwy murmured, 'there's been no talk of sending me home.'

'Gwystyl tells us many of Arawn's liegemen are already marching,' Coll said to her. 'The Valley Cantrevs are too dangerous, whatever. Otherwise, Princess,' he added with a grin, 'you would long since have been on your way to Caer Dallben.'

Well before dawn Gwydion and Fflewddur Fflam rode from Caer Cadarn, each to follow his separate path. King Smoit, girded for battle, set out from the castle, and with him went Lord Gast and Lord Goryon, who had learned belatedly of the attack on their king and now hastened to join him. Faced with the common danger, the two rivals had put aside their quarrel. Goryon declined to take insult at Gast's every word, Gast refrained from giving offence to Goryon, and neither so much as mentioned cows.

That same morning a gnarled, grey-headed farmer strode up to Taran in the castle courtyard. It was Aeddan, who had befriended him long before in Smoit's cantrev. The two clasped hands warmly, but the farmer's face was grim.

'There is no time now to speak of time past,' Aeddan said. 'I offer you friendship – and this,' he added, unsheathing a rusted sword. 'It has served once and can serve again. Say where you ride and I will go with you.'

'I value the sword, and value more the man who bears it,' answered Taran. 'But your place is with your King. Follow him and hope that you and I will meet on a happier day.'

As Gwydion had ordered, Taran and the remaining companions waited at Smoit's castle, hoping Kaw might arrive with further tidings. But when the following day brought no sign of the crow, they made ready for their own departure. Eilonwy's needlework had gone unscathed and she carefully unfolded it.

'You're a war leader now,' she said proudly to Taran, 'but I've never heard of a war leader without a battle flag.'

With leather thongs she bound the still-unfinished embroidery to the end of a spear.

'There,' said Eilonwy. 'As an emblem Hen Wen may not be properly terrifying. And yet, for an Assistant Pig-Keeper, she's very likely the most fitting.'

They rode through the gates. Gurgi, at Taran's side, raised the spear high and the wind caught at the banner of the White Pig. Above the smoke-blackened fortress and the burial mound, whose fresh earth was already frost-covered, the clouds had grown heavy. Soon there would be snow.

CHAPTER 8

The Messengers

From the moment he left Caer Dallben, Kaw had flown directly towards Annuvin. Though it was the bird's pleasure, aloft, to revel in the limiltess reaches of the sky, to swoop and soar above the white sheep flocks of clouds, he now put aside all temptation to sport with the wind and held steadily to his course. Far below, Avren glinted like a long trickle of molten silver; fallow fields spread in patches; the treetops of pine forest following the curves of the hills. Kaw pressed ever northwestward, resting seldom during the hours of daylight. Only at dusk, when even the crow's keen eyes could not search beyond the gathering shadows, did he drop to earth and find haven among the branches of a tree.

Days he flew high above the clouds to profit from the wind tides that bore him swiftly as a leaf in a stream. But, as he passed over the Forest of Idris, drawing closer to the harsh peaks of Annuvin, Kaw checked his gliding flight and drove earthward, alert for any stirring among the mountain passes. Shortly he glimpsed a column of heavily armed warriors marching northward. At closer range, he saw them to be Huntsmen of Annuvin. For a time he followed them and, when they halted amid the scrub and stunted trees, flapped to a low branch and settled there. Squatting at their cook fires, the Huntsmen prepared their midday meal. The crow cocked his head and listened intently, but their muttered speech told him little, until he heard the words 'Caer Dathyl'.

Kaw shifted his position and cast about for a closer branch. One of the Huntsmen, a brutish warrior garbed in bearskin, caught sight of the bird. Grinning cruelly at this chance for sport, the warrior reached for his bow and nocked an arrow to the string. Quickly he aimed, and loosed the shaft. Rapid though the Huntsman's movements were, the crow's sharp eyes followed them as quickly. Kaw flapped his wings and dodged the arrow that went rattling through the dead branches a little distance over his head. The Huntsman cursed both his lost arrow and the crow, and made to draw again. Delighted with himself, jeering raucously, Kaw sped above the trees, intending to circle back and find a safer listening post.

It was then the gwythaints appeared.

For an instant, bent on returning to the Huntsmen's camp, Kaw did not see the flight of three huge birds. From a bank of clouds they plunged downward in a rush of black, beating wings. Kaw's self-satisfaction vanished. The crow veered from their attack and strove desperately to climb higher, not daring to allow the deadly creatures to command the air above him.

The gwythaints, too, swiftly veered. One broke from his fellows to pursue the fleeing crow: the others, with powerful strokes of their wings, rose towards the clouds to renew their assault.

Kaw forced himself ever upward and the gwythaint had gained only slightly when the crow burst through a sea of mist into a sunswept vastness that nearly blinded him.

The other two gwythaints were waiting. Shrieking in fury, they dropped towards him. Behind the crow his pursuer drove him closer to the oncoming creatures. Kaw glimpsed the flash of glistening beaks and blood-red eyes. The gwythaints' screams of triumph ripped the empty sky. The crow suddenly checked his flight, feigning confusion. When the gwythaints were nearly upon him, he summoned all his strength in a single lunge that carried him beyond the talons slashing like daggers.

The crow had not gone unscathed. One of the gwythaints had struck him beneath the wing. Despite the pain that dizzied him, Kaw fluttered free of his attackers. The open sky was no refuge for him. No longer could he rely on swiftness of flight to save him. He plunged earthward.

The gwythaints were not outwitted. The scent of blood had maddened them, and they would not be deprived of their kill. They streaked after the crow to overtake and prevent him from reaching the forest below.

The highest trees rose up towards Kaw. He avoided them to drop closer to the underbrush. The tangle of branches slowed his pursuers. Without slackening speed, Kaw skimmed above the ground, deeper and deeper into the maze of bushes. The huge wings of the gwythaints which had served so well aloft now kept them from their prize. They screamed in rage, but made no attempt to venture farther into the woods. The crow, like a fox, had gone to earth.

The day had begun to fade. Kaw settled himself painfully for the night. At dawn, he fluttered cautiously to a treetop. The gwythaints had gone, but his senses told him he had been driven far east of Annuvin. Stiffly he launched himself from the tree and flapped his way aloft. Southward, Caer Cadarn lay beyond the reach of his ebbing strength. He must decide quickly, while life still remained to him. Kaw circled once, then flew heavily towards his new goal and his only hope.

His flight was now a constant torment. Often his wings faltered and only the wind-tides held him aloft. He could no longer travel a full day's distance. Long before sundown, his wound forced him to alight and hide himself amid the trees. Nor could he fly closer to the sun's warmth, but made his way only a little above the ground, nearly brushing the treetops. Below him, the countryside was springing to life with warriors, both on horseback and afoot. During the times he halted to husband his strength, he learned their destination, like that of the Huntsmen, was the fortress of the Sons of Don. His alarm grew sharper than his pain and he flew onward.

At length, in the numbing cold of the mountains northeast of the River Ystrad, he dimly spied what he had been seeking. Surrounded by sheer walls of cliffs, the valley was a green nest amid the snow-capped summits. A small cottage came into sight. The blue surface of a lake flashed in the sunlight. Against the protected side of a hill slope stretched a long, boat-like shape, the vessel's ribs and timbers overgrown with moss. Beating his wings feebly, Kaw dropped like a stone into the valley.

He was vaguely aware, as his eyes closed, of jaws firmly about him, lifting him from the grass; then a deep voice asking, 'Now, Brynach, what have you brought us?'

The crow knew nothing more.

When he opened his eyes again, he lay upon a soft nest of rushes in a sunny chamber. He was weak, but his pain had left him; his wound had been bound up. As he feebly fluttered his wings, a pair of strong hands deftly reached to hold and calm him.

'Gently, gently,' said a voice. 'I fear you will be earthbound for a time.'

The man's white-bearded face was as gnarled and weathered as an ancient oak in a snowdrift. White hair hung below broad, knotted shoulders, and a blue gem sparkled from the golden band circling his brow. Kaw, without his customary squawking and jabbering, humbly bowed his head. Never before had he flown to this valley, but his heart had always known such a refuge awaited him. A secret sense, like some hidden memory he shared with all the forest creatures of Prydain, had guided him unerringly; and the crow understood he had come at last into the abode of Medwyn.

'Let me see, let me see,' Medwyn continued, knitting his heavy brows in search of something long stored in a corner of his mind. 'You would be – yes – the family likeness is unmistakable: Kaw Son of Kadwyr. Yes, of course. Forgive me for not recognizing you immediately, but there are so many crow clans I sometimes get them mixed. I knew your father when he was a spindly-legged fledgling.' Medwyn smiled at his own recollections. 'The rogue was no stranger to my valley – a broken wing to be mended, a leg out of joint, one scrape after the other.

'I hope you do not follow his example,' Medwyn added. 'I have already heard much of your bravery and – a certain bent, shall we say, for boisterousness? It has reached my ears, as well, that you serve an Assistant Pig-Keeper at Caer Dallben. Melynlas is his name, I believe. No – forgive me. That is his steed. Of course, Melynlas Son of Melyngar. The Pig-Keeper's name escapes me at the moment. But no matter. Serve him faithfully, Son of Kadwyr, for his heart is good. Among all the race of men, he was of the few I allowed within my valley. As for you, I judge you and the gwythaints have been at close quarters. Have a care. Many of Arawn's messengers rove aloft these days. But you are safe now, and will soon be up and winging.'

Perched on the back of Medwyn's chair, an enormous eagle studied the crow. Beside the old man, the wolf Brynach sat on his haunches. Lean and grey, with yellow eyes, he wagged his tail and grinned up at the crow. A moment later, another wolf, smaller and with a white blaze on her breast, trotted in and crouched beside her mate.

'Ah, Briavael,' said Medwyn. 'Have you come to greet our visitor? Like his father, no doubt, he will have a bold tale to tell us.'

Kaw spoke then in his own tongue which Medwyn easily understood. The old man's features turned grave as he listened. When the crow had finished, Medwyn was silent for a time, deeply frowning. Brynach whined uneasily.

'It is come,' Medwyn said heavily. 'I should have guessed so, for I sense a strange fear among the animals.

More and more find their way here, fleeing what they themselves only dimly know. They tell of Huntsmen abroad in force, and armed men. Now I understand the meaning of those tidings. The day I had feared has come upon us. Yet my valley cannot hold all who would seek refuge.'

Medwyn's voice had begun to rise like a wrathful gale. 'The race of men face the slavery of Annuvin. So, too, the creatures of Prydain. In the shadow of the Land of the Dead, the nightingale's song will choke and die. The galleries of badgers and moles will become prison houses. No beast, no bird will roam or fly with the joy of a free heart. Those who are not slain – theirs will be the fate of the gwythaints, long ago made captive, tormented, broken, and their once-gentle spirits twisted to Arawn's vile ends.'

Medwyn turned to the eagle. 'You, Edyrnion, fly swiftly to the mountain eyries of your kindred. Bid them rise up in all their strength and all their numbers.

'You, Brynach, and you, Briavael,' he commanded, as the wolves pricked up their ears, 'spread the alarm among your own brethren; among the bears, with paws to smite and arms to crush; among the sharp-antlered stags; and all forest dwellers, large and small.'

Medwyn had risen to his full height. His hands clenched as tree roots clench the earth. The crow watched, awe-struck and silent. Medwyn's eyes flashed and his deep voice came as a wave of thunder.

'Speak to them in my name and tell them such are the words of one who built a ship when the dark waters flooded Prydain, of one who bore their ancient sires to safety. Now, against this flood of evil, each nest, each lair must be a stronghold. Let every creature turn tooth, beak, and claw against all who serve Arawn Death-Lord.'

Side by side, the wolves loped from the cottage. And the eagle took flight.

CHAPTER 9

The Banner

Light snow fell before the companions had journeyed a day from King Smoit's castle, and by the time they reached the Valley of Ystrad the slopes were white-cloaked and ice had begun to sheathe the river. They forded while frozen splinters cut at the legs of their horses, and wended through the bleak Hill Cantrevs, pressing eastward towards the Free Commots. Of all the band, Gurgi suffered most grievously from the cold. Though bundled in a huge garment of sheepskin, the unhappy creature shivered wretchedly. His lips were blue, his teeth chattered, and ice droplets clung to his matted hair. Nevertheless, he kept pace at Taran's side and his numbed hands did not loosen their grip on the banner.

Days of harsh travel brought them across Small Avren to Cenarth, where Taran had chosen to begin the rallying of the Commot Folk. But even as he rode into the cluster of thatch-roofed cottages, he saw the village thronged with men; and among them Hevydd the Smith, barrel-chested and bristle-bearded, who shouldered his way through the crowd and clapped Taran on the back with a hand that weighed as much as one of his own hammers.

'A good greeting to you, Wanderer,' called the smith. 'We saw you afar and gathered to welcome you.'

'A good greeting to good friends,' Taran replied, 'but I bring a stern task in exchange for a warm welcome. Hear me well,' he went on urgently. 'What I ask is not asked lightly nor granted lightly: the strength of your hands and the courage of your hearts, and, if it must be, even your lives.'

As the Commot Folk, murmuring, pressed around him,

Taran spoke of what had befallen Gwydion and of the rising of Arawn. When he had finished, the men were grim-faced, and for a long moment all stood silent. Then Hevydd the Smith lifted his voice.

'The Folk of the Free Commots honour King Math and the House of Don,' he said. 'But they will answer only to one they know as a friend, and follow him not in obligation but in friendship. And so let Hevydd be the first to follow Taran Wanderer.'

'All follow! All!' cried the Commot men as with a single voice, and on the instant the once-peaceful Cenarth stirred like a gathering storm as each man hastened to arm himself.

But Hevydd gave Taran and the companions a hard grin. 'Our will is strong but our weapons lack,' he declared. 'No matter, Wanderer. You toiled bravely in my smithy; now shall my smithy toil for you. And I will send word to every metalsmith in the Commot lands to labour as hard for you as I myself will do.'

While the men readied their mounts and Hevydd set his forge to blazing, Taran led the companions to the neighbouring Commots. His task became quickly known and each day brought its throng of herdsmen and farmers who needed no urging to march in the growing host following the banner of the White Pig. For Taran, days and nights merged into one another. In the marshalling camps, astride unflagging Melynlas, he rode among the gatherings of peaceful men turned warriors, seeing to their provisions and equipment, and by the embers of watch fires held council with the new-formed war bands.

When he had accomplished all he could at Cenarth, Hevydd rejoined Taran to serve as his master armourer.

'You have done your work well, but we still go too lightly armed,' Taran said, speaking apart with the smith. 'I fear all the forges in Prydain will not be enough to serve our need. Somehow I must find a way . . .'

'And so you shall, with luck!' called a voice.

Taran turned to see a horseman who was riding up beside him, and blinked in surprise for this was the strangest-garbed of all the Commot warriors. The man was tall, lank-haired, with legs as spindly as a stork's and so long they almost touched the ground on either side of his mount. Bits of iron and odds and ends of metal were stitched closely all over his jacket; he carried a wooden staff with a scythe blade at the end; on his head he wore what had once been a cook-pot, now worked and shaped into a makeshift helmet that sat so low on the man's forehead it nearly covered his eyes.

'Llonio!' Taran cried, warmly, clasping the new arrival's hand. 'Llonio Son of Llonwen!'

'None other,' answered Llonio, pushing back his peculiar headpiece. 'Did you not suppose I'd be along sooner or later?'

'But your wife and family,' Taran began. 'I would not ask you to leave them. Why, of children I remember half a dozen.'

'And another merrily on the way,' Llonio replied, grinning happily. 'Perhaps twins, with my kind of luck. But my brood will be safe enough till I return. Indeed, if there is ever to be safety in Prydain I must follow the Wanderer now. But your concern is not babes in arms but men-at-arms. Hear me, friend Wanderer,' Llonio went on. 'I have seen pitchforks and hay-rakes among the Commot Folk. Could not the tines be cut off and set in wooden shafts? Thus would you gain three, four, and even more weapons where you had only one to begin with.'

'Why, so we could!' burst out Hevydd. 'How did I not see that myself?'

'Nor more did I,' admitted Taran. 'Llonio sees more sharply than any of us, but calls luck what another would call keen wits. Go, friend Llonio, find what you can. I know you'll find more than meets the eye.'

As Llonio, with the help of Hevydd the Smith, gleaned the Commots for sickles, rakes, fire tongs, scythes, and pruning hooks, and found ways to make even the most unlikely objects serve a new purpose, the store of weapons grew.

While each day Taran rallied followers in greater numbers, Coll, Gurgi, and Eilonwy helped load carts with gear and provisions, a task by no means to the liking of the Princess, who was more eager to gallop from one Commot to the next than she was to plod beside the heavy-laden wagons. Eilonwy had donned man's garments and braided her hair about her head; at her belt hung a sword and short dagger wheedled from Hevydd the Smith. Her warrior's garb was ill-fitting, but she took pride in it and was therefore all the more vexed when Taran refused to let her go afield.

'You'll ride out with me,' Taran said, 'as soon as the pack animals are tended and their loads secured.'

The Princess reluctantly agreed; but next day, when Taran cantered past the horse lines at the rear of the camp, she furiously cried to him, 'You've tricked me! These tasks will never be done! No sooner do I finish with one string of horses and carts than along come some more. Very well, I shall do as I promised. But war leader or no, Taran of Caer Dallben, I'm not speaking to you!'

Taran grinned and rode on.

Bearing northward through the Valley of Great Avren, the companions entered Commot Gwenith and had scarcely dismounted when Taran heard a crackling voice call out, 'Wanderer! I know you seek warriors, not crones. But tarry a moment and give a greeting to one who has not forgotten you.'

Dwyvach, the Weaver-Woman of Gwenith, stood in her cottage doorway. Despite her white hair and wizened features she looked as lively and untired as ever. Her grey eyes scanned Taran sharply, then turned to Eilonwy. The ancient Weaver-Woman beckoned to her. 'Taran Wanderer I know well enough. And who you may be I can guess well enough, even though you go in the guise of a man and your hair could stand a little washing.' She glanced shrewdly at the Princess. 'Indeed, I was sure, when the Wanderer and I first met, that he had a pretty maiden in his thoughts.'

'Humph!' Eilonwy sniffed. 'I'm not sure if he did then, and even less sure if he does now.'

Dwyvach chuckled. 'If you are not, then no one else can be. Time will tell which of us is right. But meanwhile, child,' she added, unfolding a cloak she held in her withered hands and setting it about Eilonwy's shoulders, 'take this as a gift from a crone to a maiden, and know there is not so much difference between the two. For even a tottering granddam keeps a portion of girlish heart, and the youngest maiden a thread of old woman's wisdom.'

Taran had now come to the cottage door. He warmly greeted the Weaver-Woman and admired the cloak she had given Eilonwy. 'Hevydd and the Commot smiths labour to make arms for us,' he said. 'But warriors need warmth as much as weapons. Alas, we have no garments like this.'

'Do you think a weaver-woman less hardy than a metal-smith?' Dwyvach replied. 'As you wove patiently at my loom, now my loom will weave the more quickly for you. And in every Commot, shuttles will fly for the sake of Taran Wanderer.'

Heartened by the Weaver-Woman's promise, the companions departed from Gwenith. A short distance from the Commot, Taran caught sight of a small band of horsemen riding towards him at a quick pace. Leading them was a tall youth who shouted Taran's name and raised a hand in greeting.

With a glad cry Taran urged Melynlas to meet the riders. 'Llassar!' Taran called, reining up beside the young man. 'I did not think you and I would meet so far from your sheepfold in Commot Isav.'

'Your news travels ahead of you, Wanderer,' Llassar replied. 'But I feared you would deem our Commot too small and pass it by. It was I,' he added, with shy hesitation that could not altogether conceal his boyish pride, 'it was I who led our folk to find you.'

'The size of Isav is no measure of its courage,' Taran said, 'and I need and welcome all of you. But where is your father?' he asked, glancing at the band of riders. 'Where is Drudwas? He would not let his son journey so far without him.'

Llassar's face fell. 'The winter took him from us. I grieve for him, but honour his memory by doing what he himself would have done.'

'And what of your mother?' Taran asked, as he and Llassar trotted back to join the companions. 'Was it her wish, too, that you leave home and flock?'

'Others will tend my flock,' the young shepherd answered. 'My mother knows what a child must do and what a man must do. I am a man,' he added stoutly, 'and have been one since you and I stood against Dorath and his ruffians that night in the sheepfold.'

'Yes, yes!' cried Gurgi. 'And fearless Gurgi stood against them, too!'

'I'm sure all of you did,' Eilonwy remarked sourly, 'while I was curstying and having my hair washed on Mona. I don't know who Dorath is, but if I should ever meet him, I promise you I'll make up for lost time.'

Taran shook his head. 'Count yourself lucky you don't know him. I know him all too well, to my sorrow.'

'He has not troubled us since that night,' said Llassar. 'Nor will he likely trouble us again. I have heard he has left the Commot lands and roves westward. He has put his sword in the service of the Death-Lord, it is said. Perhaps it may be so. But if Dorath serves anyone, it is himself.'

'Your service freely given counts more for us than any the Lord of Annuvin could hire,' Taran said to Llassar. 'Prince Gwydion will be grateful to you.'

'To you, rather,' said Llassar. 'Our pride is not in fighting but in farming; in the work of our hands, not our blades. Never have we sought war. We come now to the banner of the White Pig because it is the banner of our friend, Taran Wanderer.'

The weather worsened as the companions continued through the valley, and the growing host of Commot men forced them to travel at a slower pace. The days were too short for the work to be done, but Taran rode grimly on. Beside him galloped Coll, uncomplaining and ever cheerful. His broad face, reddened and roughened by cold and wind, was nearly hidden by the collar of a great fleece-lined jacket. A sword belt of heavy iron links bound his girth, and at his back hung a round shield of ox hide. He had found a helmet of beaten metal, but deemed it did not sit as comfortably on his bald crown as had his old leather cap.

Taran was grateful for Coll's wisdom and gladly sought his counsel. It was Coll who gave him the thought, as the marshalling camps grew crowded, to send smaller, swifter bands directly to Caer Dathyl rather than march from one Commot to the next with a force becoming ever more cumbersome. Llassar, Hevydd, and Llonio would not leave Taran's vanguard and stayed ever close at hand; but when Taran wrapped himself in a cloak and stretched on the frozen ground for rare moments of sleep, it was Coll who stood watch over him.

'You are the oaken staff I lean on,' Taran said. 'More than that.' He laughed. 'You are the whole sturdy tree, and a true warrior.'

Coll, instead of beaming, looked wryly at him. 'Do you mean to honour me?' he asked. 'Then say, rather, I am a true grower of turnips and a gatherer of apples. No warrior whatever, save that I am needed thus for a while.

My garden longs for me as much as I long for it,' Coll added. 'I left it unready for winter, and for that I will pay a sorry reckoning at spring planting.'

Taran nodded. 'We shall dig and weed together, true grower of turnips – and true friend.'

The watch fires flickered in the night. The horses stirred in their lines. About them, a mass of deep shadows, dark against darkness, lay sleeping warriors. The chill wind cut at Taran's face. He was suddenly weary to the marrow of his bones. He turned to Coll.

'My heart, too, will be easier,' he said, 'when I am once more an Assistant Pig-Keeper.'

Word reached Taran that King Smoit had raised a strong host among the cantrev lords and was now turning northward. The companions learned, too, that certain of Arawn's liegemen had sent war parties across Ystrad to harass the columns marching to Caer Dathyl. Taran's task thus grew more urgent, but he could do no more than press onward with all haste.

The companions made their way to Commot Merin. For Taran, it had been among the fairest he had known in all his wanderings. Even now, amid the tumult of warriors arming, of neighing horses and shouting riders, the white, thatched cottages of the little village seemed to stand peaceful and apart. Taran galloped past the common fields ringed by hemlocks and tall firs. His heart laden with memories, he reined up at a familiar hut, whose smoking chimney betokened a warm fire within. The door opened and out stepped a stocky, hale old man garbed in a coarse, brown robe. His iron-grey hair and beard were cropped short; his eyes were blue and undimmed.

'Well met,' he called to Taran, and raised a huge hand crusted with dried clay. 'You left us a wanderer, and return to us a war leader. As for your skill in the latter, I have heard much. But I ask: Have you forgotten your skill at my potter's wheel? Or have I wasted my own to teach you?'

'Well met, Annlaw Clay-Shaper,' Taran answered, swinging down from Melynlas and fondly clasping the old potter's hand. 'Wasted, in truth,' Taran laughed, following him into the hut, 'for the master had a clumsy apprentice. My skill lacks, but not my memory. What little I could learn, I have not forgotten.'

'Show me, then,' challenged the potter, scooping a handful of wet clay from a wooden trough.

Taran smiled sadly and shook his head. 'I halted only to give you greeting,' he replied. 'Now I labour with swords, not earthen bowls.' Nevertheless, he paused. The hearth light glowed on shelves and rows of pottery, of graceful wine jars, of ewers handsomely and lovingly crafted. Quickly he took the cool clay and cast it upon the wheel which Annlaw had begun to spin. Time pressed him too closely, Taran knew; yet, as the work took form under his hands, for a moment he put down the burden of his other task. The days turned back and there was only the whirring of the wheel and the shape of the vessel born from the shapeless clay.

'Well done,' said Annlaw in a quiet voice, then added, 'I have heard how smiths and weavers throughout the Commots labour to give you arms and raiment. But my wheel cannot forge a blade nor weave a warrior's cloak, and my clay is shaped only for peaceful tasks. Alas, I can offer nothing that will serve you now.'

'You have given me more than all the others,' Taran answered, 'and I treasure it the most. My way is not the warrior's way; yet, if I do not bear my sword now, there will be no place in Prydain for the usefulness and beauty of any craftsman's handiwork. And if I fail, I will have lost all I gained from you.'

His hand faltered, for Coll's booming voice was shouting his name. Taran sprang from the wheel and, while Annlaw watched in alarm, strode out of the hut, calling a hurried farewell to the potter. Coll had already drawn his sword. In another moment, Llassar joined them. They galloped towards the camp a little way from Merin, as Coll hastily told Taran that the guard posts had sighted a band of marauders.

'They shall soon be upon us,' Coll warned. 'We should meet them before they attack our trains. As a grower of turnips, I advise you to rouse a company of bowmen and a troop of good riders. Llassar and I shall try to lure them with a smaller band of warriors.'

Quickly they set their plans. Taran rode ahead, calling to the horsemen and foot soldiers, who hastily caught up their weapons and followed after him. He ordered Eilonwy and Gurgi to safety among the carts; without waiting to hear their protests, he galloped towards the fir forest covering the outlying hills.

The marauders were armed more heavily than Taran had expected. Swiftly they sped down from the snow-covered ridge. At a sign from Taran, the bowmen raced and flung themselves into a shallow gully, and the mounted warriors of the Commots wheeled to the charge. The riders met in a turmoil of hoofs and clash of blades. Then Taran raised his horn to his lips. At the piercing, echoing signal, the bowmen rose from cover.

It was, Taran knew, little more than a skirmish, but sharply and hotly fought; only at the last, when Coll and Llassar's band drew off many of the foe, did the marauders break and flee. Yet it was the first battle Taran had commanded as a war leader for the Prince of Don. The Commot folk had carried the day, with none of their number slain and only a few wounded. Though weary and drained of his strength, Taran's heart pounded with the joy of victory as he led the exulting warriors from the forest and back towards Merin.

As he reached the hill crest he saw flames and black billows of smoke.

At first he thought the camp had taken fire. He spurred Melynlas at top speed down the slope. As he drew closer, as the crimson tongues wavered against the sky in a blood-stained sunset and the smoke rose and spread over the valley, he saw it was the Commot burning.

Outdistancing the troop, he galloped into Merin. Among the warriors from the camp, Taran glimpsed Eilonwy and Gurgi struggling vainly to quench the flames. Coll had reached the village before him. Taran leaped from Melynlas and ran to his side.

'Too late!' Coll cried. 'The raiders circled and stormed the Commot from the rear. Merin has been put to the torch, and its folk to the sword.'

With a terrible cry of grief and rage Taran ran past the blazing cottages. The thatch had burned from the roofs, and many of the walls had split and crumbled. So it was with the hut of Annlaw, which still smouldered, its ruins open to the sky. The body of the potter lay amid the rubble. Of the work of his hands, all had been shattered. The wheel was overturned, the bowl flung into pieces.

Taran dropped to his knees. Coll's hand was on his shoulder, but he drew himself away and stared up at the old warrior. 'Did I shout for victory today?' he whispered hoarsely. 'Small comfort to folk who once befriended me. Have I served them well? The blood of Merin is on my hands.'

Later, Llassar spoke apart with Coll. 'The Wanderer has not stirred from the potter's hut,' the shepherd murmured. 'It is harsh enough for each man to bear his own wound. But he who leads bears the wounds of all who follow him.'

Coll nodded. 'Leave him where he chooses to be. In the morning he will be well,' he added, 'though likely never healed.'

By midwinter, the last of the war bands had been gathered and the Commot warriors dispatched to Caer Dathyl. In addition to a troop of horsemen, Llassar, Hevydd, and Llonio still remained with Taran, who now led the companions northwestward through the Llawgadarn Mountains. The force was strong enough to safeguard their progress without slowing their journey.

Twice, marauders attacked them, and twice Taran's followers beat them off, inflicting heavy losses. The raiders, having learned a bitter lesson from the war leader who rode under the ensign of the White Pig, slunk away and dared harass the columns no further. The companions passed swiftly and unhindered through the foothills of the Eagle Mountains. Gurgi still proudly carried the banner which snapped and fluttered in the sharp winds lashing from the distant heights. In his cloak Taran bore one talisman: a shard of broken, fire-blackened pottery from Commot Merin.

At the approaches to Caer Dathyl outriders brought word of still another host. Taran galloped ahead. In a vanguard of spearmen rode Fflewddur Fflam.

'Great Belin!' shouted the bard, urging Llyan to Taran's side. 'Gwydion shall rejoice! The northern lords arm in all their strength. When a Fflam commands – yes, well, I did rally them in the name of Gwydion, otherwise they might not have been so willing. But no matter, they're on the way. I've heard King Pryderi, too, has raised his armies. Then you'll see a battle host! I daresay half the western cantrevs are under his command.

'Oh, yes,' Fflewddur added, as Taran caught sight of Glew perched atop a swaybacked, heavy-hoofed, grey horse, 'the little fellow is still with us.'

The former giant, busily gnawing a bone, gave Taran only a scant sign of recognition.

'I didn't know what to do with him,' said Fflewddur in a low voice. 'I hadn't the heart to send him packing, not in the midst of all the armies gathering. So here he is. He's not stopped whining and complaining; his feet hurt one day, his head the next, and little by little all the rest of him. Then, in between meals, he goes on with his endless tales of when he was a giant.

'The worst of it is,' Fflewddur went on in some dismay, 'he's given my ears such a drubbing that he's made me almost feel sorry for him. He's a small-hearted weasel, always was and always will be. But as you stop and think on it – he *has* been considerably mistreated and put upon. Now, when Glew was a giant . . .' The bard interrupted himself and clapped a hand to his forehead. 'Enough! Any more of this chatter, and I'll end by believing it! Come, join us,' he cried, unslinging his harp from the tangle of bows, quivers of arrows, bucklers and leather strapping he bore on his back. 'All friends are met again. I'll play you a tune to celebrate and keep us warm at the same time!'

Cheered by the bard's music, the companions journeyed on together. Soon the high fortress of Caer Dathyl rose golden in the winter sunlight. Its mighty bastions sprang up like eagles impatient for the sky. Beyond the walls and circling the fortress stood the camps and flag-decked pavilions of lords come in allegiance to the Royal House of Don. Yet it was not the sight of the banners or the wind-tossed emblems of the Golden Sunburst that made Taran's heart leap, but rather the knowledge that the companions and Commot warriors had come safe to the end of one journey, to warmth and rest for a little time at least. Safe – Taran halted in his own thoughts, and the memories returned: of Rhun King of Mona who slept silent before the gates of Caer Cadarn; of Annlaw Clay-Shaper. And his fingers clenched around the fragment of pottery.

CHAPTER 10

The Coming of Pryderi

Caer Dathyl was an armed camp, where sparks like blazing snowflakes whirled from the armourers' forges. Its widespreading courtyards rang with the iron-shod hooves of war horses and the sharp notes of signal horns. Although the companions were now safe within its walls, the Princess Eilonwy declined to exchange her warrior's rough garb for more befitting attire. The most she agreed to do – and that reluctantly – was to wash her hair. A few ladies of the court remained, the rest having been sent to the protection of the eastern strongholds, but Eilonwy flatly refused to join them in their spinning and weaving chambers.

'Caer Dathyl may be the most glorious castle in Prydain,' she declared, 'but court ladies are court ladies wherever you find them, and I've had more than my share with Queen Teleria's hen flock. Listening to their giggling and gossiping – why, it's worse than having your ears tickled with feathers. For the sake of being a Princess, I've been half-drowned with soapy water and that's quite enough. My hair still feels clammy as seaweed. As for skirts, I'm comfortable just as I am. I've lost all my robes, anyway, and I certainly shan't bother to be measured for others. The clothes I'm wearing will do very nicely.'

'No one has considered asking *me* whether *my* clothing is suitable,' Glew testily remarked, although the former giant's garments, as far as Taran could judge, were in better repair than those of the companions. 'But shabby treatment is something I've grown used to. In my cavern, when I was a giant, things were very different. Generosity! Alas, gone forever. Now, I recall when the bats and I . . .'

Taran had neither strength to dispute Eilonwy's words nor time to listen to Glew's. Gwydion, hearing of the companions' arrival, had summoned Taran to the Hall of Thrones. While Coll, Fflewddur, and Gurgi secured gear and provisions for the warriors who had journeyed with them, Taran followed a guard to the Hall. Finding Gwydion in council with Math Son of Mathonwy, Taran hesitated to draw closer; but Math beckoned to him, and Taran dropped to one knee before the whitebearded ruler.

The High King touched Taran's shoulder with a hand withered but firm, and bade him rise. Not since the battle between the Sons of Don and the armies of the Horned King had Taran been in the presence of Math Son of Mathonwy, and he saw the years had borne heavily upon the monarch of the Royal House. The face of Math was even more care-worn and more deeply furrowed than Dallben's; upon his brow the Gold Crown of Don seemed a cruel burden. Yet his eyes were keen and filled with stern pride. More than this, Taran sensed a sorrow so profound that his own heart grieved and he bowed his head.

'Face me, Assistant Pig-Keeper,' Math commanded in a quiet voice. 'Fear not to see what I myself know. The hand of death reaches toward mine and I am not loath to clasp it. I have long heard the horn of Gwyn the Hunter, that summons even a king to his barrow home.

'With a glad heart would I answer it,' said Math, 'for a crown is a pitiless master, harsher than the staff of a pig-keeper; while a staff bears up, a crown weighs down, beyond the strength of any man to wear it lightly. What grieves me is not my death; but at the end of my life to see blood spilled in the land where I sought only peace.

'You know the history of our Royal House; how, long ago the Sons of Don voyaged in their golden ships to Prydain, and how men sought their protection against

Arawn Death-Lord, who had robbed Prydain of its treasures and turned a rich, fair land into a fallow field. Since then the Sons of Don have stood as a shield against the ravages of Annuvin. But if the shield now be riven, then all shatters with it.'

'We will gain victory,' Gwydion said. 'The Lord of Annuvin stakes all upon this venture, but his strength is also his weakness, for it may be that if we withstand him his power will shatter forever.

'Good tidings, as well as bad, have reached us,' Gwydion went on. 'For the latter, King Smoit and his armies are embattled in the Valley of Ystrad. He cannot, for all his boldness, force his way farther northward before the end of winter. He serves us well, nonetheless, since his warriors engage the traitors among the southern lords and keep them from joining Arawn's other battle hosts. The more distant kings in the northern realms come but slowly, for winter, to them, is a sterner enemy than Arawn.

'More heartening is word that the armies of the West Domains are but a few days march from our stronghold. Scouts have already sighted them. It is a host greater than any ever raised in Prydain, and Lord Pryderi himself commands them. He has done all I prayed from him, and more. My only unease is that Arawn's liegemen may give battle and turn him aside before he reaches Caer Dathyl. But, if so, we will have warning and our forces will march to relieve him.

'Not least among our good tidings,' Gwydion added, a smile lightening his drawn and haggard features, 'is the coming of Taran of Caer Dallben and the warriors led from the Commots. I have counted heavily upon him and shall ask still more.'

Gwydion spoke then of the ordering of Taran's horsemen and unmounted troops. The High King listened closely and nodded his agreement.

'Go now to your task,' said Math to Taran. 'For the day

is come when an Assistant Pig-Keeper must help bear the burden of a king.'

During the days that followed, the companions served wherever need arose and as Gwydion commanded them. Even Glew shared, to some extent, in the toil – at the forceful insistence of Fflewddur Fflam and not through his own choice. Under the watchful eye of Hevydd the Smith, the former giant was set to pumping bellows at the forges, where he compained unstintingly of the blisters on his pudgy hands.

More than a stronghold of war, Caer Dathyl was a place of memory and a place of beauty. Within its bastions, in the farther reaches of one of its many courtyards, grew a living glade of tall hemlocks, and among them rose mounds of honour to ancient kings and heroes. Halls of carved and ornamented timbers held panoplies of weapons of long and noble lineage, and banners whose emblems were framed in the songs of the bards. In other buildings were stored treasures of craftsmanship sent from every cantrev and Commot in Prydain; there, Taran saw, with a twinge of heart, a beautifully fashioned wine jar from the hands of Annlaw Clay-Shaper.

The companions, when spared from their tasks, found much of wonder and delight. Coll had never before journeyed to Caer Dathyl, and he could not help staring at the archways and towers that seemed to soar higher than the snow-capped mountains beyond the walls.

'Handsome enough it all is,' Coll admitted, 'and skilfully worked. But the towers make me think my apple trees should have been better pruned. And left to itself, my garden will yield as much as the stones of this courtyard.'

A man called out to them and beckoned from the doorway of one of the smallest and plainest of the buildings. He was tall, his face deeply weathered; white hair fell straight to his shoulders. The coarse cloak of a warrior was flung loosely about him, but neither sword nor dagger hung at his unadorned leather belt. As the companions followed, Fflewddur ran instantly to the man and, heedless of the snow, dropped to one knee before him.

'Perhaps it is I who should bow to you, Fflewddur Fflam Son of Godo,' said the man, smiling, 'and ask your pardon.' He turned to the companions and offered his hand. 'I know you better than you know me,' he said, and laughed good-heartedly at their surprise. 'My name is Taliesin.'

'The Chief Bard of Prydain,' said Fflewddur, beaming proudly and delightedly, 'made me a gift of my harp. I am in his debt.'

'Of that I am not altogether sure,' replied Taliesin, as the companions followed him through the doorway and into a spacious chamber lightly furnished with only a few sturdy seats and benches, and a long table of curiously grained wood that glowed in the light of a cheery hearth-fire. Ancient volumes, stacks and rolls of parchment crowded the walls and rose high into the shadows of the raftered ceiling.

'Yes, my friend,' the Chief Bard said to Fflewddur, 'I have thought often of that gift. Indeed, it has been a little on my conscience.' He gave the bard a glance that was shrewd but filled with kindness and good humour. Taran at first had seen Taliesin as a man of many years; now he could not guess the Chief Bard's age. Taliesin's features, though heavily lined, seemed filled with a strange mixing of ancient wisdom and youthfulness. He wore nothing to betoken his rank; and Taran realized there was no need for such adornment. Like Adaon, his son and Taran's companion of long ago, his eyes were grey, deep-set, seeming to look beyond what they saw, and there was, in the Chief Bard's face and voice, a sense of authority far greater than a war leader's and more commanding than a king's.

'I knew the nature of the harp when I gave it to you,' the Chief Bard continued. 'And, knowing your own nature, suspected that you would always have some small trouble with the strings.'

'Trouble?' cried Fflewddur. 'Why, not a bit of it! Never for a moment . . .' Two strings broke with such a twang that Gurgi started in alarm. Fflewddur's face turned bright red to the tip of his nose. 'The fact of the matter is, as I stop and think on it, the old pot's forced me to tell the truth – ah, shall we say a little more than I normally would. But it does occur to me, telling the truth has harmed no one, least of all myself.'

Taliesin smiled. 'Then you have learned no small lesson. Nonetheless, my gift was in jest, yet not entirely in jest. Say, perhaps, the laughter of one heart to another. But you have borne it willingly. Now I offer you any of your choosing,' he said.

Taliesin pointed to a shelf where stood a number of harps, some newer, some older, and a few even more gracefully curved than the instrument Fflewddur carried. With a joyful cry Fflewddur hastened to them, lovingly touching the strings of each, admiring the workmanship, turning from one to the next and back again.

He hesitated some while, looking dolefully at the newly broken strings of his own instrument, at the scratches and chips scarring the frame. 'Ah – yes, well, you honour me,' he murmured in some confusion, 'but this old pot is quite good enough for me. There are times, I swear, when it seems to play of itself. None has a better tone; when the strings are fixed, that is. It sits well against my shoulder. Not to belittle these, but what I mean is that somehow we're used to each other. Yes, I'm most grateful. But I would not change it.'

'So be it, then,' replied Taliesin. 'And you others,' the Chief Bard added to the companions, 'you have seen many of the treasures of Caer Dathyl. But have you seen its true pride and priceless treasure? It is here,' he said quietly, gesturing around the chamber. 'Stored in this Hall of Lore is much of Prydain's ancient learning. Though Arawn Death-Lord robbed men of their craft secrets, he could not gain the songs and sayings of our bards. Here they have been carefully gathered. Of your songs, my gallant friend,' he said to Fflewddur, 'there are not a few.

'Memory lives longer than what it remembers,' Taliesin said. 'And all men share the memories and wisdom of all others. Below this chamber lie even richer troves.' He smiled. 'Like poetry itself, the greater part is the more deeply hidden. There, too, is the Hall of Bards. Alas, Fflewddur Fflam,' he said regretfully, 'none but a true bard may enter it. Though one day, perhaps, you shall join our company.'

'Oh, wisdom of noble bards!' cried Gurgi, his eyes popping in wonderment. 'It makes humble Gurgi's poor tender head spin with whirlings and twirlings! Alas, for he has no wisdom! But he would go without crunchings and munchings to gain it!'

Taliesin put a hand on the creature's shoulder. 'Do you believe you have none?' he asked. 'That is not true. Of wisdom there are as many patterns as a loom can weave. Yours is the wisdom of a good and kindly heart. Scarce it is, and its worth all the greater.

'Such is that of Coll Son of Collfrewr,' said the Chief Bard, 'and added thereto the wisdom of the earth, the gift of waking barren ground and causing the soil to flourish in a rich harvest.'

'My garden does that labour, not I,' said Coll, his bald crown turning pink from both pleasure and modesty. 'And as I recall the state I left it in, I shall wait long for another harvest, whatever.'

'I was to gain wisdom on the Isle of Mona,' put in Eilonwy. 'That's why Dallben sent me there. All I learned was needlework, cooking, and curtsying.'

'Learning is not the same as wisdom,' Taliesin interrupted with a kindly laugh. 'In your veins, Princess, flows the blood of the enchantresses of Llyr. Your wisdom may be the most secret of all, for you know without knowing; even as the heart itself knows how to beat.'

'Alas for my own wisdom,' said Taran. 'I was with your son when he met his death. He gave me a brooch of great power, and while I wore it there was much I understood and much that was hidden grew clear to me. The brooch is no longer mine, if indeed it ever truly was. What I knew then I remember only as a dream lingering beyond my power to grasp it.'

A shade of sorrow passed over Taliesin's face. 'There are those,' he said gently, 'who must first learn loss, despair, and grief. Of all paths to wisdom, this is the cruellest and longest. Are you one who must follow such a way? This even I cannot know. If you are, take heart nonetheless. Those who reach the end do more than gain wisdom. As rough wool becomes cloth, and crude clay a vessel, so do they change and fashion wisdom for others, and what they give back is greater than what they won.'

Taran was about to speak, but the notes of a signal horn rang from the Middle Tower and shouts rose from the guardians at the turrets. Watchers cried out the sighting of King Pryderi's battle host. Taliesin led the companions up a broad flight of stone steps where, from atop the Hall of Lore, they could see beyond the walls of the fortress. Taran could only glimpse the gleam of the westering sun on ranks of spears across the valley. Then, mounted figures broke away from the mass and galloped across the snow-flecked expanse. Against the rolling meadow, the leading rider of the band was sharply brilliant in trappings of crimson, black, and gold, and sunlight sparkled on his golden helmet. Taran could watch no longer, for guards were shouting the names of the companions, summoning them to the Great Hall.

Catching up the banner of the White Pig, Gurgi hastened after Taran. The companions quickly made their way to the Great Hall. A long table had been placed there and at its head sat Math and Gwydion. Taliesin took his seat at Gwydion's left hand; to the right of Math stood an empty throne draped in the colours of King Pryderi's Royal House. On either side sat the Lords of Don, cantrev nobles, and war leaders.

Circling the Hall stood the banner-bearers. Gurgi glanced about him in dismay; but, at a gesture from Gwydion, stationed himself among their ranks. The poor creature looked miserable and frightened out of his wits amid the stern warriors. But the companions turned encouraging eyes on him, and Coll gave him such a huge grin and a wink that Gurgi raised both his shaggy head and his makeshift banner more proudly than any in the Great Hall.

Taran himself felt no little awkwardness when Gwydion signalled for him and the others to take seats among the war leaders; though Eilonwy, still in her warrior's attire, smiled happily and seemed altogether at ease.

'Humph!' she remarked. 'I think Hen Wen shows up quite handsomely and, for the matter of that, better than most. You were so disagreeable about whether her eyes were blue or brown. Well, I can tell you that's not half as strange as the colours they've embroidered on some of these banners . . .'

Eilonwy stopped speaking, for the portals were flung open and King Pryderi entered the Great Hall. All eyes were on him as he strode towards the council table. He was as tall as Gwydion himself, and his rich raiment glittered in the torchlight. He wore no helmet; what Taran had seen was his long hair that shone like gold about his brow. At his side hung a naked sword, for it was Pryderi's custom, as Fflewddur whispered to Taran, never to sheathe his blade until the battle was won. Behind him followed falconers with hooded hawks on their gauntleted wrists; his war leaders, with the crimson hawk emblem of the House of Pwyll broidered on their cloaks; and spearmen flanking his banner-bearer.

Gwydion, clothed like the Chief Bard in the unadorned garb of a warrior, stood to greet him, but Pryderi halted before reaching the council table and, arms folded, glanced around the Hall at the waiting cantrev kings.

'Well met, Lords,' Pryderi cried. 'I rejoice to see you gathered here. The threat of Annuvin makes you forget your own quarrelling. Once more you seek protection from the House of Don, like fledglings who see the hawk circling.'

Pryderi's voice rang with unhidden scorn. Taran started at the King's harsh speech. The High King himself looked sharply at Pryderi, though when he spoke his words were measured and grave.

'How, then, Lord Pryderi? It is I who summoned all who will stand with us, for the safety of all hangs in the balance.'

Pryderi smiled bitterly. His handsome features were flushed, whether from the cold or from anger Taran could not tell; blood tinged Pryderi's high, jutting cheekbones as he threw back his golden head and unflinchingly met the High King's stern glance.

'Would any have lingered, seeing himself threatened?' replied Pryderi. 'Men answer only to an iron fist or a sword at their throats. Those who bear you allegiance bear it as it serves their own ends. Among themselves, these cantrev rulers are never at peace, but each is eager to profit from the weakness of his neighbour. In their secret hearts, are they less evil than Arawn Death-Lord?'

Shocked and angry murmurs arose from the cantrev kings. Math silenced them with a quick gesture.

Then Gwydion spoke: 'It is beyond any man's wisdom to judge the secret heart of another,' he said, 'for in it are good and evil mixed. But these are matters to ponder over the embers of a campfire, as you and I have often done; or at the end of feasting, when the torches burn low. Our deeds now must safeguard Prydain. Come, Pryderi Son of Pwyll. Your place awaits you and we have many plans to set.'

'You summoned me, Prince of Don,' Pryderi answered in a hard voice. 'I am here. To join you? No. To demand your surrender.'

CHAPTER II

The Fortress

For an instant, none could speak. The silver bells at the legs of Pryderi's hawks tinkled faintly. Then Taran was on his feet, sword in hand. The cantrev lords shouted in rage and drew their weapons. Gwydion's voice rang out, commanding them to silence.

Pryderi did not move. His retainers had unsheathed their blades and formed a circle about him. The High King had risen from his throne.

'You sport with us, Son of Pwyll,' Math said severely, 'but treachery is no fitting matter for a jest.'

Pryderi still stood with arms folded. His golden features had turned the colour of iron. 'Call it no jest,' he answered, 'and call me no traitor. This I have pondered long and closely and with much anguish of heart. I see now that only thus can I serve Prydain.'

Gwydion's face was pale and his eyes grave. 'You speak in madness,' he replied. 'Have Arawn's false promises blinded you to reason? Would you tell me that a liegeman of the Death-Lord serves any realm but Annuvin?'

'To me, Arawn can promise nothing I do not already have,' answered Pryderi. 'But Arawn will do what the Sons of Don failed to do: make an end of endless wars among the cantrevs, and bring peace where there was none before.'

'The peace of death and the silence of mute slavery,' Gwydion replied.

Pryderi glanced around him. A harsh smile was on his lips. 'Do these men deserve better, Lord Gwydion? Are all their lives together worth one of ours? Crude brawlers, these self-styled cantrev lords are unfit to command even their own households.

'I choose what is best for Prydain,' he continued. 'I do not serve Arawn. Is the axe the woodcutter's master? At the end, it is Arawn who will serve me.'

With horror, Taran listened to the words of Pryderi as he spoke to the High King.

'Lay down your arms. Abandon the weaklings who cling to you for protection. Surrender to me now. Caer Dathyl shall be spared, and yourself, and those I deem worthy to rule with me.'

Math raised his head. 'Is there worse evil?' he said in a low voice, his eyes never leaving Pryderi's. 'Is there worse evil than that which goes in the mask of good?'

One of the cantrev lords sprang from the council table and, blade upraised, started towards Pryderi.

'Touch him not!' cried Math. 'We welcomed him as a friend. He leaves as a foe, but he shall leave in safety. If any harm even a feather of his hawks, his life shall be forfeit.'

'Go from here, Pryderi Son of Pwyll,' Gwydion said, the coldness of his tone making his wrath the more terrible. 'The anguish of my heart is no less than yours. Our comradeship is broken. Between us there can be only the lines of battle, and our only bond the edge of a sword.'

Pryderi did not answer, but turned on his heel and with his retainers strode from the Great Hall. Even as he mounted his steed, word spread among the warriors, and they stared silently in their ranks. Beyond the walls, the armies of Pryderi had lit torches and the valley flamed as far as Taran's eyes could see. Pryderi rode through the gates, the crimson and gold of his raiment shimmering like the torches themselves, and galloped towards his waiting host. Taran and the Commot men watched, sick with despair; they knew, as did all in Caer Dathyl, this glittering King, like a hawk of death, had snatched their lives and now bore them away with him.

*

Gwydion had expected the army of King Pryderi to attack at first light, and the men in the fortress had laboured through the night making ready to withstand a siege. When dawn came, however, and the pale sun rose higher, Pryderi's battle host was seen to have advanced but little. From the wall Taran, Fflewddur, and Coll, with the other war leaders, watched beside Gwydion, who stood scanning the valley, and the heights that dipped in raw ridges to the flatlands. Snow had not fallen for some days; gullies and rocky fissures still held streaks and patches of white, caught among the crevices like tufts of wool, but the broad meadowland was, for the most part, clear. The dead turf showed in dark brown splotches under a ragged mantle of frost.

Scouts had brought word that Pryderi's warriors held the valley in strength and barred passage through the battle lines. Nevertheless, no skirmishers or flanking columns of riders had been seen abroad; and the scouts judged, from this and the stationing of the foot soldiers and horsemen, that the attack would come in a great forward thrust, as an iron fist against the gates of Caer Dathyl.

Gwydion nodded. 'Pryderi means to strike in all his might, though it will cost him dearly. He can be spendthrift of his warriors' lives, knowing we can ill afford to pay an equal price.'

He frowned and rubbed his chin with the back of a gauntleted hand. His green eyes narrowed as he peered across the valley, and his lined face was that of a wolf scenting his enemies. 'Lord Pryderi is arrogant,' he murmured.

Gwydion turned sharply to the war leaders. 'I will not await a siege. To do so would be sure defeat. Pryderi has numbers enough to flood us like a wave. We shall give battle beyond the fortress, and we ourselves strike against the wave before it reaches its crest. Math Son of Mathonwy shall command the inner defences. Only at the last, if so it must be, shall we retreat into the fortress and make our stand there.'

Gwydion looked for a long moment at the halls and towers of the castle which had now caught the early rays of the sun. 'The Sons of Don raised Caer Dathyl with their own hands, and built it not only as a shield against Arawn but as safeguard for the wisdom and beauty of Prydain. As I would do all in my power to shatter Pryderi, so would I do all to spare Caer Dathyl from destruction. It may be that we shall gain both these ends, or lose both. But we must battle not as sluggish oxen but as swift wolves and cunning foxes.'

The Prince of Don spoke quickly to the war leaders, clearly setting forth the tasks of each. Taran felt uneasy. As a boy, he had dreamed of taking a man's place among men; and, as a boy, had deemed himself well fit to do so. Now, amid the grizzled, battle-wise warriors, his strength seemed feeble, his knowledge clouded. Coll, sensing Taran's thoughts, winked encouragement at him. The stout old farmer, Taran knew, had paid heed to Gwydion's words. Yet Taran guessed that a corner of Coll's heart was distant, busily and happily occupied with his turnip patch.

For much of the morning Pryderi's host held its position while the defenders quickly formed their own battle lines. At some distance beyond the walls of Caer Dathyl, heavily armed fighting men stood ready to bear the brunt of Pryderi's assault, and there Gwydion himself would command. Fflewddur and Llyan, with Taliesin and a company of warrior-bards, held a post across the valley. The Commot horsemen would be at the flank of Pryderi's attack and it would be their task to slash into the onrushing wave, to disrupt and sap the strength from the enemy's arms.

Taran and Coll at the head of one troop, and Llassar entrusted to lead another, galloped to their stations. Gurgi, silent and shivering in his huge jacket, drove the banner of the White Pig into the frozen ground to mark a rallying point. Taran felt the eyes of the foe watching every move, and an odd impatience, mixed with fear, drew him taut as a bowstring.

Gwydion, astride Melyngar, rode up for a last glance at the ordering of the Commot men, and Taran cried out to him, 'Why does Pryderi wait? Does he mock us? Are we no more than ants to him, labouring at a hill, to be crushed at his pleasure?'

'Patience,' answered Gwydion in a tone that was both the reassurance of a friend and the command of a war leader. 'You are swords added to my hands,' Gwydion went on. 'Do not let yourselves be shattered. Move quickly, stay not over long in one fray, but start many.' He took Taran's hand and Coll's and Gurgi's. 'Farewell,' Gwydion said almost brusquely, then spun Melyngar about and rode swiftly to his warriors.

Taran watched him until he had disappeared, then turned towards the distant towers of Caer Dathyl. Eilonwy, along with Glew, had been commanded to remain in the fortress under the High King's protection. Taran strained his eyes in the vain hope of glimpsing her on the walls. What she might feel for him he was no more sure than he had been at Caer Dallben; but, despite his resolve, he was on the verge of speaking his own heart fully. Then, suddenly, like a man swept away in a flood, he had been caught up in the rallying of warriors, without even a moment to say his farewell. Yearning pierced him, and regret for his unspoken words was an iron hand gripping his throat.

He started and clenched the reins as Melynlas, snorting a white cloud, began to paw the ground. At a glance he saw Pryderi's host had risen and was surging into the valley. The battle was upon him.

It came quickly, not as the slow-cresting wave Taran had expected. First was a swelling sea of shouting men.

The Sons of Don were not awaiting Pryderi's charge but were racing ahead to grapple with the attacking foe. He saw Gwydion on the rearing white shape of Melyngar. But Taran could not tell the instant of the first clash of arms; for in a moment, instead of two tides there was only one that spun and shifted in a great convulsion, a whirlpool of spears and swords.

Taran sounded his horn and, as an answering shout came from Llassar, clapped heels into the flanks of Melynlas. Coll and the Commot horsemen spurred their mounts after him. From a swift canter the powerful legs of Melynlas stretched to a gallop. The stallion's muscles heaved beneath him and Taran, sword raised, plunged into the sea of men. His head spun and he gasped as if drowning. He realized he was terrified.

Around him swirled the faces of friends and foes. He glimpsed Llonio flailing right and left. The man's makeshift helmet bobbed over his eyes, his long legs were drawn up high in the stirrups, and he looked like nothing so much as a scarecrow come to life; yet, where Llonio passed, attackers fell as wheat to a scythe. Hevydd's burly frame rose like a wall in the midst of the combat. Of Llassar there was no sign, but Taran thought he could hear the young shepherd's high-pitched battle cry. Then a furious roaring reached his ears and he knew Llyan, with Fflewddur, had entered the fray. In another moment, aware of nothing beyond the blade in his hand, Taran was locked in a blind madness with warriors who thrust at him and whose blows he strove to return.

Again and again Taran and the Commot horsemen slashed deep into the attackers' flanks, then wheeled to gallop free of the iron whirlpool, only to plunge back again. In a flash of clarity Taran saw glittering gold and crimson. It was King Pryderi on a black charger. Taran struggled to engage him. For an instant their eyes met, but the Son of Pwyll made no attempt to answer the challenge of a ragged horseman. Instead, he looked away and continued to press ahead. Then he was gone. And it was Pryderi's scornful glance that stung Taran more sharply than the blade which swung up from the mass of foemen to lash across his face.

Once, the swell of the armed tide flung Taran to the fringes of the battle. He caught sight of Gurgi's banner and tried to rally the horsemen around it. A trough had opened up amid Pryderi's ranks. In another moment a horse pounded towards him: Lluagor. A warrior armed with a long lance clung to the steed's back.

'Go back!' Taran shouted at the top of his voice. 'Have you lost your wits?'

Eilonwy, for it was she, half-halted. She had tucked her plaited hair under a leather helmet. The Princess of Llyr smiled cheerfully at him. 'I understand you're upset,' she shouted back, 'but that's no cause to be rude.' She galloped on.

For a time, Taran could not believe he had really seen her.

Moments later, he was struggling against a band of warriors who slashed at Melynlas, threw themselves against the stallion's flanks, and strove to bear down horse and rider. Taran was vaguely aware of someone seizing his mount's bridle and dragging him to the side. Pryderi's warriors fell away. Free of the press, he turned in the saddle, and blindly flung up his sword against the new attacker.

It was Coll. The stout farmer had lost his helmet. His bald crown was as scratched as if he had plunged headlong into briars. 'Save your sword for your foes, not your friends!' he cried.

Taran's surprise left him speechless an instant, before he stammered, 'You saved my life, Son of Collfrewr.'

'Why, so perhaps I did,' replied Coll, as though the idea had suddenly come to him.

They looked at each other and burst out laughing like a pair of fools.

Only towards sundown, when the sky itself seemed streaked with blood, did Taran gain a new sense of the battle. Gwydion's warriors, flung across the path of Pryderi's advance, had met the full fury of their attackers. The hosts of Pryderi had faltered, as though stumbling over their own dead. The wave had crested and hung poised. Now a fresh wind surged over the valley. Taran's heart leaped as shouts of renewed strength rang from the warriors of Don. They pressed onward, driving all before them. Taran sounded his horn and with the Commot horsemen galloped to join the sweeping tide.

The ranks of the enemy parted like a shattered wall. Taran clutched at his reins, Melynlas reared and whinnied in alarm. A shudder of horror racked the valley. Taran saw and understood why, even before the rising current of outcries reached his ears.

'The Cauldron-Born! The deathless warriors!'

The men of Pryderi fell back to let them pass, as if in fearful homage. In ghastly silence, their pace neither fast nor slow, the Cauldron-Born filled the breach and the valley rang with the tread of their heavy boots. In the crimson haze of the dying sun their faces seemed all the more livid. Their eyes were cold and dull as stones. Unfaltering, the column of deathless warriors bore towards Caer Dathyl. Among them, slung about with ropes, they carried an iron-capped battering ram.

The foemen flanking the Cauldron-Born now turned suddenly to launch a fresh attack against the Sons of Don. In horror, Taran realized why Pryderi had delayed, and understood his arrogance. Only now had the traitor King's plan reached its fulfilment. Behind the long column of Cauldron-Born fresh fighting men streamed from the heights. For Pryderi, the long day of battle had been no more than a mockery. The slaughter had begun.

At the fortress, bowmen and spearmen of the inner defences thronged the walls. The mute Cauldron-Born did not falter in the storm of arrows. Though every shaft found its mark, the foe moved steadily onward, pausing only to rip the arrows from their unbleeding flesh. Their features showed neither pain nor anger, and no human cry, no shout of triumph passed their lips. From Annuvin they had journeyed as though from the grave, their task only to bring death, unpitying, implacable as their own lifeless faces.

Against the pounding of the battering ram the gates of Caer Dathyl groaned and trembled. The massive hinges loosened, while echoes of the driving ram shuddered through the fortress. The portal splintered, the first breach gaped like a wound. The Cauldron-Born gathered strength once more to force the ram forward. The gates of Caer Dathyl shattered and fell inward. Trapped between the ranks of Pryderi's warriors, the Sons of Don fought vainly to reach the fortress. Sobbing with fury and despair, Taran, helpless, saw the Cauldron-Born stride past the broken gates.

Before them stood Math the High King. He was attired in the raiment of the Royal House, belted with links of gold, and on his brow glittered the Gold Crown of Don. About his shoulders was a cloak of fine white wool, wrapped as though it were a burial garment. Outstretched, his withered hand gripped a naked sword.

The deathless warriors of Annuvin halted as if at the faint stirring of some clouded memory. The moment passed and they strode on. The field of battle was silent now; an awed hush had fallen even upon the men of Pryderi. The High King did not turn away as the Cauldron-Born drew closer, his eyes fixed theirs as he raised his sword defiantly. Unflinching he stood in pride and ancient majesty. The first of the pallid warriors was upon him.

Grasping the flashing sword in his frail hands, the High King swung it downward in a sweeping blow. The warrior's blade turned it aside, and the Cauldron-Born struck heavily. King Math staggered and dropped to one knee. The mass of mute warriors pressed forward, their weapons thrusting and slashing. Taran covered his face with his hands and turned away weeping, as Math Son of Mathonwy fell and the iron-shod boots of the Cauldron-Born pressed their relentless march over his lifeless body. From the dark hills then there rose the long notes of a hunting horn, trembling, echoing among the crags, and a shadow seemed to brush the sky above the fortress.

Now behind the Cauldron-Born the men of Pryderi streamed through the broken gates, while waves of attackers drove the remnants of Gwydion's army into the heights, scattering them amid snow-filled gullies. From Caer Dathyl came new claps of thunder as the ram of the Cauldron-Born turned against the walls to breach them in turn. Flames rose above the Great Hall, above the Hall of Lore, and from the Middle Tower was unfurled the crimson hawk of Pryderi.

Beside it, blotting out the dying sun, spread the black banner of Arawn Lord of Annuvin.

Caer Dathyl had fallen.

CHAPTER 12

The Red Fallows

All night the destruction raged and by morning Caer Dathyl lay in ruins. Fires smouldered where once had stood the lofty halls. The swords and axes of the Cauldron-Born had levelled the hemlock grove near the mounds of honour. In the dawn light the shattered walls seemed bloodstained.

The army of Pryderi, denying even the right of burial for the slain, had driven the defenders into the hills east of Caer Dathyl. It was there, amid the turmoil of the makeshift camp, the companions found one another again. Faithful Gurgi still bore the banner of the White Pig, though its staff had been broken and the emblem slashed almost beyond recognition. Llyan, with Fflewddur beside her, crouched in the scant shelter of a rocky outcropping; her tail twitched and her yellow eyes still glowed with anger. Hevydd the Smith built a campfire, and Taran, Eilonwy, and Coll tried to warm themselves at the embers. Llassar, though sorely wounded, had lived through the battle; but the enemy had taken cruel toll of the Commot men. Among those who lay stark and silent on the trampled battleground was Llonio Son of Llonwen.

One of the handful of survivors from the inner defences of the fortress was Glew. A warrior of Don, finding him lost and dazed outside the walls, had taken pity on his plight and brought him to the camp. The former giant was pathetically glad to rejoin the companions, though he was still too terrified and trembling to do more than mumble a few words. With a torn cloak over his shoulders, he huddled beside the fire and held his head in his hands.

Gwydion stood alone. For long, his eyes did not leave

the column of black smoke staining the sky above the ruins of Caer Dathyl. At last he turned away and ordered all who had lived out the day to assemble. Taliesin came to stand before them and, taking up Fflewddur's harp, sang a lament for the slain. Amid the black pines the voice of the Chief Bard rose in deep sorrow, yet it was sorrow without despair; and while the notes of the harp were heavy laden with mourning they held, as well, the clear strains of life and hope.

As the melody died away Taliesin lifted his head and spoke quietly. 'Each broken stone of Caer Dathyl shall be a mark of honour, and the whole valley a resting place for Math Son of Mathonwy and all our dead. But a High King still lives. As I honour him, so do I honour all who stand with him.' He turned to Gwydion and bowed deeply. The warriors drew their swords and cried out the name of the new King of Prydain.

Gwydion then called the companions to him. 'We meet only to part,' he said. 'Pryderi's victory gives us one choice and one hope. Though messengers bear tidings of our defeat to King Smoit and his army, and to the lords of the north, we dare not await their help. What we do must be done now. Not even a battle host tenfold greater than Pryderi's can withstand the Cauldron-Born. Army after army can be flung against them only to swell the ranks of the slain.

'Yet here is the seed of our hope,' Gwydion said. 'Never in man's memory has Arawn sent his deathless warriors abroad in such strength. He has taken the greatest risk for the greatest gain. And he has triumphed. But his triumph has become his moment of greatest weakness. Without the Cauldron-Born to guard it, Annuvin lies open to attack. So must we attack it.'

'Do you believe then that Annuvin is unguarded?' Taran asked quickly. 'Are there none other who serve Arawn?'

'Mortal warriors, surely,' replied Gwydion, 'and perhaps a force of Huntsmen. But we have strength to overcome them, if the Cauldron-Born do not reach Annuvin in time to aid them.'

Gwydion's blood-streaked face was hard as stone. 'They must not reach Annuvin. As their power dwindles the longer they remain beyond the Death-Lord's realm, so at all cost must they be hindered, delayed, turned from every path they follow.'

Coll nodded. 'Indeed, this is our only hope, whatever. And it must be done quickly, for now they will seek to return quickly to their master. But can we overtake them once they are on the march? Can we hinder them and at the same time mount our own attack against Annuvin?'

'Not if we journey as one army,' Gwydion said. 'Instead, we must separate into two bands. The first, and smaller, shall be given as many horses as can be spared, and hasten to pursue the Cauldron-Born. The second shall make their way to the Valley of Kynvael and follow its river north-west to the coast. The valley land is gentle, and with forced marches the sea can be reached in no more than two days.

'The sea must aid our venture,' Gwydion continued, 'for Pryderi can too easily forbid our army's journey overland.' He turned to Taran. 'Math Son of Mathonwy spoke to you of the ships that bore the Sons of Don from the Summer Country. These vessels were not abandoned. Still seaworthy, they have ever been held ready against a day of need. A faithful folk guard them in a hidden harbour near the mouth of the river Kynvael. They will carry us to the western shore of Prydain, close to the bastions of Annuvin itself.

'Two men alone have knowledge of the harbour,' Gwydion added. 'One was Math Son of Mathonwy. The other is myself. I have no choice but to lead the seaward march. As for the other journey,' he said to Taran, 'will you accept to lead it?'

Taran raised his head. 'I serve as you command.'

'I do not command this,' replied Gwydion. 'I order no man to such a task against his will. And all who follow you must do so willingly.'

'Then it is my will to do so,' Taran answered.

The companions murmured their assent.

'The vessels of the Sons of Don are swift,' Gwydion said. 'I ask you to delay the Cauldron-Born but a little while. Yet all hangs on that little.'

'If I fail,' Taran said, 'how shall I send word to you? Should the Cauldron warriors reach Annuvin ahead of you, your plan cannot succeed and you must turn back.'

Gwydion shook his head. 'There can be no turning back, for there is no further hope. Should either of us fail, all our lives are forfeit.'

Llassar, Hevydd, and all the other Commot folk chose to follow Taran. With them were joined the surviving warriors of Fflewddur Fflam, and together they made the greater portion of Taran's band. To the surprise of the companions, Glew chose to ride with them.

The former giant had recovered from his fright, at least enough to regain much of his customary peevishness. He had, however, regained all of his appetite and demanded food in great quantity from Gurgi's wallet of provisions.

'I've had my fill of being dragged here and there by the scruff of the neck,' said Glew, licking his fingers, 'and now I'm either to be put on a ship or cast among a herd of horses. Very well, I shall take the latter, for at least it's not so wet and salty. But I assure you I would have agreed to neither, when I was a giant.'

Fflewddur glowered at the former giant and spoke apart with Taran. 'It seems we're doomed, on top of all our other woes, to put up with that whining weasel at every step. And I can't help feeling that in the back of that puny little mind he's hoping somehow to feather his own nest.' The bard shook his head and gave Taran a sorrowful look. 'But are any nests left to feather? There's not a safe place even for Glew to hide his head.'

Gurgi had tied the banner of the White Pig to a new staff, but he sighed mournfully at the tattered emblem. 'Poor piggy!' he cried. 'None can see her now, for she is torn into threadings and shreddings!'

'I promise to sew another,' Eilonwy said. 'As soon as . . .' She stopped abruptly and said no more, as she climbed astride Lluagor. Taran saw her troubled glance. The Princess of Llyr would wait long, he feared, before her hands worked with an embroidery needle. And, unspoken but in his heart was the dread that none of them might see Caer Dallben again. At the end of their grim race, death might be the only prize.

Armed with spears and swords, the warriors were mounted and ready. With a last farewell to Gwydion, the companions rode westward from the hills.

It was Coll's judgement that the Cauldron-Born would march directly to Annuvin, following the straightest and shortest path. At the head of the column winding its way from the snow-swept heights, Llassar rode beside Taran. The skill of the young shepherd eased their passage, and he guided them swiftly towards the lowlands, unseen by Pryderi's army which had begun to withdraw from the valley around Caer Dathyl.

For some days they journeyed, and Taran began to fear the retreating Cauldron-Born had outdistanced them. Nevertheless, they could do no more than press on as quickly as possible, southward now, passing through long stretches of sparse woodland.

It was Gurgi who first sighted the deathless warriors. The creature's face went grey with fright as he pointed to an expanse of rock-strewn plain. Glew blinked, choked, and could barely swallow the food he was munching. Eilonwy watched silently, and the bard gave a low whistle of dismay.

Taran's heart sank at the sight of the column moving like a long serpent over the flatlands. He turned questioningly to Coll. 'Can we hold them off at all?'

'A pebble can turn aside an avalanche,' said Coll, 'or a twig stem a flood.'

'I daresay,' muttered Fflewddur. 'What happens to the twig or pebble afterwards I should rather not think about.'

Taran was about to signal the warriors to form for an attack, but Coll took his arm. 'Not yet, my boy,' he said. 'First, I would be sure of the path these creatures of Arawn mean to follow to Annuvin. If the twig is to do its work, it must be well placed.'

For the rest of that day and the morning of the next, the companions matched their own progress with the march of the Cauldron-Born, sometimes ahead, sometimes along their flank, but never losing sight of the deathless warriors. It seemed to Taran that the Cauldron-Born had slowed their pace. The dark column moved without faltering, but heavily, as though burdened. He spoke of this to Coll, who nodded in satisfaction.

'Their strength ebbs a little,' Coll said. 'Time works for us, but I think we must soon work for ourselves.'

They had reached a broad, winding belt of wasteland where grassless earth stretched away on either side as far as the eye could see. The dead ground was broken, rutted as though ill-ploughed, slashed with deep ditches and gullies. No tree, no shrub rose from the dull red earth, and nowhere did Taran see the faintest sign that any growing thing had ever flourished there. He looked at it uneasily, chilled not only by the bitter wind but by the silence that hovered like frozen mist about the lifeless land.

He asked, in a low voice, 'What place is this?'

Coll grimaced. 'The Red Fallows, it is called now. At the moment,' he added wryly, 'I fear it is much the way my garden looks.'

'I have heard it spoken of,' Taran said, 'though I believed it to be no more than a traveller's tale.'

Coll shook his head. 'No traveller's tale, whatever. Men have long shunned it, yet once it was the fairest realm in Prydain. The land was such that all manner of things would grow, as if overnight. Grains, vegetables, fruits – why, in size and savour the apples from the orchards here would have made mine look like shrivelled windfalls beside them. A prize it was, to be won and held, and many lords fought for its possession. But in the fighting over it, year after year, the hooves of steeds trampled the ground, the blood of warriors stained it. In time the land died, as did those who strove to claim it from their fellows, and soon its blight crept far beyond the battle grounds.' Coll sighed. 'I know this land, my boy, and it does not please me to see it again. In my younger days I, too, marched with the battle hosts, and left not a little of my own blood in the Fallows.'

'Will they never flourish?' Taran asked, looking with dismay at the wasted expanse. 'Prydain could be a rich land with the abundance they might bear. It would be a shame worse than bloodshed to leave these fields thus. Would the soil not yield again if it were laboured well?'

'Who can say?' answered Coll. 'Perhaps. No man has tilled it for years long past. But for us now that is all by-the-by.' He gestured towards the heights rising sharply at the distant edge of the fields. 'The Red Fallows stretch along the Hills of Bran-Galedd, southwestward almost to Annuvin. From here it is the longest but easiest path to Arawn's realm, and if I judge aright the Cauldron-Born will follow it swiftly to their master.'

'We must not let them pass,' Taran replied. 'Here we

must make our first stand and hinder them as best we can.' He glanced towards the heights. 'We must force them into the hills. Among rocks and broken ground, we might set snares or lure them into ambush. It is all we can hope to do.'

'Perhaps,' said Coll. 'Though before you choose, know this: the Hills of Bran-Galedd also give a path to Annuvin, and a shorter one. They rise sharper as they go westward and turn soon to steep crags. There stands Mount Dragon, the highest peak, guarding the Iron Portals of the Land of Death. It is a harsh passage, cruel and dangerous – more so for us than for the deathless Cauldron-Born. We can lose our lives. They cannot.'

Taran frowned anxiously, then said with a bitter laugh, 'Indeed, there is no happy choice, old friend. The path of the Red Fallows is easier but longer; the mountain way, harder and shorter!' He shook his head. 'I have not the wisdom to decide. Have you no counsel for me?'

'The choice must be yours, war leader,' answered Coll. 'Yet, as a grower of turnips and cabbages, I might say if you trust your strength, the mountains may be friend as much as foe.'

Taran smiled at him sorrowfully. 'Little trust do I put in the strength of an Assistant Pig-Keeper alone,' he said after a long moment, 'but much in the strength and wisdom of his companions. So be it. We must drive the Cauldron warriors into the hills.'

'Know this, too,' said Coll. 'If such is your choice, it must be done at this place and at all cost. Farther southward, the Fallows widen, the plain grows broad and flat; and there is danger the Cauldron-Born may escape our reach if we fail here.'

Taran grinned. 'Now that is simple enough for an Assistant Pig-Keeper to understand.'

Taran rode back through the column of warriors to tell them of the plan they were to follow. Though he cautioned

Eilonwy and Gurgi to hold themselves as far as possible from the fray, he could judge, with little difficulty, that the Princess of Llyr had no intention of heeding his warning. As for Taran himself, the decision he had taken lay heavily on him; his doubts and fears only sharpened as the horsemen rallied at the fringe of woodland and as the moment for their advance across the Fallows drew closer. He felt cold; the wind muttering across the rutted fields seeped through his cloak like an icy flood. He caught sight of Coll, who winked at him and nodded his bald crown in a quick gesture. Taran raised the horn to his lips and signalled the warriors forward.

At Coll's counsel the companions and each horseman had cut stout branches from the trees. Now, like ants burdened with straws, the column entered the wasteland, struggling across the ruts and gullies. To their right rose the ruins of a wall, some ancient boundary, useless now, whose broken slabs stretched over much of the Fallows' width and ended near the steep ascent of the Bran-Galedd Hills.

It was there that Taran, with all haste, led the toiling band of warriors. The Cauldron-Born, it seemed to him, had already glimpsed them, for the dark column quickened its own pace, thrusting rapidly across the Fallows. Taran's horsemen had dismounted and raced to fling their branches between the gaps in the wall. The column of Cauldron-Born marched closer. Beside them rode mounted Huntsmen garbed in heavy jackets of wolfskin, the troop captains whose harsh commands reached Taran's ears like the snapping of a lash. Their orders rang in a language unknown to him, but Taran well understood their scornful tone and the brutal laughter that spat from their lips.

As at Caer Dathyl, the Cauldron-Born held their ranks, striding onward, unwavering. They had drawn their swords from their belts of heavy bronze. The bronze studs covering their leather breastplates glinted dully. Their pallid faces were frozen, as empty as their staring eyes.

Suddenly the horns of the captains screamed like hawks. The Cauldron warriors stiffened, and in another moment lunged forward at a faster gait, running heavily across the dark red earth.

The men of the Commots leaped to their makeshift barrier of rocks and branches. The Cauldron-Born flung themselves against the ruined wall and strove to clamber upwards. Fflewddur, leaving Llyan with Glew amid the other steeds, had snatched up a long branch and, shouting at the top of his voice, thrust it like a spear, into the mass of climbing warriors. Beside him, Gurgi flailed a huge staff, striking desperately at the rising wave. Heedless of Taran's warning outcry, Eilonwy plied her spear and it was under her furious onslaught that the first Cauldron warrior toppled and fell, struggling to regain his footing amid the ranks that streamed silently over him. Taran's band redoubled their efforts, slashing, sweeping, fending off the mute foe with all their strength.

Others among the deathless troops lost their footing as the surging attackers threw themselves blindly against the barrier, only to be struck down by the lashing staves and spear shafts of the Commot men.

'They fear us!' cried the bard in frenzied joy. 'See! They turn away! If we can't slay them, Great Belin, we can still push them back!'

In the turmoil of warriors and the shrilling of the Huntsmen's horns, Taran glimpsed the ranks of Cauldron-Born veer from the threatening hedge of spears. His heart leaped. Were the captains indeed fearful of the hindrance, of the waning power of their mute host? Even now the attacking wave semed weaker, though he could not be sure that it was no more than his hope that made it appear so. No longer was he even sure how long they struggled at the wall. Wearied by the endless thrusts of his spear, he felt it had been forever, although the sky was still light.

Of a sudden, he realized Fflewddur was right. The silent mass of deathless warriors had fallen back. The Huntsmen captains had taken their decision. Like beasts that find their prey too well hidden, and unworthy of their efforts, the mounted leaders sounded a long, wavering note on their horns. The ranks of Cauldron-Born swung towards the Hills of Bran-Galedd.

Cheers burst from the Commot warriors. Taran spun about to find Coll. But the old warrior was hastening farther along the wall. Taran cried out to him, then in dismay realized what Coll had seen. A band of Cauldron-Born had broken from the main force and now strove to clamber through an undefended breach.

Coll reached it as the first Cauldron warrior had begun to force himself over the stones. The old man was upon him in an instant and, dropping his spear, seized the warrior in his burly arms and flung him downward. While other Cauldron-Born swarmed to the breach, Coll snatched out his sword and laid about him right and left, heedless of the attackers' hacking and stabbing blades. Shouting in wrath as the weapon shattered in his hands, the stout farmer cast it away and struck out with his heavy fists. The deathless warriors clung to him, striving to pull him into their midst, but he shook them off, ripped a sword from the grasp of a tottering Cauldron-Born, and swung it as if he meant to fell an oak with a single blow.

Taran was at Coll's side in a moment. The horns of the Huntsmen screamed the signal to retreat. Now Taran realized the attack had truly ended with this last convulsion. The Cauldron-Born had begun to scale the heights. The Red Fallows were barred to them.

Coll was bleeding heavily from the head; his fleece-lined coat, bloodsoaked, was slashed and tattered by the blades of the Cauldron-Born. Quickly, Taran and Fflewddur carried him between them to the bottom of the wall. Gurgi, whimpering in distress, hurried to aid them. Eilonwy had torn off her cloak to cushion the old farmer against the harsh stones.

'After them, my boy,' Coll gasped. 'Give them no rest. The twigs have turned the flood, but it must be turned again, and many times, if you would block the way to Annuvin.'

'One stout oak tree has turned it,' Taran replied. 'Once again, I have leaned on it.' He took Coll's work-hardened hands and gently tried to lift him.

Coll's broad face grinned and he shook his head. 'I am a farmer,' he murmured, 'but warrior enough to know my own death wound. Go along, my boy. Carry with you no more burden than you must.'

'What then,' answered Taran, 'will you have me break the promise I made? That we will dig and weed together?' But the words came painfully as a dagger wound.

Eilonwy, her face drawn, looked anxiously at Taran.

'I had hoped one day to sleep in my own garden,' Coll said. 'The drone of bees would have pleased me more than the horn of Gwyn the Hunter. But I see the choice was not to be mine.'

'The horn of Gwyn does not blow for you,' said Taran. 'You hear the Cauldron-Born summoned to retreat.' Yet even as he spoke, the faint notes of a horn rose above the hills and its dying echoes trembled like shadows over the wasteland. Eilonwy covered her face with her hands.

'See to our plantings, my boy,' said Coll.

'We shall both do so,' answered Taran. 'The weeds will no more stand against you than did Arawn's warriors.'

The stout old farmer did not answer. It was a long moment before Taran realized that Coll was dead.

While the grieving companions gathered stones from the ruined wall, with his own hands Taran hollowed out a grave in the harsh earth, allowing none other to aid him in this task. Even when the humble mound had risen above Coll Son of Collfrewr, he did not move from it, but ordered Fflewddur and the companions to press on into the Hills of Bran-Galedd, where he would join them before nightfall.

For long he stood silently. As the sky darkened, at last he turned away and climbed heavily astride Melynlas. He halted another moment by the mound of red earth and rough stones.

'Sleep well, grower of turnips and gatherer of apples,' Taran murmured. 'You are far from where you longed to be. So, too, am I.'

Alone he rode across the darkening Fallows to the waiting hills.

CHAPTER 13

Darkness

In the days that followed, the companions strove to overtake the Cauldron-Born and again fling themselves across the path of the retreating warriors, but their progress was agonizingly slow. Taran knew Coll had spoken truly when he had called the Hills of Bran-Galedd both friend and foe: the rocky troughs and narrow defiles, the sudden drops where the ground fell away sharply into frozen gorges offered the companions their only hope of delaying the deathless host moving onward like a river of iron. But at the same time, from the high crags of the west, gusts of snow-laden wind battered the struggling band with icy hammers. The winding trails were slippery and treacherous. The ravines held deep pits filled with snow, where horse and rider might founder beyond rescue.

In the hills, Taran's most trusted guide was Llassar. Surefooted, long used to mountain ways, the Commot youth was now shepherd to a different, grimmer flock. More than once, Llassar's keen senses kept the companions from the icy traps of snow-hidden crevices, and he discovered pathways no other eye could see. But the progress of the ragged band was nonetheless slow, and all suffered cruelly from the cold, men and animals alike. Only the great cat, Llyan, showed no concern for the bitter blasts that drove frosty needles against the faces of the companions.

'She seems to be enjoying herself,' Fflewddur sighed, huddling in his cloak. He had been obliged to dismount, for Llyan had suddenly taken it into her head to sharpen her huge claws against a tree trunk. 'And so should I,' he added, 'if I had her coat.'

Gurgi ruefully agreed. Since entering the hills, the poor

creature had grown more and more to resemble a drift of hairy snow. The cold had even stopped Glew's endless whining; the former giant pulled his hood over his face and little could be seen of him but the frostbitten end of his flabby nose. Eilonwy, too, was unwontedly silent. Her heart, Taran knew, was as heavy as his own.

Yet Taran forced himself, as far as he was able, to put grief aside. His dogged pursuit had at last brought his warriors within striking distance of the Cauldron-Born, and now he thought only of the means to slow their march to Annuvin. As at the Red Fallows, the companions laboured to build barriers of tree limbs, and set them across a narrow gorge, toiling until the sweat drenched their garments and froze in the bitter wind. This time the livid warriors overran them, mutely hacking away the branches with their swords. In despair, the men of the Commots clashed hand-to-hand with the oncoming foe; but the Cauldron-Born slashed mercilessly through their ranks. Taran and the Commot men sought to block the way with heavy boulders; but even with the help of Hevydd's mighty arms this labour was beyond their strength, and the toll of the slain only rose higher.

The days were a white nightmare of snow and wind. The nights were frozen with hopelessness, and like exhausted animals the companions found respite amid rocky overhangs and the scant shelter of the mountain passes. Yet concealment served little purpose, the presence of the Commot warriors was known and their movements quickly sighted by the enemy captains. At first, the Cauldron-Born had chosen to disregard the ragged band; now the deathless marchers not only quickened their pace, they swung closer to Taran's riders as though eager to join battle.

This puzzled Fflewddur, who rode beside Taran at the head of the column.

Taran frowned and shook his head grimly. 'I understand it all too well,' he said. 'Their power had waned when they were farther from Annuvin. Closer, it returns to them, and as we grow weaker, they grow stronger. Unless we halt them, one time for all, our efforts will do no more than sap our own strength. Soon,' he added bitterly, 'we shall defeat ourselves more sharply than Arawn's warriors could ever hope to do.'

But he said nothing of another fear that lay in all their hearts. Each passing day showed more clearly the Cauldron-Born were turning south, away from the Hills of Bran-Galedd and once again towards the swifter, easier way of the Red Fallows. With dour satisfaction, Taran judged this to mean the enemy still feared the pursuers and would strive to any lengths to be rid of them.

Snow fell that night, and the companions halted, blinded by the whirling flakes and by their own weariness. Before dawn the Cauldron-Born attacked their camp.

At first, Taran believed only one company of the mute warriors had overrun his outposts. As the Commot warriors sprang to arms amid the terrified shrieking of horses and the clang of blades, he quickly realized the entire enemy column was slashing across his lines. He spurred Melynlas into the fray. Fflewddur, with Glew clinging to his waist, was astride Llyan, who sped in great bounds to join the embattled defenders. Taran had lost sight of Eilonwy and Gurgi among the rush of warriors. Like a ruthless sword, the Cauldron-Born had split the Commot horsemen's ranks and were streaming through unhindered, crushing all who stood against them.

All day the uneven battle raged while the men of the Commots struggled vainly to rally their forces. By dusk the path of the Cauldron-Born was a bloody wake of wounded and slain. In one deadly blow, the Cauldron host had broken free of their pursuers to move swiftly and unfaltering from the hills.

Eilonwy and Gurgi were missing.

Fearful and dismayed, Taran and Fflewddur pressed

their way through the shattered remnants of the war band struggling to regain their ranks. Torches had been lit to signal rallying points for the stragglers, who stumbled wounded and bewildered among the bodies of their fallen comrades. Throughout the night Taran searched frantically, sounding his horn and shouting the names of the lost companions. With Fflewddur, he had ridden beyond the battleground, hoping for some sign of either one of them. There was none, and the new snowfall, which began towards dawn, covered all tracks.

By midmorning, the survivors had gathered. The passage of the Cauldron-Born had taken heavy toll of both mounts and men; of the Commot warriors, one out of three had fallen beneath the swords of the deathless foe; and of the steeds, more than half. Lluagor galloped empty-saddled. Eilonwy and Gurgi were among neither the slain nor the living.

Desperate now, Taran made ready to search through the farther hills. But Fflewddur, his face grave and filled with concern, took Taran's arm and drew him back.

'Alone, you can't hope to find them,' warned the bard. 'Neither can you spare time nor men for a search party. If we're to stop those foul brutes before they reach the Fallows, we shall have to move with all speed. Your Commot friends are ready to march.'

'You and Llassar must lead them,' Taran replied. 'Once Eilonwy and Gurgi are found, we'll join you somehow. Go quickly. We shall meet soon again.'

The bard shook his head. 'If that's your command, so be it. But, as I have heard it, Taran Wanderer it was who called the Commot folk to his banner, and for the sake of Taran Wanderer they answered. They followed where you led. For none other would they have done as much.'

'What, then,' Taran cried, 'would you have me leave Eilonwy and Gurgi in danger?'

'It is a heavy choice,' Fflewddur said. 'Alas, none can

lighten it for you.'

Taran did not reply. Fflewddur's words grieved him all the more because of their truth. Hevydd and Llassar had asked no more than to fight at his side. Llonio had given his life at Caer Dathyl. There was no Commot warrior who had not lost kinsman or comrade. If he left them to seek Eilonwy, would she herself deem his choice good? The horseman awaited his orders. Melynlas impatiently pawed the ground.

'If Eilonwy and Gurgi are slain,' Taran said in an anguished voice, 'they are beyond my help. If they live, I must hope and trust they will find their way to us.' He swung heavily into the saddle. 'If they live,' he murmured.

Without daring a backward glance at the silent, empty hills, he rode towards the war band.

By the time the Commot men were on the march again, the Cauldron-Born had well outdistanced them and were moving without delay to the foothills of Bran-Galedd. Even at their fastest pace, halting only for moments of fitful rest, the Commot riders regained little of the precious time that had been lost.

Each day Taran strained his eyes for a sign of Eilonwy and Gurgi, hoping against hope that the Princess would find some means of reaching the war band again. But the two companions had vanished, and Fflewddur's desperate cheerfulness and assurance that both would appear from one moment to the next rang false and hollow.

At midmorning on the third day of their march an outrider galloped in with tidings of strange movements in the pine forest at the column's flank. Taran halted his warriors, hastily ordering them to stand ready for combat, then rode with Fflewddur to see for himself. Through the trees a little below him he could make out no more than a vague stirring, as if shadows of branches flickered across the drifts. But in another instant the bard shouted excitedly and Taran quickly sounded his horn.

From the woods tramped a long procession of short, stocky figures. Garbed in white cloaks and hoods, they were all but invisible against the snow, and not until they had begun to move across a bare stretch of rocky ground could Taran distinguish one marcher from the next. Their stout leather boots, laced and bound with thongs, barely showed below their cloaks, and looked like nothing so much as rapidly moving tree stumps. The shapes that bulked on their shoulders or at their waists were, Taran guessed, weapons or sacks of provisions.

'Great Belin!' cried Fflewddur. 'If that's who I think it is . . .'

Taran had already dismounted and was racing down the slope, waving at the bard to follow him. At the head of the band, which seemed to number well over a hundred, trudged a familiar, stumpy figure. Though he, too, was heavily muffled in white, his crimson hair flamed out beyond the fringe of his hood. In one hand he carried a short, heavy-bladed axe, and in the other, a thick staff. He had caught sight of Taran and Fflewddur and strode to meet them.

In another instant the bard and Taran were clasping his hands, pummelling his burly shoulders, and shouting so many greetings and questions that the new arrival clapped his hands to his head.

'Doli!' Taran cried. 'Good old Doli!'

'I heard you clearly the first few times,' the dwarf snorted. 'If I ever doubted you recognized me, you've fully convinced me that you do.' He put his hands on his hips and looked up sharply, trying, as always, to appear as gruff as he could. Despite himself his bright red eyes flashed with pleasure and his features broke into a grin, which he tried, without success, to change to his usual scowl.

'You've led us a chase,' Doli declared, motioning the warriors to follow Taran up the slope. 'We had word you'd gone into the hills, but saw nothing of you until today.'

'Doli!' Taran exclaimed, still amazed at the unexpected sight of this long-absent companion. 'What good luck brings you to us?'

'Good luck?' grumbled Doli. 'Do you call tramping day and night in snow and wind good luck? All of us Fair Folk are abroad, one place or another – Orders of King Eiddileg. Mine were to find you and put myself at your service. No offence, but I could guess that if anybody in Prydain needed help it would turn out to be you. So, here we are.'

'Gwystyl has done his work well,' Taran said. 'We knew he was journeying to your realm, but we feared King Eiddileg might not heed him.'

'I can't say he was overjoyed,' Doli answered. 'In fact, he nearly burst. I was there when our gloomy friend brought word of your plight and I thought my ears would split with Eiddileg's bellowing. Great gawks! Lumbering oafs! Giant clodpoles! All his usual opinions about humans. But he agreed willingly enough despite his bluster. He's really fond of you, no matter what he says. Above all, he remembers how you saved the Fair Folk from being turned into frogs, moles, and whatever. It was the greatest service any mortal ever did for us, and Eiddileg means to repay the debt.

'Yes, the Fair Folk are on the march,' Doli continued. 'Alas, we came too late to Caer Dathyl. But King Smoit has cause to thank us. There's a host of Fair Folk fighting side by side with him. The northern lords are ready for battle, and we'll take a hand in that, too, you can be sure.'

Doli, for all his gruffness, was obviously proud of his own tidings. He had finished, with great relish, an account of one fray in which the Fair Folk had baffled the enemy by making an entire valley so resound with echoes that the foe fled in terror, believing themselves surrounded, and had begun another tale of Fair Folk valour, when he stopped abruptly, seeing the look of concern on Taran's face. Doli listened while Taran told what had befallen the other companions, and it was the dwarf's turn to be grave and thoughtful. When Taran finished, Doli did not reply for a time.

'As for Eilonwy and Gurgi,' the dwarf said at last, 'I agree with Fflewddur. They'll manage, somehow. And if I know the Princess, I wouldn't be surprised to see her galloping up at the head of her own army.

'With the Cauldron-Born, we're all in bad straits,' Doli continued. 'Even we Fair Folk can do little against such creatures. All the tricks that would gull a common mortal are useless. The Cauldron-Born aren't human – I should say they're less than human. They've no memory of what they were, no fear, no hope – nothing can touch them.' The dwarf shook his head. 'And I see that any victory we might gain elsewhere would be wasted unless we find some way to deal with that spawn of Annuvin. Gwydion is quite right. If they aren't stopped – well, my friends, among us we'll have to do it, and that's flat.'

By this time the Fair Folk band had reached Taran's lines and a murmur of wonder spread through the ranks of the Commot men. All had heard of the skill and prowess of King Eiddileg's fighting forces, but none had seen them face to face. Hevydd the Smith marvelled at their axes and short swords, pronouncing them sharper and better tempered than any he could make. For their own part, the Fair Folk seemed not the least uneasy; the tallest of Eiddileg's warriors stood barely higher than Llassar's knee, but the Fair Folk soldiers looked on their human comrades with the friendly indulgence they might show to overgrown children.

Doli patted Llyan's head and the huge animal purred happily in recognition. The sight of Glew, hunched on a rock and staring sourly at the new arrivals, brought a cry of surprise from the crimson-haired dwarf. 'Whoever – or whatever – is that? It's too big for a toadstool and too small for anything else!'

'I'm glad you asked,' replied Glew. 'It's a tale I'm sure you will find most interesting. I was once a giant, and my present unhappy state comes, no more and no less, from a complete lack of concern from those – ' he looked dourly at Taran and the bard – 'who might have been expected to show at least a small amount of consideration. My kingdom – yes, I would appreciate it if you addressed me as King Glew – was the finest cavern, with the finest bats, on the Isle of Mona. A cavern so vast . . .'

Fflewddur clapped his hands to his ears. 'Leave off, giant! Enough! We've no time for your prattle about caverns and bats. We know you've been ill-used. You've told us so yourself. Believe me, a Fflam is patient, but if I could find a cavern I'd pop you into it and leave you there.'

Doli's face had turned deeply thoughtful. 'Caverns,' the dwarf muttered. He snapped his fingers. 'Caverns! Hear me well,' he said quickly. 'No more than a day's march from here – yes, I'm sure of it – there's a Fair Folk mine. The best gems and precious stones are gone, and Eiddileg's had no one working there as long as I can remember. But I think we can get into it. Of course! If we follow the main shaft it should bring us out almost at the edge of the Red Fallows. You'll catch up with the Cauldron-Born in no time at all. With all our warriors together we'll stop them one way or another. How, I don't know. That doesn't matter for the moment. We'll cross that bridge when we come to it.'

Doli grinned broadly. 'My friends, you're with Fair Folk now. When we do something, it's done right. The first half of your worries are over. The second half,' he added, 'might be something else again.'

For the first time since leaving Caer Dallben, Glew

appeared in good spirits. The idea of anything resembling a cavern seemed to cheer him, although the result of his improved temper was a further spate of rambling tales about his own feats as a giant. However, after a hard day and night of marching, when Doli halted at the sheer face of a high cliff, the former giant began glancing about fearfully. His nose twitched and his eyes blinked in dismay. The entrance to the ancient mine towards which the dwarf beckoned was no more than a fissure in the rock, barely wide enough for the horses, overhung with icicles glistening like sharp teeth.

'No, no,' stammered Glew. 'This doesn't compare with my realm on Mona. Not half the size. No, you can't expect me to go stumbling around a shabby den like this.'

He would have drawn back had not Fflewddur taken him by the collar and dragged him along.

'Have done, giant!' cried the bard. 'In you go with the rest of us.' But Fflewddur himself seemed none too eager to lead Llyan through the rocky crevice. 'A Fflam is valiant,' he murmured, 'but I've never been fond of underground passages and all such. No luck with them. Mark my words, we'll be grubbing like moles before we're through.'

At the mouth of the cavern Taran halted. Beyond this point there was no hope of finding Eilonwy. Once more he battled the wish of his heart to seek her again before she would be forever lost to him. With all his strength he fought to wrench these thoughts from his mind. But when at last he ruthlessly forced himself to follow the bard, it was as though he had left all of himself behind. He stumbled blindly into the darkness.

At Doli's orders the warriors had fashioned torches. These they now lit, and in the flickering light Taran saw the dwarf had brought them into a shaft that dipped gradually downward. Its walls of living rock rose no higher than Taran's upraised hands. Dismounted, the

Commot men led their fearful horses past sharp outcroppings and over broken stones.

This, Doli explained, was not the mine itself, but only one of many side-tunnels the Fair Folk had used when carrying sacks of gems above ground. Indeed, as the dwarf foretold, the passageway soon grew much wider and the rocky ceiling soared three times Taran's height. Narrow platforms of wood, one above the other, followed the walls on either side, though many had fallen over the earthen floor. Lengths of half-rotted timbers shored up the archways leading from one gallery to the next, but of these some had partly crumbled, forcing warriors and steeds to pick their way most cautiously over or around the piles of rubble. The air was stifling after the icy wind above ground, and hung heavy with ancient dust and decay. Echoes flitted like bats through the long-abandoned chambers as the war band moved in a wavering file, with torches raised high above their heads. The twisting shadows seemed to muffle the sound of their footsteps; only the piercing whinny of a frightened steed broke the silence.

Glew, who had not left off his complaining since entering the mine, gave a sharp cry of surprise. He stooped and snatched something from the ground. In the flare of his torch, Taran saw the former giant held a glittering gem as big as a fist.

Fflewddur had seen it, too, and he sternly ordered, 'Put that down, little man. This is a Fair Folk trove, not that bat-ridden cave of yours.'

Glew clutched his find to his chest. 'It's mine!' he squealed. 'None of you saw it. If you had, you'd have kept it for yourselves.'

Doli, who glanced at the gem, snorted scornfully. 'It's rubbish,' the dwarf said to Taran. 'No Fair Folk craftsman would waste his time on it. We use better quality than that to mend a roadbed. If your mushroom-faced friend wants to burden himself, he's more than welcome.'

Without waiting to be told twice, Glew hastily thrust the gem into the leather pouch dangling at his side, and his flabby features took on an expression Taran had seen only when the former giant was in the midst of a meal.

From then on, as the companions progressed steadily through the mine, Glew's beady eyes darted everywhere and he strode forward with unwonted energy and interest. The former giant was not disappointed, for soon the torchlight glinted on other gems half-buried in the ground or protruding from walls. Glew fell upon them instantly, scrabbling away with his pudgy fingers and popping the glittering crystals into his sack. With each new find he grew more excited, giggling and mumbling to himself.

The bard looked pityingly at him. 'Well,' he sighed, 'the little weasel has at last sniffed out something to profit himself. Much good it may do him once we're above ground again. A handful of rocks! The only use I can see is if he throws them at the Cauldron-Born.'

But Glew, absorbed in gathering as many gems as quickly as he could, paid no heed to Fflewddur's remarks. In little time the former giant's pouch was crammed with jewels of bright red and brilliant green, with gems clear as water or, in their glittering depths, flecked with gold and silver.

Taran's thoughts were not on the abandoned riches of the mine, although the jewels seemed to grow more plentiful as the long column of warriors made their way farther into the tunnel. As far as Taran could judge, it was no later than midday, and already the companions had journeyed a considerable distance. And, as the tunnel widened and the path straightened, their pace gained even more speed.

'Easy as whistling,' declared Doli. 'Another day and a half at most and we'll come above ground at the Fallows.'

'It's our only hope,' Taran said, 'and, thanks to you, the

best hope we've had. But the Fallows trouble me. If the land is barren we'll have little protection for ourselves, and little means to hinder the Cauldron-Born.'

'Humph!' cried Doli. 'As I told you, you're dealing with Fair Folk now, my lad. When we set to a task there's nothing paltry or small about it. You'll see. Something will come to hand.'

'Speaking of paltry and small,' interrupted Fflewddur, 'where is Glew?'

Taran halted and quickly looked around. At first he saw nothing of the former giant. He lifted his torch and called Glew's name. A moment later he caught sight of him and ran forward in alarm.

Glew, in his search for treasure, had clambered up to one of the wooden platforms. Just above the arch leading to the next chamber a sparkling gem as big as his own head was embedded amid the rocks; Glew, having swung precariously to a narrow ledge, was trying with all his might to dislodge it.

Taran cried out to him to come down, but Glew tugged and heaved all the harder. Dropping the reins of Melynlas, Taran was about to swing up after him, but Doli seized his arm.

'Don't do it!' snapped the dwarf. 'The beams won't hold you.' He whistled through his teeth and signalled two of the Fair Folk warriors to climb to the platform which, under Glew's furious struggle with the gem, had begun to sway dangerously. 'Hurry!' Doli shouted. 'Bring that idiot down here!'

Just then Glew's pouch, already filled to bursting, tore apart. The gems streamed down in a glittering shower and Glew, with a yell of dismay, spun around to clutch at them. His foothold slipped, he clawed frantically at the platform and as he did so the arch gave way beneath him. Now shrieking not for his lost jewels but for his life, Glew flailed wildly and caught one of the swaying timbers.

With a crash he toppled to earth. Behind him the archway lurched, the ceiling rumbled. Glew picked himself up and scuttled madly from the hail of falling stones.

'Back!' Doli shouted. 'Back! All of you!'

The horses reared and whinnied as the warriors strove to turn them. With an earsplitting crack, the upper platforms collapsed, an avalanche of boulders and broken beams thundered into the gallery. Blinding, choking dust filled the tunnel, the mine seemed to shudder all along its length, then settled into deathly silence.

Shouting for Doli and Fflewddur, Taran stumbled to the heap of wreckage. None of the warriors or animals had been caught in it; behind them, the tunnel had held firm and kept them safe. But the way forward was hopelessly blocked.

Doli had scrambled on to the heap of stones and wood and was tugging at the end of a long beam. But after a moment he stopped, breathless, and turned a despairing face to Taran. 'It's no good,' he gasped. 'If you want to keep on we'll have to dig our way through.'

'How long?' Taran asked urgently. 'How much time dare we lose?'

Doli shook his head. 'Hard to say. Even with Fair Folk it will be a long task. Days, very likely. Who knows how far the damage has gone?' He snorted angrily. 'You can thank that half-witted, undersized, two-legged toadstool of a giant for it!'

Taran's heart sank. 'What then?' he asked. 'Must we retrace our steps?' From the expression on Doli's face, he feared what the dwarf's answer would be.

Doli nodded curtly. 'We're badly delayed, no matter what. But if you want my advice, I say turn around and go back. Make our way to the Fallows above ground as best we can. The whole mine is weakened now; there'll be more cave-ins, or I'll miss my guess. Next time we may not be so lucky.'

'Lucky!' moaned the bard, who had slumped down on a rock. He put his head in his hands. 'Days wasted! The Cauldron-Born will be in Annuvin before we have another chance at them. The only luck that would suit me now would be to see that greedy weasel under a pile of his own worthless gems!'

Glew, meanwhile, had ventured to crawl from under one of the remaining platforms. His garments were torn, his pudgy face smeared with dust.

'Days wasted?' he wailed. 'Cauldron-Born? Blocked up tunnels? But has any one of you stopped to consider I've just lost a fortune? My gems are gone, all of them, and you don't give it a second thought. I call that selfish. Selfish! There's no other word for it.'

CHAPTER 14

Daylight

The Princess Eilonwy was doubly angry. First, she was lost; second, she was a prisoner. Swept away from Taran and Fflewddur during the attack, she would surely have fallen among the slain had not Gurgi dragged her from the fray. When the assault had shifted beyond them, she had stumbled blindly, with Gurgi at her side, over the darkening crags. At nightfall, when they could search no longer for Taran, Gurgi had found a shallow cave where they crouched and shivered until first light. During the next day, as the two companions sought Taran's trail, the marauders had suddenly leaped upon them.

Biting, kicking, and scratching, Eilonwy struggled vainly to free herself from the burly man who had seized her. Another had flung Gurgi to the ground and, with dagger drawn, set his knee in the small of the hapless creature's back. In a trice the two companions were bound hand and foot and hoisted like mealsacks on their assailants' shoulders. Eilonwy had no idea of the direction in which she was being carried, but in a little while she glimpsed a campfire flickering through the gathering dusk and hunched around it a ruffianly band of a dozen or more.

The man squatting nearest the fire looked up. Garbed in dirty sheepskins and a rough cloak, he was heavy-faced and stubble-bearded, his long hair yellowish and tangled.

'I sent you for game, not prisoners,' he called out hoarsely. 'What have you found?'

'Lean pickings,' answered Eilonwy's captor, dropping his furious burden to the turf beside Gurgi. 'A brace of churls, for what they may be worth.'

'Nothing, very likely.' The heavy-faced man spat in the

fire. 'You should have slit their gullets and spared yourself the burden.' He climbed to his feet and strode to the companions. With a grimy, broken-nailed hand he seized Eilonwy by the throat as if he meant to throttle her. 'Who are you, boy?' he demanded in a grating voice. His cold blue eyes narrowed. 'Who do you serve? What ransom will you bring? Answer quickly when Dorath asks a question.'

At the sound of the name Eilonwy caught her breath. Taran had spoken of Dorath. From Gurgi's terrified whimpering she judged he, too, had recognized the outlaw.

'Answer!' Dorath cried with a curse. He struck Eilonwy across the face. The girl stumbled and fell, her head singing from the blow. The golden sphere dropped from her jacket. Eilonwy strained at her bonds and tried to fling herself on top of the bauble. A booted foot kicked it from her. Dorath bent and snatched up the sphere, turning it curiously in the firelight.

'What is it?' questioned one of the ruffians, pressing closer to gape at the bauble.

'Gold it is,' said another. 'Come, Dorath, chop the thing apart and share it out.'

'Hands off, you swine,' Dorath growled. He thrust the bauble into his sheepskin. Mutters of protest rose from the band, but Dorath silenced them with a glance. He bent down to Eilonwy. 'Where did you steal such a trinket, you young thief? Will you keep your head on your shoulders? Then tell me where we can find more treasure like this.'

Eilonwy, though furious, kept silent.

Dorath grinned. 'You will speak soon enough,' he said, 'and only wish you had spoken earlier. First, let me see if your fellow has a tongue looser than yours.'

Gurgi, teeth chattering violently, had sunk his head deep into his sheepskin coat and tightly hunched his shoulders.

'Do you play turtle with me?' Dorath cried with a harsh

laugh. He knotted his thick fingers in Gurgi's hair and jerked the creature's head upright. 'Small wonder you hide your face! It's ugly as ever I've seen!'

Dorath stopped suddenly and squinted closer. 'Ugly it is, and not one easily forgotten. So ho! We are old friends, you and I. You share my hospitality once more! When last we met, you were comrade to a pig-keeper.' He turned his glance on Eilonwy. 'But this is not the swineherd.'

Dorath gripped Eilonwy's face and roughly turned it from side to side. 'This beardless boy . . .' He grunted in surprise. 'What, then? Boy? – No boy at all! A wench!'

Eilonwy could no longer contain herself. 'Wench indeed! I'm Eilonwy Daughter of Angharad Daughter of Regat Princess of Llyr. I don't like being tied up, I don't like being smacked. I don't like being pawed, and I'll thank you to stop doing all of that immediately!' Despite her bonds she kicked vigorously at the outlaw.

Dorath laughed and drew back a pace. 'My memory is that the Lord Swineherd spoke once of you.' He gave a mocking bow. 'Welcome, Princess Vixen. You are a choicer prize than any ransom. A long score lies between Dorath and your pig-keeper. You give me and my company the pleasure of settling a little of it.'

'I'll give you the pleasure of setting Gurgi and me loose this very instant,' Eilonwy flung at him. 'And I shall have my bauble again.'

Dorath's face had grown mottled. 'You shall go free,' he said between his teeth, 'after a time, my pretty Princess, after a time. When you shall be fitting company for pig-keepers, perhaps you may join the swineherd again. Perhaps he will even recognize your charms, whatever may be left of them.'

'Have you considered what will be left of *you* when Taran finds you?' Eilonwy retorted. Until now the Princess of Llyr had kept her self-possession. But she could sense the outlaw's thoughts behind his cold eyes and for the first time she was deeply afraid.

'Lord Swineherd and I will finish our reckoning when the time comes,' Dorath replied. Grinning, he bent towards her. 'But your time is now.'

Gurgi thrashed wildly in his bonds. 'Do not harm wise and kindly Princess!' he shouted. 'Oh, Gurgi will make you pay for hurtful wickedness!' He flung himself against Dorath and tried to sink his teeth into the outlaw's leg.

Cursing, Dorath turned on Gurgi and snatched out his sword. Eilonwy cried aloud.

But before the outlaw could begin his downward stroke a long shape sprang suddenly from the overhanging rocks. Dorath gave a stifled shout. His weapon fell from his hand and he toppled backwards, the furry shadow snarling and tearing at his throat. At the campfire the other outlaws leaped to their feet and screamed in terror. Grey shadows were all about, closing swiftly on them. Vainly the marauders sought to flee, but on all sides they were flung back, borne to the ground by the force of lean bodies and slashing fangs.

Gurgi began yelling fearfully. 'Help, oh help! Oh, evil spirits come to slay us all!'

Eilonwy forced herself upright. Behind her she could feel something sharp gnawing and worrying at her bonds. In another moment her hands were free. She stumbled forward while the grey shadow tore away the thongs holding her feet. In front of her lay the motionless body of Dorath. Quickly Eilonwy knelt and drew the bauble from the outlaw's sheepskin jacket. From her cupped hand the sphere shed golden rays on a huge wolf crouching before her. By the campfire she glimpsed other wolves, withdrawing as swiftly as they had come. Behind them all was silent. Eilonwy shuddered and looked away. The wolves had done their work well.

Gurgi had been freed by a grey she-wolf with a white blaze on her breast and, pleased though he was to be out of the warriors' clutches, he wrinkled his forehead and cast a distrustful glance at his rescuer. The wolf Briavael blinked her yellow eyes and grinned at him. Gurgi, nevertheless, chose to keep his distance.

For her own part, Eilonwy surprisingly felt no fear or uneasiness. The wolf Brynach sat on his haunches, watching her closely. Eilonwy put her hand on the animal's shaggy, muscular neck.

'I hope you know we're trying to thank you,' she said, 'though I'm not sure whether you understand or not. The only wolves I ever met personally lived far from here in Medwyn's valley.'

At this Brynach whined and wagged his tail.

'Well, you do understand that,' said Eilonwy. 'Medwyn . . .' She hesitated. 'There were two wolves . . .' She clapped her hands. 'It must be! I don't mean to say I can tell one wolf from another, at least not at first glance. But there's something about you that reminds me . . . In any case, if that's who you are, we're very glad to see you again. We're obliged to you and now we'll be on our way. Though I'm not exactly sure which way our way is, if you see what I mean.'

Brynach grinned and showed no sign of leaving. Instead, he remained on his haunches, opened his jaws, and gave a high-pitched bark.

Eilonwy sighed and shook her head. 'We're lost and trying to find our companions, but I haven't any idea how to say Assistant Pig-Keeper in wolf speech.'

Gurgi, meantime, had picked up his wallet of food and slung it over his shoulder. At last seeing the wolves meant him no harm, he drew a little closer to Brynach and Briavael and looked at them with great interest, while they studied him no less curiously.

Eilonwy turned to Gurgi. 'I'm sure they're willing to

help us. Oh, if I could only understand them! What good is it being half an enchantress if you can't even tell what a wolf is trying to say to you?' Eilonwy stopped short. 'But – but I think I did understand! I must have! There, one of them just said "Tell us!" I could hear – no, not *hear*; I could feel it!'

She looked at Gurgi in amazement. 'It's not words at all. It's like listening without your ears or hearing with your heart. I know it, but I can't imagine how I do. And yet,' she added wonderingly, 'that's what Taliesin told me.'

'Oh, great wisdom!' Gurgi cried. 'Oh, clever listenings! Gurgi listens, too, but inside hears only rumblings and grumblings when his poor belly is empty! Oh, sorrow! Gurgi will never hear deep secret things like Princess.'

Eilonwy had dropped to her knees beside Brynach. Hurriedly she spoke of Taran, of all the companions and what had befallen them. Brynach pricked up his ears and barked sharply. The huge wolf rose from his haunches, shook the snow from his shaggy coat, and with his teeth gently plucked at Eilonwy's sleeve.

'He says we're to follow them,' Eilonwy told Gurgi. 'Come, we're in safe hands now. Or, should I say paws?'

The wolves padded silently and swiftly, following hidden trails and passages whose existence the girl would have never guessed. The two companions strove to keep up with Brynach's rapid pace; yet often, despite themselves, they were forced to halt and rest. At those times the wolves seemed satisfied to wait patiently until the companions were ready to journey once again. Brynach crouched at Eilonwy's side, his grey head between his paws, seldom drowsing, his ears alert and moving at every faint sound. Briavael, too, served as sentinel and guide, springing lightly to the rocky peaks, sniffing the air; then, with a gesture of her head, beckoning the companions to follow.

Of the rest of the pack Eilonwy saw little. Now and

then, however, she would awaken from a brief slumber to find the wolves sitting in a protective circle about her. Soon the lean grey animals would vanish into the shadows while Brynach and Briavael alone remained. The girl shortly became aware the wolves were not the only creatures in the Hills of Bran-Galedd. Once she glimpsed a large company of bears lumbering in single file along a ridge. They halted a moment, peered curiously, then resumed their march. In the cold, clear air she heard the barking of foxes in the distance and other sounds which might have been echoes or answers to some unknown signal.

'They're scouting all through the hills,' Eilonwy whispered to Gurgi, pointing to a bare summit where a tall stag had suddenly appeared. 'I wonder how many other bands of outlaws are roaming around. If the bears and wolves have anything to say about it, I somehow don't think there's very many.'

The wolf Brynach glanced at her, as though he had overheard Eilonwy's words. He lolled out his tongue and blinked his yellow eyes. Around the sharp rows of gleaming teeth his lips turned slightly in an unmistakable smile.

They continued on their path. At nightfall Eilonwy lit her bauble and held it aloft. The full wolf pack, she saw, had joined them once again, moving in long files on either side of her, just beyond the circle of golden light. The bears, too, were following, and the other forest creatures whose presence she sensed rather than saw.

There were, in the Hills of Bran-Galedd, many places of danger and death. Of these, the Princess of Llyr was unaware, for she and Gurgi passed them by unharmed, safe amid the watchful band of silent guardians.

Late in the morning of the next day Briavael, who had spent most of her time scouting the passages ahead, grew excited and eager. The she-wolf barked and leaped atop high-standing rocks where she faced westward, wagging her tail briskly and urging the companions to greater speed.

'I think they've found Taran!' Eilonwy cried. 'I can't quite make out what they're saying, but it sounds very much as if they have. Men and horses! A mountain cat – that must be Llyan! But what are they all doing in this direction? Are they going to the Red Fallows again?'

Neither Eilonwy nor Gurgi could check their impatience to join the companions once more; they refused to halt for food or rest and Brynach frequently had to fasten his teeth in Eilonwy's cloak to keep the girl from taking needless risks among the ever-steepening hills. Soon the travellers reached the rim of a deep mountain cup, and a cry of joy burst from Eilonwy's lips.

'I see them! I see them!' She hastily pointed downward, into the wide valley. Gurgi had run up beside her and began to leap with excitement.

'Oh, it is kindly master!' he shouted. 'Oh, yes, and brave bard! No bigger than ants, but sharp-eyed Gurgi sees them!'

Only by straining her eyes could Eilonwy distinguish the tiny figures, so distant were they. The long descent into the valley, she knew, would take the rest of the day, and she was anxious to reach the companions before nightfall. She was about to scramble down the cliff when she stopped suddenly.

'What can they be doing?' she cried. 'They're going straight into the wall of rock. Is it a cave? Look, there's the last horseman. Now I can't see any of them. If it's a cave, it must be the biggest one in Prydain! I don't understand a bit of it. Is there a passage of some kind? Or a tunnel? Oh, that's vexing! You might know an Assistant Pig-Keeper would take it into his head to vanish the moment he's been found!'

Hurriedly, Eilonwy began picking her way down the steep slope. For all her haste the descent seemed endless.

Even with the help of Brynach and Briavael the two had gone little more than half the distance by the time the sun had dropped westward and the shadows had begun to lengthen. Brynach suddenly halted and growled deeply in his throat. His hackles rose and he bared his teeth. The eyes of the wolf were fixed on the valley, and his muzzle twitched uneasily. In another moment, Eilonwy saw what had made Brynach stop. A long column of warriors had appeared and was moving rapidly westward.

Briavael whined shrilly. From the voice of the she-wolf, Eilonwy sensed fear and hatred. She understood the reason.

'Huntsmen!' the girl cried. 'It looks like hundreds of them on the way back to Annuvin. Oh, I hope they don't see Taran's tracks, though he's very likely safe enough where he is.'

No sooner had she said this than a movement at the distant wall of rock made her clap a hand to her mouth. From the deepening shadows she saw, one by one, the tiny figures of Taran and his band reappear.

'No!' Eilonwy gasped. 'They're coming out again!'

From her vantage point, the girl could scan the valley, and it was suddenly, coldly clear to her that the Commot warriors and the Huntsmen, as yet unseen by one another, were moving closer together.

'They'll be trapped!' Eilonwy cried. 'Taran! Taran!'

The echoes died in the vast, snowy expanse. Taran could neither see nor hear her. Darkness had now fallen over the valley, blinding the girl to the inevitable clash of the warrior bands. It was a nightmare in which all action was useless, in which she could only wait for the slaughter bound to come. She felt as though her hands were tied and her voice stifled.

Still calling Taran's name, Eilonwy snatched the bauble from her cloak. She lifted the sphere high. Brighter and brighter it glowed. The wolves turned away fearfully and

Gurgi threw his arms over his face. The beams spread and rose towards the clouds, as though the sun itself were bursting from the mountainside. The dark cliffs and black branches of the trees were drenched in light, brilliant and clear. The whole valley had turned bright as noon.

CHAPTER 15

The River of Ice

Under the sudden outpouring of golden light, the Huntsmen shouted in alarm and a wave of fear rippled along the marching column as they faltered and fell back into the protection of a deep gorge. Instantly Taran realized how closely he had come to leading the Commot horsemen into a fatal trap, but a cry of joy sprang from his lips.

'Eilonwy!'

He would have urged Melynlas across the valley to the mountainside had not Fflewddur put out a restraining hand.

'Hold, hold,' cried the bard. 'She's found us, right enough. Great Belin, there's no mistaking the light from that girl's bauble! She's saved our lives with it. Gurgi's sure to be with her, too; but if you go galloping after them, none of you will get back. We've seen the Huntsmen, and they could hardly help seeing *us*.'

Doli had clambered atop a boulder and stood peering after the retreating Huntsmen. Eilonwy's signal winked out as quickly as it had appeared, and in another moment the winter darkness fell once more over the valley.

'A fine plight!' growled the dwarf. 'Of all times to be caught above ground! The mine is useless to us, and there's no other passage within a week's march. Even if there were, we couldn't reach it with an army of Huntsmen blocking the way.'

Fflewddur had drawn his sword. 'I say attack! Those foul villains had a good scare. They'll have no stomach for a fight now. We'll set upon them without warning. Great Belin, that's something they won't expect!'

Doli snorted at him. 'You've left your wits in the mineshaft! Set upon the Huntsmen? Slay one and make the others that much stronger? Even Fair Folk would think twice about attacking those ruffians. No, my friend, it won't answer.'

'When I was a giant,' put in Glew, 'it would have been a simple matter for me to put them all to flight. However, through no fault of my own, times have changed, and I can hardly say they've changed for the better. On Mona, for example, one day I had decided something really had to be done about those impudent bats. It's an interesting tale . . .'

'Silence, you puny thing,' commanded the bard. 'You've said enough and done enough.'

'That's right, lay all the blame on me,' sniffed Glew. 'It's my fault Gwydion's sword was stolen, my fault the Cauldron-Born escaped, my fault every other disagreeable thing has happened.'

The bard did not deign to answer the former giant's whining outburst. Taran, having ordered the Commot warriors into the relative safety of the tunnel mouth, returned and stood beside the companions.

'I fear Doli is right,' Taran said. 'By attacking the Huntsmen we can only destroy ourselves. Our strength is slight enough as it is, and we dare not waste it. We have been long delayed, and already may be too late to aid Gwydion. No, we must find some means to make our way despite the Huntsmen.'

Doli shook his head. 'Still won't answer. They know we're here; they'll know if we try to move. All they need to do is track us. For the matter of that, I'll be surprised if we're not attacked before dawn. Look to your skins, my friends. It may be the last time you'll see them whole.'

'Doli,' Taran said urgently, 'you're the only one who can help us now. Will you spy out the Huntsmen's camp? Learn all you can of their plans. I know how you feel about turning yourself invisible, but . . .'

'Invisible!' shouted the dwarf, clapping a hand to his head. 'I knew it would come to that sooner or later. It always does! Good old Doli! Turn invisible! I'm not sure I can do it any more, I've tried to forget how. It hurts my ears. I'd sooner have my head stuffed with hornets and wasps. No, no, out of the question. Ask anything else you like, but not that.'

'Good old Doli,' Taran said. 'I was sure you'd do it.'

After a further show of reluctance, which deceived no one except perhaps Doli himself, the crimson-haired dwarf consented to do as Taran had asked. Doli wrinkled his eyes shut, took a deep breath, as though making ready to plunge into icy water, and flickered out of sight. Had it not been for a stifled sound of irritable grumbling, Taran would not have believed Doli to be there at all. Only the faint click of pebbles stirred by unseen feet told Taran that the dwarf had moved from the tunnel towards the enemy lines.

At Doli's orders the Fair Folk troop took guard posts in a wide half-circle beyond the tunnel's mouth, where their sharp eyes and ears could catch any threatening movement or sound. Taran was amazed at how still these warriors remained, silent and nearly as invisible as Doli. Their white garb made them seem no more than ice-covered stones or frosted hummocks under the moon, which had now begun to drift from behind the clouds. The horsemen drowsed among their steeds for warmth. Glew curled up nearby. Just within the tunnel Fflewddur sat with his back against the wall of rock, one hand on his harp, the other resting on the huge head of Llyan, who had stretched out beside him and was gently purring.

Muffled in his cloak, Taran gazed once more in wonder at the mountainside where first had appeared Eilonwy's signal light. 'She's alive,' he murmured to himself. 'Alive,' he whispered again and again, and his heart leaped each time he spoke the words. Gurgi would be with her, of this he was somehow sure. All his senses told him both companions had survived. Over the chill air came the baying of a wolf. There were other sounds, as of distant shouting, but they soon faded, and he gave them no thought, filled as he was with his new-found hope.

Half the night had worn away when Doli flickered back into sight. The dwarf, too excited to complain of his buzzing ears, hurriedly beckoned Taran and Fflewddur to follow him. Ordering the horsemen to stand alert, Taran hastened after the companions. The Fair Folk warriors were already jogtrotting behind Doli, silent as white shadows.

Taran at first thought the dwarf meant to lead them directly to the Huntsmen's camp; instead Doli turned off a little distance before it and began scrambling up a slope rising high above the gorge.

'The Huntsmen are still there,' Doli muttered under his breath as they climbed. 'No wish of their own. We have some friends we didn't know about – bears and wolves, dozens of them, all along the rim of the gorge. A band of Huntsmen tried to climb out. Good thing they couldn't see me or I wouldn't be here. But *they* were seen. The bears got to them first. Quick work they made of those villains. Bloody work, but quick.'

'They slew a party of Huntsmen?' Taran frowned. 'Now the others are even stronger.'

'Be that as it may,' replied Doli. 'The bears and wolves can attend to them better than we can. I doubt the Huntsmen will attack tonight. They fear the animals. They'll stay in the gorge until morning. And that's where I want them. I think I've struck on something.'

By this time they had reached the summit and had come to the rim of an ice-bound lake. At the sheer drop over the edge of the bluff, a frozen waterfall glittered under the moon; like fingers on a huge fist, vast icicles clawed at the steep slope, as though holding the lake in its frigid grip. A river of hard silver twisted downward towards the gorge where the Huntsmen were sheltering. Taran glimpsed their campfires glowing like baleful eyes in the darkness. Though he could not be sure, it seemed to him that shadowy shapes stirred among the rocks and stunted brush of the higher ground; perhaps the bears and wolves of which the dwarf had spoken.

'There!' Doli said. 'What do you think of that?'

'What do I think?' cried the bard. 'My old friend, I think you're the one who left your wits in the mine. You've led us on a good climb, but I should hardly call this a moment to admire the beauties of nature.'

The dwarf put his hands on his hips and looked at Fflewddur with exasperation. 'Sometimes I think Eiddileg's right about you humans. Can't you see past your nose? Can't you see at all? We're nearly atop those ruffians. Free the lake! Free the waterfall! Let it go pouring down! Straight into the camp!'

Taran caught his breath. For a moment, his heart leaped hopefully. Then he shook his head. 'The task is too great, Doli. The ice will defeat us.'

'Then melt it!' shouted the dwarf. 'Cut branches, bushes, all that will burn. Where the ice is too thick, chop it away! How many times must I tell you? You're dealing with Fair Folk!'

'Can it indeed be done?' Taran whispered.

'Would I have said it if I didn't think so?' the dwarf snapped.

Fflewddur gave a low whistle of admiration. 'You think in large terms, old fellow. But it appeals to me. Great Belin, if we could pull it off we'd strike them all down at one blow! And rid ourselves of them once and for all!'

Doli was no longer listening to the bard, but was passing hasty orders to the Fair Folk warriors, who unslung their axes and, with all speed, began chopping and hacking at the trees, uprooting underbrush and racing with their burdens to the lake.

Casting his doubts aside, Taran drew his sword and hewed at the branches. Fflewddur toiled beside him. Despite the bitter cold air, their brows streamed; their panting breath hung in a white haze before their faces. At the frozen waterfall the axes of the Fair Folk rang upon the ice. Doli dashed among the warriors, adding to the pile of bushes and branches, dislodging rocks and boulders to form a straighter, swifter channel.

The night was waning quickly. Taran stumbled in exhaustion, his cold-numbed hands torn and bleeding. Fflewddur was barely able to keep his feet. But the efforts of the Fair Folk never slackened. Before dawn the lake and the watercourse were piled high, as though a forest had overgrown them. Only then was Doli satisfied.

'Now, we'll set it alight,' he cried to Taran. 'Fair Folk tinder burns hotter than anything you humans know. It will blaze in no time.' He whistled shrilly through his teeth. All along the lake the torches of the Fair Folk flamed, then arched like shooting stars as the warriors flung them into the pyre. Taran saw the first branches catch fire, then the rest. A fierce crackling filled his ears, and over it he heard Doli shouting for the companions to race clear of the blaze. A wave of heat like the breath of a furnace caught at Taran as he struggled for a foothold among the stones. The ice was melting. He heard the hiss of quenched flames. But the fire, too high to be altogether extinguished, raged even more hotly. From the watercourse came the crack and groan of boulders shifting under the growing pressure of the rising flood. In a moment, like a gate ripped from its hinges, like a wall collapsing, the side of the bluff gave way, and through the channel burst a sheet of water carrying all before it. Huge blocks of ice thundered down the slope, bounding and rolling as if they had been no more than pebbles. The swift outpouring bore with it the flaming branches; above the streaming mass, clouds of sparks billowed and swirled, and the watercourse blazed all along its length.

In the gorge below, the Huntsmen shouted and strove to flee. It was too late. The rushing waters and careering boulders flung back the warriors as they sought to scramble up the ravine. Screaming and cursing, they fell beneath the cascade or were tossed in the air like chips, to be dashed against the sharp rocks. A few gained higher ground, but as they did, Taran saw dark shapes spring to grapple with them, and now it was the turn of the waiting animals to take vengeance on those who had ever mercilessly hunted and slaughtered them.

Silence fell over the gorge. In the dawn light Taran saw the glint of the dark water that had flooded the ravine. Some of the branches still burned, others smouldered, and a grey mist of smoke hung in the air. A rattle of stones behind him made Taran spin about and snatch his blade from the scabbard.

'Hallo!' said Eilonwy. 'We're back again!'

'You have an odd way of welcoming people,' Eilonwy went on, as Taran, his heart too full to speak, stared speechless at her. 'You might at least say something.'

While Gurgi, yelping joyfully, tried to greet everyone at once, Taran stepped quickly to Eilonwy's side, put his arms about her and drew the Princess close to him. 'I had given up hope . . .'

'A silly thing to do,' Eilonwy answered. '*I* never did. Though I admit having a few uneasy moments with that ruffian Dorath, and I could tell you tales you wouldn't believe about wolves and bears. I'll save them for later, when you can tell me all that's been happening to you. As for the Huntsmen,' she continued, as the reunited companions made their way to the tunnel, 'I saw the whole thing. At first I hadn't any idea what you were up to. Then I understood. It was wonderful. I should have known

Doli had a hand in it. Good old Doli! It looked like a river of burning ice . . .' The Princess stopped suddenly and her eyes widened. 'Do you realize what you've done?' she whispered. 'Don't you see?'

'Know what we've done?' laughed Fflewddur. 'Indeed we do! We've rid ourselves of the Huntsmen, and a good job it was. A Fflam couldn't have done better. As for what I see, I'm more pleased with what I *can't* see, if you take my meaning, namely, not a sign of those villains.'

'Hen Wen's prophecy!' Eilonwy cried. 'Part of it's come true! Have all of you forgotten? *Night turn to noon and rivers burn with frozen fire ere Dyrnwyn be regained.* Well, you've burned a river, or so it seems to me. Frozen fire could just as well mean all that ice and flaming branches, couldn't it?'

Taran looked closely at the Princess. His hands trembled as the words of the prophecy echoed in his memory. 'Have you seen what we ourselves did not see? But have you not done as much as we did? Without realizing it yourself? Think! *Night turn to noon.* Your bauble made daylight of darkness!'

It was Eilonwy's turn to be surprised. 'So it did!' she exclaimed.

'Yes, yes!' shouted Gurgi. 'Wise piggy told the truth! Mighty blade will be found again!'

Fflewddur cleared his throat. 'A Fflam is always encouraging,' he said, 'but in this case I should remind you, the prophecy also said Dyrnwyn's flame would be quenched and its power would vanish, which leaves us no better off than we were, even if we did manage to find it. And I also recall something about asking mute stones to speak. So far I've heard not a word from any of the stones here, though in the matter of boulders and rocks, there's hardly a short supply. The only message they've given me is that they're hard to sleep on. Moreover, if you want my opinion, I'd say don't trust prophecies in the first place. It's been my experience they're as bad as enchantments and lead only to one thing: trouble.'

'I do not understand the meaning of the prophecy myself,' Taran said. 'Are these signs of hope, or do we deceive ourselves by wishing them to be? Only Dallben or Gwydion has wisdom to interpret them. And yet I can't help feeling there is some hope at last. But it is true. Our task is no easier than it was.'

Doli grimaced. 'No easier? It's impossible now. Do you still mean to gain the Red Fallows? I warn you the Cauldron-Born are far out of reach.' He snorted. 'Don't talk to me about prophecies. Talk about time. We've lost too much of it.'

'I have thought long about this, too,' Taran answered. 'It has been in my mind ever since the tunnel fell. I believe our only chance is to go straight across the mountains and try to hold back the Cauldron-Born as they turn northwest to Annuvin.'

'Slim hope,' Doli replied. 'The Fair Folk can't venture that far. It's forbidden land. That close to Arawn's realm, Fair Folk would die. Gwystyl's waypost was nearest to the Land of Death, and you've seen what it did to his digestion and disposition. The best we could do is to put you well on your way. One of us might go with you,' he added. 'You can imagine who that is. Good old Doli! I've spent so much time above ground with you humans that being in Annuvin can't harm me.

'Yes, I'll go with you,' Doli went on, scowling furiously. 'I see nothing else for it. Good old Doli! Sometimes I wish I didn't have such an agreeable temper. Humph!'

CHAPTER 16

The Enchanter

Like a weary child, the old man hunched over the book-strewn table, his head upon his arm. Across his bony shoulders he had flung a cloak; the fire still flickered in the hearth, but the chill of this winter sank into him more deeply than any other he could remember. At his feet, Hen Wen stirred restlessly and whimpered in a high, plaintive voice. Dallben, who was neither altogether asleep nor awake, reached down a frail hand and gently scratched her ear.

The pig would not be calmed. Her pink snout twitched, she snorted and muttered unhappily and tried to hide her head in the folds of his robe. The enchanter at last roused himself.

'What is it, Hen? Is our time upon us?' He gave the pig a reassuring pat and rose stiffly from the wooden stool. 'Tut, it is a moment to pass, no more than that, whatever the outcome.'

Without haste he took up a long ash-wood staff and, leaning on it, hobbled from the chamber. Hen Wen trotted at his heels. At the cottage door, he pulled the cloak tighter about him and stepped into the night. The moon was at its full, riding distant in a deep sky. Dallben stood, listening carefully. To another's ears, the little farm would have seemed silent as the moon itself, but the old enchanter, his brow furrowed, his eyes half closed, nodded his head. 'You are right, Hen,' he murmured. 'I hear them now. But they are still far. What then,' he added, with a wrinkled smile, 'must I wait long for them and freeze the little marrow left in my bones?'

Nevertheless, he did not return within the cottage but

moved a few paces across the dooryard. His eyes, which had been heavy with drowsiness, grew bright as ice crystals. He peered sharply past the leafless trees of the orchard, as though to see into the shadows entwining the circling forest like black ivy tendrils. Hen Wen stayed behind, sitting uneasily on her haunches and watching the enchanter with much concern on her broad, bristly face.

'I should say there are twenty of them,' Dallben remarked, then added wryly, 'I do not know whether to be insulted or relieved. Only twenty? It is a paltry number. Yet more than that would be too cumbersome for the long journey, especially through the fighting in the Valley of Ystrad. No, twenty would be deemed ample and well chosen.'

For some time the old man stood quietly and patiently. At last, through the clear air, a faint sound of hoofbeats grew more insistent, then stopped, as if the riders had dismounted and were walking their steeds.

Against the dark tangle of trees where the forest rose at the edge of the stubble field, the darting shapes could have been no more than shadows cast by the bushes. Dallben straightened, raised his head, and blew out his breath as gently as if he were puffing at thistledown.

In an instant a biting gale shrieked across the field. The farm was calm, but the wind ripped with the force of a thousand swords into the forest, where the trees clashed and rattled. Horses whinnied, men shouted as branches suddenly lashed against them. The gale beat against the warriors, who flung up their arms to shield themselves from it.

Still, the war band pressed on, struggling through the wind-whipped forest and at last gaining the stubble field. At the onset of the gale, Hen Wen, squealing fearfully, had turned tail and dashed into the cottage. Dallben raised a hand and the wind died as quickly as it had risen.

Frowning, the old man smote his staff on the frozen turf.

Deep thunder muttered, the ground shuddered; and the field heaved like a restless sea. The warriors staggered and lost their footing, and among the attackers many fled to the safety of the forest, hastening to escape, fearful the earth itself might open and swallow them. The rest, urging each other on, drew their swords and stumbled across the field, racing towards the cottage.

With some vexation Dallben thrust out his arm with fingers spread as though he were casting pebbles into a pond. From his hand a crimson flame spurted and stretched like a fiery lash, in blinding streaks against the black sky.

The warriors cried out as ropes of crackling flame caught at them and twined about their arms and legs. The horses broke loose and galloped madly into the woods. The attackers threw down their weapons and tore frantically at their cloaks and jackets. Howling in pain and terror, the men reeled and plunged in full flight back to the forest.

The flames vanished. Dallben, about to turn away, glimpsed one figure which still pressed across the empty field. Alarmed, the old man gripped his staff and hobbled as quickly as he could into the cottage. The warrior was striding past the stables and into the dooryard. With footfalls pounding behind him, Dallben hurried across the threshold, but the old man had no sooner gained the refuge of his chamber than the warrior burst through the doorway. Dallben spun about to face his assailant.

'Beware!' cried the enchanter. 'Beware! Take no step closer.'

Dallben had drawn himself up to his full height, his eyes flashed, and his voice rang with such a commanding tone that the warrior hesitated. The man's hood had fallen back and the firelight played over the golden hair and proud features of Pryderi Son of Pwyll.

Dallben's eyes never faltered. 'I have long awaited you,

King of the West Domains.'

Pryderi made as if to take a step forward. His hand dropped to the pommel of the naked sword at his belt. Yet the old man's glance held him. 'You mistake my rank,' Pryderi said mockingly. 'Now I rule a larger realm. Prydain itself.'

'What then,' replied Dallben, feigning surprise, 'is Gwydion of the House of Don no longer High King of Prydain?'

Pryderi laughed harshly. 'A king without a kingdom? A king in rags, hunted like a fox? Caer Dathyl has fallen, the Sons of Don are scattered to the wind. This you already know, though it seems the tidings have reached you swiftly.'

'All tidings reach me swiftly,' Dallben said. 'Swifter, perhaps, than they reach you.'

'Do you boast of your powers?' Pryderi answered scornfully. 'At the last, when you most needed them, they failed. Your spells did no more than frighten a handful of warriors. Does the crafty Dallben take pride in putting churls to flight?'

'My spells were not meant to destroy, only to warn,' Dallben replied. 'This is a place of danger to all who enter against my will. Your followers heeded my warning. Alas, Lord Pryderi, that you did not. These churls are wiser than their king, for it is not wisdom that a man should seek his own death.'

'Again you are mistaken, wizard,' Pryderi said. 'It is your death I seek.'

Dallben tugged at the wisps of his beard. 'What you may seek and what you may find are not always one, Son of Pwyll,' he said quietly. 'Yes, you would take my life. That is no secret to me. Has Caer Dathyl fallen? That victory is hollow so long as Caer Dallben stands and so long as I live. Two strongholds have long stood against the Lord of Annuvin: a golden castle and a farmer's cottage. One lies in ruins. But the other is still a shield against evil, and a sword ever pointed at Arawn's heart. The Death-Lord knows this, and knows as well that he cannot enter here, nor can his Huntsmen and Cauldron-Born.

'Thus have you come,' Dallben added, 'to do your master's bidding.'

A flush of anger spread over Pryderi's face. 'I am my own master,' he cried. 'If power is given me to serve Prydain, shall I fear to use it? I am no Huntsman, who kills for the joy of killing. I do what must be done, and shrink not from it. My purpose is greater than the life of a man, or a thousand men. And if you must die, Dallben, then so be it.'

Pryderi ripped the sword from his belt, and in a sudden movement struck at the enchanter. But Dallben had taken a firmer grip on his staff and raised it against the blow. Pryderi's blade shattered upon the slender wood, and the shards fell ringing to the ground.

Pryderi cast the broken hilt from him. Yet it was not fear that filled his eyes, but scorn. 'I have been warned of your powers, wizard. I chose to prove them for myself.'

Dallben had not moved. 'Have you been truly warned? I think not. Had you been, you would not have dared to face me.'

'Your strength is great, wizard,' Pryderi said, 'but not so great as your weakness. Your secret is known to me. Strive against me as you will. At the end it is I who must conquer. Of all powers one is forbidden you on pain of your own death. Are you master of winds? Can you make the earth tremble? This is useless toying. You cannot do what the lowest warrior can do: you cannot kill.'

From his cloak Pryderi had drawn a short black dagger whose pommel bore the seal of Annuvin. 'No such ban is laid upon me,' he said. 'As I have been warned, so have I been armed. This blade comes from the hand of Arawn himself. It can be wielded despite all your spells.'

A look of pity and deep sorrow had come over Dallben's wrinkled face. 'Poor foolish man,' he murmured. 'It is true. This weapon of Annuvin can take my life and I cannot stay your hand. But you are blind as the mole that toils in the earth. Ask now, Lord Pryderi, which the master and which the slave. Arawn has betrayed you.

'Yes, betrayed you,' Dallben said, his voice sharp and cold. 'You thought to make him serve you. Yet all unwitting you have served him better than any of his hirelings. He sent you to slay me, and gave you the means to do it. Indeed, perhaps you shall slay me. But it will be Arawn's triumph, not yours. Once you have done his bidding, you are a useless husk to the Lord of Annuvin. He knows full well that never will I let you depart alive from Caer Dallben. You are a dead man, Lord Pryderi, even as you stand here.'

Pryderi raised the black dagger. 'With words you seek to ward off your death.'

'See from the window,' Dallben answered.

As he spoke, a crimson glow poured through the casement. A broad belt of flames had sprung up to circle Caer Dallben. Pryderi faltered and stepped back. 'You have believed half-truths,' Dallben said. 'No man has ever suffered death at my hands. But those who scorn my spells do so at their own peril. Slay me, Lord Pryderi, and the flames you see will sweep over Caer Dallben in an instant. There is no escape for you.'

Pryderi's golden features were drawn in a look of disbelief, mingled with growing fear at the enchanter's words. 'You lie,' he whispered hoarsely. 'The flames will die, even as you will die.'

'That, Lord, you must prove for yourself,' Dallben said.

'I have my proof!' Pryderi cried. 'Arawn would not destroy what he seeks most. There were two tasks! In all your wisdom you did not guess them. Your death was only one. The other, to gain *The Book of Three*.'

Dallben shook his head sadly and glanced at the heavy, leather-bound tome. 'You have been doubly betrayed, then. This book will no more serve Arawn than it will serve any evil end. Nor will it serve you, Lord Pryderi.'

The force of the old man's voice was like a cold wind. 'You have steeped your hands in blood, and in your pride sought to pass judgement on your fellow men. Was it your concern to serve Prydain? You chose an evil means to do it. Good cannot come from evil. You leagued yourself with Arawn for what you deemed a noble cause. Now you are a prisoner of the very evil you hoped to overcome, prisoner and victim. For in *The Book of Three* you are already marked for death.'

Dallben's eyes blazed and the truth of his words seemed to grip Pryderi's throat. The King's face had turned ashen. With a cry, he flung away the dagger and clutched at the huge book. Desperately his hands reached out as if they would rip it asunder.

'Touch it not!' Dallben commanded.

But Pryderi had already seized it. As he did so a blinding bolt of lightning sprang like a blazing tree from the ancient tome. Pryderi's death shriek rang through the chamber.

Dallben turned away and bowed his head as though some heavy grief had come upon him. Beyond the little farm the circle of fire dwindled and faded in the quiet dawn.

CHAPTER 17

The Snowstorm

The Fair Folk warriors, all save Doli, had turned back at the line of treeless crags marking the westernmost edge of the Hills of Bran-Galedd, for beyond that point the land lay under the sway of Arawn Death-Lord. For some days now the companions had toiled painfully through a wilderness of stone, where not even moss or lichen flourished. The sky was grey, and the few thin clouds no more than shreds of darker grey. It was as though an evil mist had seeped from the stronghold of Annuvin, stifling all living things and leaving only this rocky waste.

The companions spoke little, husbanding their strength. From the first day within the borders of the Land of Death, they had been obliged to dismount and go on foot, leading the weary horses through the treacherous passes. Even the stallion Melynlas showed signs of fatigue; the steed's powerful neck drooped and his gait sometimes faltered. Llyan, however, padded skilfully along the narrowest and most dangerous of ledges. Often, while the companions laboured down one sharp descent to clamber up an even sharper slope, the enormous cat leaped from one crag to the next, and they would come upon her sitting with her tail coiled about her haunches, waiting for Fflewddur to scratch her ears, after which she would bound off once more.

Doli, firmly gripping his staff, his white hood pulled well down over his face, trudged at the head of the little band. Taran had never ceased to wonder at the tireless dwarf who found, as though by secret sense, hidden footpaths and narrow ways that helped speed the harsh journey.

Yet, after a time, Doli's pace seemed to flag. Taran saw with growing concern and uneasiness that from time to time the dwarf would lose his footing and his step turn suddenly unsure. When Doli staggered and dropped to one knee, Taran ran to his side, alarmed, and tried to lift up the dwarf. The companions hurried to join him.

Doli's usually ruddy face had grown mottled and he breathed only in painful gasps. He struggled to regain his feet.

'Curse this evil realm,' he muttered. 'Can't stand it as well as I thought. Don't gawk! Give me a hand up.'

Stubbornly, the dwarf refused to mount one of the horses, insisting he felt better when his feet were on the ground. When Taran urged him to rest, Doli angrily shook his head. 'I said I'd find a passage for you,' he snapped. 'And I mean to. Can't stand a botched job. When the Fair Folk set about a task, they do it right, and don't dawdle over it.'

Nevertheless, after a short while Doli reluctantly consented to climb astride Melynlas. He fumbled with the stirrups but grumbled irritably when Fflewddur helped him into the saddle.

Even this relief was not long lasting. The dwarf's head soon drooped weakly forward, he swayed unsteadily and, before Taran could reach him, lurched from the stallion's back and pitched to the ground.

Taran quickly signalled a halt. 'We'll go no further today,' he told the dwarf. 'By morning you'll have your strength again.'

Doli shook his head. His face was white, his crimson eyes had turned dull. 'No use waiting,' he gasped. 'I've been too long here. It will grow worse. Must keep on while I can still guide you.'

'Not at the cost of your life,' Taran said. 'Hevydd the Smith will ride with you to the border. Llassar Son of Drudwas will help the rest of us find our way.'

'Won't do,' muttered the dwarf. 'Take too long without Fair Folk skill. Tie me to the saddle,' he commanded.

He strove to raise himself from the ground, but fell back and lay motionless. His breathing grew rasping and violent.

Taran cried out in alarm. 'He's dying. Hurry, Fflewddur. Help me put him on Llyan. She is the swiftest mount. Ride back with him. There may still be time.'

'Leave me here,' Doli gasped. 'You can't spare Fflewddur. His sword is worth ten. Or six, at least. Go quickly.'

'That I will not do,' replied Taran.

'Fool!' choked the dwarf. 'Heed me!' he commanded. 'It must be done. Are you a war leader or an Assistant Pig-Keeper?'

Taran knelt by the dwarf, whose eyes were half-closed, and gently put a hand on Doli's shoulder. 'Need you ask, old friend? I'm an Assistant Pig-Keeper.'

Taran rose to meet the bard, who had hastened up with Llyan, but when he turned back to the dwarf, the ground was empty. Doli had vanished.

'Where has he gone?' shouted Fflewddur.

An irritable voice came from somewhere near a boulder. 'Here! Where else do you think?'

'Doli!' cried Taran. 'You were close to your death, and now . . .'

'I've turned invisible, as any clodpole with half an ounce of sense can plainly see,' snorted Doli. 'Should have thought of it before. Last time in Annuvin, I was invisible most of the way. Never realized how it protected me.'

'Can it serve you now?' asked Taran, still a little bewildered. 'Dare you keep on?'

'Of course,' the dwarf retorted. 'I'm better already. But I'll have to stay invisible. As long as I can stand it, that is! Invisible! Hornets and wasps in my ears!'

'Good old Doli!' Taran cried, seeking vainly to pump the dwarf's unseen hand.

'Not that again!' snapped the dwarf. 'I'd not do this

willingly – oh, my ears – for any mortal in Prydain – oh, my head – but you! And don't shout! My ears won't stand it!'

Doli's staff, which had dropped to the ground, seemed to rise of itself, as the invisible dwarf picked it up. From the motion of the staff Taran could see that Doli had once more begun trudging ahead.

Guiding themselves by the length of wood, the companions followed. Yet even without sight of the staff they could have found their way, led by the sound of loud and furious grumbling.

Fflewddur was first to sight the gwythaints. In the distance, above a shallow ravine three black-winged shapes soared and circled. 'What have they found?' the bard cried. 'Whatever it is, I hope we're not the ones to be found next!'

Taran sounded his horn and signalled the war band to find whatever protection they could among the huge boulders. Eilonwy, disregarding Taran's orders, scrambled to the top of a high, jutting stone and shaded her eyes.

'I can't tell for sure,' Eilonwy said, 'but it looks to me as though they've cornered something. Poor creature. It will not last long against them.'

Gurgi crouched fearfully against a rock and tried to make himself as flat as a fish. 'Nor will Gurgi, if they see him,' he wailed. 'They will seize his poor tender head with gashings and slashings!'

'Pass on! Pass on!' Glew shouted, his little face puckered in fright. 'They're busy with their prey. Don't stop here like fools. Get as far away as we can. Oh, if I were a giant again, you'd not find me lingering!'

The gwythaints narrowed their circle and had begun to swoop downward, seeking their kill. But suddenly what appeared to be a black cloud, with a dark shape leading it, streaked down from the eastern quarter of the sky. Before the surprised companions could follow its swift movement overhead, the cloud shattered as if at its leader's command into winged fragments that drove straight upon the huge birds. Even at this distance Taran could hear the furious screams of the gwythaints as they veered aloft to face these strange assailants.

Fflewddur had leaped up beside Eilonwy and, as Taran and Doli clambered to a vantage point, the bard shouted excitedly: 'Crows! Great Belin, I've never seen so many!'

Like great black hornets, the crows swarmed over their enemy; it was not a single combat of bird against bird, but a battle in which whole troops of crows grappled and clung to the gwythaints' lashing wings, heedless of sharp beaks and talons, forcing the creatures earthward. When, by sheer strength, the gwythaints shook off their attackers, a new troop would form and renew the charge. The gwythaints sought to break free of their burden by plunging downward, scraping as closely as they dared against the sharp stones. But as they did, the crows pecked furiously at them and the gwythaints spun and fluttered dizzily, losing their course and falling once again victim to the relentless onslaught.

In a last burst of power, the gwythaints beat their way aloft; they turned and sped desperately northward, with the crows in hot pursuit. They vanished over the horizon, all save a solitary crow that flew swiftly towards the companions.

'Kaw!' Taran shouted and held out his arms.

Jabbering at the top of his voice, the crow swooped down. His eyes glittered in triumph and he flapped his shiny wings more proudly than a rooster. He gabbled, croaked, squawked, and poured forth such a torrent of yammering that Gurgi clapped his hands over his ears.

From his perch on Taran's wrist, Kaw bobbed his head and clacked his beak, thoroughly delighted with himself and never for a moment ceasing his chatter.

Taran, trying vainly to interrupt the crow's raucous

and boastful clamour, had despaired of learning any tidings from the roguish bird when Kaw flapped his wings and sought to fly off again.

'Achren!' Kaw croaked. 'Achren! Queen!'

'You've seen her?' Taran caught his breath. He had given little thought to the once-powerful Queen since her flight from Caer Dallben. 'Where is she?'

The crow fluttered a little distance away, then returned, his beating wings urging Taran to follow him. 'Close! Close! Gwythaints!'

Eilonwy gasped. 'That's what we saw. The gwythaints have slain her!'

'Alive!' Kaw answered. 'Hurt!'

Taran ordered the Commot horsemen to await him, then leaped to the ground to follow after Kaw. Eilonwy, Doli, and Gurgi hastened to join him. Glew refused to budge, remarking that he had already skinned himself on enough rocks and had no intention of going out of his way for anyone.

Fflewddur hesitated a moment. 'Yes, well, I suppose I shall go along, too, should you need help in carrying her. But it doesn't sit well with me. Achren was eager enough to go her own way, and I rather think we shouldn't meddle. Not that I fear her, not for a moment – ah, the truth of it is,' he hurriedly added, as the harp strings tensed, 'the woman makes me shudder. Since the day she threw me into her dungeon. I've noticed something unfriendly about her. She has no fondness for music, I can tell you. Nevertheless,' he cried, 'a Fflam to the rescue!'

Like a tattered bundle of black rags the still form of Queen Achren lay in the fissure of a massive rock where she had, in her last hope, pressed to escape the gwythaints' vicious beaks and talons. Yet her refuge, Taran saw pityingly, had offered the Queen scant protection. Achren moaned faintly as the companions carefully lifted her from the crevice. Llyan, who had ›llowed along with the bard, crouched silently nearby, and lashed her tail uneasily. Achren's face, drawn and deathly pale, had been badly slashed, and her arms bore many deep and bleeding wounds. Eilonwy held the woman and tried to revive her.

'Llyan shall carry her back with us,' Taran said. 'She will need more healing herbs than I have brought; more than her wounds, a fever has weakened her. She has gone long without food or drink.'

'Her shoes are in ribbons,' Eilonwy said. 'How far must she have wandered in this awful place? Poor Achren! I can't say I'm fond of her, but it makes my toes curl up just imagining what could have happened.'

Fflewddur, after helping move the unconscious Queen to more level ground, had stayed a few paces away. Gurgi, too, chose to keep some distance between Achren and himself. Nevertheless, at Taran's bidding they drew closer and the bard, with many soothing words, held Llyan steady while the other companions lifted Achren to the great cat's back.

'Hurry along,' called the voice of Doli. 'It's starting to snow.'

White flakes had begun drifting from the heavy sky; within little time a biting wind swirled around the companions and snow drove against them in an ever-thickening cloud. Needles of ice stung their faces, it grew more and more difficult to see, and as the storm gained in fury even Doli could no longer be sure of the path. The companions staggered blindly in a file, each clutching the other, with Taran gripping an end of Doli's staff. Kaw, almost entirely covered with snow, hunched up his wings and tried desperately to keep his perch on Taran's shoulder. Llyan, burdened with the motionless Queen, bent her great head against the gale and plodded onward; but the sure-footed cat often stumbled over hidden boulders and snow-filled pits. Once Gurgi yelled in terror and vanished as suddenly as if the earth had swallowed him.

He had tumbled into a deep crevice and by the time the companions were able to haul him out, the hapless creature had nearly turned into a shaggy icicle. He trembled so violently he could scarcely walk, and between them, Taran and Fflewddur bore him along.

The wind did not slacken, the snow fell in an impenetrable curtain; and the cold, already bitter, grew even more intense. Breathing was painful and with each laboured gasp Taran felt the frigid draught like daggers in his lungs. Eilonwy half-sobbed with cold and exhaustion, and she clung to Taran, striving to keep her footing as Doli led them through drifts that now had risen more than knee-high.

'We can't go on,' the dwarf shouted above the wind. 'Find shelter. Make our way to the horsemen when the snow lets up.'

'But the warriors, how shall they fare?' Taran replied anxiously.

'Better than we!' the dwarf cried. 'Where they are, there's a good-sized cave I noticed along the cliff wall. Your young shepherd is bound to find it, never fear. Our trouble is finding something for ourselves.'

However, even after long and painful searching, the dwarf discovered nothing more than a shallow gully below an overhanging ledge. The companions stumbled gratefully into it; here they were protected against the worst battering of the wind and snow. But the cold still gripped them, and no sooner had they halted than their bodies seemed to stiffen and they moved arms and legs only with the greatest difficulty. They clung together for warmth and pressed against Llyan's thick coat of fur. Even this gave them little comfort for, as night fell, the chill deepened. Taran stripped off his cloak and covered Eilonwy and Achren; Gurgi insisted on adding his sheepskin jacket and he crouched with his shaggy arms wrapped around himself, his teeth chattering loudly.

'I fear that Achren will not live the night,' Taran murmured to Fflewddur. 'She was too close to death when we found her. She will not have strength to stand such cold.'

'Will any of us?' answered the bard. 'Without a fire, we might just as well say farewell to each other right now.'

'I don't know what you're complaining about,' Eilonwy sighed. 'I've never been so comfortable in all my life.'

Taran looked at her in alarm. The girl did not stir under the cloak. Her eyes were half-shut, her voice faltered with drowsiness.

'Quite warm,' she rambled on happily. 'What a lovely goosefeather quilt I have. How odd. I dreamed we were all caught in a terrible storm. It wasn't pleasant at all. Or am I still dreaming? No matter. When I wake up, it will all be gone away.'

Taran, his face drawn with anxiety, shook her roughly. 'Don't sleep!' he cried. 'If you sleep it will be your death.'

Eilonwy did not answer him, but only turned her head away and closed her eyes. Gurgi had curled up beside her and could not be roused. Taran himself felt a fatal drowsiness spreading over him. 'Fire,' he said, 'we must build a fire.'

'From what?' Doli brusquely replied. 'There's not a twig to be found in this wilderness. What will you burn? Our boots? Our cloaks? We'll freeze all the faster.' He flickered back into sight. 'And if I'm going to freeze, I won't do it with hornets buzzing in my ears.'

Fflewddur, who had been silent this while, reached behind him and unslung his harp. At this, Doli gave a furious shout.

'Harp music!' he cried. 'My friend, your wits are frozen solid as ice!'

'It shall give us the tune we need,' replied Fflewddur.

Taran dragged himself to the side of the bard. 'Fflewddur, what do you mean to do?'

The bard did not answer. For a long moment he held the harp lovingly in his hands and gently touched the strings, then with a quick motion raised the beautiful instrument and smashed it across his knee.

Taran cried out in anguish as the wood shattered into splinters and the harp strings tore loose with a discordant burst of sound. Fflewddur let the broken fragments drop from his hands.

'Burn it,' he said. 'It is wood well-seasoned.'

Taran seized the bard by the shoulders. 'What have you done?' he sobbed. 'Gallant, foolish Fflam! You have destroyed your harp for the sake of a moment's warmth. We need a greater fire than this wood can ever give us.'

Doli, however, had quickly taken flint from his pouch and had struck a spark into the pitiful heap of splinters. Instantly, the wood blazed up and sudden warmth poured over the companions. Taran stared amazed at the rising flames. The bits of wood seemed hardly to be consumed, yet the fire burned all the more brightly. Gurgi stirred and raised his head. His teeth had ceased their chattering and colour was returning to his frost-pinched face. Eilonwy, too, sat up and looked about her as though waking from a dream. At a glance she understood what fuel the bard had offered, and tears sprang to her eyes.

'Don't give it a second thought,' cried Fflewddur. 'The truth of the matter is that I'm delighted to be rid of it. I could never really play the thing, and it was more a burden than anything else. Great Belin, I feel light as a feather without it. Believe me, I was never meant to be a bard in the first place, so all is for the best.'

In the depths of the flames several harp strings split in two and a puff of sparks flew into the air.

'But it gives a foul smoke,' Fflewddur muttered, though the fire was burning clear and brilliant. 'It makes my eyes water horribly.'

The flames had now spread to all the fragments, and

as the harp strings blazed a melody sprang suddenly from the heart of the fire. Louder and more beautiful it grew, and the strains of music filled the air, echoing endlessly among the crags. Dying, the harp seemed to be pouring forth all the songs ever played upon it, and the sound shimmered like the fire.

All night the harp sang, and its melodies were of joy, sorrow, love, and valour. The fire never abated, and little by little new life and strength returned to the companions. And as the notes soared upward a wind rose from the south, parting the falling snow like a curtain and flooding the hills with warmth. Only at dawn did the flame sink into glowing embers and the voice of the harp fall silent. The storm had ended, the crags glistened with melting snow.

Wordless and wondering, the companions left their shelter. Fflewddur lingered behind for a moment. Of the harp, nothing remained but a single string, the one unbreakable string which Gwydion had given the bard long ago. Fflewddur knelt and drew it from the ashes. In the heat of the fire the harp string had twisted and coiled around itself, but it glittered like pure gold.

CHAPTER 18

Mount Dragon

As Doli had foretold, Llassar had led the warriors to shelter in a cave and had saved them from the full fury of the snowstorm. The companions now made ready to continue their journey. The sharp crags that were their last obstacle lay not far distant. The crest of Mount Dragon loomed dark and forbidding. With the help of Taran's healing potions and Eilonwy's care, Achren had regained consciousness. Fflewddur was still reluctant to come within fewer than three paces of the black-robed Queen, but Gurgi had finally taken enough courage to open his wallet and offer food to the half-starved woman – although the creature's face wrinkled uneasily and he held out the morsels at arm's length, as if fearful of being bitten. Achren, however, ate sparingly; Glew, for his part, lost no time in snatching up what remained, popping it into his mouth and glancing about to see whether more might be forthcoming.

Achren's fever had left her weakened in body, yet her face had lost none of its haughtiness; and after Taran had briefly recounted what had brought the companions so close to Annuvin it was with ill-disguised scorn that she answered him.

'Does a pig-keeper and his shabby followers hope to triumph where a queen failed? I would have reached Annuvin long since, had it not been for Magg and his warriors. By chance, his war band came upon me in Cantrev Cadiffor.' Her broken lips drew back in a bitter grimace. 'They left me for dead. I heard Magg laugh when they told him I had been slain. He, too, shall know my vengeance.

'Yes, I lay in the forest like a wounded beast. But my hatred was sharper than their sword thrusts. I would have crept after them on hands and knees and given my last strength to strike them down, though indeed I feared that I would die unrevenged. But I found refuge. There are still those in Prydain who pay homage to Achren. Until I could journey once again, they sheltered me; and for that service they shall be rewarded.

'Yet I failed even within sight of my goal. The gwythaints were more ruthless than Magg. They would have made certain of my death – I, who once commanded them. Sharp will be their punishment.'

'I have the awful feeling,' Eilonwy whispered to Taran, 'that Achren sometimes thinks she's still Queen of Prydain. Not that I mind, so long as she doesn't take it into her head to try to punish *us*.'

Achren, overhearing Eilonwy's remarks, turned to the girl. 'Forgive me, Princess of Llyr,' she said quickly. 'I spoke half in a rambling dream and the cold comforts of memory. I am grateful to you for my life and shall repay you far beyond its worth. Hear me well. Would you pass the mountain bastions of Annuvin? You follow the wrong path.'

'Humph!' Doli cried, popping visible for a moment. 'Don't tell one of the Fair Folk he's on the wrong path.'

'Yet it is true,' Achren replied. 'There are secrets unknown even to your people.'

'It's no secret that if you cross mountains you choose the easiest way,' Doli snapped back. 'And that's what I plan. I'm taking my bearings from Mount Dragon, but you can believe me, once we're closer, we'll turn aside and find a passage through the lower slopes. Do you think I'm such a fool as to do otherwise?'

Achren smiled contemptuously. 'In so doing, dwarf, you would indeed be a fool. Of all the peaks surrounding Annuvin, Mount Dragon alone can be breached. Heed me,' she added, as Taran murmured in disbelief. 'The crags are lures and traps. Others have been deceived, and their bones lie in the pitfalls. The lower mountains beckon with promise of easier passage, but no sooner are they crossed than they fall away into sheer cliffs. Does Mount Dragon warn you to shun its heights? The western descent is a very roadway to the Iron Portals of Annuvin. To reach it there is a hidden trail, where I shall guide you.'

Taran looked closely at the Queen. 'Such are your words, Achren. Do you ask us to stake our lives on them?'

Achren's eyes glittered. 'In your heart you fear me, Pig-Keeper. But which do you fear the more – the path I offer you or the certain death of Lord Gwydion? Do you seek to overtake Arawn's Cauldron warriors? This you cannot do, for time will defeat you unless you follow where I lead. This is my gift to you, Pig-Keeper. Scorn it if you choose, and we shall go our separate ways.'

Achren turned and muffled herself with her ragged cloak. The companions drew away from her and spoke among themselves. Doli, thoroughly vexed and disgruntled by Achren's judgement of his skill, nonetheless admitted that he could have unwittingly led them astray. 'We Fair Folk have never dared to journey here, and I can't prove what she says one way or the other. But I've seen mountains that look sheer on one side – and on the other you could roll down without so much as a bump. So she could be telling the truth.'

'And she could be trying to get rid of us the fastest way she knows,' the bard put in. 'Those pitfalls with bones in them make my flesh creep. I think Achren would be delighted if some of those bones were ours. She's playing her own game, you can be sure of that.' He shook his head uneasily. 'A Fflam is fearless, but with Achren, I prefer being wary.'

Taran was silent a moment, searching for the wisdom to choose one way or the other, and again felt the weight of the burden Gwydion had set upon him to be more than he could bear. Achren's face was a pallid mask; he could read nothing of her heart in it. More than once the Queen would have taken the lives of the companions. But, as he knew, she had served Dallben well and faithfully after her own powers had been shattered. 'I believe,' he said slowly, 'that we can do no less than trust her until she gives us clear reason to doubt. I fear her,' he added, 'as do all of us. Yet I will not let fear blind me to hope.'

'I agree,' said Eilonwy, 'which makes me think in this case, at least, your judgement is quite right. I admit that trusting Achren is like letting a hornet sit on your nose. But sometimes you only get stung when you try to brush it off – the hornet, I mean.'

Taran went to Achren's side. 'Lead us to Mount Dragon,' he said. 'We will follow you.'

Another day's travel brought the companions across a harsh, uneven valley that lay within the shadow of Mount Dragon itself. The summit had been well named, for Taran saw its peak was in the rough shape of a monstrous, crested head with gaping jaws, and on either side the lower slopes spread like outflung wings. The great blocks and shafts of stone that rose to form its jagged bulk were dark, mottled with patches of dull red. Before this last barrier, poised as though to swoop downward and crush them, the companions fearfully halted. Achren strode to the head of the waiting column and beckoned them onward.

'There are other, easier paths,' Achren said, as they entered a narrow defile that twisted between towering walls of sheer cliffs, 'but they are longer and those who travel them can be seen before they reach the stronghold of Annuvin. This one is known only to Arawn and his most trusted servants. And to me, for it was I who showed him the secret ways of Mount Dragon.'

Taran, however, soon began to fear Achren had deceived them, for the path rose so steeply that men and horses could barely keep their footing. Achren seemed to be leading them deep into the heart of the mountain. Mighty shelves of overhanging rocks rose like arches above the toiling band, blotting the sky from their sight. At times, the path skirted yawning chasms and more than once Taran stumbled, buffeted by a sudden chill blast that flung him against the walls. His heart pounded and his head reeled at the sight of the deep gorges opening at his feet, and terrified he clung to the sharp edges of jutting rocks. Achren, whose step did not falter, only turned and silently glanced at him, a mocking smile on her ravaged face.

The path continued to rise, though not so abruptly, for it no longer followed the slope of the mountain but seemed almost to double back on itself, and the companions gained the higher reaches of the trail only by small degrees. The huge stone jaws of the dragon's head loomed above. The trail which, for some of its course, had been hidden by grotesque formations of rocks, now lay exposed, and Taran could see most of the mountain slope dropping sharply below him. They were almost at the highest ridge of the dragon's shoulder, and it was there that Kaw, scouting ahead, returned to them and clacked his beak frantically.

'Gwydion! Gwydion!' the crow jabbered at the top of his voice. 'Annuvin! Haste!'

Taran sprang past Achren and raced to the ridge, clambering upward among the rocks, straining his eyes for a glimpse of the stronghold. Had the Sons of Don already begun their attack on Annuvin? Had Gwydion's warriors themselves overtaken the Cauldron-Born? His heart pounding against his ribs, he struggled higher. Suddenly the dark towers of Arawn's fastness were below him. Beyond the high walls, beyond the massive Iron Portals, ugly and brooding, he glimpsed the spreading courtyards, the Hall of Warriors where once the Black Cauldron had stood. Arawn's Great Hall rose, glittering like black, polished marble, and above it, at the highest pinnacle, floated the Death-Lord's banner.

The sight of Annuvin sickened him with the chill of death that hung over it, his head spun and shadows seemed to blind him. He pressed higher. Struggling shapes filled the courtyard, the clash of blades and shouted battle cries struck his ears. Men were scaling the western wall; Dark Gate itself had been breached, and Taran believed he saw the flash of Melyngar's white flanks and golden mane, and the tall figures of Gwydion and Taliesin.

The Commot men had not failed! Arawn's deathless hosts had been held back and victory was in Gwydion's hands. But even as Taran turned to shout the joyous tidings, his heart froze. Southward he glimpsed the hastening army of Cauldron-Born. Their iron-shod boots rang and clattered as the mute warriors raced towards the heavy gates and the horns of the troop captains shrieked for vengeance.

Taran leaped from the ridge to join the companions. The shelf of stone crumbled at his feet. He pitched forward, Eilonwy's scream rang in his ears; and the sharp rocks seemed to whirl upward against him. Desperately he clutched at them and strove to break his fall. With all his strength he clung to the sheer side of Mount Dragon, while jagged stones bit like teeth into his palms. His sword, ripped from his belt, clattered into the gorge.

He saw the horrified faces of the companions above him and knew he was beyond their reach. His muscles trembling, his lungs bursting with his efforts, he fought to climb upward to the path.

His foot slipped and he twisted about to regain his balance. It was then that he saw, plunging from the peak of Mount Dragon, the gwythaint speeding towards him.

CHAPTER 19

The Death Lord

The gwythaint, greater than any Taran had ever seen, screamed and beat its wings, churning a wind like a gale of death. Taran saw the curved, gaping beak and blood-red eyes, and in another instant the gwythaint's talons sank into his shoulders, seeking to grip the flesh beneath his cloak. The relentless bird pressed so closely that the reek of its feathers filled Taran's nostrils. Its head, deeply scarred by an old wound, thrust against him.

Taran turned his face away and waited for the beak to rend his throat. Yet the gwythaint did not strike. Instead, it was pulling him from the rocks with a strength Taran could not resist. The gwythaint no longer screamed, but made soft keening sounds, and the bird's eyes fixed upon him not in fury but in a strange gaze of recognition.

The bird seemed to be urging him to loosen his grasp. A sudden memory from his boyhood flooded Taran, and again he saw a fledgling gwythaint in a thorn bush; a young bird wounded and dying. Was this the ragged bundle of feathers he had nursed back to life? Had the creature come at last to pay a debt so long remembered? Taran dared not hope, yet as he clung, weakening, to the side of Mount Dragon, it was his only hope. He relaxed his grip and let himself fall free.

The weight of its burden made the gwythaint falter and drop earthward for a moment. Below Taran, the crags reeled. With all his strength, the huge bird beat its wings and Taran felt himself borne upward, higher and higher, as the wind whistled in his ears. Its black wings heaving and straining, the gwythaint pressed steadily aloft until at last its talons opened and Taran fell to the stone-crested peak of Mount Dragon.

Achren had spoken the truth. The short, downward slope lay before him, clear and unhindered to the Iron Portals, which now swung open as the hastening army of Cauldron-Born streamed into Annuvin. The deathless host had drawn their swords. Within the stronghold, Gwydion's warriors had seen the foe, and shouts of despair rose from the embattled Sons of Don.

A troop of Cauldron-Born, sighting the lone figure of Taran atop the mountain's summit and the companions who now had crossed the ridge, broke from the main body of the host and turned their attack upon Mount Dragon. Brandishing their weapons, they sped up the slope.

The gwythaint, circling overhead, screamed a war cry. Sweeping its wings, the giant bird flew straight to the onrushing warriors and plunged into their ranks, striking out with beak and claws. Under the violence of the gwythaint's unexpected charge, the first rank of Cauldron-Born fell back and stumbled to the ground, but one of the mute warriors lashed out with his sword, striking again and again until the gwythaint dropped at his feet. The huge wings fluttered and trembled, then the battered body lay still.

Three of the Cauldron-Born had leaped past their comrades and raced towards Taran, who read his own death in their livid faces. His eyes darted about the summit, vainly seeking a last means of defence.

At the highest peak of the dragon's crest rose a tall rock. Time and tempest had gnawed it into a grotesque shape. The wind, blowing through the eroded crannies and hollows, set up a baleful keening, and the stone shrieked and moaned as if with human tongue. The weird wail seemed to command, to beseech, to draw Taran closer. Here was his only weapon. He flung himself against the rock and wrestled against the unyielding bulk, struggling to uproot it. The Cauldron-Born were nearly upon him.

The stone crest seemed to move a little as Taran redoubled his efforts. Then suddenly it rolled from its socket. With a final heave Taran sent it crashing amid his assailants. Two of the Cauldron-Born tumbled backward and their blades spun from their hands, but the third warrior did not falter in his upward climb.

Driven by despair, as a man casts pebbles at the lightning that would strike him down, Taran groped for a handful of stones, of loose earth, even a broken twig to fling in defiance of the Cauldron warrior who strode closer, blade upraised.

The socket from which the dragon's crest had been torn was lined with flat stones, and in it, as in a narrow grave, lay Dyrnwyn, the black sword.

Taran snatched it up. For an instant, his mind reeling, he did not recognize the blade. Once, long before, he had sought to draw Dyrnwyn and his life had been almost forfeit to his rashness. Now, heedless of the cost, seeing no more than a weapon come to his hand, he ripped the sword from its sheath. Dyrnwyn flamed with a white and blinding light. It was only then, in some distant corner of his mind, Taran dimly understood that Dyrnwyn was blazing in his grasp and that he was still alive.

Dazzled, the Cauldron-Born dropped his sword and flung his hands to his face. Taran leaped forward and with all his strength drove the blazing weapon deep into the warrior's heart.

The Cauldron-Born stumbled and fell; and, from lips long mute burst a shriek that echoed and re-echoed from the Death-Lord's stronghold as though rising from a thousand tongues. Taran staggered back. The Cauldron-Born lay motionless.

Along the path and at the Iron Portals the Cauldron warriors toppled as one body. Within the stronghold the deathless men locked in combat with the Sons of Don screamed and crumpled to earth even as Taran's foe had fallen. A troop hastening to fill the breach at Dark Gate pitched headlong at the feet of Gwydion's warriors, and those who strove to slay the soldiers at the western wall dropped in mid-stride and their weapons clattered on the stones. Death at last had overcome the deathless Cauldron-Born.

Shouting for the companions, Taran raced from the peak of Mount Dragon. The Commot horsemen leaped to their saddles and urged their steeds to a gallop, plunging after Taran and into the fray.

Taran sped across the courtyard. At the death of the Cauldron-Born, many of Arawn's mortal guards threw down their weapons and sought vainly to flee the stronghold. Others fought with the frenzy of men whose lives were already lost; and the remaining Huntsmen, who had gained new strength as their comrades fell under the blades of the Sons of Don, still shouted their war cry and flung themselves against Gwydion's warriors. One of the Huntsmen troop captains, his branded face twisted in rage, slashed at Taran, then shouted in horror and fled at the sight of the flaming sword.

Taran fought his way through the press of warriors that swirled about him and raced towards the Great Hall where he had first glimpsed Gwydion. He burst through the portals and as he did so, sudden fear and loathing plucked at him. Torches flared along the dark, glittering corridors. For a moment he faltered, as though a black wave had engulfed him. From the far end of the corridor Gwydion had seen him and he strode quickly to Taran's side. Taran ran to meet him, shouting triumphantly that Dyrnwyn had been found.

'Sheathe the blade!' Gwydion cried, shielding his eyes with a hand. 'Sheathe the blade, or it will cost your life!'

Taran obeyed.

Gwydion's face was drawn and pale, his green-flecked eyes burned feverishly. 'How have you drawn this blade, Pig-Keeper?' Gwydion demanded. 'My hands alone dare touch it. Give me the sword.'

The voice of Gwydion rang harsh and commanding, yet Taran hesitated, his heart pounding with a strange dread.

'Quickly!' Gwydion ordered. 'Will you destroy what I have fought to win? Arawn's treasure trove lies open to our hands, and power greater than any man has dreamed awaits us. You will share with me in it, Pig-Keeper. I trust no other.

'Shall some base-born warrior keep these treasures from us?' Gwydion cried. 'Arawn has fled his realm, Pryderi is slain and his army scattered. None has strength to stand against us now. Give me the sword, Pig-Keeper. Half a kingdom is in your grasp, seize it now before it is too late.'

Gwydion reached out his hand.

Taran flung himself back, his eyes wide with horror. 'Lord Gwydion, this is not the counsel of a friend. It is betrayal . . .'

Only then, as he stared bewildered at this man he had honoured since boyhood, did he understand the ruse.

In another instant Taran ripped Dyrnwyn from its sheath and raised the glittering blade.

'Arawn!' Taran gasped, and swung the weapon downward.

Before the blade struck home, the Death-Lord's disguised shape blurred suddenly and vanished. A shadow writhed along the corridor and faded away.

The companions now pressed into the Great Hall and Taran hurried towards them, crying the warning that Arawn still lived and had escaped.

Achren's eyes blazed with hatred. 'Escaped you, Pig-Keeper, but not my vengeance. The secret chambers of

Arawn are no secret to me. I shall seek him out wherever he has taken refuge.'

Without waiting for the companions, who ran to follow her, Achren set off with all speed down the winding halls. She sprang past a heavy portal which bore the Death-Lord's seal branded deeply in the iron-studded wood. At the far end of the long chamber Taran glimpsed a hunched, spidery figure scuttling to a high, skull-shaped throne.

It was Magg. The Chief Steward's face was ghastly white, his lips trembled and slavered, and his eyes rolled in his head. He stumbled to the foot of the throne, snatched at an object that lay on the flagstones, clutched it to him, and whirled to face the companions.

'No closer!' shrieked Magg, in such a tone that even Achren halted and Taran, about to draw Dyrnwyn from its scabbard, was gripped in horror at Magg's contorted features.

'Will you keep your lives?' Magg cried. 'To your knees, then! Humble yourselves and beg mercy. I, Magg, shall favour you by making you my slaves.'

'Your master has abandoned you,' replied Taran. 'And your own treachery has ended.' He strode forward.

Magg's spidery hands thrust out in warning, and Taran saw that the Chief Steward held a strangely wrought crown.

'I am master here,' Magg shouted. 'I, Magg, Lord of Annuvin. Arawn pledged that I should wear the Iron Crown. Has it slipped from his fingers? It is mine, mine by right and promise!'

'He has gone mad,' Taran murmured to Fflewddur, who stared in revulsion as the Chief Steward raised high the crown and gibbered to himself. 'Help me take him prisoner!'

'No prisoner shall he be,' cried Achren, drawing a dagger from her cloak. 'His life is mine for the taking, and he shall die as all who have betrayed me. My vengeance begins here, with a treacherous slave, and next, his master.'

'Harm him not,' commanded Taran, as the Queen struggled to make her way past him to the throne. 'Let him find justice from Gwydion.'

Achren fought against him, but Eilonwy and Doli hastened to hold the raging Queen's arms. Taran and the bard strode towards Magg, who flung himself to the seat of the throne.

'Do you tell me Arawn's promises are lies?' the Chief Steward hissed, fondling and fingering the heavy crown. 'It was promised I should wear this. Now it is given into my hands. So shall it be!' Quickly, Magg lifted the crown and set it on his brow.

'Magg!' he shouted. 'Magg the Magnificent! Magg the Death-Lord!'

The Chief Steward's triumphant laughter turned to a shriek as he clawed suddenly at the iron band circling his forehead. Taran and Fflewddur gasped and drew back.

The crown glowed like red iron in a forge. Writhing in agony, Magg clutched vainly at the burning metal which now had turned white hot, and with a last scream toppled from the throne.

Eilonwy cried out and turned her face away.

Gurgi and Glew had lost track of the companions and were now pelting through the maze of winding corridors trying vainly to find them. Gurgi was terrified at being in the heart of Annuvin and at every step shouted Taran's name. Only the echoes from the torch-lit halls came back to him. Glew was no less fearful. Between gasps, the former giant also found enough breath to complain bitterly.

'It's too much to bear!' he cried. 'Too much! Is there no end to the wretched burdens put upon me? Thrown aboard a ship, hustled off to Caer Dallben, half frozen to death, dragged through mountains at the risk of my life, a fortune snatched from my hands! And now this! Oh, when I was a giant I'd not have stood for such high-handed treatment!'

'Oh, giant, leave off pinings and whinings!' replied Gurgi, miserable enough at being separated from the companions. 'Gurgi is lost and lorn, but he tries to find kindly master with seekings. Do not fear,' he added reassuringly, though it was all he could do to keep his voice from trembling, 'bold Gurgi will keep plaintful little giant safe, oh, yes.'

'You're not doing very well at it,' snapped Glew. Nevertheless, the pudgy little man clung to the side of the shaggy creature and, his stubby legs pumping, matched him stride for stride.

They had come to the end of one corridor where a squat and heavy iron portal stood open. Gurgi fearfully halted. A bright cold light poured from the chamber. Gurgi took a few cautious paces and peered within. Beyond the doorway stretched what seemed to be an endless tunnel. The light came from heaps of precious stones and golden ornaments. Farther on, he glimpsed strange objects half-hidden by shadows. Gurgi drew back, his eyes popping in wonder and terror.

'Oh, it is treasure house of evil Death-Lord,' he whispered. 'Oh, glimmerings and shimerings! This is a very secret place and fearsome, and not wise for bold Gurgi to stay.'

Glew, however, pressed forward, and at the sight of the gems his pale cheeks twitched and his eyes glittered. 'Treasure, indeed!' he said, choking in his excitement. 'I've been cheated of one fortune, but now I'll be repaid. It's mine!' he cried. 'All of it! I spoke first! No one shall deprive me of it!'

'No, no,' protested Gurgi. 'It cannot be yours, greedy

giant! It is for mighty Prince to give or take. Come with hastenings and seek companions even faster. Come with tellings and warnings, for Gurgi also fears snappings and trappings. Costly treasures without guardings? No, no, clever Gurgi sniffs evil enchantments.'

Heedless of the creature's words, Glew thrust him aside. With an eager cry the former giant sprang past the threshold and into the tunnel, where he plunged his hands into the largest heap of jewels. Gurgi, seizing him by the collar, tried vainly to drag him back, as flames burst from the walls of the treasure-trove.

Before the Great Hall of Annuvin, Gwydion rallied the last survivors of the Sons of Don and the Commot horsemen. There the companions, with Kaw squawking jubilantly overhead, joined them. For a moment, Taran stared searchingly at Gwydion, but his doubts vanished when the tall warrior strode quickly to him and clasped his hand.

'We have much to tell each other,' Gwydion said, 'but no time for the telling. Though Annuvin is in our hands the Death-Lord himself has escaped us. He must be found and slain, if it is in our power to do so.'

'Gurgi and Glew are lost in the Great Hall,' Taran said. 'Give us leave to find them first.'

'Go quickly, then,' answered Gwydion. 'If the Death-Lord is still in Annuvin, their lives are in as much danger as ours.'

Taran had unbuckled Dyrnwyn from his belt and held out the sword to Gwydion. 'I understand now why Arawn sought possession of it – not for his own use but because he knew it threatened his power. Only Dyrnwyn could destroy his Cauldron-Born. Indeed, he dared not even keep it in his stronghold, and believed it harmless buried atop Mount Dragon. When Arawn disguised himself in your shape, he nearly tricked me into giving him the weapon.

Take it now. The blade is safer in your hands.'

Gwydion shook his head. 'You have earned the right to draw it, Assistant Pig-Keeper,' he said, 'and thus the right to wear it.'

'Indeed so!' put in Fflewddur. 'It was magnificent the way your struck that Cauldron-Born. A Fflam couldn't have done better. We're rid of those foul brutes forever.'

Taran nodded. 'Yet I hate them no longer. It was not their wish to bend in slavery to another's will. Now they are at peace.'

'In any case, Hen Wen's prophecy came true after all,' Fflewddur said. 'Not that I ever doubted it for a moment.' He glanced instinctively over his shoulder, but this time there came no jangling of harp strings. 'But she did have a curious way of putting things. I still haven't heard any stones speaking.'

'I have,' answered Taran. 'Atop Mount Dragon, the sound from the crest was like a voice. Without it, I'd have paid no heed to the stone. Then, when I saw how hollowed and eaten away it was, I believed I might be able to move it. Yes, Fflewddur, the voiceless stone spoke clearly.'

'I suppose so, if you think about it in that way,' Eilonwy agreed. 'As for Dyrnwyn's flame being quenched, Hen was quite mistaken. Understandably. She was very upset at the time . . .'

Before the girl could finish, two frightened figures burst from the Great Hall and raced to the companions. Much of Gurgi's hair had been singed away in ragged patches; his shaggy eyebrows were charred and his garments still smouldered. The former giant had fared worse, for he seemed little more than a heap of grime and ashes.

Taran had no time to welcome the lost companions, for the voice of Achren rose in a terrible cry.

'Do you seek Arawn? He is here!'

Achren flung herself at Taran's feet. Taran gasped and

froze in horror. Behind him coiled a serpent ready to strike.

Taran sprang aside. Dyrnwyn flashed from its scabbard. Achren had clutched the serpent in both hands, as though to strangle or tear it asunder. The head of the snake darted towards her, the scaly body lashed like a whip, and the fangs sank deep into Achren's throat. With a cry she fell back. In an instant, the serpent coiled again; its eyes glittered with a cold, deadly flame. Hissing in rage, jaws gasping and fangs bared, the serpent shot forward, striking at Taran. Eilonwy screamed. Taran swung the flashing sword with all his strength. The blade clove the serpent in two.

Flinging Dyrnwyn aside, Taran dropped to his knees beside Gwydion, who held the limp body of the Queen. The blood had drained from Achren's lips and her glazed eyes sought Gwydion's face.

'Have I not kept my oath, Gwydion?' she murmured, smiling vaguely. 'Is the Lord of Annuvin slain? It is good. My death comes easily upon me.' Achren's lips parted as though she would speak again, but her head fell back and her body sagged in Gwydion's arms.

A horrified gasp came from Eilonwy. Taran looked up as the girl pointed to the cloven serpent. Its body writhed, its shape blurred. In its place appeared the black-cloaked figure of a man whose severed head had rolled face downward on the earth. Yet in a moment this shape too lost its form and the corpse sank like a shadow into the earth; and where it had lain was seared and fallow, the ground wasted, fissured as though by drought. Arawn Death-Lord had vanished.

'The sword!' cried Fflewddur. 'Look at the sword!'

Quickly, Taran caught up the blade, but even as he grasped the hilt the flame of Dyrnwyn flickered, as though stirred by a wind. The white brilliance dimmed like a dying fire. Faster then the glow faded, no longer white but filled with swirling colours which danced and trembled. In another moment, Taran's hand held no more than a scarred and battered weapon whose blade glinted dully, not from the flame that once had burned within it but only from the mirrored rays of the setting sun.

Eilonwy, hurrying to his side, called out, 'The writing on the scabbard is fading, too. At least I think it is, unless it's just the dim light. Here, let me see better.'

She drew the bauble from her cloak and brought it closer to the black scabbard. Suddenly, in the golden rays, the marred inscriptions glittered.

'My bauble brightens the lettering! There's more than what used to be there!' cried the surprised girl. 'Even the part that was scratched out – I can see most of it now!'

The companions hastily gathered and, while Eilonwy held the bauble Taliesin took the scabbard and scanned it closely.

'The writing is clear, but fading quickly,' he said. 'Indeed, Princess, your golden light shows what was hidden. "DRAW DYRNWYN, ONLY THOU OF NOBLE WORTH, TO RULE WITH JUSTICE, TO STRIKE DOWN EVIL. WHO WIELDS IT IN GOOD CAUSE SHALL SLAY EVEN THE LORD OF DEATH." '

In another moment the inscription had vanished. Taliesin turned the black scabbard back and forth in his hands. 'Perhaps now I understand what was only hinted in the lore, that once a mighty king came upon great power and strove to use it for his own advantage. I believe Dyrnwyn was that weapon, turned from its destiny, long lost and found again.'

'Dyrnwyn's task is ended,' Gwydion said. 'Let us leave this evil place.'

In death the face of Achren, no longer bitterly haughty, was at last tranquil. Shrouding the woman in her tattered cloak, the companions bore the body to rest in the Great Hall, for she who had once ruled Prydain had died not without honour.

At the pinnacle of the Death-Lord's tower, the dark banner suddenly burst into flames and fell away in blazing shreds. The walls of the Great Hall trembled, and the stronghold shuddered deep within itself.

The companions and the warriors rode from the Iron Portals, behind them the walls shattered and the mighty towers crumbled. A sheet of flame reached skyward from the ruins where Annuvin had stood.

CHAPTER 20

The Gift

They were home again. Gwydion had led the companions westward to the coast where the golden ships waited. From there, with Kaw proudly perched on the highest mast, the great vessels with their gleaming sails bore them to Avren harbour. Word of Arawn's destruction had spread swiftly; and even as the companions disembarked, many cantrev lords and their battle hosts gathered to follow the Sons of Don, to do homage to King Gwydion, and to cry greetings to the Commot folk and Taran Wanderer. Gurgi unfurled what remained of the banner of the White Pig and raised it triumphantly.

Yet Gwydion had been strangely silent. And Taran, as the little farm came into sight, felt more heartache than joy. The winter had broken; thawing earth had begun to stir, and the first, hardly visible traces of green touched the hills like a faint mist. But Taran's eyes went to Coll's empty garden, and he grieved afresh for the stout grower of turnips, far distant in his lonely resting place.

Dallben hobbled out to greet them. The enchanter's face had grown even more deeply lined, his brow seemed fragile, the wrinkled skin almost transparent. Seeing him, Taran sensed that Dallben already knew Coll would not return. Eilonwy ran to his outstretched arms. Taran, leaping from the back of Melynlas, strode after her. Kaw flapped his wings and gabbled at the top of his voice. Fflewddur, Doli, and Gurgi, who looked more than ever patchy and scraggly, hastened to add their greetings, attempting to tell Dallben, all at the same time, what had befallen them.

Hen Wen was squealing, grunting, and wheezing, and

very nearly climbing over the bars of the pen. As Taran jumped into the enclosure to fling his arms about the delighted pig, he suddenly heard shrill squeakings and his jaw dropped in surprise.

Eilonwy, who had hurried to the enclosure, gave a joyful cry. 'Piglets!'

Six small pigs, five white as Hen Wen and one black, stood squealing on their hind legs beside their mother. Hen Wen chuckled and grunted proudly.

'We have had visitors,' said Dallben. 'One of them a very handsome boar. During the winter, when there was much stirring among the forest creatures, he came seeking food and shelter, and found Caer Dallben more to his liking than the woods. He is roaming about somewhere now, for he is still a little wild and unused to so many new arrivals.'

'Great Belin!' cried Fflewddur. 'Seven oracular pigs! Taran, my friend, your tasks will be harder than they were in the Hills of Bran-Galedd.'

Dallben shook his head. 'Sturdy and healthy they are, and as fine a litter as I have seen, but their powers are no greater than those of any other pig – which should be quite enough to satisfy them. Hen Wen's own gift began to fade when the letter sticks shattered and now is gone past recall. It is for the best; such power is a heavy burden, for men as well as pigs, and I daresay she is much happier now.'

For two days, the companions rested, grateful and content to be together in the peacefulness of the little farm. The sky had never seemed clearer, filled with happier promise of spring, or greater joy. King Smoit had arrived with his guard of honour, and through a night's feasting the cottage rang with merriment.

Next day Dallben summoned the companions to his chamber, where Gwydion and Taliesin already waited. He peered deeply and kindly at all gathered there, and when he spoke his voice was gentle.

'These have been days of welcome,' he said, 'but also days of farewell.'

A questioning murmur rose from the companions. Taran, with alarm, looked searchingly at Dallben. Fflewddur, however, clapped a hand to his sword and exclaimed, 'I knew it would be so! What task remains to be done? Have the gwythaints returned? Is a band of Huntsmen still abroad? Have no fears! A Fflam stands ready!'

Gwydion smiled sadly at the excited bard. 'Not so, gallant friend. Like the Huntsmen, the gwythaints have been destroyed. Yet it is true: one task remains. The Sons of Don, their kinsmen and kinswomen, must board the golden ships and set sail for the Summer Country, the land from which we came.'

Taran turned to Gwydion as though he had not grasped the High King's words. 'How then,' he quickly asked, not daring to believe he had heard aright, 'the Sons of Don leave Prydain? Must you sail now? To what purpose? How soon shall you return? Shall you not first rejoice in your victory?'

'Our victory is itself the reason for our voyage,' Gwydion answered. 'This is a destiny long ago laid upon us: When the Lord of Annuvin shall be overcome, then must the Sons of Don depart forever from Prydain.'

'No!' Eilonwy protested. 'Not now, of all times!'

'We cannot turn from this ancient destiny,' Gwydion replied. 'King Fflewddur Fflam, too, must join us, for he is kin to the House of Don.'

The bard's face filled with distress. 'Fflam is grateful,' he began, 'and under ordinary circumstances I should look forward to a sea voyage. But I'm quite content to stay in my own realm. Indeed, dreary though it is, I've found myself rather missing it.'

Taliesin spoke then. 'It is not for you to choose, Son of Godo. But know that the Summer Country is a fair land, fairer even than Prydain, and one where all heart's desires are granted. Llyan shall be with you. A new harp you shall have. I myself shall teach you the playing of it, and you shall learn all the lore of the bards. Your heart has always been the heart of a true bard, Fflewddur Fflam. Until now, it was unready. Have you given up that which you loved most for the sake of your companions? The harp that awaits you shall be all the more precious, and its strings shall never break.

'Know this, too,' Taliesin added. 'All men born must die, save those who dwell in the Summer Country. It is a land without strife or suffering, where even death itself is unknown.'

'There is yet another destiny laid upon us,' Dallben said. 'As the Sons of Don must return to their own land, so must there come an end to my own powers. I have long pondered the message Hen Wen's last letter stick might have given us. It is clear to me now why the ash rods shattered. They could not withstand such a prophecy, which could only have been this: Not only shall the flame of Dyrnwyn be quenched and its power vanish, but all enchantments shall pass away, and men unaided guide their own destiny.

'I, too, voyage to the Summer Country,' Dallben continued. 'I do so with sorrow but with even greater joy. I am an old man and weary, and for me there shall be rest and a laying down of burdens which have grown all too heavy upon my shoulders.

'Doli, alas, must return to the realm of the Fair Folk, and so must Kaw,' the enchanter went on. 'The wayposts are being abandoned. King Eiddileg will soon command the barring of all passages into his kingdom, just as Medwyn has already closed his valley forever to the race of men, allowing only the animals to find their way to him.'

Doli bowed his head. 'Humph!' he snorted. 'It's about

time to stop dealing with mortals. Only leads to trouble. Yes, I'll be glad enough to go back. I've had my fill of good-old-Doli this and good-old-Doli that, and good-old-Doli would you mind turning invisible just once more!' The dwarf strove to look as furious as he could, but there were tears in his bright red eyes.

'Even the Princess Eilonwy Daughter of Angharad must voyage to the Summer Country,' Dallben said. 'So it must be,' he went on, as Eilonwy gasped in disbelief. 'At Caer Colur, the Princess gave up only the usage of her magical powers. They are still within her, as they have been handed down to all daughters of the House of Llyr. Therefore must she depart. However,' he went on quickly, before Eilonwy could interrupt, 'there are others who have well-served the Sons of Don: faithful Gurgi; Hen Wen, too, in her own fashion; and Taran of Caer Dallben. It is their reward that they may journey with us.'

'Yes, yes!' shouted Gurgi. 'All go to land of no sighings and no dyings!' He bounded joyously and waved his arms in the air, shedding a good portion of what hair remained to him. 'Yes, oh yes! All together forever! And Gurgi, too, will find what he seeks. Wisdom for his poor tender head!'

Taran's heart leaped as he cried out Eilonwy's name and hastened to the side of the Princess to take her in his arms. 'We shall not part again. In the Summer Country we shall be wed – ' He stopped short. 'If – if that is your wish. If you will wed an Assistant Pig-Keeper.'

'Well, indeed,' replied Eilonwy, 'I wondered if you'd ever get round to asking. Of course I will, and if you'd given half a thought to the question you'd have already known my answer.'

Taran's head still spun from the enchanter's tidings, and he turned to Dallben. 'Can this be true? That Eilonwy and I may voyage together?'

Dallben said nothing for a moment, then he nodded.

'It is true. No greater gift lies in my power to grant.'

Glew snorted. 'That's all very well, bestowing never-ending life right and left. Even on a pig! But no one's given a thought to me. Selfishness! Lack of consideration! It's plain that if that Fair Folk mine hadn't come tumbling down – robbing me of my fortune, I might add – we'd have taken a different path, we'd never have gone to Mount Dragon, Dyrnwyn would never have been found, the Cauldron-Born never slain . . .' For all his indignation, however, the former giant's brow puckered wretchedly and his lips trembled. 'Go, by all means! Let me stay this ridiculous size! I assure you, when I was a giant . . .'

'Yes, yes!' Gurgi shouted. 'Whining giant, too, has served, even as he says. It is not fair to leave him lone and lost in smallness! And in treasure house of evil Death-Lord, when all rich treasures fall in flames, a life was saved from hot and hurtful blazings!'

'Yes, even Glew has served, though all unwitting,' Dallben replied. 'His reward shall be no less than yours. In the Summer Country he may grow, if he so desires, to the stature of a man. But do you tell me,' Dallben said, looking sternly at Gurgi, 'that he saved your life?'

Gurgi hesitated a moment. Before he could answer, Glew quickly spoke. 'Of course he didn't,' said the former giant. 'A life was saved. Mine. If he hadn't pulled me out of the treasure house I'd be no more than a cinder in Annuvin.'

'At least you've told the truth, giant!' cried Fflewddur. 'Good for you! Great Belin, I think you've already grown a little taller!'

Gwydion stepped forward and gently put his hand on Taran's shoulder. 'Our time is soon upon us,' he said quietly. 'In the morning, we shall depart. Make ready, Assistant Pig-Keeper.'

That night Taran drowsed fitfully. The joy that so lightened his heart had strangely flown, fluttering out of reach like a bird of brilliant plumage he could not lure back to his hand. Even thoughts of Eilonwy, of happiness awaiting them in the Summer Country could not regain it.

At last he rose from his pallet and stood, uneasy, by the chamber window. The campfires of the Sons of Don had burned to ashes. The full moon turned the sleeping fields to a sea of silver. From far beyond the hills a voice began to lift in song, faint but clear; another joined it, then still others. Taran caught his breath. Only once, long ago in the Fair Folk realm, had he heard such singing. Now, more beautiful than he remembered, the song swelled, in a long flood of melody shimmering brighter than the moonbeams. Suddenly it ended. Taran cried out in sorrow, knowing he would never hear its like again. And, perhaps in his own imaginings, there echoed from every corner of the land the sound of heavy portals closing.

'What, sleepless, my chicken?' said a voice behind him.

He turned quickly. Light filling the chamber dazzled him, but as his vision cleared he saw three tall and slender figures; two garbed in robes of shifting colours, of white, gold, and flaming crimson; and one hooded in a cloak of glittering black. Gems sparkled in the tresses of the first, at the throat of the second hung a necklace of shining white beads. Taran saw their faces were calm, beautiful to heartbreak, and though the dark hood shadowed the features of the last, Taran knew she could be no less fair.

'Sleepless and speechless, too,' said the middle figure. 'Tomorrow, poor dear, instead of dancing with joy he'll be yawning.'

'Your voices – I know them well,' Taran stammered, barely able to speak above a whisper. 'But your faces – yes, once have I seen them, a time long past, in the Marshes of Morva. Yet you cannot be the same. Orddu? Orwen, and – Orgoch?'

'Of course we are, my gosling,' Orddu replied, 'though

it's true whenever you met us before we were hardly at our best.'

'But good enough for the purpose,' Orgoch muttered from the depths of her hood.

Orwen giggled girlishly and toyed with her beads. 'You mustn't think we look like ugly old hags *all* the time,' she said. 'Only when the circumstances seem to require it.'

'Why have you come?' Taran began, still baffled at the familiar tones of the enchantresses coming from such fair shapes. 'Do you, too, journey to the Summer Country?'

Orddu shook her head. 'We are journeying, but not with you. Salt air makes Orgoch queasy, though it's very likely the only thing that does. We travel to – well – anywhere. You might even say everywhere.'

'You shall see no more of us, nor we of you,' added Orwen, almost regretfully. 'We shall miss you. As much, that is, as we can miss anyone. Orgoch especially would have loved to – well, best not to dwell on that.'

Orgoch gave a most ungentle snort. Orddu, meanwhile, had unfolded a length of brightly woven tapestry and held it out to Taran.

'We came to bring you this, my duckling,' she said. 'Take it and pay no heed to Orgoch's grumbling. She'll have to swallow her disappointment – for lack of anything better.'

'I have seen this on your loom,' Taran said, more than a little distrustful. 'Why do you offer it to me? I do not ask for it, nor can I pay for it.'

'It is yours by right, my robin,' answered Orddu. 'It does come from our loom, if you insist on strictest detail, but it was really you who wove it.'

Puzzled, Taran looked more closely at the fabric and saw it crowded with images of men and women, of warriors and battles, of birds and animals. 'These,' he murmured in wonder, 'these are of my own life.'

'Of course,' Orddu replied. 'The pattern is of your

choosing and always was.'

'My choosing?' Taran questioned. 'Not yours? Yet I believed . . .' He stopped and raised his eyes to Orddu. 'Yes,' he said slowly, 'once I did believe the world went at your bidding. I see now it is not so. The strands of life are not woven by three hags or even by three beautiful damsels. The pattern indeed was mine. But here,' he added, frowning as he scanned the final portion of the fabric where the weaving broke off and the threads fell unravelled, 'here it is unfinished.'

'Naturally,' said Orddu. 'You must still choose the pattern, and so must each of you poor, perplexed fledglings, as long as thread remains to be woven.'

'But no longer do I see mine clearly,' Taran cried. 'No longer do I understand my own heart. Why does my grief shadow my joy? Tell me this much. Give me to know this, as one last boon.'

'Dear chicken,' said Orddu smiling sadly, 'when, in truth, did we really give you anything?'

Then they were gone.

CHAPTER 21

Farewells

Through the remainder of the night, Taran did not move from the window. The unfinished weaving lay at his feet. By dawn, a still greater number of Commot folk and cantrev nobles came to throng the fields and hillsides around Caer Dallben, for it had become known the Sons of Don were departing Prydain, and with them the Daughters of Don who had journeyed from the eastern strongholds. At last Taran stirred and made his way to Dallben's chamber.

The companions were already gathered, even Doli, who had flatly refused to set out for the Fair Folk realm without taking a last leave of each and every friend. Kaw, quiet for once, perched on the dwarf's shoulder. Glew seemed excited and pleased to be on his way. Taliesin and Gwydion stood near Dallben, who had donned a heavy travel cloak and bore an ash-wood staff. Under his arm the enchanter carried *The Book of Three*.

'Kindly master, hasten!' shouted Gurgi, as Llyan at Fflewddur's side twitched her tail impatiently. 'All are ready for floatings and boatings!'

Taran's eyes went to the faces of the companions; to Eilonwy, who was watching him eagerly; to the weathered features of Gwydion, and the face of Dallben, furrowed with wisdom. Never had he loved each of them more than at this moment. He did not speak until he came to stand before the old enchanter.

'Never shall I have greater honour than the gift you offer me,' Taran said. The words came slowly, yet he forced himself to continue. 'Last night my heart was troubled. I dreamed that Orddu – no, it was not a dream.

She was indeed here. And I have seen for myself your gift is one I cannot take.'

Gurgi's yelping stopped short and he stared at Taran with wide and unbelieving eyes.

The companions started and Eilonwy cried out, 'Taran of Caer Dallben, do you have any idea what you're saying? Has the flame of Dyrnwyn scorched your wits?' Suddenly her voice caught in her throat. She bit her lips and turned quickly away. 'I understand. In the Summer Country we were to be wed. Do you still question my heart? It has not changed. It is your heart that has changed towards mine.'

Taran dared not look at Eilonwy, for his grief was too keen in him. 'You are wrong, Princess of Llyr,' he murmured. 'I have long loved you, and loved you even before I knew that I did. If my heart breaks to part from our companions, it breaks twice over to part from you. Yet, so it must be. I cannot do otherwise.'

'Think carefully, Assistant Pig-Keeper,' Dallben said sharply. 'Once taken, your choice cannot be recalled. Will you dwell in sorrow instead of happiness? Will you refuse not only joy and love but never-ending life?'

Taran did not answer for a long moment. When at last he did, his voice was heavy with regret, yet his words clear and unfaltering.

'There are those more deserving of your gift than I, yet never may it be offered them. My life is bound to theirs. Coll Son of Collfrewr's garden and orchard lie barren, waiting for a hand to quicken them. My skill is less than his, but I give it willingly for his sake.

'The seawall at Dinas Rhydnant is unfinished,' Taran continued. 'Before the King of Mona's burial mound I vowed not to leave his task undone.'

From his jacket Taran drew the fragment of pottery. 'Shall I forget Annlaw Clay-Shaper? Commot Merin and others like it? I cannot restore life to Llonio Son of

Llonwen and those valiant folk who followed me, never to see their homes again. Nor can I mend the hearts of widows and orphaned children. Yet if it is in my power to rebuild even a little of what has been broken, this must I do.

'The Red Fallows once were a fruitful place. With labour, perhaps they shall be so again.' He turned and spoke to Taliesin. 'Caer Dathyl's proud halls lie in ruins, and with them the Hall of Lore and the treasured wisdom of the bards. Have you not said that memory lives longer than what it remembers? But what if memory be lost? If there are those who will help me, we will raise the fallen stones and regain the treasure of memory.'

'Gurgi will help! He will not voyage, no, no!' Gurgi wailed. 'He stays always. He wants no gift that takes him from kindly master!'

Taran put a hand on the creature's arm. 'You must journey with the others. Do you call me master? Obey me, then, in one last command. Find the wisdom you yearn for. It awaits you in the Summer Country. Whatever I may find, I must seek it here.'

Eilonwy bowed her head. 'You have chosen as you must, Taran of Caer Dallben.'

'Nor will I gainsay you,' Dallben said to Taran, 'but only warn you. The tasks you set yourself are cruelly difficult. There is no certainty you will accomplish even one, and much risk you will fail in all of them. In either case, your efforts may well go unrewarded, unsung, forgotten. And at the end, like all mortals, you must face your death; perhaps without even a mound of honour to mark your resting place.'

Taran nodded. 'So be it,' he said. 'Long ago I yearned to be a hero without knowing, in truth, what a hero was. Now, perhaps, I understand it a little better. A grower of turnips or a shaper of clay, a Commot farmer or a king – every man is a hero if he strives more for others than for himself alone. Once,' he added, 'you told me that the seeking counts more than the finding. So, too, must the striving count more than the gain.

'Once, I hoped for a glorious destiny,' Taran went on, smiling at his own memory. 'That dream has vanished with my childhood; and though a pleasant dream it was fit only for a child. I am well-content as an Assistant Pig-Keeper.'

'Even that contentment shall not be yours,' Dallben said. 'No longer are you Assistant Pig-Keeper, but High King of Prydain.'

Taran caught his breath and stared with disbelief at the enchanter. 'You jest with me,' he murmured. 'Have I been prideful that you would mock me by calling me King?'

'Your worth was proved when you drew Dyrnwyn from its sheath,' Dallben said, 'and your kingliness when you chose to remain here. It is not a gift I offer you now, but a burden far heavier than any you have borne.'

'Then why must I bear it?' cried Taran. 'I am an Assistant Pig-Keeper and such have I always been.'

'It has been written in *The Book of Three*,' Dallben answered, and raised his hand for silence before Taran could speak again. 'I dared not tell you this. To give you such knowledge would have defeated the prophecy itself. Until this very moment, I was not sure you were the one chosen to rule. Indeed, yesterday I feared you were not.'

'How then?' Taran asked. 'Could *The Book of Three* deceive you?'

'No, it could not,' Dallben said. 'The book is thus called because it tells all three parts of our lives: the past, the present, and the future. But it could as well be called a book of "if". *If* you had failed at your tasks; *if* you had followed an evil path; *if* you had been slain; *if* you had not chosen as you did – a thousand "ifs", my boy, and many times a thousand. *The Book of Three* can say no more than "if" until at the end, of all things that might have been, one alone becomes what really is. For the deeds of a man, not the words of a prophecy, are what shape his destiny.'

'I understand now why you kept my parentage a secret,' Taran said. 'But shall I never be given to know it?'

'I did not keep it secret from you entirely through my own wish,' Dallben answered. 'Nor do I keep it so now. Long ago, when *The Book of Three* first came into my hands, from its pages I learned that when the Sons of Don departed from Prydain the High King would be one who slew a serpent, who gained and lost a flaming sword, who chose a kingdom of sorrow over a kingdom of happiness. These prophecies were clouded, even to me; and darkest was the prophecy that he who would come to rule Prydain would be one of no station in life.

'Long did I ponder these things,' Dallben continued. 'At last, I left Caer Dallben to seek this future king and to hasten his coming. For many years I searched, yet all whom I questioned well knew their station, whether shepherd or war leader, cantrev lord or Commot labourer.

'The seasons turned; kings rose and fell, wars turned to peace, and peace to war. Indeed, on a certain time, as many years ago as you yourself have years, a grievous war was upon the land, and I despaired of my quest and turned my steps once more towards Caer Dallben. On that day I chanced to pass a field where a battle had raged. Many lay slain, noble as well as humble folk; even the women and children had not been spared.

'From the forest nearby I heard a piercing cry. An infant had been hidden among the trees, as though his mother had sought, at the last, to keep him safe. From his wrappings I could judge nothing of his parentage and only sensed with certainty that both mother and father lay upon that field of the slain.

'Here, surely, was one of no station in life, an unknown babe of unknown kin. I bore the child with me to Caer Dallben. The name I gave him was Taran.

'I could not have told you of your parentage, even had I wished to,' Dallben continued, 'for I knew it no more than you did. My secret hope I shared only with two others: Lord Gwydion and Coll. As you grew to manhood, so our hopes grew, though never could we be certain you were the child born to be High King.

'Until now, my boy,' said Dallben, 'you were always a great "perhaps".'

'What was written has come to pass,' Gwydion said. 'And now in truth we must say farewell.'

The chamber was silent. Llyan, sensing the bard's distress, nuzzled him gently. The companions did not move. It was Glew who stepped forward and spoke first.

'I've been carrying this with me ever since I was so shabbily hustled away from Mona,' he said, drawing from his jacket a small blue crystal which he pressed into Taran's hand. 'It reminded me of my cavern and those grand days when I was a giant. But for some reason I don't want to be reminded of them any longer. Since I don't want it – here, take it as a small remembrance of me.'

'He's still hardly the most generous spirit in the world,' muttered Fflewddur, 'but I've no doubt it's the first time he's ever given anybody anything. Great Belin, I swear the little fellow's actually grown another inch!'

Doli had taken the handsomely crafted axe from his belt. 'You'll need this,' he told Taran, 'and it should serve you well in many tasks. It's Fair Folk quality, my lad, and you'll not blunt it easily.'

'It can serve me no better than did its owner,' Taran replied, clasping the dwarf's hand, 'and its metal cannot be as true as your own heart. Good old Doli . . .'

'Humph!' The dwarf snorted furiously. 'Good old Doli! I've heard that somewhere before.'

Kaw, on Doli's shoulder, bobbed up and down while Taran gently ran a finger over the crow's sleek feathers.

'Farewell,' Kaw croaked. 'Taran! Farewell!'

'Farewell to you,' Taran answered, smiling. 'If I have despaired of teaching you good manners, I have rejoiced in your bad ones. You are a rogue and a scamp, and a very eagle among crows.'

Llyan had padded up to rub her head affectionately against Taran's arm, which she did so vigorously that the enormous cat nearly knocked him off his feet.

'Bear my friend good company,' Taran said, stroking Llyan's ears. 'Cheer him with your purring when his spirits are low, as I wish you might cheer me. Stray not far from him, for even such a bold bard as Fflewddur Fflam is no stranger to loneliness.'

Fflewddur himself had drawn near, and in his hand held the harp string he had taken from the fire. The heat of the flame had caused the string to curl and twine in a curious pattern that seemed without beginning or end, constantly changing as from one melody to another even as Taran looked at it.

'I'm afraid it's all that's left of the old pot,' Fflewddur said, offering the string to Taran. 'Truthfully, I'm just as well pleased. It was forever jangling and going out of tune . . .' He paused, glanced behind him nervously, and cleared his throat. 'Ah – what I meant to say was that I shall miss those snapping strings.'

'No more than I shall miss them,' Taran said. 'Remember me as well and fondly as I remember you.'

'Have no fear!' cried the bard. 'There are still songs to be sung and tales to be told. A Fflam never forgets!'

'Alas, alas!' wailed Gurgi. 'Poor Gurgi has nothing to give kindly master for fond rememberings. Woe and misery! Even wallet of crunchings and munchings now is empty!'

The tearful creature suddenly clapped his hands together.

'Yes, yes! Forgetful Gurgi has one gift. Here, here it is. From burning treasure house of wicked Death-Lord, bold Gurgi seized it with catchings and snatchings. But his poor tender head was so filled with fearful spinnings that he forgot!'

With this, Gurgi drew from his leather pouch a small, flame-scarred, battered coffer of unknown metal and held it out to Taran, who took it, studied it curiously, then broke the heavy seal which kept it locked.

The coffer held no more than a number of thin, closely written parchments. Taran's eyes widened as he scanned them, and he turned quickly to Gurgi.

'Do you know what you have found?' he whispered. 'Here are the secrets of forging and tempering metals, of shaping and firing pottery, of planting and cultivating. This is what Arawn stole long ago and kept from the race of men. This knowledge is itself a priceless treasure.'

'Perhaps the most precious of all,' said Gwydion, who had come to study the parchments in Taran's hand. 'The flames of Annuvin destroyed the enchanted tools that laboured of themselves and would have given carefree idleness. These treasures are far worthier, for their use needs skill and strength of hand and mind.'

Fflewddur gave a low whistle. 'Who owns these secrets is truly master of Prydain. Taran, old friend, the proudest cantrev lord will be at your beck and call, begging for anything you choose to grant him.'

'And Gurgi found it!' shouted Gurgi, springing into the air and madly whirling about. 'Yes, oh yes! Bold, clever, faithful, valiant Gurgi always finds things! Once he found a lost piggy and once he found evil black cauldron! Now he finds mighty secrets for kindly master!'

Taran smiled at the excited Gurgi. 'Indeed, you have found many mighty secrets. But they are not mine to keep. These will I share with all in Prydain, for by right they belong to all.'

'Then share this, as well,' said Dallben, who had been

listening closely and now held out the heavy, leather-bound volume he had kept under his arm.

'*The Book of Three?*' Taran said, looking wonderingly and questioningly at the enchanter. 'I dare not . . .'

'Take it, my boy,' Dallben said. 'It will not blister your fingers, as once it did with an over-curious Assistant Pig-Keeper. All its pages are open to you. *The Book of Three* no longer foretells what is to come, only what has been. But now can be set down the words of its last page.'

The enchanter took a quill from the table, opened the book, and in it wrote with a bold, firm hand:

And thus did an Assistant Pig-Keeper become High King of Prydain.

'This, too, is a treasure,' said Gwydion. '*The Book of Three* is now both history and heritage. For my own gift, I could give you nothing greater. Nor do I offer you a crown, for a true king wears his crown in his heart.' The tall warrior clasped Taran's hand. 'Farewell. We shall not meet again.'

'Take Dyrnwyn, then, in remembrance of me,' Taran said.

'Dyrnwyn is yours,' Gwydion said, 'as it was meant to be.'

'Yet Arawn is slain,' Taran replied. 'Evil is conquered and the blade's work done.'

'Evil conquered?' said Gwydion. 'You have learned much, but learn this last and hardest of lessons. You have conquered only the enchantments of evil. That was the easiest of your tasks, only a beginning, not an ending. Do you believe evil itself to be so quickly overcome? Not so long as men still hate and slay each other, when greed and anger goad them. Against these even a flaming sword cannot prevail, but only that portion of good in all men's hearts whose flame can never be quenched.'

Eilonwy, who had been standing in silence, now drew close to Taran. The girl's eyes did not waver from his as she held out the golden sphere.

'Take this,' she softly said, 'though it does not glow as brightly as the love we might have shared. Farewell, Taran of Caer Dallben. Remember me.'

Eilonwy was about to turn away, but suddenly her blue eyes flashed furiously and she stamped her foot. 'It's not fair!' she cried. 'It's not my fault I was born into a family of enchantresses. I didn't ask for magical powers. That's worse than being made to wear a pair of shoes that doesn't fit! I don't see why I have to keep them!'

'Princess of Llyr,' said Dallben. 'I have waited for you yourself to say those words. Do you truly wish to give up your heritage of enchantment?'

'Of course I do!' Eilonwy cried. 'If enchantments are what separates us, then I should be well rid of them!'

'This lies within your power,' Dallben said, 'within your grasp, and, for the matter of that, upon your finger. The ring you wear, the gift Lord Gwydion gave you long ago, will grant your wish.'

'What?' Eilonwy burst out, in both surprise and indignation. 'Do you mean to say that all the years I've worn my ring I could have used it to have a wish granted? You told me nothing of it! That's worse than unfair. Why, I could simply have wished to destroy the Black Cauldron! Or to find Dyrnwyn! I could have wished Arawn conquered! Without the least danger! And I never knew!'

'Child, child,' Dallben interrupted, 'your ring can indeed grant you a wish, and one wish alone. But evil cannot be conquered by wishing. The ring will serve only you, and grant only the deepest wish of your own heart. I did not tell you before because I was uncertain that you truly knew what you longed for.

'Turn the ring once upon your finger,' Dallben said. 'Wish with all your heart for your enchanted powers to vanish.'

Wondering and almost fearful, Eilonwy closed her eyes and did the enchanter's bidding. The ring flared suddenly, but only for a moment. The girl gave a sharp cry of pain. And in Taran's hand the light of the golden bauble winked out.

'It is done,' Dallben murmured.

Eilonwy blinked and looked around her. 'I don't feel a bit different,' she remarked. 'Are my enchantments truly gone?'

Dallben nodded. 'Yes,' he said gently. 'Yet you shall always keep the magic and mystery all women share. And I fear that Taran, like all men, shall be often baffled by it. But, such is the way of it. Come, clasp hands the two of you, and pledge each other your troth.'

When they had done so, the companions pressed around the wedded couple to wish them happiness. Then Gwydion and Taliesin went from the cottage and Dallben took up his ashwood staff.

'We can tarry no longer,' the enchanter said, 'and here our ways must part.'

'But what of Hen Wen?' Taran asked. 'Shall I not see her one last time?'

'As often as you please,' answered Dallben. 'Since she was free to go or stay, I know she will choose to remain with you. But I suggest you first let those visitors trampling about the fields see there is a new High King in Prydain, and a new Queen. Gwydion will have proclaimed the tidings and your subjects will be impatient to hail you.'

The companions following, Taran and Eilonwy left the chamber. But at the cottage door, Taran drew back and turned to Dallben. 'Can one such as I rule a kingdom? I remember a time when I jumped headfirst into a thorn bush and I fear kingship will be no different.'

'Very likely more nettlesome,' put in Eilonwy. 'But should you have any difficulties, I'll be happy to give you my advice. Right now, there's only one question: Are you going in or out of this doorway?'

In the waiting throng beyond the cottage, Taran glimpsed Hevydd, Llassar, the folk of the Commots, Gast and Goryon side by side near the farmer Aeddan, King Smoit towering above them, his beard bright as flame. But many were the well-loved faces he saw clearly only with his heart. A sudden burst of cheering voices greeted him as he took Eilonwy's hand tightly in his own and stepped through the door.

And so they lived many happy years, and the promised tasks were accomplished. Yet long afterwards, when all had passed away into distant memory, there were many who wondered whether King Taran, Queen Eilonwy, and their companions had indeed walked the earth, or whether they had been no more than dreams in a tale set down to beguile children. And, in time, only the bards knew the truth of it.

Fontana Paperbacks: Fiction

Fontana is a leading paperback publisher of both non-fiction, popular and academic, and fiction. Below are some recent fiction titles.

☐ SEEDS OF YESTERDAY Virginia Andrews £2.50
☐ SONG OF RHANNA Christine Marion Fraser £2.50
☐ JEDDER'S LAND Maureen O'Donoghue £1.95
☐ THE WARLORD Malcolm Bosse £2.95
☐ TREASON'S HARBOUR Patrick O'Brian £2.50
☐ FUTURES Freda Bright £1.95
☐ THE DEMON LOVER Victoria Holt £2.50
☐ FIREPRINT Geoffrey Jenkins £2.50
☐ DEATH AND THE DANCING FOOTMAN Ngaio Marsh £1.75
☐ THE 'CAINE' MUTINY Herman Wouk £2.50
☐ LIVERPOOL DAISY Helen Forrester £1.95
☐ OUT OF A DREAM Diana Anthony £1.75
☐ SHARPE'S ENEMY Bernard Cornwell £1.95

You can buy Fontana paperbacks at your local bookshop or newsagent. Or you can order them from Fontana Paperbacks, Cash Sales Department, Box 29, Douglas, Isle of Man. Please send a cheque, postal or money order (not currency) worth the purchase price plus 15p per book for postage (maximum postage required is £3).

NAME (Block letters) ______________________________

ADDRESS ______________________________

____

____

While every effort is made to keep prices low, it is sometimes necessary to increase them at short notice. Fontana Paperbacks reserve the right to show new retail prices on covers which may differ from those previously advertised in the text or elsewhere.

Stephen Donaldson

The Chronicles of Thomas Covenant, the Unbeliever

'Comparable to Tolkien at his best . . . will certainly find a place on the small list of true classics.' *Washington Post*

'An irresistible epic.' *Chicago Daily News*

'The most original fantasy since *Lord of the Rings* and an outstanding novel to boot.' *Time Out*, London

'Intricate, absorbing, these volumes create a whole new world.' *Sunday Press*, Dublin

The First Chronicles of Thomas Covenant, the Unbeliever

LORD FOUL'S BANE
THE ILLEARTH WAR
THE POWER THAT PRESERVES

The Second Chronicles of Thomas Covenant

THE WOUNDED LAND
THE ONE TREE
WHITE GOLD WIELDER

FONTANA PAPERBACKS